July 2024

To Bill,

THE
LINDEN TREE

Fair Winds and Following Seas.

S.D.M. Carpenter

Clovercroft Publishing

The Linden Tree

©2020 by S. D. M. Carpenter

Published by Clovercroft Publishing, Franklin, Tennessee.
www.clovercroftpublishing.com

Edited by Gail Fallen

Cover and Interior Design by Suzanne Lawing

Illustration by Adept Content Solutions

ISBN: 978-1-950892-57-0

Printed in the United States of America

For Linda, as always.

Also by the Author

Military History by Stanley D.M. Carpenter

Military Leadership in the British Civil Wars: 'The Genius of This Age'

The English Civil War (editor)

Southern Gambit: Cornwallis and the British March to Yorktown

The American War of Independence, 1775-83 (coauthor), forthcoming in 2022

Historical Fiction by S.D.M. Carpenter

Genesis of ANTIMONY

Resurrection of ANTIMONY

The Last Med, forthcoming in 2022

The Flying Squadron: ANTIMONY's Challenge, forthcoming in 2023

Preface

Great cataclysmic events often turn on a single episode of random chance. As an example, the assassination of the Austro-Hungarian heir, the Archduke Franz Ferdinand, in Sarajevo on 28 June 1914, set in motion a chain of events that led ultimately to the First World War. But what if a US Navy submarine on patrol near the Hawai'ian Islands detected and reported the Imperial Japanese Navy *Kido Butai* or 1st Air Fleet (Mobile Force) preparing to attack US military installations on Oahu? How might that dynamic, clearly an episode of random chance, have altered the history of World War II and perhaps even that of the world? That is the precept of this World War II action-adventure, espionage, alternate history thriller.

To set up the action by having a US Navy submarine detect the Japanese strike force and to give it technical authenticity, the prologue is, by design, heavy in "navalese" and technical jargon. Anyone who has served in any military branch recognizes that commands and orders must be given in crisp, succinct, and easily recognizable form. However, for the purposes of fiction dialogue, this dynamic can be a death trap. Readers who do not know the "lingo" may be turned off and never read past the first chapter. How to get around this conundrum? *The Linden Tree* prologue is written so as to capture the technical aspects of a Navy submarine in 1941 while at the same time providing enough contextual narrative and description so that readers can follow the action with minimal confusion. From there, starting with chapter 1 where the alternate fictional history begins with the main story line, the technical jargon is presented where needed, but the novel becomes more standard narrative storytelling.

A second dynamic is language usage in the dialogue and narrative. Many of the characters in *The Linden Tree* are either Swiss or German. To give the flavor of the language in the dialogue, German phrases, terms, or words (e.g., common terms such as good morning, good day, yes and no, and personal titles) are interspersed with English text such that the reader can easily understand the dialogue. To assist the reader, the preface provides many of these German phrases, words, terms, etc. with a brief translation. Additionally, the preface includes a list by nationality of characters with a short description of their role or position. Since this novel is also an historical fiction work, many of the characters are actual personalities. Fictitious characters are intermingled with actual personages, which then creates the flow of events. The reader will find in the author's notes some brief comments on actual personages.

World War I and II alternate history has been very popular over the years. Two such novels come immediately to mind—Len Deighton's *SS-GB*, published in the 1970s, and Philip K. Dick's *The Man in the High Castle*, published in the 1960s and now a popular television drama series. With this dynamic in mind, *The Linden Tree* launches readers into the world of "what might have happened if . . . ." In this case, what if that episode of random chance—the discovery of the Japanese Pearl Harbor attack force—set in motion a chain of earthshaking events.

American Characters

Lieutenant Tom Garrold, USNR, Officer of the Deck (OOD), USS *Swordfish* (SS-193)

Ensign Charlie McDaniel, USN, Junior Officer of the Deck (JOOD), USS *Swordfish*

Chief Petty Officer Albert Smith, USN, Chief of the Boat (COB), USS *Swordfish*

Commander Rich Noland, USN, Commanding Officer (CO), USS *Swordfish*

Lieutenant Herb Newcomb, USN, Executive Officer (XO), USS *Swordfish*

Brigadier General Leslie Groves, USA, Head of the Manhattan Project

Brigadier General William Donovan, USA, Head of the Office of Strategic Services (OSS)

Cordell Hull, Secretary of State

Henry Stimson, Secretary of War

Frank Knox, Secretary of the Navy

Franklin Delano Roosevelt, President of the United States

General George Marshall, USA, Army Chief of Staff

Admiral William Leahy, USN, Chief of Staff to the Commander-in-Chief

Admiral Ernest King, USN, Chief of Naval Operations and Commander-in-Chief, US Fleet

General Henry Arnold, USA, Commander of US Army Air Forces

Congressman Samuel Rayburn, Speaker of the House of Representatives

Senator Alben Barkley, Senate Majority Leader

British, Polish, and Swiss Characters

Piper MacDougall, Argyll and Sutherland Highlanders

Company Sergeant Major (CSM) Hamish Mackenzie, Argyll and Sutherland Highlanders

Major Frank Walsh, R.A.M.C.

Lech Kwiatkowski, Polish Special Operations Executive (SOE) agent

Józef Mowak, Polish Special Operations Executive (SOE) agent

Winston Leonard Spenser Churchill, Prime Minister of the United Kingdom

Major-General Sir Stewart Menzies, Head of MI6, Secret Intelligence Service

William Stephenson (INTREPID), Head of British Security Coordination (BSC)

Air Commodore Sir Charles Hambro, Chief of the Special Operations Executive (SOE)

Frederick Lindemann (Baron Cherwell), Churchill's Science Adviser

General Sir Alan Brooke, Chief of the Imperial General Staff (CIGS)

MAUD Committee physicists

Group Captain Reginald Blanton, RAF, bomber group commander

Flight Sergeant Pearce, RAF, flight engineer

Pilot Officer Colin Jones, RAF, navigator

Sergeant O'Bannon, RAF, wireless operator

Air Chief Marshal Sir Arthur Harris, RAF, Air Officer Commander-in-Chief (AOC-in-C), Bomber Command

King George VI, British monarch

Lieutenant R. M. Brooker, Commandant of Camp X

Lieutenant William Fairbairn, Instructor at Camp X

Baroness Amelia Anne Marie Ramsour-Fritsch (AGATHA), SOE agent

Major Kevin Shirley, (CHRISTIE) SOE agent, aka *Ulrich* Todt

Colonel Michael Jones, Camp X briefer

Major David Niven, SOE agent in Zürich

Mary Elizabeth Nesbitt, MI5 counter-intelligence agent

Löwen Proprietor, Zimmerwald, Switzerland

Peter Ruffener, Count of Fontenot, Swiss Ambassador to Germany

German Characters

Generalleutnant Peter Christian von Zimmermann, Baron Zimmermann, *Luftwaffe* pilot

Feldwebel Freitag, Grenadier Company, 1st Prussian Foot Guards

Feldwebel Schmidt, Kline's clerk at the Air Ministry

Generaloberst Karl von Kline, Commander, *Luftwaffe Luftflotte* 1

Feldwebel Holtzmann, Zimmermann's driver

Eva von Zimmermann, Zimmerman's younger sister

Helga von Zimmermann, Zimmermann's older sister

Dowager Baroness Zimmermann, Zimmermann's mother

Heinz, butler at Linden Hall

Major Hans Pieper, *Luftwaffe* pilot

Reichsführer Heinrich Himmler, head of the *Schutzstaffel (SS)*

Hauptmann Steiner, Himmler's aide

Hauptmann Klemperer, Zimmermann's escort at *Der Gevatter Tod*

Professor *Doktor* István Tisza, Hungarian atomic physicist

Oberleutnant Fritz Fischer, *Luftwaffe* navigator

Generaloberst Ernst Krause, Head of Project Armageddon

Professor *Doktor* Franz Zwilling, German atomic physicist

Stabsfeldwebel Weber, *Luftwaffe* crew chief and flight engineer

CHARLEMAGNE, German *Abwehr* double agent

Frau Schultz, proprietor of *Edelweiss* teashop

Sturmbannführer Johann Maas, SS officer

Joseph Goebbels, *Reich* Minister of Propaganda

Generaloberst Kurt Zeitzler, *Wehrmacht* Chief of the General Staff

Karl Reinhardt, member of German resistance

Deppen, Reinhardt's assistant

Oberst Klaus Boorstein, *Luftwaffe* fighter group commander

German WWII Rank Equivalents to US and UK

Reichsführer-SS—Head of *SS*/no US/UK equivalent

Reichsmarschall—Head of *Luftwaffe*/no US/UK equivalent

Grossadmiral-Kriegssmarine—Grand Admiral /US Fleet Admiral/ UK Admiral of the Fleet

Generalfeldmarschall-Wehrmacht—US General of the Army/UK Field Marshal/Marshal of the RAF

Generaloberst-Luftwaffe—US General/UK Air Chief Marshal

Generaloberst-Wehrmacht—US General/UK General

Generalleutnant-Luftwaffe—US Major General/UK Air Vice-Marshal

Generalmajor-Luftwaffe—US Brigadier General/UK Air Commodore

Oberst-Luftwaffe—US Colonel/UK Group Captain

Oberstleutnant-Luftwaffe—US Lieutenant Colonel/UK Wing Commander

Major-Luftwaffe—US Major/UK Squadron Leader

Hauptmann-Luftwaffe—US Captain/UK Flight Lieutenant

Oberleutnant-Luftwaffe—US First Lieutenant/UK Flying Officer

Stabsfeldwebel-Luftwaffe—US Master Sergeant/UK Warrant Officer

Feldwebel-Luftwaffe—US Staff Sergeant/UK Sergeant

Feldwebel–Imperial Army—US Sergeant/UK Sergeant

Unteroffizier-Wehrmacht—US Corporal/UK Corporal

Sturmbannführer SS–equivalent to a *Wehrmacht* or *Luftwaffe Major*/ no US or UK equivalent

Schütze—private in the *SS*/no US or UK equivalent

German Terms, Expressions, and Phrases

Abwehr—German military intelligence service, 1920–45

Altpörte—Speyer, "old gate," part of medieval city wall

Amerikabomber—heavy bomber capable of attacking North America

Bitte—please

Danke—thank you

Der Gevatter Tod—Godfather Death or the Grim Reaper

Der Lindenbaum—The Linden Tree

Deutschland über alles—"Germany above all, above all in the world"—opening lines of German national anthem, adopted in 1922

Freikorps—irregular volunteer military units, typically demobilized soldiers

Gasthaus—inn or guesthouse

Geschwader—*Luftwaffe* squadron

Grosser Zapfenstreich March—"Grand Tattoo," military ceremony "Salute to the Colors"

Gott im Himmel—God in Heaven

Gottverdammt—"Goddamn!"

Guten Abend—good evening

Guten Morgen—good morning

Guten Tag—good day

Heereswaffenamt—*Wehrmacht* weapons administrative office, Ordnance Office

Herr Botschafter—Mr. Ambassador

Ja/Jawohl—yes, less and more formal

Jagdgeschwader—*Luftwaffe* air superiority fighter wing

Junkers—landowning aristocracy of Prussia and eastern Germany

Kampfgeschwader—*Luftwaffe* battle wing

Kriegsmarine—German Navy, 1935–45

Kriegsverdienstkreuz—War Merit Crosse, issued to civilians and military

Kübelwagen—light military vehicle built by Volkswagen

Leibfraumilch—semisweet white German wine

Luftflotte—*Luftwaffe* air fleet

Luftwaffe—German Air Force, 1933–46

Me 108 *Taifun*—Messerschmitt Me 108 Typhoon, four-seat civilian aircraft

Meine Damen und Herren—"Ladies and Gentlemen"

Mein Gott—"My God!"

Oberkommando der Luftwaffe—Air Force High Command

Ordnungspolizei—German uniformed police force, 1936–45

Pickelhaube—spiked leather helmet popular in the nineteenth century

Reich—German state, 1933–45, Third *Reich*

Reichsluftfahrt Ministerium—Air Ministry

Reichsmark—German currency, 1924–48

Reichssicherheitsdienst—security service, provided bodyguards for Hitler/leading officials

Reichswehr—German Army of the Weimer Republic, 1919–35

Sauerbraten—marinated meat dish

Scheisse—"Shit!"

Schlosswälder—castle woods

Schmeisser—MP 40 machine pistol

Schneewalzer—"The Snow Waltz," Austrian waltz

Schnell—speedy or quickly

Schutzstaffel—"protection squad"—Nazi paramilitary organization, SS

Schweinehund—insult meaning bastard or swine, literally "pig dog"

Schwarzwälder schinken—Black Forest smoked ham

Sehr gut—very good

Spaetzle—pasta noodle dish

Stahlhelm—German steel helmet introduced in 1916

Sturmabteilung-SA—"Brownshirts, "Storm Detachment," Paramilitary organization, 1923–34

Teufel in Röcken—Devil in Skirts—German WWI term for Scottish Highland troops

Uranverein—German nuclear weapons program

Uranmaschine—nuclear reactor

Verdammt—"dammit!"

Verwundeten abzeichen—badge for combat injuries

Vesperplatte—meat, cheese, and bread platter, similar to charcuterie

Volk—"folk," the German people

Waffen—SS—military arm of the SS, operated as troops and police

Wehrmacht—German armed forces, 1935–45: *Heer* (Army), *Luftwaffe* (Air Force), *Kriegsmarine* (Navy)

Willkommen—welcome

Wolfschanze—Wolf's Lair, Hitler's command HQ in East Prussia

Wunderbar—wonderful

Würstchen—thin parboiled pork sausage

Zentral Flughafen Tempelhof—Berlin *Tempelhof* Airport

Prologue

Great cataclysmic events often turn on a
single episode of random chance.

Latitude 032N, Longitude 160W, 660 Nautical Miles NNW of Pearl Harbor, Hawai'i, 6 December 1941

0245. "Bridge, sonar," came the scratchy voice over the "bitch box," the sailors' affectionate term for the ship's internal intercom.

The Officer of the Deck (OOD) flipped down the lever, opening the transmit circuit on the intercom box. "Bridge, aye."

"Sir, I hold sonar contacts—many—bearing 320 relative."

"Officer of the Deck, aye," responded Lieutenant Tom Garrold, US Naval Reserve, doing his annual active duty training. As Officer of the Deck (OOD), he was the captain's representative who controlled all the submarine's movement, speed, etc., when the "old man" was not on the bridge or in the conning tower or control room below the bridge. The OOD coordinated all the routine reports from the various departments, maintaining a complete picture of the submarine's status. The OOD, then, represented the submarine's brain in a way. At least, that was how he always conceived of it when he tried to explain it to his high school students back in Maine. "Bearing 320 degrees relative," he mumbled to himself. If a ship or contact was at 320 degrees relative, that meant if straight ahead represented 000 relative bearing in a 360-degree circle, the contacts must be off to the left and slightly ahead of them. He swung around to the opposite side of the sub's open bridge, peered through the high-powered binoculars, and scanned the dark horizon. *Nothing yet.*

The boat had been running on the surface since 1800 when the captain ended the emergency crash dive drills and the sub was secured for routine patrol cruising. She ran on four General Motors V16 diesel engines on the surface, recharging batteries at night, the usual routine. On course 035 at ten knots since midnight, what was not routine was "many" sonar contacts, certainly not in this patrol area. A light, cool breeze flipped up his khaki collar. Even in the Central Pacific just north of Hawai'i, it was still winter. He shivered.

He toggled the intercom box. "Sonar, bridge. How many contacts?"

In the conning tower below, the petty officer pulled himself up closer to the tiny scope, squinting to get a better focus on the display of pulsing green dots in the red glow of the night lighting. "I count at least a dozen—probably more. They look big, but it's hard to get a solid return, sir. They're still pretty far out."

"Bridge, aye." Garrold knew that this particular petty officer was one of the best at the new sonar and underwater passive detection technology. "Go down for a look see," he said to the other officer on the bridge, Ensign Charlie McDaniel, the Junior Officer of the Deck (JOOD). A new officer just out of Submarine School in New London, Connecticut, McDaniel was green and inexperienced but trustworthy.

"Aye, sir."

Garrold turned his binoculars to 320 degrees again toward the contacts but still saw nothing but water. It had been, up until now, a quiet midwatch for USS *Swordfish* (SS-193). For Garrold, a Naval Reserve officer on his second patrol in *Swordfish*, it was also his first watch as a qualified OOD. He was no longer "under instruction" under the careful tutelage of the Commanding Officer (CO). *Why was it that the Navy always made your first qualified watch a mid-*

watch? He always wondered about that dynamic. *It seems to me that if anything bad happened, most likely it would be in the middle of the night when the boat was in the lowest readiness condition,* he thought as he scanned the empty horizon in search of the mysterious contacts.

"Request permission to come on the bridge?" asked the Chief of the Boat (COB), Chief Petty Officer Albert Smith, the highest-ranking enlisted man on board. His head had just popped out of the hatch leading down into the conning tower.

"Permission granted, Chief."

The COB had just come into the conning tower with his usual cup of strong coffee—a "cuppa joe"—from the crew's mess when the sonar operator reported the contacts. He came just to check up on his "new boy." All of the junior officers were the COB's "boys" until they had a few patrols under their belts. He pushed himself up onto the bridge.

"What do you think, Chief?"

"Not sure, sir. I wonder if it might be the USS *Lexington* Task Force. TF 12, I believe? Isn't that aircraft carrier taking some fighter planes to Midway Island?"

"I thought of that too, but they should be well south of here." He keyed the intercom for the conning tower. "Sonar, bridge. JOOD, check the last reported position of *Lexington.*"

McDaniel glided down the vertical ladder to the control room below. Hovering over the chart table, the petty officer on duty as Quartermaster of the Watch (QMOW) and in charge of maintaining a record of their location had just finished marking the estimated 0245 position. The QMOW shifted to let the newcomer in to examine the chart spread over the table.

"We're right here, sir," the sailor explained, pointing to a spot in the ocean. Since *Swordfish* had maintained a constant speed and steady course all night, the position would be fairly close.

"Here is the *Lexington* Task Force over near Midway Island," responded McDaniel, pointing to a small triangle drawn on the chart in red pencil, "at—" he craned his neck to read the numbers in the dim red glow, "at 1800." *No, can't be it.* The task force cruised several hundred miles distant and moving away from the submarine. He keyed the intercom. "Bridge, control. It can't be the *Lexington* force unless Pearl is really screwed up."

"I think, Chief, it's time to roust out the skipper. I hate to do that, but this isn't what we should be finding way out here," responded Garrold, now becoming tenser by the minute. He took another look in the invisible contacts' direction. Still nothing.

"Yes, sir. I'll get him myself."

"Thanks, Chief," he mumbled through cold-numbed lips.

On his way through the control room, the COB dropped his empty mug into the metal rack welded onto the bulkhead, then headed forward to the CO's stateroom. His next stop after that would be the crew berthing compartment to roust out the cook to brew up some more of the heavy, oil-black liquid. Smith suspected it would be a long night ahead for *Swordfish*.

* * * * * * * *

"Bearing to the lead ship?" shouted the captain, Commander Rich Noland, through the open hatch.

"Lead ship bears 330 relative, Skipper," came the Radarman's response from below.

"Very well. Helm. Right 10 degrees rudder, steady on new course 060."

"Right 10 degrees coming to new course 060, Helm, aye," answered the quartermaster manning the ship's wheel below in the conning tower. The "old man," the skipper, had the conn, which meant he would now give the course and speed directions to the helmsman. Meanwhile, the Executive Officer (XO), the second-in-command, Lieutenant Herb Newcomb, had arrived on the bridge, also awakened by the chief.

"What do you think, Skipper?" Newcomb asked, squinting through his binoculars into the murky predawn haze.

"Damned if I know," replied Noland. He looked at his watch, barely readable on the dark bridge. The froth thrown up by the swelling sea striking the bow turned to a fine salt spray. It enveloped the open bridge, encrusting the binocular lenses. The CO wiped his lenses for the umpteenth time in the past two hours. On the surface, USS *Swordfish* ran at 15 knots. She had been running on an intercept course to the unknown formation. Soon she would take a station ahead of and to starboard of the lead contact. She would approach the unknown ships submerged, quietly running on battery power.

"Request permission to come on the bridge?" It was the COB with a mug of steaming java freshly obtained from the wardroom.

"Permission granted."

"Coffee, Skipper?"

"Thanks, Chief."

The COB handed the CO's mug to him with a nod. The men resumed their shivering, pre-dawn vigil. Far off to the east, just over the bow, the morning's first light now streaked over the horizon, stabbing in bands of ivory light. It had been foul weather in the patrol area for several days as still evidenced by the swells that rolled the sub more than uncomfortably. The cloud cover, though, looked about to break. At least now they might get a visual identification of the many contacts to the north.

* * * * * * * *

0515. "Lead ship bears 300 relative," reported the Radarman.

"It's about that time, XO."

"Yes, sir." Newcomb patted his gloved hands together to get the circulation going, lifted the glasses over his head, and placed them into the watertight box. He clambered down the vertical ladder into the conning tower followed by the COB.

"Helm, right 10 degrees rudder. Come to new course 125."

"Right 10 degrees, coming to new course 125, Helm, aye."

Swordfish steadied out on a course parallel to the unknown formation.

"Lookouts below. Clear the bridge!" shouted the captain.

With the thunk and banging of hard leather soles against the metal deck as the lookouts scrambled through the open hatch, only the captain remained on the bridge. Two screeching "Ahhooogahs" reverberated through the metal hull as foamy water enveloped the bow. "Dive! Dive!" he shouted into the intercom box. As he slid down the ladder, he pulled the hatch shut with the lanyard. Before his feet barely touched the deck, the quartermaster spun the crank wheel, locking the hatch tight. A clean dive—no water spilled into the conning tower. "Make your depth six zero feet."

"Six zero feet, aye!" shouted the COB, who had assumed the diving officer position and now controlled the sub's movements with the flooding of ballast tanks, causing it to submerge. At 60 feet, the boat settled out. Now on battery power, she slipped silently through the murky water, away from the pitch and roll of the surface.

"Up scope," ordered the captain.

* * * * * * * *

0532. "Jesus H. Christ! They're Japs!" shouted the astonished Newcomb, his arms draped over the periscope arms.

"Are you sure?" shot back an equally astonished Noland.

"Yes, sir. That large boy . . . it's a Jap carrier . . . I'm sure of it!"

"Let me see," exploded the skipper, fairly shoving aside the gawking XO and peering into the periscope eyepiece. He felt a tug on his shirtsleeve. The navigator extended his hand, offering the international ship recognition chart for the Imperial Japanese Navy. Noland peered through the high-power periscope across the choppy, black water at the intruders' silhouettes, just barely above the horizon. "Close enough, but we need a better look. Let's angle in."

"Sounds good, Skipper," the XO said, gushing with excitement at the prospect.

Noland slapped the folding periscope handle arms back into the up position. "Down scope!" With an electric hum, the metal tube slid back down into its sheath. "Helm. Left 10 degrees rudder, steady on new course 080."

"Left 10 degrees rudder coming to new course 080. Helm, aye."

"Make your depth five zero feet."

Swordfish slowly but perceptibly closed with the contacts.

* * * * * * * *

0610. USS *Swordfish* closed to 8,000 yards ahead of the Japanese formation. At the much slower submerged speed, she would pass close to the lead ship, confirmed to be a carrier. Two more periscope observations confirmed it. Noland wiped his moist brow with the back of his hand. He gazed down at the metal deck plate and asked, "Bearing to the lead ship?"

"Lead ship bears 280 relative," responded the Radarman.

"Very well. Helm. Right standard rudder, come to new course 125."

"Right standard rudder coming to new course 125. Helm, aye."

Swordfish gently rolled to the right, to starboard, as the propellers bit into the water, which washed over the rudder as she moved into an attack position. *The world is a nasty place*, thought Noland as he took in a deep breath of the heavy, dank air of the crowded conning tower. From far back in his past, he thought of a phrase, a watch-word drilled into him his plebe year at the Naval Academy. *Authority equals responsibility equals accountability.*

"Officer of the Deck, go to battle stations."

"Battle stations, aye," responded Garrold. The general alarm sounded throughout the boat, the loud clanging reverberating off the metal bulkheads. Men still in the racks leapt out and threw on clothes and shoes, then raced to their assigned battle stations. At that moment, a thought occurred to Garrold: *Now I'm damned not likely to be back teaching high school history any time soon!*

In the control room, Chief Smith bit his lower lip. The world was about to fall apart.

0616. Unofficially, *Swordfish* had been at battle stations for some time. Ever since the word spread throughout the boat that they had stumbled upon a Japanese carrier task force, the atmosphere had become electric. In ones and twos, men downed a last swallow of coffee and made their way to their battle stations. Only a few men had still been asleep when the general alarm sounded. In spite of the tension, there was very little talking, only some nervous chatter and the professional voices of more senior petty officers making their spaces ready. *Was the skipper going to attack? What if they sank a Japanese carrier? Were the men of Swordfish being propelled into World War II?* With the tension that mounted throughout the autumn as American-Japanese tensions ratcheted up and especially with the war warning message of late November, *Swordfish* was practically on a war footing already with torpedoes in their tubes and deck gun ammunition stowed in the watertight ready service lockers. The torpedoes were all war shots—no practice "fish," slang for the deadly weapon that could break apart even the largest ship. Hadn't SUBPAC, the commander of all Pacific Fleet submarines, all but admitted before their patrol began on 1 December that war with Japan was imminent? "Sweat pumps" ran at full blast in Washington, in Pearl Harbor, and in the Pacific Fleet. This was not just another drill. Within seconds, manned and ready reports started coming in. In 40 seconds, the phone talker reported to the captain, "all stations manned and ready." In the cramped conning tower, the feverish sweat of several men added to the already hot, humid atmosphere.

"Battle stations set throughout the boat," advised Garrold.

"Very well," responded the captain.

USS *Swordfish*, like a medieval knight, prepared for battle. She had eight Mk 14 torpedoes loaded and ready, four in the forward torpedo tubes and four in the stern tubes. The slow churning of the propellers and the faint hiss of high-pressure compressed air that would thrust the torpedoes out of their tubes could not be heard by the ships on the surface above. Within the submarine's metal pressure hull, every man could now hear the whoosh, whoosh, whoosh sound of multiple propeller blades above them. On the captain's order, the boat came back left to course 035, now running perpendicular to the task force at barely three knots.

"OOD. Take her to periscope depth," ordered Noland, who earlier had passed the conn back to Garrold.

"Periscope depth, aye. Diving officer. Make your depth five zero feet."

"Five zero, aye," responded Smith.

The diving planes, rudder-like fins that caused the sub to move up or down vertically in the water much like an airplane's ailerons, bit into the water. Slowly and gracefully, the sub rose toward the surface.

"Six zero feet . . . five five feet . . . five eight . . . five zero . . ." called off Smith.

"Very well. Up scope!"

They heard an electric hum as the attack periscope slid up the tube. Unlike the observation periscope that provided a broad wide-angle view of the sea and sky, the attack periscope showed only a narrow picture of the target and was used to calculate its position relative to the submarine, as well as the target's speed, distance, and course, all vital data needed for a successful torpedo attack. Noland slapped down the periscope's handles and draped his arms over them, twirling the tube around, searching for his target, face pressed tight against the eyepiece.

"I hold the lead carrier . . . bearing . . . mark . . . range . . . mark . . . down scope," he called off the data rapid-fire, which the XO calculated quickly to estimate the target's speed, course, and distance from them. The periscope slid back down quickly. He didn't want the scope out of the water except for very short periods lest the enemy lookouts spot it.

"Bearing 315 . . . range . . . 2 divisions . . . high power . . ."

"Range . . . 3,000 yards."

"Angle on the bow?"

"Starboard four five."

"Set."

"Initial observation on the target?"

"Speed . . . three knots."

"Depth five zero feet."

"Up scope!" The whirr of electric motors filled the conning tower again. "I make her an *Akagi*-class aircraft carrier. XO, confirm."

Newcomb stepped up to the attack periscope. He only needed a second to confirm the target. The Imperial Japanese Navy ensign fluttered in the early morning breeze. He saw clearly the flag as well as the rakish angle of the bow and the compact superstructure jutting out of the flight deck.

"Confirmed as *Akagi*-class carrier. Imperial Japanese Navy."

"Down scope. Quartermaster, how far are we from the exclusion zone boundary?"

"Sir," he paused, "we are just inside the northern exclusion zone." With the threat of war, the US Navy established zones around Hawai'i. Any non-US ship, especially Japanese, risked attack.

The two men hovered by the attack periscope, their eyes not six inches apart. A bead of sweat welled up on the captain's forehead and rolled down onto his khaki collar. It settled onto the silver oak leaf rank device pinned to the collar. In spite of their hushed whispers, every ear in the conning tower clearly heard their words—and their anguish—even over the noise of tense, nervous breathing. *Authority equals responsibility equals accountability.*

"What do you think, XO?" questioned Noland.

Newcomb took a deep breath of the heavy air, then let it out slowly and deliberately, knowing the importance of his next few words. Each man in the conning tower huddled over his particular piece of gear, but their attention lay elsewhere.

"Well, Skipper, we both know what they're up to. Pearl has to be warned. But . . . jeez . . . if we can take out even one of those carriers . . . well . . . the bastards may have to think about proceeding on with an attack." He looked straight into the CO's eyes, searching for any sign of approval or even acknowledgement. There was none. Not yet. The "old man" waited for the other half of the equation he knew had to be stated. He demanded recommendations and solutions from his officers, not statements of the problem.

"On the other hand?" the CO prompted.

"On the other hand," the XO said, pausing, "do we want to be the ones to fire the first shot? I mean . . . it's one thing for those bastards to start it. But us? I don't know, Skipper. I just don't know. And we are just within the exclusion zone. There's room for navigational error here."

The captain concurred. There was the rub.

"Another thing. We'll never have a better shot than we have right now . . . at this moment . . . but . . . even if we get a hit, what if their destroyers get us before we can alert Pearl? We wouldn't have done a damn thing."

So there it is. The XO had done his job. He laid out the options and the consequences. An old military axiom says that no matter how good the staff recommendations, the ultimate decision lay with the person in command. Noland dropped his head, his chin touching his chest, contemplating his options . . . his onerous options.

"XO. Man the TDC," he shouted.

"Aye, aye, Skipper!" responded Newcomb.

The TDC, the Torpedo Data Computer, received data on bearing and range, course and speed, and calculated the firing solution. It served as the primary fire control mechanism for a torpedo attack, As Newcomb turned toward the TDC, he stopped, then turned back to Noland.

"You know, I'll back you up, whatever the decision, whatever it takes."

Noland shook his head. He paused, then made the decision. "Up scope. Open outer doors on all forward tubes." The atmosphere in the conning tower felt charged as if lightning had struck. The captain had initiated "firing point procedures," those rapid-fire orders and final calculations made as a submarine lines up the target and launches its deadly weapons.

"Outer doors open."

"Very well. Observation on the target . . . bearing . . . mark . . . range . . . mark . . . down scope!"

"Bearing 325 . . . range . . . 2.5 divisions high power."

"Range . . . 2,000 yards."

"Angle on the bow."

"Starboard three five."

"Set."

"Observation on the target?"

"Speed . . . three knots."

"Depth five zero feet."

"Firing point procedures on the target, torpedo tubes 1, 2, 3, and 4!"

Months of training, hundreds of drills, ever so precise, ever so tedious, now proved their worth. In the stifling, sweaty air of the conning tower, the men of USS *Swordfish* performed their tasks with precision. They did what they trained to do—their only mission, their reason for being—a submarine on an attack run.

"Ship ready!"

"Solution ready!"

"Weapons ready!"

"Final bearing and shoot!"

"Speed . . . three knots."

"Bearing 330."

"Depth five zero feet."

"Up scope! Bearing . . . mark . . . down scope."

"Bearing 332."

"Set!"

"Standby."

I know what you're up to, you sorry bastards. I can get at least one of you before you get me. You get me . . . and then you'll attack Pearl Harbor anyway. How many hundreds, no, thousands of guys will you kill if you get me before I can alert Pearl? How many guys . . . you sorry bastards . . . I hate you! Another day, mates! Noland slammed the periscope casing. It bruised his hand.

"Down scope. Helm. Right full rudder, all ahead 2/3, make your depth one zero, zero feet!"

"Right full rudder, Helm, aye."

"All ahead 2/3, Helm, aye."

"One zero feet, aye."

"Close outer doors on all tubes. XO, get the leading Radioman up here ASAP!" shouted Noland.

"Roger," responded Newcomb.

* * * * * * * *

Minutes later a FLASH message, with the highest precedence for speed of delivery, went out to Pearl Harbor from *Swordfish* warning them of the Japanese task force presumably headed for an air attack on Oahu military installations. It read

FLASH

061930 Z DEC 41

FROM: USS SWORDFISH

TO: COMSUBPAC

INFO: CINCPAC; CINCPACFLT

SUBJ: CONTACT REPORT

BT

1. SIGHTED JAPANESE REPEAT JAPANESE AIRCRAFT CARRIER TASK FORCE, LAT 031.30N. LONG 159.00W. CSE 125. SPD 15 KTS.

2. POSITIVE ID AT LEAST FOUR REPEAT FOUR CARRIERS. POSSIBLE SIX CARRIERS REPEAT SIX CARRIERS. POSITIVE ID LEAD CARRIER AS AKAGI CLASS. POSSIBLE BATTLESHIPS. MANY ESCORTS.

3. TRAILING IN TATTLETALE.

BT

* * * * * * * *

Naval Station Pearl Harbor, Hawai'i Territory, 6 December 1941

1035. USS *Arizona* (BB-39), flagship of Rear Admiral Isaac Kidd's Battleship Division One, rounded Hospital Point. Within minutes, she made the open sea, followed by the *Oklahoma* (BB-37) and *Nevada* (BB-36). Captain Franklin Van Valkenburgh ordered maximum speed and set course for the fleet rendezvous point northwest of Oahu as the United States Pacific Fleet responded to the general emergency sortie order directing all ships to get underway and depart the harbor as rapidly as possible. By early afternoon, all ships that could get underway had cleared the channel.

1630 Hawai'i time, 6 December 1941. Admiral Yamamoto Isoroku, Commander-in-Chief, Combined Fleet, Imperial Japanese Navy, issued the recall order. Within a few minutes, the six aircraft carriers and their escort cruisers and destroyers of the Mobile Force, the 1st Air Fleet of the *Kido Butai*, came about to a course of 280 degrees headed for Japanese home waters. A day later, the Japanese imperial government issued an apology to the United States for the "accidental intrusion into Hawai'ian waters of Japanese naval forces on a training cruise." War had indeed been averted by that random chance encounter—an American submarine on patrol in the right place at the right time. Averted . . . for now.

PART I.
Armageddon

CHAPTER 1

The Cabaret Paris

Selle River, Northeast France, 23 October 1918

The artillery barrage ceased. Across the trench line came screams of agony—the wounded, the maimed, and the soon to be dead. A few shells had landed directly into the German trench. Men of the Grenadier Company of the 1st Foot Guards Regiment of the Prussian Guards raced to their comrades, binding horrific wounds with whatever scraps of cloth that could be found. Pools of blood mixed with the rain of the early morning compounded by the ever-present mud made it even more treacherous. Men cursed and stumbled over prostrate bodies in the carnage left by the artillery barrage. Pitiful cries from shattered men welled up into a crescendo, then died down again as men "crossed over the river" or simply fell into unconsciousness. Lesser men might have run for safety, but not these men. They were Prussians, soldiers of the Imperial Guard, warriors of the first order. They would stand their ground and meet whatever came at them. The barrage lasted 20 minutes. All quiet.

Hauptmann (captain) Peter von Zimmermann, scion of an old Brandenburg noble family, raised the binoculars up and observed the empty field separating the hastily constructed trench line from the

British enemy occupying the woods beyond. A dank early morning mist hanging over the line mixed with the cordite odor of exploded artillery rounds gave the battlefield a surreal, eerie feel. As he moved the glasses around back and forth across the area in front of the Guard's position in search of what he knew came next, he mused that this must be what Dante's Hell had to be.

"*Herr Hauptmann, Herr Hauptmann!*"

"*Ja, Feldwebel* (sergeant). What is it?"

"Report, sir. Many casualties. Both machine gun crews are completely wiped out."

"Steady on, Freitag." He lowered the glasses and stared directly at the noncommissioned officer. "We have been in this position before, have we not? The men will hold. They have never broken before."

"Just so, sir. Just so. I'll see to a casualty count."

"*Danke*, Freitag."

Zimmerman turned back toward the area immediately before them. The mist had only grown dimmer. Just as the company senior sergeant turned to assess the damage and count the casualties, a strange, almost shrieking sound came from within the mist. Freitag turned sharply and leaned against the sandbag parapet, straining to make out the noise. It grew louder and louder by the second, no doubt amplified by the wet, sticky mist.

"*Teufel in Röcken! Herr Hauptmann. Teufel in Röcken!*" shouted a man further down the trench line.

Zimmermann only shook his head, already sensing what came at them across the way. *Teufel in Röcken*—the Devil in Skirts. Scottish Highlanders. Coming from across the far side of the copse of trees several hundred yards ahead of his position, Zimmermann heard a familiar and terrifying sound of bagpipes. The first time he had heard the terrific noise had been in 1915 on his second day in the trenches. Fellow officers laughed at the noise drifting across the devastated patch of shell-pocked mud that stank of putrid-smelling, decaying flesh where a stand of old oaks once stood. One trench mate likened it to beating an old cat with a broom. They all laughed. They were all dead now.

Across the field from the Prussian position emerged Piper MacDougall from the woods piping the tune for a charge—"Monymusk." Shielded by the trees stood B Company, 10th Battalion, The Argyll and Sutherland Highlanders of the 97th Brigade, 32nd Division, X Corps of Sir Henry Rawlinson's British Fourth Army, primed to race across the mist-shrouded "No Man's Land" directly at the Prussian position.

"*Teufel in Röcken,*" whispered Freitag over and over, an enigmatic frown on his grimy, mud- and powder-streaked face. Zimmermann could not tell if it was fright, disgust, or malice. He looked left, then right. The young men who now made up his company—boys, really, and a few older men not actually fit for forward area service—fidgeted and squirmed. One looked about to cry. One simply stood silent, jaw set, but with no expression on his youthful face. All knew what the dreadful sound coming from the far trees meant.

He had done the best he could in erecting makeshift defensive works. The regiment had fallen back many miles in the past week, pounded by British artillery and strafed by the ever- constant Royal Air Force fighters. *Where were the German air squadrons? No matter. Can't be helped.* Still, the enemy was relentless, pressing ever deeper into the area so long safely occupied by the *Kaiser's* forces. The Allied Hundred Days Offensive that began on 8 August near Amiens had since simply rolled on and on and on. General Erich von Ludendorff had called it the "Black Day of the German Army." Now, in late October, as the German lines collapsed everywhere along the Western Front, the battalion, decimated with every new attack and with no reinforcements in weeks, sought to hold back the advancing Allied tide. Retreat, reform, then retreat again. Build new defensive works. Then retreat again, losing even more precious men with each new encounter. The Allied juggernaut rolled on, beefed up by hundreds of thousands of new troops—Americans, Yanks, the doughboys.

"*Teufel in Röcken*," the *Feldwebel* whispered again. Zimmermann lifted the binoculars up and scanned the far woods, but nothing appeared. Only the squealing sound came across the open ground between his makeshift trench and the woods beyond. He gripped the glasses harder and muttered under his breath, *Gott im Himmel*—God in Heaven.

Slowly the noise formed a new melody, a jaunty melody—"Highland Laddie." Zimmermann recognized it from his travel days before the war. He shook his head in recognition. He turned to the *Feldwebel*. "*Ja*, Freitag. You are correct. Devil in Skirts."

Across the way, the Argyll and Sutherlands gathered at the wood's edge around Piper MacDougall. The early morning misty air amplified the shrill melody and whine of drones, making it a primeval screech that rolled across the open ground toward the German position. One by one, men appeared beside the piper, kilted men, Highlanders, descendants of an age-old warrior race. Hundreds of them gathered on the wood's edge, grim-faced, determined, and seething.

Zimmermann looked up and down his line once again. Less than 40 men remained of his company. In August, they had numbered over 200. He lowered his head, not in shame, but in recognition that within minutes, his company would likely disappear. "*Gott im Himmel*," he whispered again as the *Feldwebel* merely shook his head in understanding and recognition.

Across the way, MacDougall finished "Highland Laddie" and launched into "All the Bluebonnets are o'er the Border," the signal for the assault. An officer raised his cane in the air and blew his silver whistle. A great shout came from up and down the line and, like a swarm of ants, they came forward in an inexorable wave, bent on mayhem and carnage. It started with a slow walk, then a quick step, and, as the human wave gathered momentum, finally turned into a run.

With bayonets fixed on the muzzles of their Lee-Enfield rifles—British cold steel—the wave surged forward in an age-old rush of a headlong assault, a throwback to warfare of ancient times.

Zimmermann looked behind him. The artillery pre-assault barrage had churned up the ground behind them but had done less damage than it might have. The advance had moved so rapidly that the Royal Artillery had not been able to range their field guns accurately. Nonetheless, they had landed a few rounds on top of the Germans finding shelter as best as possible. *Thank goodness for small miracles,* he thought. *There could have been many more casualties.* He observed that he had not lost too many men in the barrage, which typically devastated the troops hunkered down in their shallow trench before an assault. Fortunately, there was no poison gas. Many of his men had lost their gas masks in the headlong retreat. Many had no helmets. Some lost their bayonets as well. In better days, Maxim machine guns would have cut down the attacking Britons like harvested wheat, but not this day. He had started the retreat days earlier with six machine guns, but all had been put out of action. Now the men faced the assault with nothing but Mauser rifles, a few bayonets, and some pistols. Little ammunition remained. *Very well then. A Mauser makes an excellent war club.* A few still had their trench knives for close-in hand-to-hand fighting. He turned back toward the oncoming horde, now only 200 yards distant and coming on fast. He drew his service pistol, a *Parabellum*—commonly known as a *Luger.* It was a good weapon, but he had only a single clip remaining. *It will have to do.* As the kilted men came closer, he thought of his home in Brandenburg and the rows of beautiful linden trees that lined the drive leading up to the main house. He envisioned how gorgeous they were in springtime and in bloom. His great-grandfather had planted the neat rows of linden saplings and so impressive were they that the estate came to be called *Der Lindenbaum*—The Linden Tree. He had not been home in months. Now he doubted he would ever see the wonderful linden trees again. The early morning mist cleared. All he could think of now was the admonition of some American militia general from the

War of American Independence, who reportedly shouted to his men, "Don't fire until you see the whites of their eyes." He chuckled. *Fire with what now? Fire with what?*

The first wave of Highlanders struck the trench. The hand-to-hand combat began as the firing ceased. Zimmermann later recalled how deathly silent all seemed for a few brief seconds. Perhaps it was just the concussion caused by the artillery barrage. Then a great roar arose along the line as hundreds of men in khaki and kilts poured over the top and down into the hastily dug, shallow trench. Men screamed as bayonets thrust forward into human flesh. There were few shots, only the cries and shouts of men struggling with each other, of clubbed rifles striking human bodies, and a clang of metal as his men desperately warded off the oncoming bayonets of the frenzied Scots.

Amazingly, no one appeared ahead of him. The shape of the ground, which sloped down on either side just in front of his position, must have channeled the enemy to his left and right. But more on-rushers poured into the trench, overwhelming his outnumbered men. He aimed his pistol at the nearest enemy to his right and fired, but the shot went wide—no damage. As he re-aimed for a second shot, in his peripheral vision he saw a huge, monstrous, looming presence barreling down on him. No time to fire, Zimmermann wheeled about to face the oncoming man.

With bayonet and Enfield extended out, Company Sergeant-Major (CSM) Hamish Mackenzie raced over the parapet and down into the trench aiming directly at Zimmermann with rage in his eyes. In the three years since the CSM first arrived on the Western Front, he had seen many friends and comrades die or become maimed and crippled. There was no pity in his eyes, even though everyone already knew the Hun was beaten. No pity, only rage. He thrust forward with the bayonet, aimed squarely at Zimmermann's abdomen.

In a swift move that surprised both himself and Mackenzie, Zimmermann parried the thrust with the pistol barrel. Deftly, he brought the muzzle around and over the bayonet to set up a shot.

Mackenzie had survived three years in the trenches and learned too well to be fooled by such a move. He jerked the rifle upward and struck the pistol's trigger guard. The shot went high. For a fraction of a second, the words of Zimmermann's fencing master, a Hungarian sabre Olympic champion, struck him: *Play off his strength. If he thrusts, you dodge. Let the opponent overextend. Catch him off balance as you jump aside. Then strike down atop his helmet. Strike!* Zimmermann dodged the next thrust, surprised at how nimble he still was despite the exhaustion from days of marching, retreating, and few rations. Off-balance with having thrust forward and expecting the target to be dead ahead, Mackenzie stumbled, but only for a moment. As he regained his footing, Zimmermann struck. The now empty pistol came down hard on the Scot's shoulder, staggering the man. Mackenzie reeled backward, and only the forward trench wall caught his fall. Advantage, Zimmermann.

"Bloody Hun bastard!" he shouted. He brought the rifle up into a defensive stance expecting the German to thrust back. But Zimmermann had nothing—no bayonet, no trench knife, nothing but an empty pistol. Undaunted, he tried to strike the enemy with the pistol butt. Too late! Mackenzie had recovered his stance and thrust forward again with the bayonet.

This time, the exhaustion of too many days on short rations, of worry for his men, of retreat after retreat, finally took hold. He was spent. Although he swung the pistol around in a parry motion, he was simply too slow. The blow was too weak and just glanced off the oncoming bayonet. It did, though, deflect the thrust enough to carry the bayonet point away from his stomach and down toward his thigh. The 18-inch long bayonet found the mark. It sliced through his uniform trousers and deep into his right thigh. Strangely though, he felt nothing—only a slight prick feeling. What he did not and could not know was that the CSM's bayonet had not only penetrated deep, it had nicked the femoral artery. He staggered backward and fell against the trench rear wall. As he fell, Mackenzie yanked the bayonet from his thigh. Zimmermann was stunned. His vision suddenly blurred.

His arms flailed, uncontrolled. Mackenzie drew back the weapon and poised it for another strike, this time for the killing thrust.

"Sergeant-Major! Over here, on the double!"

Mackenzie stopped his thrust in mid-poise, the bayonet's tip only inches from the prostrate Zimmermann's chest. Mackenzie looked over to his right at his company commander waving his swagger stick. He looked back down at the enemy, prostrate and helpless with crimson blood now pouring from the gash. "Another day, Fritz. Another day." With that, Mackenzie drew back his rifle and raced off toward the officer as all up and down the line, more and more Highlanders poured into the trench and just as quick over the other side in hot pursuit of the fleeing survivors of the Grenadier Company of the Prussian 1st Foot Guards, a proud unit that literally existed no more.

Zimmermann tried to stand. He wobbled, then collapsed again back against the trench wall. He tried to raise his hand but couldn't. Even though his *stahlhelm* (helmet) had fallen off as he initially fell back, he simply could not raise his head. His chin dropped down onto his chest, onto his mud-stained tunic. He stared at his decoration—an Iron Cross 1st Class now flecked with red mud. In his welling agony, he stared at the medal for several seconds. *Why had he worn this damned thing today?* Then a thought shot through his barely conscious mind. *A silly medal really. A silly medal. Why wear it at all?* He mustered a chuckle at the irony. He had a medal and an empty pistol, but as of a few minutes' past, he had no company. The Grenadiers were all now dead, wounded, or captured. His command ceased to exist. He had only this bit of iron and ribbon—and a deadly bayonet wound delivered by an enemy in a lust for vengeance. He chuckled at the irony and muttered under his breath, "God Save the *Kaiser!*" He laughed with all the energy he could muster. As his head started to spin, he reached out his right hand and placed it on his wounded thigh, no doubt in a futile attempt to stanch the blood spurting from the ruptured artery and flowing down into his boots. The crimson fluid poured out over his leather glove, turning it a deep brownish color. As his consciousness faded, his last vision was of *Feldwebel* Freitag a few feet over, face down, and sprawled over a wooden box that had held the last of the company's rifle ammunition.

* * * * * * * *

A Field Hospital behind the Front, 25 October 1918

He awoke. Maybe it was a throbbing pain in his leg. As his vision returned from the blur of semi-consciousness, he focused on the back of the man standing next to him wearing a bloodstained, but at one time, white linen hospital apron. The man heard him move and wheeled about.

"Aah, Captain, awake now."

Zimmermann tried to sit up, but couldn't.

"There now, lad. Stay still. You have lost a lot of blood. Nasty wound that, but we have caught it in time. You are damned fortunate, I might add. Another few minutes and you would have bled out." The man in the white apron leaned over and gently touched the bandage covering the thigh. "Yes, indeed, damned lucky."

Zimmermann noted the red flash on the man's khaki blouse— R.A.M.C.—Royal Army Medical Corps. The crown device on the shoulder straps indicated that he was a major in His Majesty's forces. The British medical officer leaned down and carefully examined the thigh, gently lifting the top bandage and inspecting the now healing wound.

"Nicely done. You should recover soon assuming the gangrene or infection doesn't set in. By the way, Dr. Walsh, Dr. Frank Walsh, R.A.M.C. Welcome to our side." The doctor grinned broadly.

"How . . . how did I get here, *Herr Doktor*?"

"Aah, Captain. You are very fortunate indeed. Your sergeant there brought you in day before yesterday. Damned kind of him I should say. He saved your life." Zimmermann was only now aware of

Feldwebel Freitag in the next cot over, bandages around his head and left arm, and grinning like a Cheshire Cat.

"My men. My soldiers. Are they—?"

"Not many left, I'm afraid. And those that survived are either here or on their way to the prisoner processing site. I'm afraid your unit was completely overrun. The Argyll and Sutherlands didn't bring in many prisoners. But, young man, your war is over, as indeed, so is your Fatherland's. There is talk of an armistice. You are bloody fortunate to have survived. Well, I have other patients to tend to. You rest and you'll be right as rain soon enough."

With that, the doctor padded off down the line of cots filled with wounded men, both British and German. *Hauptmann* Peter von Zimmermann, commander of the Grenadier Company of the *Kaiser's* 1st Foot Guards Regiment of Crown Prince Rupprecht of Bavaria's 4th Army, dropped his head to his pillow. His war was indeed finished.

* * * * * * * *

The Cabaret Paris, Berlin, 23 February 1943

"Your hat, *Herr General*?" asked the perky young lady manning the hatcheck stand.

"Ja, of course. *Danke.*" He had drifted off into a haze as he entered the cabaret's dark entryway. *The Cabaret Paris.* He had not been here since his darling wife Ingrid had been killed by a drunken and careless driver. But ever the stoic and strictly formal military man, he endured in silence and never let emotion cloud his coldly rational external persona. But inside his heart and soul, he grieved mightily for his lost wife. Outwardly, he just soldiered on—Prussian warrior-aristocrat to the end.

He had not been to the Cabaret Paris in years. How could he? It had been their favorite nightspot. Zimmermann, as the gallant war hero, and Ingrid, his sophisticated, charming, beautiful soulmate, had visited the cabaret often, dancing through the night and only leaving in the early morning hours in the bohemian and carefree Berlin of the 1920s. Now, he simply could not go near the place. Although he had passed the club on *Nollendorffstrasse* many times, he always looked away and never entered.

Why he came this evening he could not say. An odd notion engulfed him as he headed back from his office at *Luftwaffe* headquarters to his elegant flat on *Kleiststrasse* in an upscale Berlin neighborhood for a solitary dinner and quiet reading. Some emotion from deep within caused him to head to the club that evening even with all the memories. Still not completely understanding why, he rang up the club to reserve a table and then his office at headquarters. As the chief of staff to a major commander, he needed to inform them of his whereabouts at all times.

As he pulled the Mercedes into a space across from the club, an odd smirk broke across his face. "Thank you, Mr. Churchill," he said, laughing aloud. Parking at the club had always been a problem until that night in late August 1940 when Royal Air Force (RAF) bombers mounted a raid on Berlin in retaliation for the accidental bombing of London's East End during the Battle of Britain. The formation of Heinkel He 111 medium bombers had lost their navigational picture and, thinking they had missed the target, aborted the mission. Assuming they were over farm pastures, they let go their bomb loads. Unfortunately, they were over the city. Thus began the bombing of British cities, which the British dubbed "the Blitz." He considered it a strategic disaster. How much longer could the RAF hold out before being forced to move to the northern airfields? A week? Maybe two? His *Luftwaffe* had been so effective in attacking RAF airfields and bases that hardly a Spitfire or Hurricane fighter could get off the ground due to the bomb holes and craters. Then that damned fool Hitler and his lapdog Göring committed an incredible blunder in changing the targets to British cities. *Damn them, damn them all! The war might be over by now and the Fatherland redeemed from the humiliation of 1919. The chaos of war!* At any rate, one of the British bombs had demolished the building across the street from the club and, once the rubble had been cleared, a nice parking lot emerged. The irony of war!

Despite the blackout, he saw clearly the club's outline and headed across the street with an inexplicable lightness in his step. That mood changed as a heavy oak door slammed behind him. Though the entranceway was dim due to the blackout regulations, he could still see the pictures adorning the walls that reminded patrons of better times. Black and white photos, neatly signed by the stars and celebrities that graced the club over the years before the war, still hung from the walls. He actually remembered many of them. But the sight of the smiling celebrities reminded him again of why he had not been to this place of mirth, music, and joy in ever so long—they reminded him of Ingrid.

"Your hat, *Herr General*?" repeated the hatcheck girl. He handed his service cap over to her. It was the bluish-gray peaked hat adorned with the silver coil that indicated a *Generalmajor* of the German *Luftwaffe*. He hated that hat with the eagle and swastika of the despised Nazi regime. He served the Fatherland, not the fools at the *Reich* chancellery. She handed him the ticket and gracefully motioned him toward the heavy black curtain that masked the club's bright interior lights. "Enjoy your evening, *Herr General*."

"*Danke.*" He turned and strode over to the curtain, parted it, and was struck immediately by the bright yellowish light from the lit candles that adorned each table. The noise of happy patrons startled him at first. Then he heard the music from the house orchestra. He had expected to hear some blaring marshal tune or perhaps some thumping Wagnerian opera—a sign of the times in wartime Berlin. Instead, the musicians played a swing tune, an American swing tune! *He knew it. What was it? Aah, yes. Something by the American Glenn Miller. What was it? "A String of Pearls." That's it. Even the Nazis recognized a good tune, I suppose.*

"*Guten Abend, Herr General.* Right this way. Your table is ready."

With only a nod, he followed the *maître d'* to a table in the corner somewhat away from the main floor but still close enough to hear the jaunty tune. Zimmermann gazed about the crowded floor.

It seemed that everyone was in a uniform of some sort, mostly of the various branches of the new national bureaucracy—Party apparatchiks he guessed. While thousands of solid German men died every day on the ghastly Eastern Front, these overbearing, self-important National Socialist hacks and functionaries drank, danced, and reveled to American dance music. He stared off onto the stage, now lit by bright yellow and red stage-floor lights. His thoughts went back to the night bombing raids over Britain. The stage lights reminded him of the ever-present searchlights, stabbing the sky, angry lights looking for his bombers, his men, his aviators. And, inevitably, there came the flash and horror of the anti-aircraft fire. Soon would come the RAF night fighters. He had lost many good men on those raids. "Göring's Folly" they called it.

"What, aah—?"

"I said, sir . . . may I help you?" The waiter spoke again, jarring him out of the trance of the past several minutes.

"*Ja*, I was just . . . just thinking of how this place used to be before the war." *Before the war. Before the war.* A time when he and Ingrid had been young, in love, and came to this cabaret to drink, to meet good friends—many now dead—and to enjoy life.

"*Jawohl, Herr General.* Before the war." The waiter had a downtrodden look on his face. Zimmermann had neither noticed the man's limp nor could he know it was a souvenir of the trenches. What he did notice was that all the waiters seemed older than he remembered. They were mostly middle-aged men, some bearing scars of the previous war as he did as well. *Was it not inevitable—the scars of war?* All the young men were in the forces now somewhere on the Eastern Front struggling against the Soviets in what he knew was the mad *Führer's* grotesque folly. Or, they manned some lonely garrison throughout the new *Reich* Empire won by the sword and brute aggression. They might be facing the wrathful British perhaps in the Navy or maybe in the North African desert in support of their Italian allies.

Finally jostled out of his reminiscences, he replied to the waiter, "I'll have a whiskey and soda."

"*Danke, Herr Generalmajor*. At once." With a deep bow made somewhat clumsy by his crippled leg, the waiter hobbled off toward the bar. Zimmermann's eyes followed the man. Just a little bit in envy, he watched the crippled waiter move slowly toward the bar. "His war is over. Mine? Well, mine goes on," he mumbled to himself to no one in particular.

"A String of Pearls" finished and the house band struck up a new tune, some patriotic mumbo-jumbo about the greater *Reich* or some such business. Zimmermann merely shook his head. Such were the times. The floodlights came up and the master of ceremonies leapt up to center stage.

"*Meine Damen und Herren. Willkommen* to the Cabaret Paris!" The band blared out what sounded like a military bugle call. From each stage wing appeared dancers, mostly female, young girls dressed in black and silver skimpy costumes. They all sported black and silver peaked service caps with the Nazi swastika prominently displayed on the crown. Immediately, the band struck up a raucous *Deutschland über alles*. The crowd roared as patrons sprang to their feet gleefully applauding and singing along. *Generalmajor* Peter von Zimmermann sat motionless, just staring at the spectacle on stage as the master of ceremonies pranced about singing louder and louder until the final crescendo. The audience roared and shouted in a hearty applause. Zimmermann still sat mute and silent.

As the noise simmered down and the dancers twirled offstage, the waiter quietly placed the drink down on the table with just a nod. Zimmermann replied in kind. As the waiter turned to head to another table, Zimmermann raised his hand.

"*Jawohl, Herr Generalmajor?* May I help you?"

"Why don't you bring another. This looks to be a two whiskey and soda night."

"At once, *Herr Generalmajor*." The waiter toddled off toward the bar, leaving Zimmermann with his thoughts.

The show went on. Zimmermann hardly noticed. He quietly sipped his drink as he stepped back into a melancholy trance. His mind went back to better times again. The shows of years gone by came to mind, typical of the more carefree days at the prewar cabaret. These were happy shows with cheerful young dancers and actors, of mirth and, truth be told, of some typically raunchy and off-color jokes. Ingrid loved the ribald jokes, the blatant naughty humor of it all. Now the show was simply a paean to National Socialism and the glory of the new Third *Reich*.

Days of old, he pondered. *Days of old*. His mind drifted back again. *How had he come to this point?* After the war, he stayed in the Army, one of the 100,000 men allowed by that noxious, humiliating Treaty of Versailles. Germany was the pariah, but he still believed in the Fatherland. He was a Prussian aristocrat, a warrior, a soldier. He had been determined to defend the Fatherland whatever it may be. But the wounded leg ended his army career. He was no longer of use as an infantry officer. His beloved regiment, the Prussian 1st Foot Guards, had been disbanded, tossed away as a relic of the old order. Yet he stayed on as was his duty in the new German Army.

He learned to fly and proved an excellent pilot, flying any aircraft he could find. The rush of the wind past his ears thrilled him no end. Ingrid was fearful for his safety, but for him, the loops and circles in the sky excited him; he thrived on the adrenaline of death-defying flight. When the new German Air Force, the *Luftwaffe*, emerged from the shambles of the Great Depression and with the rise of a new nationalism spurred on by the upstart Nazis, he gleefully volunteered. Although he was much too senior and frankly too old for a pilot by the early 1930s, the army reluctantly allowed him to transfer to the new military arm. A natural, skilled leader, he rose rapidly in the ranks. Although he envisioned himself a fighter pilot by heart, that was the province of the young bucks, so he took command of a bomber wing—*Kampfgeschwader* KG 4—in May 1938, and turned it into one of the most elite units in the new German Air Force. Like the Phoenix rising, so too did Peter von Zimmermann—recharged and re-energized with the new possibilities of airpower. Then came the war.

KG 4 went into action immediately over Poland, bombing bridges, airfields, and other strategic targets. With much of the Polish infrastructure destroyed or disabled, the group turned to close air support of the *Wehrmacht*, the new and rebuilt German Army. In the battles of 1940, the wing attacked targets in Holland, Belgium, and France before turning its attention to the British. Bombing targets in southern England began in mid-June 1940 even before the French surrendered. Participating in raid after raid through the late summer and early autumn, German fliers saw many of their comrades go down in flames. Those that managed to parachute out typically drowned in the Channel or were made prisoner. By early September, his once potent air wing had only 14 operational aircraft. Through it all, he remained a steady rock for his air crews.

Despite the loss of friends and fellow airmen, the flyers of *Kampfgeschwader* 4 remained stalwart and aggressive. Refitted with new Heinkel He 111 medium bombers, it participated from the very beginning of OPERATION BARBAROSSA, the invasion of the Soviet Union in June 1941. Anyone paying even the remotest attention to the ravings of Adolf Hitler in his book *Mein Kampf* knew that by "*Lebensraum*" or living space for the German people, he meant land in the Soviet Union. For his leadership, in May 1941, he was awarded the Knight's Cross of the Iron Cross, promoted to *Generalmajor*, and given a major operational command based out of Berlin. Not able to fly missions at this point, he chafed at the constant administrative duties and, whenever possible, "flew to observe the boys in action," which earned him rebuke from superiors. It simply would not do to have a *Luftwaffe* general officer killed or captured in action, especially over the Soviet Union. But Zimmermann, defying orders to stay on the ground, often flew "observation" missions. Superiors might grouse about his risky actions, but his stock was so high in Berlin, especially among the real "movers and shakers" such as *Reichsmarschall* Hermann Göring and Hitler himself, that the rebukes never amounted to anything serious. As much as flying thrilled him, he was quite frankly worn out. He had been in continuous action for months from the start of the war through the air campaigns in Poland, France, Britain, and finally, over Russian skies.

All the while, Zimmermann seethed at the barbarism and uselessness of bombing cities and the civilian population. *Had not Hitler and his toady Göring seen that the terror bombing had no impact on the enemy's will to continue the fight? Had not the idiots in the Air Ministry understood that the terror bombing had only steeled the resolve of the population and more importantly of the British prime minister, Winston Churchill?* He had lost over half his command in the skies over southern England—a terrible waste of men and machine. Then the imbeciles invaded the Soviet Union. Despite the "victory fever" caused by the first few successful months having reached the outskirts of Moscow and Leningrad, the campaign bogged down with the dreadful Russian winter. He had again lost half his bombers and more importantly, the aircrews. *Treacherous waste!*

Nevertheless, Berlin soon decided that his administrative ability and leadership was needed in a more passive and less risky role. In late 1942, he assumed the post of chief of staff of *Luftflotte* 1, the huge air fleet based around Berlin, responsible for air operations over the Eastern Front. He chafed at the lack of action and made that opinion known to his senior officers. Nevertheless, as a patriot to the Fatherland and a good Prussian soldier, he followed his orders and did the best job possible as chief of staff. And, in that less aggressive role, he was able to lead a more settled life, which in truth, bored him no end. Finally, that mindset led him this night back to the Cabaret Paris despite the agony of still painful memories of happier times.

"*Herr General. Herr General.* Your whisky and soda, sir."

The waiter's deep voice jolted him out of his trance-like daydream. Thoughts whirred through his mind—random thoughts, thoughts of Ingrid, thoughts of combat, thoughts of solitude and of just sitting quietly in springtime on a far hill overlooking home. *I must focus. Lack of attention means death.* His ever-sharp mind suddenly snapped back to the reality of the moment. He sat in this place of merriment, of joy, of mirth, and of happy couples all around. He sat alone with just remembrances of the past. But now he had to focus. After all, there was a war to win. That thought trumped all else.

"*Ja, danke.*" He noticed that the waiter held in one hand the drink but, in the other, a telephone with a long extension cord. "Is there something else?"

The waiter dipped his head slightly as if to acknowledge the question. "*Jawohl, Herr General.* There is a call from your headquarters. The officer said that it was urgent that he speak with you straight-away." The waiter sat the whisky and soda in front of Zimmermann and then the phone beside it. "You may take the call here or, if it is too noisy, I am certain you may take the call in the manager's office."

* * * * * * * *

Minutes later, he retrieved his hat and greatcoat from the young lady at the hatcheck stand. He made sure to leave a large gratuity as he did for the waiter. He strode out the door of the Cabaret Paris and into a gusty breeze. It was not particularly cold this February night in Berlin, but he still turned up his collar as he stood on the pavement and fumbled in his tunic pocket for the car keys. Normally, his driver, *Feldwebel* Holtzmann, would be waiting, but this evening, he felt like a drive by himself. The call had been from *LuftFlotte* 1 headquarters from the commander's adjutant. It seemed that *Herr Generaloberst* (colonel general) had an urgent need to speak privately with his chief of staff. Zimmermann glanced at his watch as he walked briskly across the street to his car in the former building now a convenient place to park. "What could be so urgent that the 'old man' needs to have a conference at 2300 at night?" he muttered to no one in particular.

Minutes later, he arrived at the massive building on *Leipziger Strasse*—the *Reichsluftfahrtministerium* (Reich Air Ministry). As he entered the outer office of the commander of *Luftflotte* 1, *Generaloberst* Karl von Kline, he had no idea that he was about to embark on a journey that would have incredible implications for himself, for Germany, and for the world.

CHAPTER 2

Linden Hall

Berlin, 23 February 1943

"*Generaloberst* von Kline will see you now, sir," *Feldwebel* Schmidt said as he held open the door to the *Luftflotte* commander's office.

Zimmermann acknowledged the polite clerk with a slight nod. The man walked with a limp, no doubt a war wound. *Poland? Perhaps in France? The Eastern Front? No matter.* Zimmermann spied the *Verwundetenabzeichen*, the wound badge decoration on the man's uniform tunic. A *Wehrmacht* infantryman now well past prime military age, he had been assigned desk duty at *Luftwaffe* headquarters, no doubt a reward for excellent service and a place where he could continue to serve the Reich. As he rose and grabbed his hat—the one with the hated swastika symbol under the German eagle—he unceremoniously fingered his own wound badge from the first war. He still wore his medals and awards from that conflict, both Iron Crosses, 1st and 2nd Class. They represented his heritage—Prussia, beloved Prussia, and the lost German Empire. He took in a deep breath as he entered the office of the *Luftflotte* 1 commanding officer.

Generaloberst Karl von Kline sat behind a great oak desk, his hands clasped in front of a bowed head, elbows squarely on the blotter beneath. *He looks pensive,* thought Zimmermann. Something is in the air and something is not all well. The door clicked behind him as the *Feldwebel* quietly exited back to his outer office. Clearly, there was a high-level talk about to occur, and the old soldier wanted no part of it. The late hour indicated something very important was about to happen.

The *Generaloberst* had been in a high dudgeon all day and frankly, for Zimmermann, the less he knew why, the better. That had been his attitude since early that morning. In a way, that was why he headed to the cabaret this evening as perhaps a tonic to the mayhem in the office caused by his commander's mood. In a few minutes, Kline would head home to his sausages and beer and the *hausfrau* he had loved and cherished for years; hopefully, whatever had created the earlier commotion would soon be resolved by this late-night meeting. Kline rarely stayed this late at the office. Something important must be up.

Zimmermann straightened his back as much as he could muster; the drinks at the cabaret relaxed him quite a bit—at least, until he received the call to report at once. He casually raised his right arm in a half-hearted salute. "*Heil* Hitler," he barely hissed. Kline looked up wearily. His eyes were sadder than Zimmermann had ever seen. The man had aged incredibly in the few months that he worked as his chief of staff.

"There is no need for that foolishness here, Peter. Please. Sit."

Zimmermann turned, and seeing a comfortable-looking red leather chair to his right, he gingerly sat, hands firmly placed on the overstuffed arms.

"After all, we are Prussian aristocrats, Peter. Not the strutting thugs and riffraff of our beloved *Führer* and his gang of cutthroats."

Zimmermann nodded acknowledgment. Both officers came from the old school where the Fatherland was all and the royal family headed it, not the upstart Austrian corporal. In public, of course, it had to be different, but in this darkened office late at night in the heart of Berlin, the two Prussian aristocrats had no need for the Nazi regime and its band of sociopaths. They fought for Germany and the German people, not for the National Socialists. "Quite so, *Herr Generaloberst*. Quite so."

Kline nodded and leaned back in his chair that squeaked with every movement. "I must have Fritz see to this. It was my grandfather's and my father's before me." Zimmermann had always admired the older general's chair and desk. They had been presented to his grandfather, a Prussian Guards officer and hero of the Wars of German Unification against the Danes in 1864, the Austrians in 1866, and finally the hated French in 1870. *Kaiser* Wilhelm I himself had presented it to *Oberst* (colonel) Otto von Kline in gratitude for his exemplary service.

Both men now sat silent for a moment, then Kline leaned back further. A glint of lamplight flickered off the medal—the "Blue Max," *Pour le Mérite*—that hung from his collar, a recognition of his courage and daring in action in Flanders during the first war. Finally, he spoke.

"Peter, I apologize for calling you away from your well-deserved leave at the cabaret. Please forgive me, my son."

Zimmermann always viewed Kline as a father figure ever since his own father perished at Verdun in 1916. "It is of no concern, *Herr Generaloberst*. I know this meeting must be of the highest importance to the Fatherland. No, sir. No bother at all."

Kline just grunted and shook his head. But it was. It was of grave concern. Both men sat silent for several uncomfortable seconds, neither one wishing to open the conversation. Finally, Zimmermann spoke.

"*Herr Generaloberst*, just why have you called me here this evening? Are there some better hours during the day?" He had to ask, even if the question may have seemed a bit impertinent toward the senior officer. Kline leaned forward in the squeaky chair, furrowed his eyebrows, and closed his fingers together in a tight fist.

"*Generalmajor* von Zimmermann, I am here to relieve you of your current position as chief of staff of *Luftflotte* 1."

Zimmermann shot upright in the chair. Perhaps the drinks from earlier? Perhaps the exhaustion of having flown over 300 missions in the past few years? Perhaps he misunderstood the *Generaloberst*? *Relieve me of my position? Why? What had gone wrong? Had he not the respect, nay, the admiration of his men? Had he not done superior administrative work as the chief of staff? Was he the victim of some petty bureaucrat at the Reich air ministry?* All these questions swirled through his mind in a fraction of a second. A spectral silence enveloped the office. Relieved? These were words no military officer ever wanted to hear spoken and dreaded.

Finally, Kline spoke again. "Rather, Peter, I should say that you are being reassigned to a very special duty. Forgive me if I stunned you. It was completely unintentional, my boy." The older officer read the look of shock and amazement on the younger man's face. "Have you ever heard of Project Armageddon?"

Project Armageddon? What the devil? Zimmermann unclenched his jaw, which had subconsciously tightened like a bear trap on hearing the word "relieved."

"Armageddon?"

"*Ja*, Armageddon. Project Armageddon."

Zimmermann paused. He turned his eyes toward the window, then down to the magnificent red and black Kermanshah carpet beneath his chair, then back to Kline.

"It seems to me that there were some whispers about the command concerning some special project at an air base in Poland or perhaps East Prussia some months back. Something about special wonder weapons. Such talk happens all the time in the officers' mess. I never discourage it. It helps the men forget that they have lost hundreds of friends and comrades in this ridiculous war. Please forgive my negative thoughts, *Herr Generaloberst*."

Kline shook his head, the lamplight flickering across his full head of silver hair. "No need for apologies, Peter. Many of us are of the same mind. But we dare not utter such treason except amongst ourselves and trusted friends."

"Then, sir, does Project Armageddon have something to do with my reassignment?" he asked, hoping to learn more.

"It does." He pulled the manila folder stamped TOP SECRET from under the blotter, opened it, and pulled out the single flimsy page. "I read."

From: *Oberkommando der Luftwaffe*

To: *Generalmajor* Peter Christian von Zimmermann

Subject: Relief and Reassignment

Upon immediate relief as Chief of Staff *Luftflotte* 1, report for duty to Commander, Special Projects, *Oberkommando der Luftwaffe*, Berlin, attention *Oberst* Hermann Rahl at Room 339 for further instructions. You are authorized 14 days leave.

Reichsmarschall Hermann Göring

Kline slowly closed the folder and tapped it with an index finger. "It seems that you have attracted the attention of the fat bastard personally," Kline said, raising his bushy, silvery-white eyebrows. Both men heartily despised the strutting, pompous *Reichsmarschall* who commanded the *Luftwaffe*. Still, they had to begrudgingly give him some credit. In his more heroic youth as a flyer in the old Imperial German Air Force, Göring scored 22 air victories over the French and British. But that was long behind him and in a different world. Still, he did proudly wear his own "Blue Max"—not a trifling thing, to be sure.

"I might add that you are to be awarded a Knight's Cross with Oak Leaves during the turnover with your relief, which by the way is scheduled for the day after tomorrow. I trust that is enough time to properly turn over the chief of staff's duties to your current number two?"

"It will have to do." Zimmermann neither smiled nor made any expression of any kind. Would that he could award the Knight's Cross of the Iron Cross to every airman and air crewman he had ever commanded. But he could not. "I will see to things straightaway, *Herr*

Generaloberst. And, might I ask, sir, what is the nature of this new duty?"

Kline only shook his head as if to say not a clue. "Peter, my son, I have no idea. It is a, shall I say, closely guarded secret. I suspect *Oberst* Rahl will fully brief you. Where will you spend your leave? *Frau* von Kline and I would welcome you to spend the days with us."

Zimmermann rested his chin on his open palm, elbow braced on his knee, eyes staring at the carpet below. "I think that I shall visit Linden Hall. I have not been home since before deployment to the Eastern Front. It will be good to see mother and my sisters again. It's been too long." He sat up in his chair, back straight, and with it, the stoic countenance expected of a Prussian warrior returned. "The truth be told, *Herr Generaloberst,* I had hoped for a command in North Africa. Rommel has been battering the damned British and Australians all over the desert—a far better task than bombing useless Russian peasants."

Kline smiled. "Quite true. And much warmer, I suspect." Both men laughed, Zimmermann's former tension now broken by the thought of seeing Linden Hall and his ancestral estate, Linden Tree. "I apologize for my cantankerous attitude today, Peter. I realize that I have made you and the entire staff uncomfortable. The truth is, my boy, I was overjoyed when they announced that you would be my new chief of staff. I realize that you want an operational command. I understand that desire completely. Sometimes I yearn for the field again. But I am an old war horse and frankly ready to retire. You, though, are still young and energetic. And what is it the Americans say? Full of 'piss and vinegar'?" Both men chuckled. "At any rate, I am grateful for the work you have done in your very short time here. I suspect this new assignment will be most challenging and you will do well."

"I will do my utmost to do my duty to the Fatherland."

"Just so, Peter. Just so." Kline's lips arched ever so slightly up in a Cheshire Cat sort of grin. He noted that Zimmermann had said

Fatherland rather than duty to the *Führer* or the Third *Reich*. The two men were of the same mind on that subject.

The business concluded, the two officers toasted with a glass of fine Napoleon Cognac recently relieved from some French *château* or other. As Zimmermann stepped out into the damp misty air, a sudden chill went through him. He did not know why but was certain all would soon be apparent. With no further word, he stepped into the dark red Mercedes, a gift from Ingrid, and slumped into the cool leather driver's seat. The Mercedes' powerful engine growled as the car sped away.

* * * * * * * *

Linden Hall, Brandenburg, 25 February 1943

The staff car ground to a stone-crunching halt. As a senior officer, he was entitled to use a Horch 853, but he thought that too ostentatious. Let Göring and those of his ilk use those flashy, expensive vehicles. He opted for the more functional and less extravagant 1939 Mercedes-Benz 170V. Zimmerman had said nothing to the driver since leaving Berlin two hours earlier. His thoughts were elsewhere this day. What was his new assignment all about? Could he still lead men into combat and, for many of them, into death? These thoughts weighed heavy on him for the past several months. In combat, one has a serious job to do, and such thoughts and doubts cannot cloud one's mind. A successful combat leader must always keep the mission in mind. He must challenge the troops to go farther than they thought possible. Most of all, a combat commander must be stoic at all times. Only then would he inspire the confidence of the troops allowing the unit to carry out their mission knowing full well the dangers. He had learned that hard lesson as a platoon and later company commander in the trenches in the previous war. He had practiced and honed those leadership qualities in the skies over Poland, France, England, and the Soviet Union. He learned that much of leadership is simply

S.D.M. Carpenter

an art. True, there is a lot of science in war—how to aim artillery, how to pilot an airplane, how to plan a combat sortie. But he learned that leading troops into combat required more than science alone.

As the farms and houses of rural Brandenburg flashed by in the distance, he came to a realization. He was not just a good combat commander, he was a superb one. He craved another operational command after months in Berlin playing the staff bureaucrat; he was eager and anxious to get back into the fray. As much as he wanted this war to be won and over, Peter von Zimmermann, the consummate Prussian warrior-aristocrat, yearned for the battle. But he made his decision. Whatever mission the high command had for him, he would carry it out to the best of his ability. He would approach the new task as he did all things—with great energy, resolve, and excellence.

As they approached Linden Tree, his thoughts turned to those of home and his extraordinary childhood wandering the dark woods that surrounded the ancient estate. Indeed, the family name that originated in the early Middle Ages—Zimmermann—meant loosely "man of the woods." His ancestors had roamed this land in Brandenburg since ancient times. They had been proud, fierce warriors and tribal leaders for generation after generation. These were the tribesmen that held the Roman legions at bay along the Rhine and Danube Rivers. Medieval Teutonic Knights, they swore their lives and fortunes in defense of Christendom. And these were the noblemen who commanded the Prussian soldiers under King Frederick the Great—*Friedrich der Grosse*—two centuries earlier. As the scion of this great warrior family, he had held up his trust in the Great War of 1914. Now, he fought again this time, but not just for the Fatherland, for Christendom, for the land. No, this time, he fought for some perverted ideology based on lies, deceit, arrogance, oppression, and racial hatred. It troubled him no end. Yet, in the end, he chose to defend and advance his Germany, his Prussia, and his countrymen and women in hopes that in time, the German people in their moral and righteous anger would rise up and crush the strutting National Socialist parasites. He often wondered how he might con-

60

tribute to that moral cause. This dilemma also occupied his thoughts as the staff car sped through the German countryside before halting at the bronze and marble gates of his home—Linden Hall, the house of the men of the woods.

"*Danke*, Holtzmann. I shall walk to the house. It will refresh me. Please park the car in the carriage house. You can room in the chauffeur's lodgings above the carriage house. He was killed in France and his rooms are now empty."

"Very good, *Herr Generalmajor*. I shall clean and service the car and be standing by for your call."

"*Danke*, Holtzmann. Relax and enjoy this leave. God knows you have had precious little of late."

"*Danke, Herr Generalmajor.*"

With no further word, Zimmermann stepped out of the car and stood straight, arching his back. Long drives or, for that matter, long flights caused a twinge in his lower back. The medical staff called it a "muscle spasm." *No matter. Gott im Himmel, how I hate getting older!* He stepped through the seventeenth-century rococo-style bronze and marble gate crowned by a gilded bear's head, the symbol of his family adopted generations back. He chuckled to himself as he strode down the Grand Drive. He had always thought the bear's head somewhat comical. It looked to him as if the bear had been hit in the private parts by surprise. At least that is what he thought as a 10-year-old. The odd expression on the statue's face struck him as somewhere between a smirk and a look of surprise. No doubt, some sculptor's joke. He suddenly laughed aloud and picked up the pace. Linden Hall.

Linden trees lined both sides of the Grand Drive, namesake of the estate. Planted by his great-grandfather, this long elegant drive was his favorite part of the estate. In years past, coaches and carriages rumbled down this alley between the linden trees to the main entrance for elegant balls and grand events. In the happier times before the Great War, these events had been routine. Affairs at Linden Hall represented a highlight of the Berlin social season, especially since the *Königlich*

Preußische Staatseisenbahnen [Royal Prussian State Railways] built a local station. Located just south of the village of Teltow, only a day's journey from Potsdam or Berlin in the old days and just a couple of hours by car or train in recent decades, Linden Hall became a center of Prussian aristocratic social life. His predecessors hosted some of the finest balls and social events in the country; aristocrats and his fellow *junkers* (landed aristocrats) came from all over the country to those affairs. The *Kaiser* himself attended several soirées. But, since the war, Linden Hall had been quiet and dark. Gone were the great noble families of the Second Empire. Gone were the summer garden parties, brightly lit by gas lanterns installed by his grandfather. He remembered the outdoor events under the lights as an orchestra played Strauss waltzes. Officers in elegant dress uniforms and ladies in the latest Paris fashions waltzed the night away. When the weather turned damp and chilly, the festivities moved inside into the magnificent ballroom adorned with portraits of ancient Zimmermanns. These thoughts floated through his consciousness as he strode down the linden-lined walk.

Reaching the front doors—massive heavy doors made of ancient oak cut on the estate and decorated with wrought iron in the medieval style—he fumbled in his tunic pocket. Then he reached into his uniform trousers. He realized that he had no keys. He had not had keys since before the war and even then, the size and heft of the huge brass keys made the uniform look odd, not crisp and smart. He cursed under his breath for his silliness and then grasped the iron knocker. Three sharp raps followed. In barely a few seconds, an elderly servant appeared dressed in fine livery from a bygone, more graceful era. The man was so anxious, he could hardly move. He expected his master at any moment and had actually seen Zimmermann walking up the Grand Drive. The old man grinned broadly and let out a hearty hello. "*Willkommen, willkommen* home, *Herr Baron, willkommen.* Come in."

"Heinz, *mein guter Mann.* It is *wunderbar* to be home. *Ja, wunderbar!*" He stepped through the cavernous entrance, extended a hand to the elderly servant, who, surprised at this gesture of informality from his master, nevertheless grasped the gloved hand with a firm handshape. The butler then bowed gracefully and with a broad sweep of his arm, motioned the master of the house into the hallway.

Linden Hall! How many times had he wandered these hallways and cavernous rooms in his youth? Zimmermann grinned, then grimaced. *In his youth.* Life seemed so easy then. The world outside the stone walls seemed a distant alien place. He stopped for a moment and stared at a portrait of a stoic figure. The huge portrait dominated the hallway—his great, great grandfather, also a Peter von Zimmermann, resplendent in his Prussian general's dress uniform. The portrait painter captured every nuance and the power of the man, one of Frederick the Great's most successful generals. This Peter had brought the family to prominence from a minor Brandenburg *junker* to one of the great houses of the new Prussia. As a youth, he spent hours gazing at the portrait of a man whose power shone through, thanks to the exceptional artist. The young Peter fantasized about his own military fortunes. Did it include a great career full of courage and honor in defense of his beloved Prussia? But then he grimaced as memories of the mud, blood, and horror of northern France came tumbling through his conscious thoughts. He had long ago recovered from the bayonet wound from that day in late 1918, but his psyche was forever marred. True, in the Interwar years, he rarely thought about the war, the trenches, and the ugly side of it all. Despite Germany's humiliation, he always believed in her revival. Ingrid, ever optimistic and cheerful, pulled him back from the abyss of melancholy about the Fatherland's woes. He had stayed in the new German Army, the *Reichswehr*. He felt that he and other honorable men might restore the German military to its place of honor. But then came the Nazis and their strutting thugs. Hitler and his minions had reduced the German military to a band of subservient automatons by the late 1930s. He spent many a day and night agonizing over whether to stay in uniform or resign his *Luftwaffe* commission, yet something within him continually said no. *You must stay. The Nazis are a temporary aberration, a cruel mischief wrought by the Allies on a helpless Germany.* In time, the German people would recover their senses and dispose of the thugs. Then he and the true German patriots would restore the nation's honor. Germany would once again resume its rightful place in the pantheon of great civilizations. He would stay and be an agent of that restored virtue and greatness. He looked up into the eyes of his ancestor, those piercing, powerful eyes. He whispered to himself, "*Herr General,* this is my true oath. This is my true quest."

My quest. My quest. He clasped his hands behind his back and stared down at the red, black, and beige carpet that ran the distance of the hallway. *My quest.* He let out a deep breath. So many thoughts had passed through his consciousness in the past 24 hours, whip-lashing him between feelings of happy remembrance to great anger to questioning why he did as he did. Some jolted old memories, some fond, and others—well—there were the harsh memories of the trenches. Countering those thoughts had been those of Ingrid and the time they had together, however brief. Those thoughts caused him to visit the cabaret.

Then there were the thoughts of war's horrors, perhaps stimulated by the meeting with Kline and his new, but unknown, assignment. Finally, the trip to Linden Hall brought back memories of his youth and of the place's former grandeur. Seeing the portraits reminded him of his duty to his Fatherland despite his political ambivalence. Those thoughts had bedeviled him for years, but above all, he chose the Fatherland and therefore did as the political authorities commanded. And now he was to step into a new and unknown role. Little did he realize as he stood in the middle of the carpeted hallway lined with portraits of previous Zimmermanns who had done their duty to King and Fatherland just how challenging that duty would be to his moral compass and sense of right and wrong.

He slowly walked down the passageway until he reached the por-trait next to last in the line. There, staring back out at him, was his father, resplendent in the parade dress of a Prussian Guards officer with elaborate gold epaulettes and a *pickelhaube* helmet perched at a jaunty angle. A wry smile broke through the otherwise stern countenance on the portrait painted just before the Great War broke out. His father was that way, he remembered. Somewhat impish at times and always good natured, the man was loved and admired. The clever artist had captured that nature while at the same time showing the stern and ever-so-proper military bearing demanded of a Guards officer. In short, the portrait captured the essence of the man.

Zimmermann smiled.

"Hello, Father. I trust you are doing well today." He chuckled. It was an old habit he first developed after the war. Every day when at home, every time he passed his father's portrait, he would ask how Father was that day. A silly habit, perhaps, but it seemed to give him peace and solitude and eased the pain of having lost the man he so admired and loved at such an early age. For Zimmermann, the portrait always inspired genuine respect and strengthened the bond between the two military men—father and son.

"*Herr Baron. Herr Baron.* Please, your sisters are eagerly awaiting you, sir!" The butler looked anxious. He need not have been.

"Of course, Heinz. Of course. I was just admiring the great general and, of course, greeting Father."

"*Jawohl, Herr Baron.* But you too are a great general and a great patriot as was he. And your father, aah, there was a magnificent man, *Herr Baron,* a truly magnificent man," responded the butler, smiling broadly. He remembered well Zimmermann's habit of greeting the portrait every morning, and unlike other house servants who considered the habit odd, Heinz thought it a wonderful gesture.

Zimmermann chuckled and grinned. "Indeed, Heinz. I thank you. But there is no need for flattery here." The butler visibly relaxed and bowed his head ever so slightly. "Lead on, Heinz. The family awaits."

They passed through the Great Hall and through the passageway leading to the main sitting room, also known as the ladies' parlor. They passed by portrait after portrait of past family members, both male and female, some great, some . . . well. . . . *Every family has its lesser members,* he thought as he glanced at each in turn.

Linden Hall started as a simple hunting lodge centuries earlier. It stood in a great forest alive with wild boar, bears, and deer, perfect terrain for a hunting lodge or just as a convenient retreat. The family lived in a castle or, more correctly, a "fortified house" of the late medieval period. The old place was called *Schlosswälder* or "castle woods." Not really a castle in the classic sense, the place could be defended if ever besieged or raided, but more than anything represented the family's rising to landed aristocratic prominence in the late Middle Ages. By the mid-seventeenth century, the Zimmermanns enjoyed great wealth and prominence, so much so that the head of the family was ennobled by the King of Prussia. To highlight the family's rise, he added more formal rooms to the old hunting lodge in the Great Woods. Over the years, Linden Hall expanded room by room until by the late nineteenth century, it reached its present grand elegance. And yet, it stood as if frozen in time, a relic of the Second *Reich* before the Great War and a monument to a more elegant age.

They passed trophy after trophy mounted on the walls—great heads of bucks and other big game, mementos from a bygone age. They passed African animals—zebra, a lion, and even a tiger's head. His grandfather had been a big game hunter in German East Africa, and, in the 1890s, organized many big game safaris in pursuit of the noble beasts. Hides of lions, tigers, and other exotic creatures used as carpets adorned the polished teak wood floors. He always admired the men that had gone out to Africa to hunt those creatures. The trophies would stay.

Observers and visitors to Linden Hall noticed the dichotomy of style. Parts of the place appeared as if King Louis XIV's own architect designed it and had a look reminiscent of the Palace of Versailles in the late seventeenth-century grand baroque style. Then there was the distinctly rococo style of the mid-eighteenth century, with softer colors and more graceful lines. Zimmermann never really cared as much for the baroque and rococo parts of the Hall. He considered them foppish, extravagant, and excessively vain. He much preferred the older parts with the hunting lodge décor such as this Great Hall with the animal trophies surrounded by a magnificent collection of bladed weapons and antique firearms, some dating back to the first age of gunpowder weapons. This room appealed to the warrior side of his ego. Let others sit about drinking tea and eating pastries; he preferred the outdoors and a life of action and adventure.

Thus, young Peter von Zimmermann spent his youth largely romping through the Great Woods or, in foul weather, sitting by his grandfather or great-grandfather's chair near the massive stone fireplace in the Great Hall, enthralled by their tales of hunting big game on the Dark Continent or in grave combat against a variety of enemies, all in defense of the Fatherland. Growing up with these influences, it was no wonder he absorbed those values of the warrior-aristocrat and reverence for the old order of monarchy, aristocracy, and the Fatherland.

They arrived in the ladies' parlor, and he was instantly cheered. His youngest sister, Eva, ran into his arms with teenaged exuberance; she hugged and kissed him, well, kissed him until he finally had to pull her away, smiling and laughing. "There, there, young Eva. Has it been that long?" She embraced him about the waist, laughing.

"Well, brother, *willkommen* home!" His eldest sister Helga stood more sedate, but she still smiled that sweet, endearing, wistful smile. A war widow, her husband died at the front in 1917, another casualty of the folly of 1914. His mother stood next to Helga with tears welling up on her aged face. "Peter, my Peter. Come, come. It has been far too long. You must be tired and hungry. Heinz, tell the staff that we shall dine at once."

The butler bowed deeply and backed out of the room to shout instructions at the staff. He was once again the master of the house. The baron had arrived. With Eva chattering away as young girls are wont to do when excited, they entered the dining room. Zimmermann only smiled and nodded as his sister rambled on about this and that and everything else. For now, he was home and the cares of the new war and the feelings of anxiety and, yes, even some guilt, bled away as they all sat down to perhaps the best meal available in wartime Germany. They talked for hours. It was glorious. Glorious.

* * * * * * *

"Tell us, Peter, how are things in Berlin? We have not been to town in ages, just ages," blurted out Helga.

Like a dark summer storm rain cloud suddenly appearing to ruin a shiny, bright day, Zimmermann's mood changed. A dour look came across his previously smiling face. Everyone at the table noticed. Helga, visibly embarrassed, looked at their mother with a shocked expression. "Mother, have I said something I shouldn't have?" She turned back to Zimmermann. "Peter, I am sorry. Should I not have asked?"

He looked down at the table. *What to say? What to say? Do I dare tell them the truth? Ja. Part of the truth at least. They deserve to know at least that.* He looked back up and across the table at Helga and let out a deep breath.

"You should know the truth. Despite the expressions of optimism and, frankly, outright lies from our heralded ministry of information, the truth, my family, is—" he paused and took a deep breath, "is that the war does not go as well as you have heard." He closed his hands together with fingertips touching, elbows on the table, and lowered his head so that his nose touched his index fingertips as if a man in deep contemplation. All at the table understood the subtlety of the move. It indicated the seriousness of what he was about to say. After a few seconds, he lifted his head back up and placed his hands palms down on the Irish linen tablecloth.

"The truth is, we are stalemated. The British are holding on in the desert. This new commander, Montgomery, is clearly more talented than his predecessors. Even the great Desert Fox himself, *Herr* Rommel, can't break the deadlock. They move back and forth across the sand losing men and machines and no one can gain the advantage. As long as the British and Australians hold the Suez Canal, we are, as I say, stalemated."

Helga broke in. "But Peter, isn't the war in the East going well? We hear every day on the wireless that the *Wehrmacht* is crushing the evil Bolshevik Army. Is this not true?" A look almost like panic came across her face.

He pondered for a moment. Should he tell them the truth about Stalingrad? Should they know that an entire German Army had been wiped out or captured because Hitler refused to allow *Generalfeldmarschall* (field marshal) Paulus to withdraw before the Soviet Red Army completely surrounded his besieged 6th Army? Even the great *Generalfeldmarschall* von Manstein with Army Group South failed to break through to relieve 6th Army and open an escape corridor. And what of Göring, who boasted that the *Luftwaffe* could supply the Stalingrad defenders with all the resources needed? *Fatal infatuation!* Although the Stalingrad Front was out of *Luftflotte* I's operational area, he knew of the aircrews' desperate attempts to fly in supplies. What with iced wings and lubrication oils turning to the consistency of putty in the harsh Russian winter weather, few planes could actually fly. With each passing day, the situation on the ground grew more desperate. And yet, the propaganda boys kept spewing out good news after good news. The war goes well! Germany is triumphant! The Soviet Union will soon collapse! In the north where he daily assessed the losses as chief of staff and reported the bad news to Kline, the situation was grim as well. The frustrating and fruitless siege of Leningrad went on and on, to no avail. The Soviets in winter moved supplies across frozen Lake Ladoga into the city while in warmer months, they brought in relief by boat. Every day the *Luftwaffe* sent sortie after sortie against the Soviet supply route, but there was never enough—never enough aircraft and never enough aircrews to stop the supplies. And so, day after day, week after week, month after month, the siege went on, draining the *Luftwaffe* of the fuel and planes that could be used to better effect elsewhere. The German Army and Air Force were simply spread too thin. The generals knew it. The pilots and air crew knew it. The common soldier on the ground, whether freezing in winter or sweltering in summer, knew it. But the high and mighty in Berlin lived in some fantasy cloud cuckoo land deceiving themselves and ultimately the German people. And so, with a simple question from Helga as to how it goes in Berlin, Zimmermann's cheery mood of finally being back at Linden Hall turned sour with the realization that once again, the war had caught up with him. He cleared his throat.

"The truth is this." With that, he unburdened and told his family the awful story of a stalemated war with no end in sight as long as the stubborn British held out and the wicked communists continued to throttle the *Wehrmacht* and *Luftwaffe* on the Soviet plains. As he told the story, it occurred to him that somehow, his new assignment had to do with a new direction in the war effort. *Was it some new tactic or strategy? Perhaps it was a new weapons system that would break the deadlock and finally defeat the British or crush the Bolsheviks.* He could not yet know, but clearly, there was something afoot. And he had the feeling now that somehow he was about to be a major player in the drama soon to unfold. What it would be would have to wait.

Meanwhile, he would enjoy the company of his family. He would walk the Great Woods and soak in the calmness and quietude that Linden Hall and the Linden Tree estate always offered him.

* * * * * * * *

Library, Linden Hall, Brandenburg, 7 March 1943

He did not know why particularly, but that morning he had been reading a collection of poems by the Roman poet Horace—the *Odes*. One particular line struck him. An odd feeling came over him as read the line over and over—"*dulce et decorum est pro patria mori*—it is sweet and proper to die for one's country." For several minutes he just stared at the page, not understanding why the phrase so engrossed his attention—"it is sweet and proper to die for one's country."[1]

Perhaps from just a late winter chill wind, a sudden shiver came over him. For a moment—a very brief moment—he felt a premonition, a feeling of some impending doom or disaster. He had only felt this way once before back in 1916. He had been on leave at home when word arrived that his father, the previous baron, had been killed by a French sniper at Verdun. In the hours before the messenger from Berlin arrived at Linden Hall that dreary autumn afternoon, he had experienced that same feeling of ill fortune, of disaster, and calamity. Despite the stoic (or as the British might say, stiff upper lip) countenance he always displayed, the combination of Horace's words and the evil premonition made his left hand shake violently. He took in a deep breath and the fit passed. Nonetheless, the episode unnerved the man who was used to addressing death and danger head on with stoic fortitude. He sat stiff and silent for several minutes just staring out the library's French doors that opened onto the English-style boxwood garden first created by his great-great grandfather. Normally, looking out at the rows of early blooming spring flowers and carefully trimmed boxwood hedge brought him calm and solace, but not this morning. The premonition so shook him that he just stared out the doors for minute after minute. His trance was only broken when the butler entered the library. Seeing the master staring into nothing in particular, the servant cleared his throat. It was enough to shake Zimmermann out of his trance.

"*Herr Baron*. There is an officer here from Berlin. He has correspondence for you."

"*Danke*, Heinz. Show the officer in."

"At once, *Herr Baron*." The butler bowed deeply and departed.

---

1 Horace, *The Odes and Carmen Saeculare of Horace,* trans. John Conington (London: George Bell and Sons, 1882).

Berlin. So now it begins, this special mission. So be it. He quietly closed the Horace book and placed it on the side table next to the other book that he had been reading that morning, the eighteenth-century Englishman Gibbon on the rise and fall of the Roman Empire. He chuckled to himself. *I wonder if Herr Hitler and his gang have ever read this. They should.* He stood to attention. Reaching down, he pulled at the jacket tails to straighten them and then adjusted his tie. This was Linden Hall. No need for uniforms here. He preferred a tweed hunting jacket and looked ever so much the country gentleman, comfortable in his surroundings and in his place in the world. But in his *Luftwaffe* uniform, it was a different world, a violent, unsettled world. And the presence of an envoy from headquarters indicated that this country aristocrat was about to be drawn back into that world of chaos, mayhem, violence, and death.

* * * * * * * *

"*Heil!*" The *Luftwaffe Major* (major) sprang to a stiff attention, right arm extended forward in the Party salute. Zimmermann raised his right arm in a haphazard acknowledgment. Such sloppy salutes were the purview of senior officers only.

"*Guten Morgen, Herr Major.* You have a packet for me?"

"*Jawohl, Herr Generalmajor.* Direct from *Reichsmarschall* Göring's office."

"And—?"

The *Major* blushed. Despite his field grade rank and obvious combat experience as indicated by his decorations, senior officers still intimidated him. He stuttered slightly in his response: "I . . . cannot . . . cannot say what the packet contains, *Herr Generalmajor.* Only that the *Reichsmarschall's* chief of staff instructed me to hand-deliver the packet to you, *Herr Generalmajor.* I suspect the papers are of some importance."

"Very well, *Herr Major.*" Zimmermann noticed that the officer had the usual official black leather briefcase handcuffed to his left wrist. He took in a deep breath and slowly exhaled without further word as the officer fumbled for his keys, quickly unlocked the handcuffs, then opened the lock on the briefcase. Out came a manila-colored envelope. Official orders. The officer handed him the envelope and the signature sheet to acknowledge receipt. With a quick flourish, Zimmermann signed the form.

"*Danke, Herr Generalmajor*," he said, replacing the signature page back in the briefcase. Zimmermann stood stiffly without a word, holding the unopened envelope in his hand.

"I am being a rude host, *Herr Major*. I'll call Heinz. Might we offer some refreshment?" The *Luftwaffe* officer, now more visibly relaxed, smiled at last. "You are most kind, sir, but I must get back to Berlin. My driver is waiting."

Zimmermann acknowledged with just a nod. Without a further word, the officer clicked his heels, stiffened to attention, and almost raised his hand in a salute, but then understood that the tall, stately officer before him did not require the formality.

"*Danke, Herr Generalmajor.*" He spun on his heels and departed, the briefcase again chained to his wrist. Zimmermann walked across the room to the French doors that overlooked the gravel driveway and waited as the *Luftwaffe* officer quickly took his seat in the staff car with no word to the driver, who swiftly closed the car door, took his seat, and drove off. As the black Mercedes staff car receded in the distance down the driveway, Zimmermann pried open the wax seal, took out the orders, and laying them on a table, read them aloud:

Report on 9 March 1943 at 0900 to the military transport office at *Zentral Flughafen Tempelhof*, Berlin at 0900 for further travel to Rastenburg by air. You will be met by representatives of *Reichsmarschall* Göring and escorted to the *Wolfsschanze* compound. You are to report to the Officer Commanding *Reichssicherheitsdienst* (RSD) where you will be escorted to the office of the *Reichsmarschall*. You are not to speak to any person regarding the nature of these orders. You are not to speak of your observations and activities while carrying out your orders. Upon completion of your assignment, report to Air Ministry *Luftwaffe*, Berlin. Attention *Reichsmarschall* Göring only.

He paused. *Most curious. Signed by the old fat bastard himself.* As he turned the paper over and over in his hands, reading and rereading the text, his anger grew with every syllable. *The old fat bastard indeed. How many good men died in that futile attempt to coerce the British into submission by terror-bombing their cities? Did he not understand that few things will so infuriate the Anglo-Saxon-Celt more than bombing civilians in their homes? Did Göring and Hitler not understand that once the British bulldog was backed into a corner and finally reacted, no power on Earth or Hell could quell their fury and resolve? Ignorant asses!* His hands trembled with his rage. *These men will be the downfall of the Fatherland.* Meanwhile, every day, his airmen, his men, perished in the insane attempt to defeat the British bulldog and the Russian bear at the same time. *Stupendous folly! It will kill us all!*

After a few minutes, his rage subsided. Despite these feelings, he was, after all, a soldier and a patriot. He would obey these orders no matter how onerous. But in his heart, he knew that he must defend the Fatherland and the German *Volk. Pray God, the people would soon rise up and drive out these characters and their thugs. Until that day, though, he must do his duty as a soldier, as an officer, and as a Prussian aristocrat bred in the ways of war.* He returned the single page orders to the envelope and resealed it. Preparations had to be made.

* * * * * * * *

The next morning, he prepared to depart and enjoyed a hearty breakfast of sausages, black bread, and jam, all produced on the estate. He craved a cup of tea, but with the British blockade, that commodity was about nonexistent even for a family of his means and influence. But the cook had saved some excellent Brazilian coffee just for his return; he savored the dark brown brew. Lingering over the coffee for several minutes, he pondered what new mission was in his future. The Eastern Front, no doubt. The distressing truth that he shared with the family a few days earlier at the dinner table returned to his thoughts. He had not thought too much of it in the interim as he enjoyed being at home among family, old friends, and old familiarities. But now these thoughts returned as he pondered the orders. *Some new operation? Some new weapon?* He could not tell from the orders, but it was clear—a trip to the Wolf's Lair, the *Führer's* military headquarters in the East Prussian woods, meant that this new assignment held great importance to the war effort, Why else would he be reporting to Hitler's own headquarters? *Oberst* Rahl had given him few details other than to take the leave and await further orders.

It has to do with the war in the East, it simply must be! The *Wehrmacht* had bogged down and been thrown on the defensive. The sickening slaughter at Stalingrad in the winter had devastated the army. Despite the *Reichsmarschall's* claim that his Air Force could supply 6th Army, the *Luftwaffe* simply could not meet the logistical demand. Manstein's attempt to reach and rescue the trapped Germans fell short by only a few miles, and Paulus had been forced to surrender. The *Führer* had promoted Paulus to *Generalfeldmarschall* to stiffen the man's resolve, claiming that no German field marshal in history had ever surrendered. Hundreds of thousands of good German lads had died or been captured in that stupid stubborn attempt to break the Soviet grip on Stalingrad. German forces all across the Eastern Front were thrown into a heartbreaking retreat following the surrender.

Fortunately, Manstein and the other commanders managed to stabilize the defensive line somewhat in recent days. Perhaps it would hold. Perhaps not. Meanwhile, the army and *Luftwaffe* continued to pour men and machines into North Africa to shore up that front and support the flailing Italian Army. And what of the Americans? How much longer would they be willing to stay neutral and out of the fight? Their isolationist wing had lost more seats in their Congress in the November elections, but still, with each passing month, pressure on President Franklin Roosevelt grew and grew for some sort of American participation on behalf of the British and Soviets. Germany knew that Roosevelt wanted the United States in the war. How long before the war mongers in his government overcame the isolationist opposition and declared war on the *Reich*? Whatever the case, in his heart he knew that he was about to play some important role.

As he pondered his future and that of the Fatherland, he suddenly thought of his nephew, Wilhelm, Helga's only son, who died in the early weeks of OPERATION BARBAROSSA. Since Ingrid had died suddenly, he had never remarried. Wilhelm had been his heir, and now there was no male left to become the next Baron von Zimmermann. He paused in his thoughts. A sense of melancholy hit him as he swirled the last of the precious coffee around and around. He stared into the cup. He had not thought of Ingrid in many months other than that brief foray to the Cabaret Paris, perhaps to his shame. He had indeed truly loved her, but a stupid, useless auto accident took her away. A drunken driver, sodded and careless, plowed into her as she crossed a busy street one summer evening. They had planned to have children—many children—another generation of Zimmermanns, another born to take his place, the title, and the estates. And now the next heir, Wilhelm, lay in the family crypt, cut down by a Soviet bullet. Perhaps his sisters would yet have more children. Certainly, he would not, or at least it did not seem likely. His melancholy deepened.

"*Herr Baron . . . Herr Baron.*" Heinz's interruption snapped him out of his trancelike stupor. He jerked his head back, almost spilling the last of his coffee. "*Ja*, Heinz, *ja*?"

"Your driver is ready, *Herr Baron*. He awaits you in the carriageway."

"*Danke*, Heinz. Tell him that I will be there directly."

The butler bowed as he backed out of the breakfast room. "*Jawohl*, Herr *Baron*."

Zimmermann gently set down the coffee cup after draining the last of the precious liquid. He sat for a moment, then stood up, straightened his tunic, reached out and grabbed the briefcase in the chair, and strode out of the room. As he passed through the Great Hall, he paused at the portrait of the eighteenth-century General von

CHAPTER 3

Destroyer of Worlds

Office of *Reichsführer* of the *Schutzstaffel (SS)* Heinrich Himmler Berlin, 5 March 1943

"Please, this way, *Herr Major*. The *Reichsführer* will see you now."

A sudden jolt of fear struck the Luftwaffe officer. A bead of cold sweat rolled down the end of his nose and fell onto the expensive Persian carpet below. He had only seen Himmler from a distance and in the constant newsreels that crowed of German and Italian victory after victory over the evil Bolsheviks and the deluded British. He had never been inside the massive building on *Prinz-Albrecht-Strasse* that served as SS headquarters. The massive door leading to the inner sanctum of the head of Hitler's *Schutzstaffel*, enforcers of Nazi ideology, swung open. The black-uniformed SS officer dipped his head ever so slightly as he motioned the *Luftwaffe* pilot into the darkened room. Only a desk lamp lit the otherwise dim room, casting shadows about. *Major* Hans Pieper squinted as his eyes adjusted to the light. He stepped forward toward the man behind the massive mahogany desk.

"*Heil* Hitler!" he fairly screeched, thinking that decibels would improve his standing. In truth, he had no clue as to why he had been summoned to appear before the *SS Reichsführer*. After all, he was a loyal Party man since the early 1930s and had an exemplary war record, having risen in rank and being highly decorated for action in Poland, France, and Britain. Now he commanded a training squadron preparing the next generation of bomber crews for the never-ending struggle against the communist Soviets. *That's it! A new assignment. A new command, perhaps a promotion.* He stood ramrod stiff, arm still extended toward the ceiling. The man behind the desk only grunted.

"You may be seated, *Major.*"

Stunned! How could one of the most powerful men in the Reich be so casual about the salute? "Jawohl, Herr Reichsführer." He sat down in the overstuffed leather chair as gingerly as possible and stared at the man who seemingly ignored him. Himmler kept scribbling on a notepad, saying nothing. Only the tick tock of the eighteenth-century grandfather clock in the corner broke the silence in the darkened room. Trained to notice minor details, and with the eagle eye vision of an aviator, he could not help but notice the irony of the writing on the antique clock's face—H. Branson and Sons, Ltd., Birmingham. Most likely, he had actually bombed the factory that made the clock, assuming it was still in business. During the Blitz, he had made many bomb runs over not only Birmingham but also Liverpool, Manchester, Bristol, and London as well.

Himmler kept writing, never looking up. Finally, after what seemed like hours, but in reality was only a couple of minutes, the man reputed to make even the most stout-hearted warrior cringe and shiver with fear finally spoke. "*Herr Major,* are you a good Party man?"

Pieper was momentarily stunned by the question—a dangerous question. *Of course, he was. Why is it even a question? What is happening here?* He stumbled for an answer. His lips quivered. Finally, words came. "*Jawohl, Herr Reichsführer.* Indeed, I have been a loyal Party—"

"I did not ask for your history, *Major.* Are you loyal to the *Führer?* Do you love the *Reich?*" interrupted Himmler.

Pieper's blood pressure began to rise. *How could anyone question his loyalty and devotion? What is happening here?*

"Would you be willing to sacrifice your life in service of the *Reich, Herr Major*?" Himmler finally looked up, peering behind gold wire-framed glasses that made him appear smaller than he actually was. A gauntlet had been laid down. Pieper stiffened his back and stared directly at the little man behind the massive desk. His military pride surged. *Had not generations of his family fought and sacrificed for the Fatherland? Had he not flown over 300 combat missions hazarding all for the Fatherland and the new Reich? How dare this upstart little chicken farmer challenge his loyalty to Germany!* He cleared his throat and gripped the chair arm. *Control, Hans. Control.* He finally answered.

"Of course, *Herr Reichsführer*. Of course. I have flown many dangerous missions for the *Reich*. My loyalty and devotion to the *Führer* and to the *Reich* and the Party are unquestioned." *There! He had stood his ground.* A smile finally broke across Himmler's previously stone-cold expression. The little man nodded.

"That is good, *Herr Major*. I am well aware of your combat record, which is why you are here today."

Himmler's comment calmed the *Luftwaffe* man. Pieper relaxed his iron grip on the chair arm, but the impression left in the soft leather told of his previous tension. "*Danke, Herr Reichsführer.* I'm honored to have been called here." *That's it. Play the game.* He still had no clue why he had been summoned. Still, at least it appeared he had not been called in for some infraction or for disciplinary reasons.

Himmler leaned back in his chair. He crossed his hands and fingers together, still smiling a malicious grin as he was wont to do. Finally, the *Reichsführer* leaned forward and peered at Pieper. "Do you know *Luftwaffe Generalmajor* Peter von Zimmermann?"

An odd question. Pieper pondered for a second before responding. "I know of the *Generalmajor* but have never met him. His reputation for courage and loyalty to the service and to the *Reich* has never been in question to my knowledge, *Herr Reichsführer*. Why, if I may, do you ask?"

Himmler just shook his head. "Then you know of no reason to question his loyalty?"

Is this a trap? What do I say? He hesitated and squinted, searching for the right words.

"Why, no, *Herr Reichsführer*. I know of nothing that would call into question the Generalmajor's loyalty or willingness to sacrifice all for the nation. To my knowledge, he is completely above reproach and I might add, sir, he might be the best bomber pilot in the *Luftwaffe*, if I may be so bold."

Himmler clapped his tiny hands and smiled gleefully. "Excellent, *Herr Major*. Excellent. That is what I was hoping that you would say. Now, I suspect that you are curious as to why you are here today, eh?" The gleeful smile turned again to the malevolent grin, almost an arrogant smirk. Pieper forced a smile. He leaned slightly forward in his chair in anticipation of some great pronouncement from the chicken farmer. "*Jawohl, Herr Reichsführer*. I am indeed curious."

Himmler stood and strode to the window with his hands clasped behind his back. He stared out the oversized window toward the garden below. A military band played a march as men in black uniforms with silver trim paraded under the *Reichsführer's* window. Himmler stood for over a minute simply staring out at the scene below. "I adore these patriotic martial tunes. Do you not as well?" he asked, never turning away from the window. Pieper did not answer. "I especially like this one—'*Grosser Zapfenstreich*.'" Himmler stood at the window humming along with the military band below. Finally, the march ended, and he turned back toward Pieper.

"We have an important mission for you, *Herr Major*. You are to join a special *Luftwaffe* squadron as the number two. Zimmermann will be the officer commanding. Your task is to fly a special mission which you will be briefed on in due course. Let me caution you that it is the most closely guarded secret in the *Reich*. Do you understand, *Herr Major*? Most closely guarded." Himmler glared at him.

"I understand, *Herr Reichsführer,*" Pieper blurted out as his back stiffened.

"Good then. *Hauptmann* Steiner will have your orders. You are to report very soon. Please put all your affairs in order. Turn over command of your present squadron to your number two and prepare to travel. Remember, *Herr Major,* speak to no one of your orders. As far as anyone is concerned, you have merely been reassigned to a new bomber squadron. Is that understood?"

"Jawohl, Herr Reichsführer."

"Then you are dismissed." As Pieper reached for his gloves and hat, the *Reichsführer* spoke again. "And, *Herr Major,* there is more. In the course of this special mission, should anyone, especially *Generalmajor* Zimmermann, fail to carry out the mission as planned and ordered, you are to execute him or anyone else immediately and take command. Is that also completely understood?"

Pieper almost collapsed. The sudden shock of the *Reichsführer's* statement hit him like a rifle round in the head. *Gott im Himmel! What is this man saying? Execute a Luftwaffe general in the middle of a mission? What in heaven's name is this?* He stammered, "I . . . I—"

"Is there a question, *Herr Major?*" asked the *Reichsführer* in a schoolmarmish, extremely condescending manner.

Pieper stiffened as the shock subsided. *"Nein, Herr Reichsführer.* I understand completely, and I will carry out my orders and mission to the letter."

"Very well, then, *Herr Major.* You are now dismissed. Good hunting and the *Reich* thanks you for your service. That is all."

Without a further word, Himmler turned back toward the window, smiling at the SS parade in the courtyard below. Throwing up his best salute and *"Heil* Hitler," *Luftwaffe Major* Hans Pieper spun on his heels and strode out of the SS inner sanctum toward an unknown future, but one he suspected would be fraught with peril, intrigue, and above all, danger.

* * * * * * * *

Wolfsschanze (Wolf's Lair), East Prussia, 9 March 1943

The flight in the Junkers Ju 52 Trimotor to Rastenburg had been brief and uneventful. On landing, two thuggish SS men, who spoke only sparingly with just enough courtesy and formality that befit Zimmermann's rank as a *Luftwaffe* general officer, hustled him into a staff car. On the drive to the Wolf's Lair compound, neither SS man spoke to him; that was just as well. The spring foliage was just coming out in this remote part of East Prussia; he loved this early springtime of the year. But he paid little attention to the wonderful flora as the staff car bumped along the recently paved road carved out of the wilderness. About five miles east of the town lay the *Wolfsschanze*, Hitler's Eastern Front command headquarters. Located in the Masurian Woods, the site was guarded by multiple layers of security; however, with his special orders as issued directly from Göring's office, he passed easily through all the security checkpoints. The *RSD* commander at Wolfsschanze was a mousy little man who nonetheless exuded a great deal of self-important arrogance. Zimmermann thought that must be his most enduring quality, that, and undying loyalty to Adolf Hitler as his personal bodyguard commander. Zimmermann reacted to the man with caution and reserve, giving him only the courtesy due his position. It would not do to make any enemies among the Nazi elite, especially with one so close to the *Führer*.

Following a very brief and curt introduction, Zimmermann was hustled into another staff car for the short drive to meet Göring himself. At this point Zimmermann still had no clue as to what his orders or new assignment entailed. The *Reichsmarschall's* quarters appeared simple on the outside. Basically a concrete-block building, it stood only a few yards away from the *Führer's* quarters. But the importance of these men was clearly indicated by the number of black-uniformed guards surrounding the entire compound. The staff officer that accompanied Zimmermann to Göring's quarters politely opened the door and ushered Zimmermann in. He then indicated a comfortable-looking leather couch, which amounted to practically the only furniture in the otherwise bare room. "*Herr Generalmajor,* please wait here. I must return to my duties, but be assured that the *Reichsmarschall's* aide will come for you shortly. *Willkommen* to *Wolfsschanze*, sir." With that, the officer snapped to attention and delivered the Party salute, spun on his heels, and exited the building.

Zimmermann could do nothing but stare at the bare walls. He was surprised that given the garrulous and showy nature of the man that his office and quarters were not decorated with great art likely stolen from some museum or another. At least, that is what he had heard. Then again, this compound was an operational headquarters with serious business. Perhaps the *Reichsmarschall* thought it better to leave the showiness at Carinhall, his sumptuous country estate near Berlin, rather than flash it about a working headquarters.

For the next 20 minutes, he sat silently, but his mind conjured up images of the past few years, mostly horrendous ones. He pondered what his future would be. He had heard some details of the development of a new generation of heavy bombers, four-engine machines with a range of over thousands of kilometers. He had long argued that the *Luftwaffe* focused far too much on ground battle close air support and not enough on strategic and high-level bombing. He had never bought into the Interwar theory that the bomber will always get through as advocated by such luminaries as Viscount Hugh Trenchard of Britain's RAF; Giulio Douhet, the Italian general; or Billy Mitchell from the United States, the three most prominent air power theorists of the 1920s. He always understood that as anti-aircraft artillery and interceptor fighters advanced and evolved, the bomber became more and more vulnerable. On the other hand, he deeply believed that the way to destroy the enemy's ability to continue the struggle was to destroy his infrastructure and industry. That meant bombing airfields, bridges, roads, railways, and perhaps most importantly, factories and refineries. What had incensed him so much about the Battle of Britain was the attack on civilian targets. He understood that breaking the morale of an opponent was a damned difficult thing to do. It was better to attack the tangible levers of enemy power; that meant bombing the enemy's infrastructure and industries. No matter how good an enemy's forces might be, if they didn't have the logistics, they became essentially toothless. But, as a good soldier, he did the best he could with the inadequate medium bombers that the *Luftwaffe* fielded at the war's start.

As he sat pondering these things, it suddenly occurred to him that perhaps his new assignment had something to do with the development of the new fleet of heavy bombers able to carry large ordnance loads and to essentially reach any target in the world. He whispered to himself, "That's it. That must be it! I am to be the sword's edge to develop a German heavy bomber fleet! That is a good assignment." He smiled broadly. Yes, he would have preferred an operational command in a frontline combat unit, but if he could help the Fatherland win this war and end the destruction of lives, then being on the front edge of developing a weapon that would accomplish that mission was a worthy endeavor.

"*Herr Generalmajor, Reichsmarschall* Göring will see you now."

"*Ja, danke.*"

Zimmermann rose to his full height of well over six feet. His physical appearance personified the archetypal Prussian aristocratic warrior. He tucked his service cap under his left arm and slapped gray gloves into his left hand, leaving the right free for the inevitable salute and even perhaps handshake greeting from the commander of the *Reich*'s Air Forces.

"This way, *Herr Generalmajor.*" The overly courteous aide smiled entirely too obsequiously for Zimmermann's taste. He genuinely detested such rear echelon staff officers—not true Teutonic warriors like his bomber pilots and aircrew. No matter, they do perform a useful and necessary, if distasteful, role in the military machine. "*Danke, Herr Oberleutnant* (senior lieutenant)."

He followed the staff aide down a brightly lit passageway ornamented with portraits of German military heroes from Prinz Eugen to Frederick the Great and, of course, Adolf Hitler. *Well then, this is more of what I expected from the Reichsmarschall.* The scenery provided for a few moments of reflection on what had brought him to a personal audience with *Reichsmarschall* Hermann Göring—a new military assignment.

They reached the *Reichsmarschall's* office. The aide knocked briskly, entered the chamber, and, with perhaps too much self-importance, announced the visitor to the Wolf's Lair. "*Herr Generalmajor von Zimmermann, Herr Reichsmarschall.*"

Göring always liked grandiose statements. It was the circus showman in the man. Zimmermann stifled a smirk. "Peter, come in, come in. Sit down. Sit down," exclaimed the man in the powder blue uniform behind the ornate Louis XIV-style desk. Göring motioned to a stiff-looking side chair.

"*Danke, Herr Reichsmarschall.*" Zimmermann carefully set his cap and gloves on the side table as Göring dismissed the aide, who backed out of the room closing the double doors. While Göring penned his signature to the last of the sheaf of orders on the desk, Zimmermann stared straight at the obese man in the ridiculous-looking un-warrior-like costume.

"Peter, old comrade. How have you been? Well, I trust," asked the effusive Göring, extending his pudgy hand across the desk. *I hardly know the man. Why the affable greeting as if we are old comrades in arms?* Zimmermann stood smartly and firmly grasped it, shaking twice. Soft, baby like, and effeminate—how unlike the colossal and firm grip of the dashing fighter pilot of 1918. Zimmermann preferred to remember the youthful Hermann Göring, last commanding officer of the famed Richthofen "Flying Circus," *Jagdgeschwader* 1, who insisted on personally inspecting every aircraft and machine gun of every plane in the squadron. Clearly, the soft life of high and mighty in the salons of Berlin had reduced the man to a caricature of the great warrior of the previous world struggle. *Where was the Teutonic knight who commanded such fearsome warriors? Was this the same man who shot down twenty-two enemies in air-to-air combat even as the Fatherland gasped its way to heinous defeat? And now? He is more of the circus clown than of the 'Flying Circus.'"*

Zimmermann did his best to disguise and suppress his distaste for the man or, rather, what the man had become. Göring plopped his heavy bulk down into the leather chair and waved toward the credenza. "A bit of sherry, perhaps?"

"*Danke, nein, Herr Reichsmarschall.* I prefer no alcohol when I am possibly flying. Please understand it affects my equilibrium. Please accept my regrets."

He lied. Zimmermann knew full well that his return flight scheduled for that evening back to Berlin was waiting on the tarmac at Rastenburg with a full crew aboard. He would only be the passenger. Rather, it struck him as unseemly to actually drink with this detestable creature who was responsible for the death of so many of his comrades and fellow flyers.

"Of course, always the perfectionist, eh, Peter? Well, then, a Cuban cigar perhaps? Despite this perfidious British blockade, I still get them straight from Havana in the diplomatic pouch."

"No, *danke*, again *Herr Reichsmarschall.* I fear I gave up on the wonderful weed before the war. It seemed to interfere with my breathing at higher altitudes."

Göring grinned. "Most understandable, we all make sacrifices for the *Reich*." *Some more than others,* thought Zimmermann, but he dared not voice that sentiment openly.

"Well, then, let's attend to business. Do you know why you're here, *Herr Generalmajor?*" Göring leaned forward in his chair. The question had an icy tone, not as friendly and jocular as questions about sherry and cigars. The question took Zimmermann aback somewhat. *Why was Göring asking him why he was here. Wasn't he here to learn why he was here? Very odd,* thought Zimmermann. *Well, this is Göring's style, so best to simply play along.*

"Why no, *Herr Reichsmarschall.* I have just received the orders to report and have received no briefing on my new assignment. However, *Generaloberst* Kline did indicate that there was a new assignment in the offing, but he could give me no specific details. Let me say though, sir, I am eagerly looking forward to any duty that will be of service to the Fatherland." He intentionally did not say service to the *Reich*. Whether or not the man in the powder blue ridiculous uniform understood that subtlety, he was not sure.

"Just so. So you have no idea of what duty we have in mind for you, eh, Peter? Well let me assure you it is of the utmost importance to the *Reich* and, I might add, to the future of Germany and the Aryan race. You have an exemplary record, *Herr Generalmajor* Zimmermann, and that is why you have been specifically chosen by the *Führer* himself for this very important duty. I cannot, or rather, will not yet tell you what that duty is. I think it is best that you witness something yourself first. That, I believe, will impress upon you the importance of the assignment that you are about to carry out. Do you understand what I am saying to you, *Herr Generalmajor*?"

The man's tone indicated one of two things to Zimmermann, Given Göring's well-known arrogance and need for showy one-up-manship, the seriousness of his tone might be simply that. Or, it might indicate the great importance of his new assignment. He could not tell. Either way, his curiosity grew and grew with each step in the odd process of what should have been a routine change in assignment or position.

"*Herr Reichsmarschall,* I believe I do. Let me assure you that whatever duty you have in mind for me, I shall do my utmost to carry it out efficiently and effectively. I say that on my honor as a German officer and a patriot."

Göring smiled broadly and slapped a knee. "And that, Peter, is what is expected. That is why you were selected for this mission. The *Führer* and I, and I may say, the *Reich* itself, expect no less. I wish you all the best in your duties. I shall not tell you anything further about the mission at this point. You will understand why after a demonstration this afternoon. Now I believe the *Oberleutnant* will escort you to the car, because you have a short trip ahead of you. I will not be there, and you will return to Berlin straightaway after our little demonstration; therefore, let me wish you all the best and a good day."

Zimmermann rose swiftly, came to a correct attention, and despite how he felt about it all, delivered an ever-so-correct Party salute and *Heil* Hitler. With that, the aide appeared at the door and, with a wave of the hand, ushered Zimmermann back out into the hallway toward the exit. But as he passed the portrait of Hitler, a queasy feeling came over him. He could not explain why other than his visceral hatred for the man. What bothered him more was that the uneasy feeling followed him out of the building and back into the staff car that had been waiting to whisk him off to some unknown destination. The fact that the *Reichsmarschall* told him nothing of the mission ahead not only whetted his curiously but also fed into his growing unease.

* * * * * * * *

Der Gevatter Tod (Godfather Death), **East Prussia, 9 March 1943**

For almost an hour, the staff car went deeper into the Masurian Lakes region, a longer drive than Zimmermann expected. As they approached the Lake Pilwag area, the driver turned off onto a side road that seemingly went nowhere. This area of northern East Prussia in the Masurian Lakes region was a remote, sparsely populated region. As such, it represented the perfect site for a secret research and development facility. Additionally, it stood near the site of the battles of Tannenberg and the Masurian Lakes campaign of autumn 1914 where *Generalfeldmarschall* Paul von Hindenberg and his subordinate Erich von Ludendorff crushed the Russian 2nd Army in a series of lightning strokes. Zimmermann wondered if there was any symbolism to the location. Although he did not know the details, he detected from all that he had observed and heard that the destination was some ultra-secret research or production facility. The remoteness would be appropriate for developing a new heavy bomber or other war-winning weapons system. Far from prying eyes nearer to Berlin or one of the many industrial sites at larger cities, enemy agents would find it far more difficult to observe discreetly. It would be very difficult for anyone to discern what actually went on at *Der Gevatter Tod*. Then there was the command and control aspect. Being relatively close to Wolf's Lair, the high muckety-mucks such as Göring, Himmler, or the *Führer* himself could maintain a watchful eye on the activities.

Then again, there was the place's symbolism. Not only did the area represent the greatest battlefield victory of Imperial Germany in the previous war, but it held great symbolism for the German people. Nearby, in July 1410, the German-Prussian Teutonic Knights were roundly defeated by the combined Polish-Lithuanian army at the Battle of Grunwald known in Germany as the First Battle of Tannenberg. The victory established the Poles as the dominant kingdom in Central Europe for centuries. From that point on, the Teutonic Order of Knights decreased in power and influence. Zimmermann's own family had been important members of the order; he had heard many tales of his ancestors' valor and dedication. It struck him that to place such a facility in the territory wrested from Prussia, the rightful rulers, by the Poles initially, but then lost again in the eighteenth century, represented a magnificent irony. Add to that the utter and swift defeat in September 1939 of the new Poland, established from the ashes of the German Empire by the new German knights—airmen and soldiers of the *Luftwaffe* and *Wehrmacht*—and it all smacked of a new irony.

Such thoughts occupied his mind as the car sped through the countryside. He actually paid very little attention to the surroundings on the drive to the secret base. He mused about how his career had taken him from the trenches of northeastern France to this unknown place in the East Prussian woods. He thought of Linden Hall and how wonderful the gardens looked in the early spring.

The staff car turned off the main road and through an innocuous-looking wooden gate. After a further four kilometers or so, it jerked to a halt. Shaken out of his daydreams by the sudden jolt as the car stopped, Zimmermann leaned forward in the backseat and gazed at a set of massive steel doors off to his right. The door opened.

"*Guten Tag, Herr Generalmajor. Willkommen to Der Gevatter Tod.* We have been eagerly awaiting your arrival, sir."

"*Danke,*" he muttered as he stepped out of the car and onto the paved driveway. Clearly the dirt road leading off the main highway had been a clever ruse so as to not attract undue attention. To a casual observer, it appeared as a simple trail into the woods, perhaps for hunter or gamekeeper access. For the last two kilometers into the facility, the dirt path turned to a paved three-lane thoroughfare. On either side, a 12-foot high chain link fence topped with menacing barbed wire coils clearly meant to deter any man or creature. Guard posts with alert sentries appeared every few yards. He shuddered for a moment. The sight of the wire caused a momentary flashback to the trenches. For a fraction of a second, he visualized the coils of barbed wire that lay before the trenches on both sides. To launch an attack, one had to surreptitiously cut and clear the wire not only in front of one's own trenches, but parties had to sneak across "No Man's Land" to snip and clear pathways through the enemy's wire. It could be a suicide mission as the party literally operated yards away from the enemy front line. He had lost many good men to the barbed wire. The moment passed, but the effect always shook him. His shoulders shuddered ever so briefly as if a chill wind had just gusted through. He took a deep breath and stood staring at the massive steel doors while adjusting his uniform, smoothing out the creases.

"I am your host and guide, *Hauptmann* Klemperer, at your service. Please, this way, sir." The cherubic young officer indicated the massive doors, which slowly opened with a pronounced metallic creak. A rush of warm air wafted out from the dark interior. Zimmermann could see four armed guards carrying MP 40 machine pistols and with at least two grenades each attached to their web gear. *Curiouser and curiouser,* he thought to himself, repeating a line from some poem; he could never remember the title or author. *No matter.* They stepped inside.

"Please, *Herr Generalmajor*. Your seat, please." The officer motioned to an odd-looking cart of some sort. Klemperer sat beside him at the wheel and turned the key. The cart hummed—clearly battery driven. With a jerk, the cart shot forward. For the next few minutes, they traveled down a dark corridor lit by electric lights placed at intervals along the concrete walls.

Zimmermann finally spoke. "*Herr Hauptmann*. Tell me, what is the nature of this compound?"

"*Herr Generalmajor*. It is not my place to brief you on the purpose of *Der Gevatter Tod*. But you will soon see what is being accomplished here."

Well, then, we shall wait to see, he mused. His orders had been very vague—simply be at this place at this time on this date and that was about it.

They finally reached the end of the long corridor and arrived at another set of equally massive steel doors with four more guards posted. Klemperer motioned to the man standing in a small window booth, who acknowledged, and started moving control levers. Slowly, the massive doors moved. A bright light shot through the dark corridor. Zimmermann winced as his eyes adjusted to the glaring light. He could make out the movement of people inside—blurry images at first until finally his eyes adjusted.

Inside stood several persons wearing the white lab coats typical of scientists or medical types. Many were older and clearly not military. *So this is some super-secret weapons project, no doubt. But why am I here? What is a bomber pilot doing amongst the wizards of science that these men clearly are?* As he walked through the doorway behind the escort officer, it suddenly occurred to him that perhaps he was there to deliver some new ultra-destructive weapon developed by these scientists. *This must be it—some new war-winning bomb or other weapon. That had to be it.* He sighed. *Well perhaps it will finally end this terrible, destructive war and the world can get on with its business. Perhaps.*

The walls held massive devices replete with meters and scopes and row after row of lighted buttons all typical of a scientific research lab. He was a simple soldier, a flyer. Let the scientists play with their toys. He had little interest in this array of the latest in German scientific engineering. Still, he was somewhat curious, though he tried to be as nonchalant as possible and not let on that he was indeed impressed by the place.

Finally, after passing through a set of rooms filled with machines and electronic gear, they reached another set of doors. Klemperer jabbed at a button to the right of the doors; they swung open revealing another lab. But in this one, only one man stood gazing at an oscilloscope. They entered and the man grunted, turning to face the intruders on his solitude. He appeared older, perhaps in his 50s. He had a bald head with little tufts of white hair about the temples; a crown of white-streaked hair circled his otherwise naked scalp. A set of small oval-shaped glasses perched on the bridge of his nose. He was short and stocky and struck Zimmermann as the stereotypical "mad scientist," or at least how the film industry tended to portray them. But something was off here. Zimmermann could sense it, but he could not determine exactly what didn't seem to fit. The scientist appeared pale and even gaunt. He had the expression of great sadness about him. Zimmermann's first impression was of a man weighed down by deep concerns, though about what Zimmermann was sure he would soon know.

"*Herr Doktor* Tisza, may I present *Generalmajor* Peter von Zimmermann." The little scientist shook his head and then dropped his eyes toward the floor below. *Very odd*, thought Zimmermann. *There is great sadness here.* "*Herr Doktor* Tisza is our lead scientist, *Herr Generalmajor.*"

Zimmermann extended a hand to the scientist, who responded with a cold, almost clammy handshake. "*Willkommen, willkommen, Herr General. Willkommen* to *Der Gevatter Tod.* You have been expected, sir." Zimmermann stared at the odd, sad man. There was a silence for several seconds as neither spoke.

"*Herr Hauptmann,* sir, a call for you," shouted the *Feldwebel* who had followed them into Tisza's lab.

"Pardon me, *Herr Generalmajor.* I must take this call. Please, *Herr Doktor,* please brief the *Generalmajor* as you wish." Klemperer clicked his heels, spun about, and strode over to the other side of the room out of earshot of the two men now staring at each other, one tall, aristocratic and stately; the other, short, balding, and clearly a troubled soul. After a few seconds, Zimmermann finally spoke.

"*Herr Doktor* Tisza. I fear that I am at a loss as to what you do here, the purpose of this facility, and why I am here."

The scientist raised his bushy, graying eyebrows in surprise. "You have not been briefed on your purpose here, *Herr Generalmajor?*"

"*Nein, Herr Doktor.* I am completely in the dark."

Tisza glanced over at Klemperer, now clearly engaged in an animated conversation and paying no attention to the two men. Zimmermann thought to himself that the man appeared to be Eastern European, clearly a Czech or perhaps Hungarian. "Please, do sit, *Herr Generalmajor,*" he said, indicating a pair of metal chairs by a small table. Both sat. Tisza folded his hands on the table after brushing away some loose breadcrumbs. "I apologize, sir. We must take our meals where and when we are able. Mine, I take here in my lab. It is the nature of my work."

Zimmermann stared directly into the scientist's gray eyes. "And, sir, what exactly is your work?" *There it is—straight to the point.* Zimmermann detested the ballet of polite chitchat when directness was required, no doubt the discipline of many years of military life.

The scientist blanched, clearly uncomfortable. He drew in a deep breath, then exhaled slowly. "*Herr Generalmajor,* are you familiar with the work of Professor Werner Heisenberg of the Kaiser Wilhelm Institute on the physics of atomic particles?"

And there it is! Atomic energy. Perhaps a super weapon. Zimmermann had heard rumors of a new super weapon being developed by the regime, and he knew a bit of the science of the atom. "*Ja,*

Herr Doktor, I am a bit familiar. Sir, are we making a super weapon? Is that why I'm here?"

The scientist looked down at the table, then up into the Luftwaffe general's stone-cold face. "*Herr Generalmajor.* It is."

Zimmermann stared directly into the scientist's sad eyes. After a few seconds, the man's countenance seemed to change from sadness to a sort of exuberance. He changed from a man deeply distressed by the notion of an atomic super weapon to an excitement that he was the cutting edge of a wholly new technology. He was the father of the "brave new world," and it was his work that produced it. Like a schoolteacher enthused about learning and excited to talk about scholarly passions, the man's countenance altered completely as he began almost babbling about his work and his achievements.

"Are you familiar with the work of the German physicist Albert Einstein, who unfortunately is actually a Jew, who—"

Zimmermann's gloved hand shot up, stopping Tisza in midsentence. "*Herr Doktor.* His religion or ethnicity is of no concern to me." A cold stare followed. Zimmermann detested the ruinous, destructive, inhumane Nazi racial policy. How many brilliant Germans like Einstein had Hitler and his Party driven away? It was a tragedy. "Please, continue. I believe *Herr* Professor Einstein theorized that matter cannot be destroyed, only turned into energy."

"Just so, *Herr Generalmajor.* And if that is true, then by breaking apart pieces of matter, one can produce tremendous energy."

"A bomb, *Herr Doktor?* A massive, killing bomb. Is that what you have here?" The scientist bowed his head almost now ashamed to admit that that was precisely what he had done—created a massively destructive weapon of war. After a pause, Tisza looked up at the *Luftwaffe* officer, who now realized why he had been brought there. He was to be the instrument of destruction. He was to be the agent of death, the man chosen to unleash the new super weapon. After several more minutes of conversation with Tisza explaining the ins and outs of his work and how the new weapon operated, Klemperer reappeared. In truth, Zimmermann had paid little attention to the scientist's tutorial. His mind drifted back to a happier time at Linden before the first war, when all seemed right with the world, before nations broke each other in barbaric destruction, before the totalitarian regimes—communist and fascist—sought to enslave the world, before he had been chosen as the instrument of death.

Though not a scholar of any subject in particular, Peter, Baron von Zimmermann, was a Renaissance man. He knew a bit about a lot and dabbled in many different endeavors. He loved reading, especially the great historians, philosophers, and poets. As he stared at the tile deck below, only half-listening to the babbling scientist drone on about the properties of atomic particles, critical mass, and so on, and so on, the title of a particularly apropos poem came to mind. He had always been intrigued by the title— "In Time of 'The Breaking of Nations'" by the British poet Thomas Hardy. Written during the Great War, the title seemed to bemoan the crushing of civilization by that war and the destruction of nations and empires. And yet, the poet's words conveyed the notion that as kingdoms, empires, and nations come and go, simple humanity continues on its way. Silently, he mouthed the words that he remembered so well: "*Yet this will go onward the same, Though Dynasties pass . . . War's annals will cloud into night, Ere their story die."[2] How could he now reconcile his new task with the optimism of Hardy's poem?*

"*Herr Generalmajor, Herr Doktor,* we are ready now. Come, come, and please follow me."

* * * * * * * *

Many minutes later and after another long ride down several corridors in the cart, they arrived at what clearly was an observation room. Zimmermann calculated that they had travelled several kilometers down the dimly lit concrete corridor. In the room, the

---

2 Thomas Hardy, "In Time of the 'Breaking of Nations,'" in *Thomas Hardy: The Complete Poems*, ed. J. Gibson (London: Palgrave, 2001).

thick glass windows, tinted green, looked out over a wide open plain where all the trees had been taken down. Nothing could be seen for at least eight kilometers except for a few remaining shrubs and bushes. There were no buildings or any evidence of man over the wide barren landscapé. Zimmermann raised the binoculars to his eyes. In the distance, he spotted what appeared to be a radio or radar tower. Suspended about halfway up was a cylindrical object. A small hut sat beside the tower with cables running out and up to the tower. Several cables ran into the cylinder as it swayed slightly in a breeze.

Herr Generalmajor Zimmermann. May I introduce *Major* Hans Pieper," said Klemperer, who then took a few steps back. Pieper shot the arm up in a salute, which Zimmermann returned somewhat less enthusiastically but still in a somewhat acceptable manner. "*Major.*"

"Sir, I am to be your copilot on this mission. I eagerly look forward to flying with you. You are, if I may say so, a legend in the bomber community. It is a great honor, *Herr Generalmajor.*"

"Indeed, *Major* Pieper. Welcome aboard." With no further word, Zimmermann turned again and stared at the odd tower in the distance, only visible with the powerful Zeiss binoculars. After a quick safety briefing, Zimmermann, Tisza, and Pieper all put on shielded goggles and stood looking out across the great expanse of open cleared ground. On the back wall, a clock's hands crept toward zero.

1500. A rumble built in intensity and raced across the open plain. Before that, a tremendous flash of light caused each man to wince and turn away, even with tinted safety goggles. A boom shook the observation room and almost bowled over the men standing behind the heavy, thick glass windows. Zimmermann grabbed the railing and steadied himself. A billowing cloud formed rising by meters a second into the sky. Inside the cloud, flashes of what appeared to be lightning and flames shot out and up. As the cloud rose, it spread out and appeared almost like the top of a tree or, better yet, like that of a mushroom. After several seconds, the rumble of noise was followed by a great boom that again shook the observation room and stabbed at the eardrums of the men inside. The sound passed quickly, but the cloud continued to rise and spread.

Awestruck, Zimmermann raised the binoculars to his eyes again and watched in a mixture of wonderment and horror at the scene across the plain. No one spoke. Tisza bowed his head, weeping. Pieper grinned, almost laughing. Zimmermann said nothing, but a thought passed through his mind at that moment. It was a line he remembered from the "Bhagavad-Gita," an ancient Hindu poem: "Now I am become death, the destroyer of worlds."[3]

* * * * * * * *

Several miles away, Lech Kwiatkowski and Józef Mowak winced as the flash of light enveloped them. Averting their eyes to avoid the burn, after a few seconds they both looked up again at the giant cloud reaching toward the sky. Seconds later, a huge boom shook the tree leaves, rattling their eardrums as well. The two men, friends since childhood and comrades in arms in a Polish cavalry regiment that had been decimated by a German panzer armored division in the early days of the war had escaped the German onslaught and the inevitable prisoner of war camp. They managed to flee through Hungary and eventually into Greece, where they took passage to Britain. Recruited by the Special Operations Executive (SOE) of Brigadier Colin Gubbins, the head of SOE Operations in 1940, they had been trained at the special commando camp in Scotland and then inserted back into Poland to operate with the Polish underground. Their mission was observation rather than aggressive action. They had been ordered to observe the strange goings-on near Lake Pilwag in Masuria and report back to London.

Every military installation had to have civilian contract workers, and this site was no different. One of the Polish vendors, who sup-

---

3 Krishna-Dwaipayana Vyasa, "The Bhagavad Gita," trans. Juan Mascaró (New York: Penguin, 2003).

plied milk to the installation, heard that some big experiment was to happen this particular day. Though professing his love of the Reich and loyalty to Hitler, the Polish dairyman secretly belonged to the underground and dutifully passed on any rumors to Kwiatkowski and Mowak. Both knew that if the dairyman reported that something appeared to be happening that day, they would certainly be in their usual watching post, well-concealed in the woods from any German observation.

When they arrived that morning, they saw in the distance, several kilometers from their observation post, the strange tower with the adjoining hut and what appeared to be electrical cables going up to a cylindrical object suspended at the top of the tower. They had no idea what was about to happen. The two men had no clue of the magnitude of what they were about to see.

Both men stared into the binoculars, astounded and in disbelief at what they witnessed. They said nothing. They simply gawked at the rising cloud of flame and smoke for several minutes. Finally, Kwiatkowski raised a camera up and took several photographs of the strange phenomenon. Although they knew they would both be summarily executed if the enemy captured them and realized what the Poles had witnessed, and, more importantly, photographed, they did not hesitate for a moment. While Kwiatkowski hurriedly snapped photo after photo, Mowak scribbled in his notebook his best description of the expanding cloud. Finally, Kwiatkowski spoke, "My friend, I do not know what we have just witnessed. It must be the Devil himself. God help us. We must get this intelligence to London straightaway."

Not speaking a word, his companion nodded in concurrence. The two men ran back down the hill toward their vehicle parked well out of German sight and raced back to their village to transmit to London perhaps the most important intelligence of their career.

* * * * * * * *

Chiefs of Staff Conference Room, War Rooms, Whitehall, London, 14 March 1943

The room was all quiet. Not a person spoke. Seated around the table were several high-ranking officers and their civilian counterparts, some staring down at the neatly arranged notepads that the clerks conveniently provided. Some stared at the map of southern England, the Channel, northern France, and the Low Countries. But most simply stared or, put more succinctly, glared at the large blown-up photographs of what appeared to be a mushroom-shaped cloud rising hundreds of feet into the sky. One participant in the secret meeting likened the image to a giant piece of broccoli, but no one really thought that comparison humorous. The only noise in the conference room came from the tapping of a pencil on a notepad. No one noticed or cared.

The door opened and in strode the prime minister—Winston Leonard Spencer Churchill. The dour expression on his face told the complete story. Almost a scowl, clearly the PM's countenance indicated the seriousness of the hastily convened meeting. All rose in recognition of the PM's arrival.

"Gentlemen, as you were. Please sit. We have much to discuss. I believe all of you have been briefed on this . . . umm . . . situation." Wordlessly, each man retook his seat. The PM cleared his throat. "Gentlemen," he said, pausing to look into the face of everyone present, "I daresay that we have a grave situation and, quite frankly, one that we have dreaded for many months." Heads bobbed in recognition and concurrence. Everyone feared the day that the Germans might win the race to operationalize an atomic weapon. That day had arrived, and the evidence hung from an artist's easel showing enlarged photographs of the test conducted five days prior at *Der Gevatter Tod* deep in the Masurian Woods of East Prussia. Taken by two Polish patriots and transmitted from hand to hand through the Polish underground, the photos were smuggled aboard a neutral Swedish airliner bound from Warsaw to Stockholm and there handed to the British naval attaché by a pro-British Swedish diplomat. Within minutes of the photographs arriving in London at the office of Wilfred Dunderdale, the liaison officer for the Polish underground operatives, the PM had been informed. Dunderdale operated out of the headquarters of Military Intelligence, Section 6 (MI6), also known as the British Secret Intelligence Service (SIS), which had responsibility for foreign intelligence gathering. Minutes later, Churchill placed a transatlantic call to the White House in Washington to Franklin Delano Roosevelt. Shortly afterward, a call went from the White House to an office on the fifth floor of the New War Department Building on C Street, NW.

"Gentlemen, may I introduce our guest from Washington, Brigadier General Leslie Groves of the United States Army Corps of Engineers. He is the head of the American atomic development program." All around the room, the men acknowledged and welcomed the American officer.

"Prime Minister, gentlemen, I apologize for my shabby appearance. When President Roosevelt called and ordered me to fly here as fast as possible, there wasn't time for niceties like a shower and a shave or even a uniform change. I shall try not to offend. It was a long flight from DC overnight." With that, lightness entered the somber war rooms for the first time that morning as some chuckled or shook their heads in acknowledgment.

"Quite all right, General Groves. We quite understand," responded Churchill with his characteristic, well-known smirk. "I suggest that we start by introducing ourselves, some of whom you no doubt already know."

With that, each introduced himself in turn. There was the head of MI6, Major-General Sir Stewart Menzies; the head of British Security Coordination (BSC), William Stephenson (also known as INTREPID), who had arrived from New York several days earlier; Chief of the SOE, Air Commodore Sir Charles Hambro; two representatives from the British MAUD Committee, the academics responsible for British atomic research; Frederick Lindemann, Baron Cherwell, Churchill's science adviser; and General Sir Alan Brooke,

Chief of the Imperial General Staff (CIGS). With the meeting called to order, Churchill posed the critical question.

"Is it possible that the Jerries actually have developed an atomic weapon? That, to my mind, is the central issue?"

One of the scientists cleared his throat and spoke in a timid, almost embarrassed tone. "Yes, Prime Minister, it is quite possible. Understand that atomic research is one of the most highly classified and well-protected aspects of German research and development. They apparently made a breakthrough last year when they were able to create a chain reaction within a laboratory atomic pile."

"Sorry, what is an atomic pile?" interjected Menzies.

"Well, General, essentially it is an enclosed structure where . . . rather . . . well, it's a device used to initiate and control a self-sustained nuclear chain reaction." The blank look on the MI6 man's face told the scientist that his definition needed some simplification. "Sir, it is a contained space where we put bits of uranium in close contact. Being what is called 'radioactive' means that the mineral throws off particles from its atomic nucleus or the center of the atom made up of what are called protons and neutrons. Uranium 235, an isotope of the basic uranium, is particularly nasty at doing this. I am embarrassed to say, sir, that it was two German scientists, Otto Hahn and Fritz Strassmann, who first achieved what was soon called nuclear fission back in December '38."

Hambro interrupted, scolding like an overbearing schoolteacher castigating an errant pupil. "You mean to tell us that the bloody Huns stole a march on us?"

The two scientists looked at each other, both with worried expressions. After a few uncomfortable seconds, the first scientist looked first at Hambro, then Churchill, and finally back at Menzies. "I fear so, sir. I fear so." He took in a deep breath. "What essentially happens is that when sufficient radioactive material comes into contact with more such material, the nucleus or center of the atom starts to disintegrate and throw off neutron particles. It basically splits into two nuclei that then bounce around striking other nuclei, breaking them apart. What you end up with is a massive release of energy called gamma radiation."

The PM grunted and mumbled under his breath, "Damn bloody wizards!" He leaned forward in his chair and looked directly at the two scientists. "And you say that you can make a weapon out of this . . . this . . . process?"

The second scientist responded, "Well, yes, Prime Minister. Theoretically, if you can create enough fissile material, in this case refined Uranium 235 isotope, you can create a massive explosion with a relatively small weapon. The problem that has to be solved now is how to refine a high enough grade of U235 isotope to create a workable device."

"Like an air-dropped bomb?" Brooke shot in.

"Sir, quite right. Like a bomb."

At this point, Groves, who had been silent thus far, spoke up. "Gentlemen. I must add that last December in Chicago, we were able to create such a sustainable chain reaction in our developmental pile. We call it CP-1. Dr. Enrico Fermi is our chief physicist. He and his team were able to create a sustainable fission reaction by slowly removing cadmium rods from the pile. You see, gentlemen, cadmium absorbs those nasty little neutrons that are bouncing about. But when you remove the rods, the little bastards go where they please, striking other little bastards, and kaboom, you have atomic fission."

No one seemed put off by Groves' earthy language and tone.

"And that, Prime Minister, puts the Germans several months ahead of us and the Americans in terms of weaponizing this process," responded the first scientist.

"Sadly, sir, we did not know until now if the Germans have been able to create such a process, let alone a workable weapon," added INTREPID, pointing at the photographs. "We do know that the eminent Hungarian physicist, Professor István Tisza, has been recruited, or rather I should say, extorted into working on their atomic program. We believe that the SS is holding his family hostage under house arrest in Budapest, forcing his cooperation."

Lindemann shot in, "And PM, Tisza is one of the very few physicists in the world believed capable of actually creating such a weapon."

The room went silent. All heads turned toward the blown-up photos taken by the two courageous Polish intelligence agents of the hideous mushroom cloud hanging from the artist's easel. Churchill lowered his head and reached out to his tumbler placed at his seat earlier by a staff aide. He glared at the straw-tan liquid—a good Glenlivet 18-year-old—and grumbled. "I am fearful, Frederick, that he already has done so."

CHAPTER 4

Dartmoor

Avord *Luftwaffe* Air Base, France, 27 April 1943
"*Willkommen* to Avord, *Herr Generalmajor.*"

Zimmermann acknowledged the man's salute as a sentry snapped to precise, heel-clicking attention. Zimmermann waved to the young *Luftwaffe* airmen nonchalantly and pressed down on the accelerator. The 1936 Mercedes-Benz 500K lurched forward, its powerful engine responding instantly. A jolt of regret welled up. Why be so rude to the sentry who is simply a cog in the vast Nazi machinery and probably should have been off to university or technical school or some such place studying architecture or literature or history instead of in the service?

He took a right turn somewhat too fast, but the powerful Mercedes took it in stride and smoothly surged ahead. He loved this car, a gift from his wife before she had been killed suddenly and tragically. He could've ridden to the air base in a *Luftwaffe* staff car with his regular driver but chose instead to drive. In truth, driving had a calming effect; he took the Mercedes out as often as his flight schedule or workload permitted. A man defined by speed and risk taking, he loved to push the car past 120 km/h on the *Autobahn* motorway.

After all, since taking up flight, he had become addicted to speed, the faster the better. It earned him promotion, high command and, most recently, the Knight's Cross of the Iron Cross with Oak Leaves.

Without thinking, his left hand raised up to his throat and fingered the shiny black metal. He squeezed it between his thumb and forefinger. *At what price? At what price?* As he motored down the tree-lined road toward the stark white base operations building, he thought of all the good airmen he had commanded and lost on so many bombing missions. Most of their bodies were never recovered; they now lay under the Channel waters or on the frozen Russian heartland—food for worms.

Of the crew on this new mission, only he and the copilot, Pieper, knew the actual details. Normally, German bombers carried a single pilot as did British bombers. But for this specific mission, two pilots were needed to ensure mission success in case of a casualty. The new He 177 bomber now sitting inside a darkened hanger accommodated two pilots. Truth be told, he did not completely trust Pieper. Zimmermann could not actually discern precisely, but there seemed something entirely too artificial about the man. True, he was a National Socialist and true believer and a competent, skilled flyer. That was pretty clear. But something else bothered Zimmermann about the man. He would bear watching closely.

He drew in a sharp breath as he braked. For over a minute, he simply stared ahead out the windscreen as the gravity of this new mission struck him again as it had so many times since the new weapon's demonstration in East Prussia weeks before. In the time since, the mission was never far from his mind. He understood that it might end the war and save millions of lives. But, in his subconscious, he also dreaded that in that case, the Nazis would literally control the world. How to rationalize this conundrum? *If the Fatherland survived, prospered, and endured, perhaps it could accommodate the rascals in Berlin. Perhaps with peace, the German people would rise up and dispose of the National Socialist contagion. Perhaps. Perhaps. . . .*

"*Herr Generalmajor. Herr Generalmajor.* The crew awaits you in the briefing room."

Suddenly, his mind jolted out of his daydream. "*Ja, danke.* Of course. *Danke.*"

The airman opened the door as Zimmermann bounded out and straightened his uniform. He appeared immaculate this day. Normally, he did not wear all his decorations and campaign ribbons, but today it seemed appropriate. His uniform blouse wore the evidence of heroism and leadership in both world wars—Iron Cross 2nd Class and two Iron Crosses 1st Class from his time in the Western Front trenches as an infantry officer. He wore the more recent Knight's Cross from the current war. Normally, he disliked showiness and wore a minimum of decorations during everyday operations. Today was different. He needed to inspire in this new crew confidence that their pilot and commander was top of the line and literally the best pilot in the entire service. A more extroverted, garrulous officer might attempt to do so with words. Zimmermann knew that these highly accomplished airmen would disregard mere words. Without saying a single syllable, the crew could get the measure of the man simply by seeing his uniform and the pieces of metal and ribbon displayed there, a testament to his leadership, performance under duress, and skill. Nothing more needed stating. He spied his former navigator standing by the door.

"Well, Fischer, let's meet our comrades, shall we?"

"*Jawohl, Herr Generalmajor,*" responded *Oberleutnant* Fritz Fischer, who had served as his navigator on many missions over Britain in 1940 and 1941 and, more recently, over the Soviet homeland. The junior officer saluted smartly and held the door as Zimmermann stepped into the darkened entryway.

* * * * * * * *

Avord Air Base sat among a cluster of tiny hamlets, farms, and villages in central France. It had been one of the French Air Force's chief operating bases before and during the Battle of France. With the German victory and the occupation, the *Luftwaffe* took over the facility and converted it to a bomber base primarily for reserve and replacement crew training. As such, it represented the ideal location for staging the operation due to its relatively backwater location and training mission in the spring of 1943. The less attention paid to the advance preparations and sudden influx of somewhat mysterious civilian personnel, the better. A forward operating airbase was likely to draw undue attention from aircrew and ground personnel and, of course, from the local Frenchmen spying for the British. It was at this isolated airfield that *Gruppe* I of *Kampfgeschwader* 1 (KG 1) arrived in late June, ostensibly to refit, train, and then launch raids against southern Britain and English Channel maritime shipping. KG 1 had a sterling reputation having served admirably over Poland, France, and in the Battle of Britain. More recently, the unit served on the Eastern Front, flying out of East Prussian bases. With so many years of experience flying the Heinkel He 111 medium bomber, it was the perfect unit to take on the new He 177 A-5 heavy bomber just coming into service. The group and airmen had come to Avord to train on the new bomber in preparation for increased sorties in support of the stalled ground offensive in the Ukraine, especially the ongoing and frustrating siege of Leningrad. The primary mission, once the group returned to East Prussia, was to interdict the supply line across Lake Ladoga that kept Leningrad fed and alive, albeit just barely. But for Zimmermann and the select members of his new aircrew, their presence at Avord heralded a far more sinister enterprise.

* * * * * * * *

Zimmermann entered the large cavernous room and took his seat. He noted the gaggle of very senior officers gathered behind him in the glass-enclosed command suite overlooking the stage. Seated in the uncomfortable metal chairs so typical of military briefing rooms were only a handful of officers and crew. Whispering among themselves, they wondered why only one aircrew was being briefed and not an entire air group. Zimmermann did not wonder. He already knew. He glanced over at the *Luftwaffe* officer sitting in the row ahead of them—the copilot, *Major* Hans Pieper. A dour-looking *Luftwaffe Oberst* stood on the stage with pointer in hand beside a map covered by a canvas drape. He cleared his throat as all whispers and conversation ceased.

"*Herr Generalmajor* Zimmermann, *Herr Major* Pieper, and crew of flight 001. You are today embarking on a mission of great importance to the *Reich* and, I might add, to the future of the world itself." A slight grin broke across his otherwise somber face. The officer nodded to the *Feldwebel* standing next to the hidden map, who promptly lifted the canvas revealing southern England. The briefing continued. "Your target is the city of Plymouth, more specifically, the Royal Navy station at Devonport." Airmen looked each other quizzically. The *Luftwaffe* had lost too many fine crew and aircraft over Plymouth; they wondered why this mission. If there was to be a raid, where were the other aircrews? A slight murmur interrupted. Zimmermann raised a gloved hand and all chatter ceased.

"You men have been specially selected for this critical mission due to your exemplary achievements. I congratulate you one and all." The briefing continued for another hour. By the time it concluded, the crew of the new He 177 bomber knew the frightening details to be sure. First, their target was the Royal Navy base at Devonport near the city of Plymouth, but should that not be an option due to weather or heavy anti-aircraft fire, they were to divert to a secondary target of less military value over the Devonshire moor. Second, they learned that they carried an entirely new weapon that would devastate an entire city. Third, they would be flying singly with just another Heinkel serving as a photography platform as well as with a heavy fighter escort out of Normandy. Fourth, they understood that not a word of the mission must leak out, and if it did, it would mean immediate execution for the leaker. What was not said was that the mission's ultimate goal was not so much the devastation of the Royal Navy base, however important. Rather, it was to force the United

Kingdom to negotiate a peace, to continue to freeze out any United States' action against the Reich and, ultimately, to crush the Soviet Union under the weight of atomic attack after atomic attack. But only Zimmermann and Pieper understood these essential objectives. For the crew of flight 001, it was sufficient for them to understand the target designation for their pending mission.

With the briefing concluded and the *Oberst* having departed the stage, all stood to attention, except for Zimmermann. He rose slowly from his seat at the back of the room. One by one, the men, some ashen-faced at what they had just been told, turned about to face the tall highly decorated officer, who now controlled their immediate destiny. He smiled broadly, in an obvious attempt to lighten the somber mood and perhaps alleviate their fears.

"Well, lads, shall we go out and inspect our winged chariot?"

With no further words, the men of Heinkel He 177, number 001, shuffled out of the briefing room toward the truck that would take them to the closed hanger across the main runway from the operations building, each one silent in his thoughts about what lay ahead and what their collective destiny might be.

Zimmermann stood but did not follow the men out. Instead, he stared for a few moments at the pale, rather too thin young man standing across the briefing room. Zimmermann had noticed him earlier and assumed that he was one of the project scientists. The ill-fitting suit, clearly intended for a heftier man, gave him the appearance of a scarecrow hung on a wooden stand overlooking the grain fields of Linden Tree with droopy sleeves and baggy trousers. While comical to any human observer, the scarecrows clearly frightened the pesky birds. Thus, they did their duty. Despite the pale, scrawny man's physical appearance, Zimmermann assumed he did his job with great effectiveness and efficiency as did the scarecrows, else why would he be present at the brief? The man spoke first as he approached Zimmermann, who had not moved.

"*Herr Generalmajor* von Zimmermann. I am pleased to finally meet you." The odd man dipped his head, a sign of if not reverence, certainly courtesy to a superior. "I am Professor *Doktor* Franz Zwilling of the Kaiser Wilhelm Institute for Physics. I have been chosen to fly with you on this mission and—"

"And your role is to do what, sir?" Zimmermann shot back. Irritated, he feared civilian interference in a purely military mission. Let the scientists at the Kaiser Wilhelm Institute and other laboratories develop this evil weapon. He did not need them actually flying on the mission with the possibility of complicating the already dangerous and delicate tasks facing the crew.

Zwilling drew back, stunned at the chilly reception. "*Herr Generalmajor*, I . . . uh . . . deeply apologize, sir. I do not mean to offend, nor do I wish to complicate your task. My role in this endeavor is to arm the weapon as we approach the target. It is a delicate and, may I add, ultra-sensitive task. I was chosen by *Generaloberst* Krause for this duty. I can only say that while I will be training and flying with your crew, I will in no way interfere, nor will I challenge your authority. My sole concern is arming the weapon." *There! I can state it no plainer.* As if to emphasize the point, he extended his hands with palms up, a sign of supplication and subservience.

Zwilling did not need the enmity of a powerful and highly respected military officer. He knew all too well the fate of several fellow scientists who had crossed Party officials. He knew only a smattering of intelligence about this tall steely-eyed *Luftwaffe* general and certainly nothing about possible connections to powerful men in the National Socialist regime. Zwilling would take care in all his actions and speech.

Zimmermann stood ramrod stiff for a few moments, arms crossed across his chest, staring coldly at the man before him. Finally, he responded, "Very well, *Herr Doktor*. Very well. As long as you understand your role in this affair and can follow orders sharply and immediately, we shall have no trouble. Agreed?"

"Agreed, *Herr Generalmajor*. Agreed."

"Then welcome aboard, *Herr Doktor* Zwilling."

With that, he extended a hand and gave the scientist a resolute and firm handshake. But he could not help feeling that something about the man seemed odd. He appeared perhaps ill or not quite strong enough. His complexion seemed too pale and wan, perhaps caused simply by the gravity of his role or the danger of the mission. Clearly *Herr* Professor *Doktor* Franz Zwilling of the Kaiser Wilhelm Institute for Physics bore careful watching, as did Pieper. "Shall we join the crew and walk to the hanger? You can then tell me about yourself."

"Indeed, *Herr Generalmajor.*" He spoke with more energy as the two men walked out of the briefing room toward the distant aircraft hangar. Zimmermann clasped his hands behind his back in a very military fashion while Zwilling, now in his element talking about the scientific and development aspects of Project Armageddon, prattled on. Zimmermann only half listened with an occasional nod. His thoughts lay elsewhere, to more immediate mission requirements and how to go about training and preparing the crew. They had to operate as an efficient team. Every man had to be at the peak of performance. There could be no room for sloppiness or carelessness. Given the timing for mission completion already laid on by *Generaloberst* Ernst Krause, the overall head of Project Armageddon, a fervent, almost demented ultra-Nazi who had advocated targeting London, he had very little time to prepare the mission and train the new crew. The recent rest and leave period at Linden Tree had reminded him of a happier, more tranquil time. Now, the real world intruded and he had no choice but to focus entirely on the challenge ahead.

"You see, *Herr Generalmajor,* the real breakthrough came in December 1938. My colleagues, the chemists Otto Hahn and Fritz Strassmann, claimed in an article in the scientific journal *Natural Sciences* that they had produced barium by bombarding uranium with neutrons. You understand that atoms are made up of tiny particles called protons, electrons, and neutrons." He paused, wondering if the *Luftwaffe* man had even a rudimentary knowledge of physics, much less atomic particles. The physicist was relieved when Zimmermann indicated that he did.

"*Ja*, proceed, *Herr Doktor*."

"Aah, quite so. *Jawohl, Herr Generalmajor.* The process was confirmed in early 1939 by Professor Otto Frisch by his own experiments. He called this bursting of the uranium atom 'nuclear fission.'"

"And why, *Herr Doktor*, is that significant?"

"Well, you see, *Herr Generalmajor*, this atomic fission, as we now call it, releases great energy as it starts a chain reaction of particles splitting off, striking other atoms, and creating tremendous energy in the process. It verifies what Professor Einstein claimed in that mass can be turned to energy." He paused. Perhaps he should not have mentioned the émigré Jewish scientist, who had been wise enough to move to the United States in the early 1930s prior to the Nazi campaign against the Jews. But since there was no reaction from the *Luftwaffe* man, he felt safe enough to proceed with his dissertation. "Given that, there was a committee of scientists formed to investigate the phenomenon and, more specifically, to determine if the splitting of atomic material had any military applications. This committee was called the *Uranverein*. Very soon, the *Wehrmacht* took over the project, specifically, the army's Ordnance Office, the *Heereswaffenamt*. I shouldn't complain. By the military taking over the program, it meant we then had the funding and resources to continue the research and development." He paused, then emitted nervous twittering laugh. Zwilling blanched, fearing he might have gone too far in his story. They continued on toward the hanger for several steps in silence.

"Go on, *Herr Doktor*. I shan't bite you."

"I am relieved, *Herr Generalmajor.* You realize that we are now delving into the most sensitive and secret aspects of the *Reich*, and I must be cautious."

Zimmermann came to a full halt and turned toward the scientist. Zwilling could not tell if it was a stare or a glare, but he understood the meaning.

"*Herr Doktor Zwilling.* Do you not think the *Reich* would have chosen me to command this mission had they any doubts about either my ability or discretion?" Zimmermann raised his left eyebrow with the comment so as to give it credibility and emphasis.

Zwilling, taken aback, stuttered and blurted out, "*Jawohl, Herr Generalmajor!* I . . . I . . . am certain of it. I . . . uh—"

"Then proceed." Zimmermann turned back toward the distant hanger and strode out, leaving the shorter Zwilling racing to catch up.

"It was felt by many physicists, including my colleague at the Institute, *Doktor* Werner Heisenberg, that while the science could be used to make a workable weapon, it would take years, perhaps, maybe six. We presented that scenario to *Herr* Speer, the *Reich* Minister for Armaments and even to the *Führer* himself. This was in late 1939."

Zimmermann stared down at the physicist but continued striding across the runway. "Yet here we are, *Herr Doktor.*"

"Indeed, *Ja*, here we are, barely three years later and on the cusp of a new world order, *Herr Generalmajor.*"

"And how, *Herr Doktor*, did this all come about if it was so, shall I say, speculative?"

The physicist was clearly now in his element discussing the program to which he had devoted the last four years of his professional life. He fairly bubbled with enthusiasm. Zimmermann thought that for a few moments the scientist seemed to forget that what they had created and what he was about to unleash on the world was the most monstrous killing weapon in the history of humanity.

"We created several committees to study and research the essential components," said Zwilling. "That included uranium, heavy water production, uranium isotope separation, and most critically, the building of the *Uranmaschine*—the nuclear reactor. We managed to actually split atoms at the Institute in July 1941 in the reactor that we built at the end of 1939. We discovered that we could refine enough fissile material to create the desired reaction. In all honesty, *Herr Generalmajor*, we were too separated and not very cohesive.

But two things happened that pushed the program along. Professor Heisenberg in April of last year managed to cause a neutron increase inside a reactor. That proved that we could actually generate an atomic fission event."

"And the other?" asked an increasingly curious Zimmermann. History and literature had been the school subjects he most enjoyed, but science and mathematics fascinated him, even though he had little aptitude for either.

"We obtained the services of Professor *Doktor* István Tisza, formerly of Budapest University of Technology and Economics in Hungary. I believe you have met Professor Tisza."

Zimmermann had. He recalled the professor at the test site in East Prussia. The man struck him as deeply depressed and melancholy, no doubt due to the presence of his SS minders. A little research showed that Professor Tisza was not altogether enthusiastic about working on the Armageddon Project. Truth be told, the man had been blackmailed or, more specifically, extorted. The SS kept a watchful eye on the scientist's family in Budapest where they were practically prisoners in their own home. While no direct threats had been made, it remained quite clear to the physicist that failure to work on the program and perhaps, more importantly, to make progress, meant a dim future for his wife and two children. The detonation at *Der Gevatter Tod* proved his worth to the regime.

"Indeed, I have met the professor. What was his role in the project?" They had almost reached the hanger where the rest of the crew waited, but Zimmermann knew that he must find out more about the physicist Tisza and perhaps find a way to help him out of his dilemma. He had done the work for the Nazi regime—let the man return to his family.

"Quite specific. Professor Tisza constructed a mechanism to refine sufficient fissile material to construct a useable weapon. He was then able to generate enough material that when two halves of a sphere of Uranium 235, which is the isotope, are thrown together at a sufficient speed, the material reaches what is called critical mass. The particles start colliding, smashing together so to speak, which creates the massive explosion. Professor Tisza was then able to design and construct a workable device."

"And perhaps the end of civilization," Zimmermann whispered under his breath.

"Pardon, *Herr Generalmajor,* what was that?" It was a deflection. Zwilling heard him perfectly well.

"Of no matter, *Herr Doktor.* We will speak more of the technical aspects of the weapon. Now let us see our aircraft. I hear it is a fine example of superior German engineering and technology."

With that, the two men stepped up to the hanger as several burly *SS* men pushed open the huge metal doors. As the doors slowly creaked on the hinges, Zimmermann turned his eyes ever so slightly toward the man standing beside him. Zwilling had bowed his head, staring at the tarmac below as if in shame or embarrassment. Zimmermann wondered if the man was as truly committed to the operation as he had appeared on the walk over from the operations building. Had that been simply a ruse? After all, in a totalitarian state, one had better show enthusiasm lest one lose his head. Or perhaps he had been caught up in the enthusiasm of explaining his life's work. Maybe the scientist had doubts about the morality of what they had embarked upon in the name of National Socialism and Third *Reich* world domination. Such doubts often crept up on Zimmermann ever since that demonstration of the weapon's power weeks earlier.

The special hanger clearly held something the regular airmen of Avord Air Base were not intended to see. As the men approached the massive building, the crew noted the heavily armed *SS* guards whose faces and scowls indicated the seriousness of their purpose. The truck came to a jolting halt by the massive doors. The crewmen had been told to sit and wait for Zimmermann's arrival. They passed the few minutes in a seemingly jovial and nonchalant manner. But everyone sitting in the truck knew that it was merely a facade—casual banter designed to hide the trepidation that every man felt but would never openly express.

"Hey, *Herr Stabsfeldwebel* Weber. Why did I volunteer for this duty, eh?" joked one of the gunners, whose duty was to man an MG 131 machine gun for aircraft self-defense.

"You didn't, you fool! You were volunteered for your good service, *Schweinehund!*" retorted the crew chief, a long service *Luftwaffe* man who also served as the aircraft flight engineer. The young airmen just laughed as he caught the crew kitbag tossed back to him by the *Stabsfeldwebel* (senior sergeant, second highest enlisted rank in the *Luftwaffe*).

Finally, the hanger doors crept open. Despite the bright spring sunshine outside, the interior appeared dark and foreboding; no one could make out anything but the dim shape of a large airplane as their pupils adjusted. Zimmermann had already seen the bomber having been shown it a day earlier on a private tour with Pieper and the base commander. They had then been briefed at the station headquarters located at the *Château d'Aubilly* some four kilometers from the airfield. He had spent a fitful night at the *Château* and now felt the fatigue, a combination of the accumulated stress of month after month of combat service compounded by the knowledge of this new and potentially war-winning mission. Despite the massive destruction he knew would follow the attack, he also rationalized that if it stopped the war, saved millions of lives, and preserved the Fatherland, he could rationalize the new weapon's use and his role.

As the crew approached the plane, all joking and conversation ceased. The new heavy bomber, powered by twin-paired Daimler-Benz DB 610 liquid-cooled piston engines that generated 2,860 horsepower, entered service in April 1942, but only in limited numbers. None of the men had yet flown the new heavy bomber, but all were eager for their first flight. The new bomber had a maximum speed of 351 miles per hour and a combat range of 1,540 kilometers, more than enough to reach the cities, factories, and airbases of southern and western England or into the Ural Mountains where the Soviets had moved most of their heavy industry following the German invasion in June 1941. Defended by a single 7.92mm MG 81 machine gun mounted in the bubble-shaped cabin and fishbowl cockpit, two 20mm MG 151 cannon with one in the tail, and four 13mm MG 131 machine guns, the plane could manage to ruin the day of any British or Soviet fighter jock foolish or bold enough to approach the plane. With an interior bomb load capacity of 15,000 pounds, the plane could do devastating damage to any target. Importantly, with a maximum service ceiling of only 26,000 feet, the plane was well within range of ground-based anti-aircraft fire as well as supercharged British fighters. The crew would soon learn what these features meant for their security.

As the crew clambered aboard, Zimmermann turned to Pieper, "Well, Hans, ready to see what she is made of?"

"Indeed, *Herr Generalmajor!*" the copilot responded enthusiastically.

A service cart pulled the plane out of the hangar and positioned it at the end of the runway. Zimmermann smiled at the smoothness of the operation. This was a real change from the muddy and rutted airstrips they had been forced to operate from in the battles of France and the forward airfields in Poland and western Soviet Union. Once the ground crew pulled away and gave the all go signal, he revved up the powerful engines; the plane slowly rolled down the runway, picking up speed with every second. Almost effortlessly, she lifted off the runway and up into the sunny, cloudless, French sky.

"She's very smooth. A fine machine," commented Pieper as he retracted the landing gear. "Ja, Hans. Very smooth indeed," responded Zimmermann. Both men knew of the initial engine troubles experienced by the first model He 177s. They had a nasty habit of catching fire in flight. The problem with the fires was resolved with the new twin-paired Daimler-Benz DB 610 power plants.

"Let's take her up to altitude and see how she does." At 10,000 feet, the crew donned oxygen masks in the thinning air. The plane performed well. But as he put the aircraft through turns and maneuvers, one thought crossed in and out of his mind: *She performs now with no bomb load, but how will she fly with the weapon she would carry into battle? And what if they encountered serious fighter opposition along the route?* It was a thought that constantly troubled him over the next few days as the crew flew more test and familiarization flights to get acquainted with their new and deadly machine.

* * * * * * * *

Avord Air Base, France, 2 May 1943

0600. The takeoff was ungainly. For security reasons, no one had actually seen the "device" (as it was simply referred to) except for Zimmermann, Pieper, Zwilling, and *Generaloberst* Krause. The weapon arrived by a heavily defended truck convoy two days prior. Covered with a heavy canvas shroud and immediately locked in a secured hanger with dozens of watchful guards surrounding the building, only the bomber's crew and a few select ground crewmen and operations officers knew what sat silently in Hanger 12. More importantly for the mission, no one really knew the effects on flight due to the weight distribution dynamic created by the massive device. The Heinkel engineers did their best to calculate the new flight characteristics, but without an actual operational test, no one really understand how the device impacted the airplane. All would soon find out.

The bomb had been loaded on board the bomber the night before under the close supervision of Krause. Just past dawn, the massive hanger doors opened as the ground crew wheeled the plane out onto the tarmac. Preflight checks had been normal. All systems appeared to be operating and functioning as planned.

In the pre-mission training flights, the aircraft performed well with no problems. What had not been accurately calculated was the fact that the He 177 had been designed and configured for a bomb load spread out over several square meters in the empty bomb bay. The massive device created havoc with the weight distribution and the aircraft's center of gravity characteristics as the crew was about to learn.

As the plane approached the end of the runway, it shuddered. Zimmermann pulled the yoke back as far as possible into his lap and called for more power. Pieper shouted nervously, "*Herr Generalmajor,* we are at maximum power now!" Had the "wizards" in their pristine white lab coats miscalculated the effect of a huge lump of metal sitting in the bomb bay? Yes, it was less than the maximum bomb load capability of the He 177, but that weight was meant to be distributed across the internal bomb bay as well as on pylons on the wings. They had apparently not calculated accurately the effect on the plane's center of gravity that the device threw woefully out of balance.

"*Herr Generalmajor,* must we abort the mission?" came a cry from Weber, the flight engineer. Zimmermann only grimaced. The determination and risk-taking character that had seen him through so many harrowing combat experiences shone through. "*Nein!* We go!" he shouted.

The plane raised off the runway, bobbled in the air, and then bounced back down. Three times it went up, then back down again. There was little wind to provide lift and the heavy, humid early spring air weighed down the wings.

At the end of the runway sat a copse of trees. The engineers had not bothered to cut them down simply because no previous aircraft ever needed the full runway to lift off. Now the Heinkel was in mortal danger of crashing into the oaks.

Sweat formed on Zimmermann's brow and rolled down his nose as the plane raced toward the trees. Slowly, agonizingly slowly, the nose lifted off the tarmac and then the wheels. Finally, she was airborne, but was it enough? *Was it enough?!*

As the now airborne plane approached the trees, Zimmermann prayed silently. He glanced at the ashen-faced copilot, whose white-knuckled hands gripped the throttle controls as if to will the engines to throw out just enough power. Gradually, seemingly in slow motion, the plane rose, foot by foot. The landing gear and underbelly scraped the top branches making a screeching sound as the plane brushed over them. But after the few tense moments, only the sound of roaring engines could be heard. Over the internal intercom, Zimmermann heard one of the gunners shout, *"Mein Gott!"* He could only silently concur. Over the tower control channel, he heard the flight controller shout, "Godspeed, *Herr Generalmajor* and crew. *Heil* Hitler!" Zimmermann said nothing.

As they reached 8,000 feet, he eased back on the yoke and Pieper throttled back the engines. They could see the He 111 chase plane off the starboard side, already climbing to altitude. The chase plane carried the film photographers and a clutch of scientists eager to see the device actually in action. As they approached the Normandy coast, they picked up a fighter escort of Messerschmitt Me 109 and Focke-Wulf 190s that would accompany them. "Coming to course 350 degrees. Next stop, Plymouth," Zimmermann said almost matter-of-factly.

* * * * * * * *

0730. Once airborne, the flight was relatively uneventful until they approached the English coast. Royal Air Force Spitfires, alerted to the enemy intrusion by the Chain Home radar system, gathered in ambush. Two squadrons had been "scrambled" by the sector station at RAF Exeter. Within a few minutes of first detection on radar as the bombers and escorts departed the French coast, No. 310 and No. 610 Squadrons were airborne and waiting over the Channel to intercept the approaching enemy. The Messerschmitts flew high cover while the Focke-Wulfs provided close support. As the Spitfires approached for a head-on attack, the Me 109s dove on the enemy and within a couple of minutes, an air battle, rarely seen since the autumn of 1940, ensued. Stricken fighters plummeted in flame and smoke, but more approached the He 177. Zimmermann realized that the aircraft was woefully underpowered for this mission. He was not even certain they could attain the 25,000-foot altitude that the scientists warned they needed to avoid the blast and shock waves. As the English coast approached, Zimmermann throttled up, but the plane responded too slowly. At 20,000 feet, she shuddered and buffeted. A worried crew chief stuck his head between the two pilot seats, a serious frown across his face.

"*Herr Generalmajor,* will she make the altitude?"

"God only knows, Chief. Only God. Have the crew assume stations."

"*Jawohl, Herr Generaloberst.* At once!"

All the crew put on the special dark-tinted glasses they had been instructed to wear and moved into the center of the plane, away from the Plexiglas windows. Zimmermann felt the plane slightly rise. Slowly, very slowly, it gained altitude. But it was not enough. A Spitfire aimed directly for the cockpit. Shaped like a round fish-bowl with multiple glass panes, the cockpit gave the pilot and crew maximum forward and down look ability. What it did not give was protection from .303 bullets coming through thin Plexiglas panes. Tracer bullets from the RAF fighter's machine guns whizzed past the cockpit. Zimmermann banked right to avoid the fusillade of bullets. None hit. As the Spitfire passed well overhead, Zimmermann banked left. But the plane was too sluggish. The yoke rattled and shook in his hands. It was all he could do to maintain positive control of the aircraft as it pitched then yawed. He glanced at over at Pieper, whose hand on the throttle had pushed the engines to full maximum power.

As they approached Plymouth and the Royal Naval Base at Devonport, the expected anti-aircraft "flak" burst about them. Occasionally, shrapnel from the anti-aircraft artillery shells bounced and pinged off the fuselage, but none penetrated nor did any serious damage. Still, it was dicey. If one random piece of shrapnel caught one of the engines, they were done for. There was no way to reach the safe altitude. As Plymouth approached in the distance, the flak grew more intense. At that moment, the crew chief stuck his head in the cockpit again with a worried look on his face. "*Herr Generalmajor.*

Oil temperature is rising in all engines. They can't take this strain for very much longer."

Zimmermann glanced at his altimeter. Just barely above 20,000 feet, it was no good. If the scientists were right, they might well hit the target with the bomb but disintegrate in the massive explosion. With no warning, tracer bullets arced across the cockpit fired from a Spitfire that had come upon the bomber from the rear and had not been noticed. They barely missed Pieper and Zimmermann, but one bullet grazed the crew chief. It was now decision time. Zimmermann stared at the altimeter and realized that the bomber was gaining altitude ever so slowly but still gaining altitude. He looked over and down at the coast coming up rapidly. He could see the naval base at Devonport, and he could make out the ships and buildings of His Majesty's Naval Base Devonport. A decision had to be made. As the flak grew more intense, Zimmermann turned to Pieper.

"Hans, this is a no go. Even if we make it over the target, we will not have sufficient altitude to drop." The copilot nodded in concurrence. Meanwhile, Zwilling appeared at the rear of the cockpit, a tense expression across his pale face. He stuck his head between the two pilot's seats. "*Herr Generalmajor,* what must we do? I must arm the bomb now!"

With the precision and judgment that he had made so many times before, Zimmermann made a snap call. "Abort primary target. Make for secondary target."

Pieper immediately broke open the seal on the envelope labeled TOP SECRET and pulled out the single paper sheet. "Come to new course 020 degrees. Target. Royal Air Force Dartmoor."

"Very well, then," whispered Zimmermann in an almost inaudible voice, the decision made. He eased the yoke and ailerons to bank right coming to new course 020. Meanwhile, Pieper sent instructions to the *Luftwaffe* fighters heavily engaged with the RAF Spitfires. The escort was to stay in the skies over Plymouth so as to make the British pilots think that was still the primary target in the hopes that the

Heinkels could, in essence, sneak away unnoticed and in doing so, gain the requisite altitude before arriving over RAF Dartmoor.

It was a huge risk. Without fighter escort, even a single Spitfire might destroy the bomber. But Zimmermann was a risk-taker. He had been all his life. Now in this moment of truth, he calculated the odds and determined to take the risk. The decision made, the Heinkel He 177 headed for the desolate granite and scrub barrens of southern Devonshire known as Dartmoor.

Dartmoor, the desolate highlands that covered thousands of square acres north and essentially between Plymouth and Exeter, had little to add to the local economy. Agriculture and animal grazing were limited due to the poor soil, rocky conditions, and somewhat cooler climate. For this reason, the moor represented an ideal location for military operations, especially gunnery practice and weapons testing. And it provided an excellent location for a major RAF bomber command base—RAF Dartmoor. Isolated and far from the usual enemy targets, RAF Dartmoor was primarily a training and replacement crew center. Many of the latest model bombers, such as the new Avro Lancaster heavy bomber, were staged at Dartmoor for crew training and familiarization. As such, the air station represented an ideal secondary target for Zimmermann and his crew should the primary target of Devonport prove problematic.

As the He 177 turned from course 350 degrees to a heading of 020, Zimmermann keyed the external radio. They were now well clear of the Plymouth area, and no British fighters appeared in the sky. It was time to implement their operational deception plan designed to make the British think the raid was over should the primary target be aborted in favor of the secondary.

As the two aircraft, the He 177 and the He 111 chase plane, struggled to climb to altitude, it was hoped that the British would not notice these two aircraft flying in a pattern not typical of a *Luftwaffe* raid. The deception worked. Alone in the sky now, Zimmermann sent the order to the fighter escort. "All escorts, break away and assume secondary escort position." Immediately, the fighters broke left and right and headed back over the Channel. They could not realistically reach sufficient altitude to avoid the shockwave to come, and for their safety were vectored by design to a spot 20 nautical miles south of Devonport. The move had a second and critically important feature. Their move would likely draw off the RAF fighters in hopes that they would go after the more tempting Messerschmitts and Focke-Wulfs rather than the lone He 177 with the accompanying He 111 or break off the engagement altogether. The ruse worked. By sections, the Spitfires broke off the engagement, satisfied that the *Luftwaffe* was in full retreat having neither dropped ordnance nor done any damage. Meanwhile, the two bombers raced northeasterly gaining altitude with each second.

"Four minutes to target," called off the copilot, his hands slowly moving toward the bomb release lever. Zimmermann glanced over and noticed that Pieper's hand twitched. Although he appeared outwardly calm as he always did on the bomb run, inside, his gut rumbled as his heart raced. "Zwilling, is the weapon set and ready to be armed?" he asked over the internal throat microphone.

"*Jawohl, Herr Generalmajor.* I am starting the arming procedure now, sir."

"Very good. Alert me when the bomb is fully armed and ready to be dropped. All crew, assume your attack positions."

Franz Zwilling had ridden in a jump seat in the compartment forward of the bomb bay since takeoff. Four other crewmen now sat in the compartment all strapped in with goggles in place and oxygen masks tightly attached. He opened the hatch leading into the bomb bay and stepped through. He had practiced it over a hundred times. Despite that drill, he nervously fumbled, his hands shaking such that twice he dropped the spanner. But finally, all was set.

To arm the bomb, Zwilling had to first remove a cover by undoing six bolts. Then he would remove a small metal box with wires attached to the bomb casing. He then had to remove the arming mechanism called the "pod" from inside the box. The pod required four sets of two numbers, each that were inputted by turning rotors.

Two sets had been inputted at Avord by two other physicists and the third set by *Generaloberst* Krause just prior to takeoff. The pod now only required a specific two number code that he alone knew.

Zwilling's hands shook as he gently stroked the bomb casing. He had been feeling ill the last few days and simply chalked it up to the stress and tension of the coming attack and, more critically, his own role in it. His scientific curiosity and, in truth, idealism, that drove him forward as the program unfolded overwhelmed all thoughts of the implications of his involvement. Now, faced with the reality in the cold, dimly lit, and cramped space of the bomb bay of a *Luftwaffe* He 177 bomber, the reality of what he was about to do finally struck him. His right hand recoiled. Despite the chill at this high altitude, he sweated profusely. Beads of sweat rolled down his cheeks. Nausea rolled up from his gut. He paused, and his mind drifted off momentarily.

"*Herr Doktor* Zwilling. Report!"

He froze. He must answer. He sucked in a deep breath, then let it out slowly with a low whistle. Finally, he keyed the throat mic. "I am arming the weapon now, *Herr Generalmajor*. I will be completed in less than a minute."

"We are three minutes from drop and now at maximum altitude. Inform me when the device is fully armed."

"At once, *Herr Generalmajor*."

Perhaps it was the cold, crisp voice of command from the man at the controls that caused him to press ahead. Perhaps it was the realization that so many German lives ultimately depended on success, the end of the war in the west, and ultimately, the Soviet Union's swift defeat. Or perhaps it was simply that as a scientist, he had to see the creation actually work. He and the small group of physicists, engineers, and mathematicians had labored so long toward overcoming every obstacle and impediment. Now at last was his chance to see it to fruition.

He lifted the spanner he had dropped earlier in his moment of hesitation and quickly turned the six bolts. Laying the box on a shelf that had been welded to the plane's internal frame for this purpose, he clamped it to the steel shelf and opened it, revealing the arming pod. He saw eight rotors. Two were still set to zero. His hands now still, he rapidly rotated the first and last rotors until the eight numbers across the pod—1-7-9-5-1-3-9-3 appeared. Two green lights came on above each of the rotors he had just set at 1 and 3. Green lights already glowed by the rotors previously set by Krause and the two physicists. A low hum emanated from the pod. A red light flashed in the center of the pod indicating that the arming was now fully completed. He inserted it back into the box, reconnected the wires, and quickly tightened the bolts. A low whirr came from inside the detonator indicating that the bomb was ready. It had been preset to explode at 300 meters, which would cause a downward blast for maximum destruction.

Zwilling wiped his brow with the back of his hand and pulled the fleece-lined leather flying glove back on. Keying the throat mic, he reported, "*Herr Generalmajor*. Device armed and set." With that, he clambered back into the cabin and strapped into his seat alongside the rest of the crew.

"Thirty seconds to target," called out Pieper. Zimmermann shook his head.

"Ten seconds to target—9-8-7-6-5-4-3-2-1 target acquired," Pieper called off.

The bomb bay doors had been modified to require both pilots to flip the toggle switch simultaneously. It was another safety mechanism to ensure against an inadvertent drop. With one minute out, both pilots flipped the switch and the bomb bay doors swung open. Cold air whistled through the bay sounding like a crowd of banshees. Zimmermann could hear the screeching noise even through his heavy flight helmet earpieces. His first thought was that it sounded like the scream of the Valkyries.

"Target acquired." Both men had their hands on the toggle to release the weapon from its cradle. "Release."

Simultaneously, both men flipped the red-painted toggles. The plane lurched as the four-ton device, freed from its shackles, plummeted toward earth from 26,000 feet. Unexpectedly, the bomber's nose raised up as the tail dipped. Again, the disrupted center of gravity caused by uneven weight distribution threw the plane off balance. Zimmermann slammed the rudder controls and pushed the yoke forward. After a few moments, the plane again leveled out, and now lightened, picked up speed. As soon as he regained control, Zimmermann turned hard to starboard while Pieper pressed the throttle forward for maximum speed. Maximum velocity, minimum drag. Speed is life! The plane angled sharply to the right. No one really knew what a safe distance and altitude to clear the blast actually was. It had all been speculation and formulas. The men of the He 177 were about to find out just how inaccurate those equations had been.

* * * * * * * *

The tiny village of Princeton represented the only significant or sizable human habitation on the otherwise desolate moor. Its primary occupation was servicing the infamous Dartmoor prison that lay just a mile away.

The prison originated in 1806 as a repository for French prisoners during the Napoleonic Wars. Later, Dartmoor Prison housed some of the most vile and notorious prisoners of Mother England. By this time in the war, only a few hundred remained. But, since 1938, the town had seen a revival with the establishment of the Bomber Command training air base just two miles distant. Despite the normal privations of wartime, Princeton prospered thanks to the hundreds of RAF men and women that came to town regularly on leave. The townsfolk were used to large aircraft constantly flying overhead, and though one or so might have looked up and noticed the contrails of a pair of aircraft high up in the clear blue early spring sky, no one thought it anything but the daily norm.

* * * * * * * *

At precisely 300 meters the arming pod sent an electrical signal to the detonator. In a microsecond, from both ends of the device, explosions occurred, sending the two halves of the thick heavy sphere together at incredible speed. The effect was instantaneous. Nuclear fission began as neutrons collided against atomic cores shattering them into numerous nuclei and releasing unheard of energy.

Zimmermann and Pieper stared out the side windows, tinted in advance to lessen the impact on their vision. Despite orders to stay strapped in, the four crewmen and Zwilling unbuckled and raced to the side windows to witness the explosion. With the plane's angle, racing away at maximum speed, everyone could clearly see the ground where a dark ugly cloud of billowing smoke and orange flame spread out from the epicenter. Within seconds, rising out of the maelstrom below, a huge column of gray smoke rose toward the sky.

The shock wave hit. The bomber pitched and yawed as if caught in a hurricane. The shock was so violent that both pilots' hands were thrown off the yokes. In the crew cabin, men tossed about, slamming against each other and the bulkheads. The plane's nose pitched up and then down violently as Zimmermann and Pieper desperately fought to regain control. The plane rolled sharply to port and almost flipped, which would likely have caused a catastrophic stall.

Few pilots had or ever would acquire the skills of *Generalmajor* Peter von Zimmermann, but as good as he was, he could simply not regain control. They needed speed to break the spin, but the DB-610 engines roared at maximum velocity already. Vainly, Zimmermann and Pieper fought the controls, praying that they could head off a stall and death spiral from 26,000 feet.

Then, as quickly as it struck, the shockwave passed. A deathly stillness followed. With only a slight chance to regain control, Zimmermann desperately worked the flaps, ailerons, rudder, and yoke. Gradually, and almost miraculously, he regained control and the plane steadied out. Meanwhile, Pieper throttled back on the engines as the plane came about to a heading of 170 degrees.

The men in the crew cabin, none miraculously badly hurt, crowded about the windows, staring in disbelief at what they now saw. The oily gray cloud now reached at least three kilometers in the sky and it started topping out and spreading. To some, it resembled a large leafy oak tree. To others, it appeared more as a giant mushroom. Zwilling did not join them. He crouched down by his seat, head in his hands, weeping. He mumbled, audible only to himself, "*Mein Gott! Mein Gott!* What have we done?"

Below them, the dark, blazing cloud spread out for several miles, consuming everything in sight. A giant crater formed where the tiny village of Princeton once stood.

At Dartmoor Prison, the stout stone and brick structures stood the blast better than the homes and buildings near ground zero where the greatest damage occurred. Though some had collapsed, some still stood. But nothing remained of the interiors but charred and burning remnants. No one survived.

At RAF Dartmoor, all the recently constructed wooden hangers, ready rooms, barracks, and mess halls had vanished. The walls of the cinder block main operations building still stood, but the structure was completely hollowed out. Only the concrete runways, now black with soot and ash, remained fairly intact.

In the cockpit, Zimmermann stared straight ahead, and every few seconds glanced down at the instruments—altimeter, air speed indicator, oil pressure, and so on. He saw the cloud in his peripheral vision. He already knew what it looked like having witnessed the detonation at *Der Gevatter Tod*. He concentrated on banking the bomber as hard as he could and still maintain positive control. The initial shock passed; they had survived.

Once clear of the blast zone, he leveled out and descended to 15,000 feet. Although the Chain Home radar system detected two enemy aircraft fleeing for the French coast and safety, no one gave chase. As they reached the Channel, he had a sudden remembrance from his youth. He had not been very keen on the Bible study at the family's Lutheran church, but he somehow remembered the phrase from the prophet Jeremiah: "Thou art my battle axe and weapons of war: for with thee will I break in pieces the nations, and with thee will I destroy kingdoms."[4]

* * * * * * * *

NNE of RAF Dartmoor, 2 May 1943

0843. The pilot at the controls of the Avro Lancaster heavy bomber sighed. Finally, he could take some well-deserved leave and head back to Colchester to spend some time with his wife and children. His eldest son Harold would be old enough for a commission in a month, and Group Captain Reginald Blanton looked forward to spending time with him before the lad headed off to his own war.

Though immensely proud of his child, Blanton was equal parts proud and worried. He had flown in two world wars now and seen his share of young men sacrificed in defense of King and Country. That aside, he welcomed his son into the Royal Air Force, his professional home for over two decades.

No. 153 Squadron had been away from RAF Dartmoor for more than a fortnight conducting navigational training in Scotland; all looked forward to returning to their home base and the 96-hour stand down that followed. In the absence of the aircraft, the ground crews enjoyed a break as well, and almost all were now on leave away from base. The ground crewmen were to report back for duty in the morning. Only a skeleton force manned the station now—enough to land the planes and roll them into the hangers. Servicing and maintenance would wait, and the returning ground crews would do their

---

4 King James Bible, Jeremiah 51:20-26.

repair, inspection, and routine maintenance tasks while the pilots and aircrew took their leave.

It was a good system, and Blanton, though exhausted by the rigors and worries of training new aircrews, especially the navigators and pilots in night navigation, felt relieved that they now returned to their station with no accidents and no loss of aircraft or crew. Though they were all exhausted, it had been a job well done by all hands. The training had been intense. It had to be. This squadron was transitioning from previous Type 156 Bristol Beaufighters to the Avro Lancaster heavy bomber. Night navigation, the trickiest part of RAF Bomber Command's war against Germany, had to be accurate for the heavy bombers to have any impact. Blanton was satisfied. The lads had done well. They knew their stuff.

"What the bloody hell?" Blanton shouted.

Up ahead in the direction of RAF Dartmoor, a giant dark gray cloud rose toward the sky. As each second passed, it grew more and more immense. Group Captain Blanton stared in awe and wonderment.

"Sir?" The flight engineer, Pearce, leapt up from his seat—the "second dicky seat" off to the right of the pilot; he too stared wide-eyed at the incredible sight.

Within seconds, a monstrous wave of energy struck the Lancaster. It bucked, then yawed wildly. Blanton gripped the yoke and held it as steady as he possibly could. Then the plane pitched and rolled—up and down and side to side. Still, the highly experienced pilot barely kept the aircraft from stalling or dropping. The shock wave passed almost as soon as it hit. Blanton eased back on the yoke as the plane stabilized. Ahead, still miles away, the strange cloud now took on the form of a tree or, more specifically, the shape of a broccoli stalk. It grew and grew thousands of feet up and into the clouds hovering over Dartmoor.

"Jones, get up here and bring your camera! On the double, lad!" shouted the pilot. The navigator grabbed his camera from under the chart table that was used to photograph a target for damage assessment. He reached out and yanked back the curtain that separated the cockpit from the navigator and wireless operator's compartment, which sat just aft of the cockpit. Jones almost dropped the Leica camera in disbelief.

"Criminy, Group Captain. What in the name of God is that, sir?"

"I don't have a bloody clue, Colin. Not a damned bloody clue. Quick, lad, get some photos. Whatever it is, we need to have it on film. London will want to see it; otherwise, they'll never believe us."

"Aye, sir. That be so true," growled the flight engineer in his archetypal Cornish brogue. He had somewhat recovered from his initial astonishment.

As Jones snapped photo after photo of the massive billowing cloud ahead, Blanton looked all around, now beginning to worry about the rest of the squadron. He counted—all 10 aircraft survived the shock, but the formation had become disjointed; some planes flew perilously close to each other. He keyed the throat mic, "O'Bannon, raise Dartmoor. Ask what the bloody hell is going on down there."

"Right away, sir," replied the wireless operator, the lone Irishman among the crew.

After a couple of minutes, the wireless operator called up to the pilot, "No good, sir. No response. All I get on all their frequencies is static, rubbishy static. It's like the station is no longer there. I'll keep trying."

With that, O'Bannon plopped back down by his wireless set and tapped out messages to every frequency that RAF Dartmoor would be monitoring. Nothing, simply nothing. Nothing but the static noise.

As the squadron approached the station—or at least where the station ought to be—they saw nothing but swirls of dust below. Blanton now faced a decision. With no response from Dartmoor and his bombers low on fuel, he had to make a command decision. He lifted the handset of the wireless radio used for flight tactical communications and keyed the microphone. He decided to dispense with the normal communications security call signs for this transmission. That seemed appropriate and all the crews knew his voice. "Well, lads, we don't know what this thing is. Disperse and find some place to land. Ring up flight control at Dartmoor as soon as you are able. Good luck, be safe, and Godspeed." He unkeyed the mic and stared straight ahead, the microphone still in his right hand by his mouth with index in the air, frozen like a marble statue. The navigator jolted him out of the momentary stupor.

"Sir, I have eight good photos. Will that be sufficient?"

"What? Oh yes, quite. No, perhaps a few more for good measure." Jones nodded, raised the camera up, and snapped yet another photo of the angry, boiling cloud that now took the shape of a tall mushroom.

Blanton leaned up in his seat to get a better view and looked in all directions. One by one, the bombers peeled off in different directions in search of airfields and safe landings. One by one, they "rogered" over the tactical net for the dispersal order. Blanton turned to Jones after the navigator had taken a few more photos. "Right then. That should do. Colin. Plot me a course to Plymouth. We must get those photographs to the intelligence boys as fast as possible. Perhaps those chaps can make some sense of what we are seeing."

"Aye, sir. Right away." The navigator plopped back down in his seat and immediately plotted a course toward the airfield at Plymouth. A minute later, the bomber turned southwesterly and skirted around the mushroom cloud, headed to safety.

Hardly a word was spoken on the flight back to Avord. Halfway across the English Channel, the portside engine sputtered and died having suffered considerable damage from the shock wave. But without the weight of the bomb in its belly, the He 177 managed to stay aloft as it limped back to base, protected by the swarm of *Luftwaffe* fighters that had been loitering off the coast for the return escort. The chase plane had suffered little damage, since it had been at a greater distance, and the film taken of the blast would soon make the point to any doubters that Germany was now the only superpower in the world.

* * * * * * * *

Hours after the blast, a set of 10 photographs arrived at Bomber Command Headquarters at RAF High Wycombe in rural Buckinghamshire. Two hours later, Air Chief Marshal Sir Arthur Harris, Air Officer Commanding-in-Chief (AOC-in-C) RAF Bomber Command, laid a plain manila folder on the desk in the prime minister's office-bedroom in the underground War Rooms beneath the Treasury Building in Whitehall.

"Prime Minister. I believe that you must see these photographs right away, sir."

"Indeed, Sir Arthur. You look as if the Devil just poked you with his pitchfork."

"Prime Minister, I would rather the Devil have done so than face what these photographs indicate." Harris spoke as his head dropped to his chin.

Churchill's eyelids narrowed to just slits as he growled—really, it was more of a low grumble. He took a sip of the excellent single malt 18-year-old Scotch that he had just poured and took a puff on a fine Cuban cigar. He reached for the folder on the desktop, tapped it twice with his forefinger, leaned forward in his chair, and flipped open the cover.

At 1800 Greenwich Mean Time the following day, two messages arrived, one at the British Embassy in Geneva and another at the United States Embassy in Berlin. Succinctly put, the one to the British demanded an immediate armistice and cessation of all British operations against the Reich and their Italian allies to be followed by formal peace negotiations. Britain was given 24 hours to respond. Failure to do so meant a similar destruction of London, Birmingham, Manchester, Liverpool, Glasgow, and Edinburgh by the same type weapon that had devastated Dartmoor.

To the United States, a different threat was issued. Even though no German aircraft could yet reach America, a threat implied that that U-boats could plant atomic mines in US harbors—Norfolk,

New York, Boston, Charleston, Jacksonville, Miami, and so on, that if exploded would create a tsunami and utter destruction. The US was to cease support of any kind to the British Empire and the Soviet Union and must stay neutral. Moreover, the US was not to interfere in any manner with Japanese actions in the Far East or China, including the transfer of the Philippine islands to Japan. Essentially, the three nations of the Tripartite Pact of 1940 had won the war.

Now the Third *Reich* turned its entire attention to the destruction and annexation of the Russian heartland, the final chapter of the Nazi drive for "*Lebensraum.*" What the United States and United Kingdom did not know and what they could not count on was that Germany had just used their only operational atomic bomb. However, there were more in production that could be operational within a few weeks.

* * * * * * * *

In his after-action report submitted the following day, *Generalmajor* Peter von Zimmermann made three critical points. First, the He 177, robust as it was, was woefully inadequate for the delivery of any future atomic weapon. It was underpowered, could not fly high enough, and was unreliable with only two engines. Second, for any future missions, Germany required a much larger, longer-range, higher ceiling capable, four-engine heavy bomber. And finally, in an appeal to basic humanity, he emphasized that only prime military targets should be chosen, not cities with a significant civilian population. He suspected his Nazi masters would ignore his plea for limiting the damage to noncombatants, as in his heart, he doubted that they had any concern about the casualty count. Germany had unleashed a whirlwind and he had driven the chariot of fire. God forgive him. God be merciful. Could Armageddon be far behind?

138

CHAPTER 5

Never Surrender

Buckingham Palace, London, 4 May 1943

The ancient warrior plodded down the dim corridor, lit only by the wash of daylight creeping through the heavy Palladian windows. In the shadows, his heavy footfalls pounded down on the floor, muffled by the heavy, antique carpet. Every once in a while, the brass tip of his walking stick struck the marble floor outside the carpet, sending up a ringing, clattering noise, which announced his presence to the somber portraits looking down. He was tired. The ancient warrior pondered. *How could he, at sixty-eight, still go on? Most men his age had long since retired. It had been a bad year of gruesome death, a bloodletting of the astronomical type. The world he knew, trusted, believed in, and fought for was crumbling, one chunk of mortar at the time under the onslaught of the new Aryan order, the new Dark Age empire. How did he go on?*

He rounded the corner, then froze in place, captured by the site before him. Ahead, on the wall to his left, hung a portrait of a man from two centuries back—the first Duke of Marlborough, General John Churchill, his great ancestor, victor at Blenheim, Ramillies, Oudenaarde, and Malplaquet. Energy seemed to seethe and rumble from beneath the haughty countenance of the official court portrait. As he stared in silence at the painting, the ancient warrior felt rejuvenated, almost as if the canvas injected new energy into the tired old warhorse. He slowly tapped the cane against the marble floor like a warrior of old striking his weapon against his shield as battle commenced. Second by second, he struck the marble faster and harder as the sound grew, reverberating through the hallway.

"Prime Minister?" his escort said, surprised by the old man's abrupt halt and cane banging against the floor. "Yes, coming along. Coming along," he growled at the king's private secretary, who turned and knocked twice, then swung open the doors to the chamber.

Winston Churchill's eyes sparkled as if charged with electricity. Renewed energy rumbled up through his body. Now charged with determination, the ancient warrior strode into the chamber.

"The Prime Minister, Your Majesty."

The tall gaunt man staring out the window at the courtyard below, hands clasped behind his back, slowly turned. His face, chalky white with weariness and worry, showed the angst he now felt. Even so, his posture was parade ground straight, regally taut. "Thank you."

"Winston," he said softly, nodding his head in recognition of the visitor.

"Your Majesty," Churchill responded in the protocol of pecking order. Superiors may address juniors by their Christian names. It was never the other way around.

"You have the letter, then?"

Yes, sir. I alone have read it." Churchill reached into his jacket breast pocket and pulled out a heavy manila envelope. He laid it on the rosewood table in the corner of the room and unwound the red tie string. He delicately lifted the paper from the envelope and handed it across the table to the king.

The man reading the letter felt as if a huge weight bore down on him—this quiet, unassuming family man—as he read the words. This was never to have been his place. It had been for his older brother Edward, the handsome worldly-wise Edward. He would bear up, though. Whatever else posterity might say about George VI, it would never say he stumbled under the burden. Yes, he would bear up.

King George VI tilted the letter toward the cold light from the window across the room and silently read the letter that had just arrived from Washington.

FOR KING GEORGE VI AND PRIME MINISTER'S EYES ONLY
THE WHITE HOUSE
Sirs:

The German ultimatum of yesterday May 3rd is absurd. This proposal reeks of the heinous blackmail and cruel barbarity we have come to expect from Mr. Hitler and the Nazi Party. Unfortunately, for the still free nations of the world, I fear he now has the means by which to carry out his threats of national genocide. The isolationists in the Congress and, sad to say, of many in the American public, have dealt us a bad hand by their reticence to commit to the great cause. This atomic blackmail by the Germans has forced the United States government to officially and unequivocally declare neutrality in the conflict, withdraw all support, both financial and logistical, from the British Empire and Soviet Union, and agree to not to interfere with the depredations of Japan in the Far East. But, Sirs, be assured that I shall never, ever acquiesce to the German demands, even though my public policy and statements may seem otherwise. Nor, can I assure you, will any other honorable American. I propose then, so far as I am able, to provide any and all assistance to your intelligence agencies in their attempts to discover and destroy the Nazis' means of employing the atomic weapon. Once accomplished, the United States will immediately commence military operations against them. It is still not too late. I have instructed Mr. Hopkins to stand by in London to convey to me your response and to work out any specific details.

> I remain, Sirs,
> Very truly yours,
> Franklin D. Roosevelt

As the king looked up from the paper in his hand, a momentary flash of hope seemed to move across his pallid, care worn face.

"I think, Mr. Churchill, that we have spawned a magnificent nation in the New World."

Churchill smiled. "Indeed so, sir, indeed so."

"Your mother was American."

"She was. My mother was from New York."

"Then, Winston, you are truly a transatlantic man."

Churchill nodded in concurrence. Outside the window, the heavy raindrops of another dreary, damp London morning tapped against the lead glass panes like tiny invaders charging the gates. The effect was instantaneous. The king's momentary cheerful mood reverted to its previous melancholy. He turned toward the window, head bowed, staring at the carpet beneath him, hands again clasped behind his back. Churchill shifted his weight from one foot to the other.

"So then, Prime Minister. What is the position of the government?"

Winston Churchill had often spoken of never surrendering, never giving in to German threats or attacks. Perhaps it had been wrung out of him by four years of war, but even now, at the summit of this crisis, he was surprisingly detached and matter-of-fact. Not at all what the king expected.

"Your Majesty, it is the position of your government that the British Empire accept and adhere to the terms of the ultimatum of May 3. Publicly, at any rate."

"And privately?" The king spun around on his heels.

Churchill drew in a deep breath, then let it out slowly, choosing each word ever so carefully. He was about to recommend to the king, the man on whose head the crown was presently so thorny, that the British government secretly violate the ultimatum's terms, thus setting up the possible death of hundreds of thousands of his subjects.

"Privately, your Majesty, your government proposes to conduct whatever operations, by whatever means, to ferret out the intelligence of the German atomic weapons program and to destroy it forever!"

The final words rose in volume in the best, most passionate Churchillian fashion.

King George just shook his head in acknowledgement, neither accepting nor rejecting the proposal from his prime minister.

"And yourself? Do you intend to turn yourself over to the Nazis? May I read for you the text of a speech you once made in the House of Commons? It was just as France collapsed."

The king reached over to a single piece of paper sitting on the top of the desk blotter. Putting on a pair of reading glasses that he never wore outside of the closed circle of family, friends, and advisers, he rustled the paper and cleared his throat.

Plagued with a speech impediment since childhood he constantly struggled to overcome, George VI was ever conscious of his handicap yet strove mightily to mask it in public. He need not have with Churchill. Although he had opposed Churchill's elevation to prime minister initially for fear that the man was a "loose cannon on deck" as the naval men would characterize, the new prime minister had proven stalwart, effective, and competent. He had used his gift of eloquence to inspire the nation to take courage and resist the German juggernaut. It had saved Britain during the Blitz and had inspired the nation through the onslaught of the *Reichsmarine* U-boat assault as the British Empire and Commonwealth stood alone against German aggression. Even with the Soviet ally thanks to Hitler's obsession with conquering the vast Russian and Ukrainian heartland, the war had simply stalemated along the two fronts in North Africa and the Eastern Front. But Britain had endured, thanks in no small part to the stalwart, pudgy man in the blue pinstripe suit now standing before the British monarch. The king came to trust and admire Churchill and his leadership. With the bond established, the two men met regularly at Buckingham Palace where Churchill briefed and, in truth, reassured George VI that the Empire and the nation stood firm and would endure. But now, with the new terror weapon and the ability to destroy great cities and thousands of citizens with a single bomb, the entire dynamic had altered. Yet there is a streak in the British personality that while perhaps slow to react initially, once backed into a corner, Britons become the fiercest of combatants and rain down all hell on the tormentor.

As the king squeezed the paper between his thumbs and index fingers, a thought—from where it came, he wasn't certain—crossed his mind: "Nothing delights the British quite like the prospect of a hopeless situation."

As the king read aloud Churchill's speech in Parliament of the fourth of June 1940 with Britain and France in the last throes of French defeat and military collapse, the prime minister stiffened almost to a military attention.

The king read: "I have, myself, full confidence that if all do their duty . . . we shall prove ourselves once again able to defend our Island home, to ride out the storm of war, and to outlive the menace of tyranny, if necessary for years, if necessary alone . . . we shall not flag or fail. We shall go on to the end, we shall fight in France, we shall fight on the seas and oceans, we shall fight with growing confidence and growing strength in the air, we shall defend our Island, whatever the cost may be, we shall fight on the beaches, we shall fight on the landing grounds, we shall fight in the fields and in the streets, we shall fight in the hills; we shall never surrender, and even if, which I do not for a moment believe, this Island or a large part of it were subjugated and starving, then our Empire beyond the seas, armed and guarded by the British Fleet, would carry on the struggle, until, in God's good time, the New World, with all its power and might, steps forth to the rescue and the liberation of the old."

Without Churchill, there was no resistance. Churchill must be saved.

"I understand, Your Majesty. INTREPID—Mr. Stephenson—has proposed a plan whereby it would appear that I die in an airplane crash while turning tail and running for South Africa. In actuality, I shall be at Camp X, protected by the Canadians and Americans. Lord Halifax is prepared to form a new national government at Your Majesty's pleasure once I resign." British intelligence, in all of its forms, was an arm of the Crown and thus directly answerable to the king. Even so, though he might feel uncomfortable with the potential for disaster, Churchill was certain that the king would authorize INTREPID'S escape plan for the prime minister.

"I see."

The king walked over to the window. He placed his fingers on the sill and leaned forward as if trying to get a better view of some bird or animal playing in the courtyard below. Churchill breathed heavily. The king was giving him no sign of the plan's acceptance or rejection, which could have such a destructive, heinous outcome or would perhaps save the world from the new Dark Ages. The king turned and walked back to the table. Churchill had not moved.

"Winston, what was it that you asked Mr. von Ribbentrop some years back? Something about why does the English bulldog's nose slant backward?"

Churchill grinned; he had his answer. By God, he had his answer! The impish, sly grin slowly transformed into a broad smile across the ancient warrior's face.

"Yes, Your Majesty. I informed the honorable German Foreign Minister that the English bulldog's nose slopes backward so that when he bites into you, he doesn't have to let go."

In one of the rarest of moments, a break in protocol and tradition seen by no other eyes,

His Majesty, George VI, by the Grace of God, of Great Britain, Ireland, and the British Dominions beyond the Seas King, Defender of the Faith, and Emperor of India, extended a hand to his prime minster. Winston Leonard Spenser Churchill, the greatest of all commoners, did not flinch. He grasped the extended hand and shook twice.

"May God have mercy on all of us, Winston."

Churchill only nodded slowly.

* * * * * * * *

The lead headline in the *Times* of London blared out the news: "Churchill dead in plane crash." The details of the Short Sunderland seaplane gave the presumed details of the crash in the Bay of Biscay off the French coast. No cause was given, though it was presumed to have been engine failure complicated by foul weather.

That afternoon, the new prime minister, Lord Halifax, read the ultimatum in the House of Commons to an audience of the Cabinet, the Commons, and the House of Lords. Germany demanded that the British Empire, its Commonwealth, all colonies, and dominions immediately cease all military operations against the Third *Reich* and its allies, the Empires of Japan and Italy. Further, both the United States and the British Empire and Commonwealth were to cease all logistical aid to the Soviet Union immediately. Both the United States and the British Empire were to declare their immediate neutrality and non-interference with any and all actions of the aforementioned states. The penalty for noncompliance of the terms of the ultimatum would be the immediate destruction of London and other British cities by atomic attack. Further, the document clarified that Germany had no wish to destroy the people of Britain or the Empire and hoped to cooperate in the future in reshaping the new world. It was a sop with no meaning. The threat was immediate, stark, and explicit. Faced with the death of hundreds of thousands of British civilians, the combined Houses of Parliament voted with only three nay votes and a dozen or so abstentions to accept the ultimatum's onerous terms.

* * * * * * * *

Special Training School No. 103 (Camp X), Ontario, Canada, 14 May 1943

Three men walked briskly toward what clearly was a training field for physical fitness as well as the martial arts. Men and women in the distance practiced jabs and throws on mats laid out on the grass. As they entered the field, they turned sharply to the left and headed toward what appeared to be either a reviewing stand or an observation shelter that somewhat resembled a baseball dugout.

"Rather a bit warm and humid today, eh, what!"

"Indeed," said the man in the middle of the trio.

"But, I might add, 'tis a far better weather day than Manhattan today. It's refreshing to be out of the city," the third man concurred.

As they approached the dugout, they turned back toward the activity on the field where a tall blonde woman had just dodged a jab from her sparring partner and then promptly tossed the even taller man to the mat.

"Well done, lassie, well done," replied Lieutenant R. M. Brooker, the commandant of Special Training School Number 103 known as Camp X.

Set in the woods of Ontario, Canada, on the northwest shore of Lake Ontario between the towns of Whitby and Oshawa, Camp X had been established in 1940 as a training base for SOE field agents destined for missions inside occupied Europe.

Covertly, since the aborted Japanese attempt to attack US naval and military facilities in Hawai'i in December of 1941, the US Federal Bureau of Investigation (FBI) and other counterintelligence agencies also trained at Camp X. Established by William Stephenson, aka INTREPID and head of BSC, the training camp was jointly operated by the British SOE and the Royal Canadian Mounted Police. Dozens of SOE agents trained at the camp operated in occupied Europe. None had been yet withdrawn despite British and Canadian acceptance of the German ultimatum.

"Who is she, Bill?" asked INTREPID, turning to the third man, Lieutenant William Fairbairn.

"The Baroness Amelia Ramsour-Fritsch, sir," he responded.

Fairbairn, a former Royal Marine who had worked for the Shanghai Police Department for many years, had been commissioned in the British Army in 1940 and charged with training operations in the arts of self-defense and deadly surreptitious attack. While a Shanghai policeman, he perfected the martial art of *Defendu*, a skill that the three men now observed the tall elegant blonde baroness executing with brutal efficiency. *Defendu* emphasized pistol and knife-fighting techniques along with traditional East Asian martial arts. Fairbairn, along with Eric A. Sykes, developed the Fairbairn-Sykes fighting knife, a razor-sharp, deadly stiletto-style dagger carried by the British and Commonwealth Special Forces and field agents. The knife had a deserved reputation for efficient slitting of sentries' throats.

Stephenson shook his head in acknowledgment. William Stephenson was the most powerful spymaster in the world. Operating out of Rockefeller Center in New York City as a lowly passport control clerk, he literally controlled all British and Commonwealth special intelligence and field operations in the Americas. From the rural fields of Manitoba, he had been a Royal Flying Corps fighter ace in the Great War and a founder of the British Broadcasting Corporation in the 1920s. Churchill sent him to New York City to stand up British Security Coordination in 1940 and charged him to be "intrepid" in his mission to flummox the Nazis. In that role, he was indeed "INTREPID." To ensure that no special operations against Germany emanated from Britain itself or could be associated in violation of the armistice, Churchill tasked INTREPID to coordinate all operations from New York and Camp X. The operation's objectives were simple in concept—discover Germany's atomic secret and destroy their program. The execution would be far more problematic.

INTREPID folded his arms across his chest and stared intently at the woman as she moved deftly to avoid a kick from the sparring partner. Clearly, she had tremendous athletic skills as her swift and graceful movements indicated. Sweat poured down off her brow. She shimmered in the glaring mid-May sunshine. Well-tanned by working in the outdoors, she gave off the aura of robustness and good health. Her skin tone highlighted her honey-blonde long silky hair pulled back into a coiled bun.

Despite the several yards between them, he clearly noted her deep blue eyes. But more than their sea-blue color, he noted the determined and, he perceived, almost fanatic look in her eyes. With her physical presence and looks, she already captured what the Nazis prized as the perfect Aryan woman. That, he recognized, would be a great asset on the mission to come.

He turned to Fairbairn. "German?"

"No sir, Swiss, actually, but clearly of German stock. I believe she is from the Zürich area."

"And why, then, is she here?" His eyes bore into the former policeman. That answer was fundamental. If he were to send this woman into harm's way behind the enemy lines, he had to be certain of her will and motivation.

Brooker spoke up. "Indeed, sir. She is Swiss, but she's also a widow. Her late husband, Baron Ramsour-Fritsch, was a Swiss citizen, but he managed to get a commission in the Czech Air Force and was an ardent anti-fascist. When the Jerries seized the rest of the country in March 1939 after the unfortunate Munich Settlement, he was marked for execution and managed to flee back to Switzerland. Since the country was strictly neutral, it was fairly easy for the baron and baroness to make their way to London where the baron joined up in the RAF. He flew Spits during the Blitz."

"Quite successfully, I might add. I believe his tally was a dozen of the buggers before they eventually got him over the Channel in spring '41," Fairbairn injected.

"Yes, indeed. Quite proficient. That's when the baroness came to us and volunteered for the SOE. I understand General Gubbins was quite impressed with her," added Brooker.

INTREPID chuckled. "That I can understand," he responded as he watched the stately, aristocratic lady deliver a lightning blow to the opponent that brought the man to the ground. One of INTREPID's great strengths as a spymaster and a successful business leader was his ability to quickly get the measure of a man or, in this case, woman. "She is quite impressive." All nodded in agreement. "She is quite athletic," noted INTREPID.

"Indeed, sir. She is quite the athlete. She competed for Switzerland in the 1932 Olympics in Los Angeles as well as the '36 games in Berlin. She is quite capable physically, sir."

"Yes, that is a tremendous asset, I am sure," responded INTREPID, a smile of satisfaction breaking across his normally stern face.

The three men stood watching the contest for several more minutes without speaking until INTREPID asked the most important question of the day. "Is she aware of what we are asking her to do?" He stared directly at the commandant, who looked first at the baroness, then at Fairbairn, and finally back at INTREPID.

"Yes, sir, she has been fully briefed and, in fact, insisted on conducting the mission. She has a passionate hatred for the Nazis, as did her husband. We believe she is well-motivated and capable."

"Let us hope so, Lieutenant. Let us hope so. Much rests on the success of her mission. Much."

With that statement, the three men turned and strolled back toward the operations building. Bowing gracefully to her somewhat worse for wear and bruised sparring partner, Amelia Anne Marie Ramsour-Fritsch, Baroness Ramsour-Fritsch, smiled as she watched the three spymasters leave the training field. Though outwardly serene, her ocean-blue eyes blazed with intensity and determination as she wiped the perspiration from her long, tanned limbs.

* * * * * * * *

The three men entered the briefing room and quickly took their seats in the front row. On the stage holding a wooden pointer stood a briefer standing beside an overhead projector with a cloth-covered easel off to the side. As he approached the front row of chairs, in his peripheral vision, INTREPID spied a lone man standing in the glass-enclosed observation booth at the rear of the briefing room. With a slight tilt of his head toward the man and an almost imperceptible wink of the eye, he took a seat in the middle. The man in the booth dipped his head ever so slightly as a smoke ring from his fine Cuban cigar wafted toward the ceiling. A bit of ash fell onto the lapel of his finely tailored dark blue pinstripe suit as the man raised a Waterford tumbler, no doubt filled with a fine single malt Scotch whisky.

"Mr. Stephenson, gentlemen, welcome to the operational briefing. If you will be seated, we can begin." With a scraping of chair legs across the polished hardwood floor, all took their seats. Colonel Michael Jones of the SOE cleared his throat a second time and began by placing the first slide on the projector. On the screen appeared an immaculate officer in the uniform of a *Generalmajor* of the German *Luftwaffe*.

"Gentlemen, this is our target. *Generalmajor* Peter, Baron von Zimmermann. He is the chap who piloted the He 177 that delivered the bomb, and he is the central figure in our drama today."

INTREPID interrupted the briefer. "Where, Colonel Jones, did we get the intelligence confirming this Zimmermann's role in the Dartmoor attack?"

Jones pursed his lips. "Excellent question, sir. We received the intelligence direct from CHARLEMAGNE." All in the room knew of the mysterious double agent code named CHARLEMAGNE. All that was known about the man was that he was a highly placed senior officer in the German *Abwehr*, the military intelligence arm of the *Wehrmacht*. It was surmised that he was a German patriot but a fervent anti-fascist. CHARLEMAGNE passed information to British agents that allowed them to counter German operations, but never enough to actually cause German losses. Clearly the man hoped for an end to the war with Germany surviving as a great power unlike how the First World War ended. To date, his information had proven reliable, substantial, and accurate. He could be believed. Zimmermann was the man, and as such, became the steely-eyed focus of British intelligence and special operations forces.

The briefing continued for almost an hour. In short, the mission, codenamed OPERATION THOR, was simple in concept but more difficult in execution. Using an introduction from the Swiss ambassador to Berlin, the baroness, codenamed AGATHA, was to get as close to the enemy pilot as possible. The objective was simply to find out as much as possible about the nature and extent of the German atomic capability. Most importantly, the British must find out how many bombs the enemy had built, where they were stored, who the principal scientists were, and how they could be nullified. From that point, a plan would develop to destroy any existing weapons and, perhaps as importantly, the mechanisms for Germany to continue producing these weapons.

"Zimmermann is a widower. His wife, shown here, died in an auto accident four years ago. We know from other sources that the general has been in deep mourning since, but that prior to his marriage in 1923, he was reputed to be quite a ladies' man."

"And now?" interjected INTREPID.

"Well, now he is apparently rather sedate in that arena. We have no evidence of his involvement with any females," responded Jones.

Fairbairn piped in. "Sir, for that reason we suspect that he may be susceptible to our agent AGATHA. As you can see, she is quite attractive and extremely . . . how do I put this delicately, sir . . . desirable."

"I believe, Lieutenant, it's called a honey trap," INTREPID said, smirking.

"Well, yes, quite so," responded Fairbairn.

Jones continued, "Additionally, we are fairly certain that he is not a Nazi Party man. He seems to be more of the old Prussian aristocrat-warrior. All for the Fatherland and honor type. Given that, he was certainly chosen for the Dartmoor mission for his military record and reputation as a first-rate pilot and leader rather than for some sort of Party loyalty."

"How do you propose to cause this plot to unfold?" INTREPID quizzed the briefing officer as the three men turned their attention back to the man wielding the pointer, who cleared his throat again.

"Indeed, sir. That is already arranged. It seems that the Swiss ambassador in Berlin is not so neutral as he appears. Our man in Zürich has been in contact and, without revealing any of the details of the operation, has arranged for the ambassador to host a diplomatic reception for senior Luftwaffe officers, most assuredly including our General von Zimmermann. At that soirée, AGATHA will be introduced as the Baroness Ramsour-Fritsch, a Swiss neutral who wholeheartedly supports the *Reich* despite her traitorous, and etc., etc., etc., RAF late husband. From there, we hope that nature takes its natural course, so to speak."

INTREPID grunted. "Well, gentlemen, I have seen worse plans," he said, sighing. "However, we have few choices. We must know what the bloody Nazis have and how we might counter it. I must emphasize, though, that this operation must be ultra-secret and close hold."

Brooker shifted uncomfortably in his seat. "What about our chaps, sir, in Whitehall?"

"Outside of this group, only General Menzies, head of MI6, and General Gubbins at SOE know of the plan."

Fairbairn stared straight at INTREPID. "And the prime minister, Lord Halifax?"

"Not even the PM," INTREPID responded, giving a not so discreet glance at the man in the observation room in the blue pinstripe suit. "No, definitely not the PM. He must have plausible deniability should the operation go sideways."

All three men shook their heads in acknowledgment. INTREPID looked up at the briefer and leaned back in his chair. It creaked as he looked side to side, first at Fairbairn, then at Brooker, and finally shifting his gaze back to the briefer.

"Continue, Colonel."

"Quite so, sir. Assuming that all goes well at the diplomatic affair, hopefully AGATHA will become friendly with Zimmermann and can observe his movements and those with whom he associates. A lonely widower and widow sort of association if you will. That will hopefully identify further intelligence targets and, if she is fortunate, potentially identify target sites for possible further actions.

"In essence, sir, she will be looking for three key pieces of intelligence. First, where are the German atomic research facilities? Second, how many weapons do they have combat ready and their location and, finally, what are the mission plans for their future use? If we are able to ferret out these three bits of intelligence, we may be able to mount a counter-operation."

The briefer moved over to the easel still covered by the cloth and lifted the flap revealing a map of central Europe. He pointed to a spot just south of Bern, capital of Switzerland.

"Once AGATHA and CHRISTIE are in country by traveling via New York and Lisbon to Bern, they will meet our agent in Zimmerwald. It's a small village just south of the city and out of the way enough to be discreet. He will pass on further instructions along with the necessary travel documents to Berlin. CHRISTIE, who you will meet this afternoon, is one of our best operatives—Major Kevin Shirley, formerly of the Welsh Guards, now one of SOE's key men. He will accompany AGATHA and serve as her invisible contact with our man in Zürich and act as the conduit. And if anything goes awry, will hopefully be able to arrange and conduct an extraction for AGATHA."

INTREPID raised a hand, which halted the briefer. "And who is this man in Zürich, Colonel?"

"Right, yes, Major Niven, codename PHANTOM," responded Jones. "He is former Highland Light Infantry, and when the war ginned up, he came back on active duty in the Rifle Brigade Prince Consort's Own but later transferred to the Commandos. We first saw him as a Commando training officer at Inverailort House in the western Highlands. That is an SOE training base. It seems that then Lieutenant Niven had quite the aptitude for this cloak and dagger show and thus transferred to the Commandos. Until recently, Major Niven commanded 'A' Squadron, General Headquarters Liaison Regiment. Those chaps are known as 'Phantom.' There is where we derived Niven's code name. The Phantom unit is specifically tasked to act as a special reconnaissance unit for intelligence gathering about German force movements and headquarters operations. Part of their mission is to keep a watch on the movements of key enemy officers, which presumably includes our Zimmermann chap. At General Gubbin's special request, our young major was seconded to SOE and sent to Zürich to act as a conduit to the *Abwehr* source known only as CHARLEMAGNE. It seems the German, whoever he is, only trusts two or three of our people, and PHANTOM is one of them. The major has a long history with Switzerland, as I believe his oldest sister was born in Geneva. His assignment seemed to fit on many fronts."

INTREPID's brow furrowed. "Niven? Niven? Do I know him?"

Fairbairn smiled. "Perhaps you do, sir. His Christian name is David. Major David Niven. You might know him as the film actor."

INTREPID jerked his head around, mouth agape in surprise. "David Niven? The film actor?"

"Aye, sir. And a damned fine one, I might add. Who better than an accomplished actor to play the role of a spy? Quite delicious. Likely this will be the most important role of his career."

"I daresay, Fairbairn. I dare say," INTREPID added with a grin. "It does have a ring of irony does it not?" All in the room chuckled.

With that, the briefing concluded with a few more operational details. Brooker, Fairbairn, and Jones departed the room leaving only INTREPID, who stood in front of the raised stage, staring at the *Luftwaffe* officer's photograph. *Well, Herr Generalmajor, Baron Peter von Zimmermann. What can you tell us about the nasty bomb that you dropped on our lads at Dartmoor? What secrets can we screw out of you?*

INTREPID stood staring at the photo for several minutes. From just the photograph, he visualized Peter von Zimmermann as the consummate military officer—courageous; bold; in complete command of himself and his subordinates; confident, but not arrogant; ethical; and dedicated to his country. And yet, there appeared a hint of sadness in his steel-gray eyes. Perhaps it was for his late wife. Perhaps he felt a duty to Germany despite the Party. Perhaps he had remorse for having been the instrument of such destruction. Only time would tell.

William Stephenson had built a career in business and industry on his ability to size up one's character and abilities from such small evidence as the way a person appeared in a photograph. He suspected he had the measure of *Generalmajor* von Zimmermann already. In the glass-enclosed observation room, the man drained the last of the Glenlivet and muttered quietly, "A wing and a prayer, indeed" as another smoke ring rose toward the ceiling and dissipated.

Two days later, a Boeing 314 flying boat departed the Marine Terminal at New York's LaGuardia airport bound for Bermuda, the Azores, and finally Lisbon, Portugal. Two Swiss nationals, code-named AGATHA and CHRISTIE, quickly passed through passport control, one a Swiss aristocrat, and the other her business manager and erstwhile bodyguard, *Herr* Ulrich Todt. The German agents who watched all incoming and outgoing flights from North America had no suspicions. Well they should have. Perhaps the daily humdrum of watching passengers come and go had dulled their observational powers. Perhaps they had just taken a quick coffee and smoke break and missed the couple boarding the flying boat. Whatever the reasons for their lack of attentiveness, their mistake would soon yield onerous consequences for the Third *Reich*. OPERATION THOR commenced on a wing and a prayer.

* * * * * * * *

Bern, Switzerland, 18 May 1943

The Swissair flight from Lisbon touched downed at the Bern airport with a slight hop and bounce, then came to a halt a few yards from the terminal as the ground crew scrambled to wheel the ladder to the rear door. With Portugal, Spain, and Switzerland all neutral, the Germans did not interfere with flights even though they crossed Occupied France.

The flight in from Lisbon was uneventful. Even in late spring in Switzerland, it can be chilly; the crewmen shivered and grunted as they moved the heavy wheeled ladder into place. The DC-3 door opened, and a smiling air stewardess waved to the crewmen. She had made the short run from Lisbon to Bern many times and knew all the ground crew. Several waved back.

As the elegant lady emerged from the doorway, assisted by helpful ground crewmen, the watcher in the tower stared at her for a few moments, then dropped his binoculars to his chest and took a sip of lukewarm coffee. As the last passenger emerged from the plane, he sighed to himself. *Nein. Nothing here today. Another wasted afternoon.* On the other hand, his alternate option for spending an afternoon observing the arriving passengers at the Bern airdrome could be the Eastern Front dodging Soviet bullets. Given that alternative, even loitering about in the passport control area observing every face and the expressions of each arriving passenger for telltale signs of stress seemed like easy duty. He should never complain.

As the last passenger passed through the Swiss customs official's inspection, a man of middling height, dark brown hair, a mustache that drooped on both sides, and with a Zürich accent who clearly was a returning Swiss businessman and traveling companion of the well-known Baroness Ramsour-Fritsch, the German agent put his notebook into a battered black leather briefcase, turned, and strode out of the airport. His supper awaited. For the second time, German airport agents failed to suspect the true nature of the two passengers traveling from New York to Bern by way of Lisbon.

* * * * * * * *

The ride to the tiny village of Zimmerwald was uneventful. Only a few miles south of the Bern city center, the ancient village sat in the rolling hills of the Canton of Bern atop the *Längenberg* (Long Mountain) mountain surrounded by a coniferous forest.

Despite its proximity to the bustling city, Zimmerwald remained a quiet and bucolic community mostly of dairymen and farmers with a few merchants and tradesmen to service the agricultural economy.

In the center of the village sat a prominent feature—the *Löwen*—a guest- house and restaurant that had first opened in the early nineteenth century. That represented the destination of the two travelers from Bern that morning—the aristocratic lady and the businessman from Zürich with the drooping mustache.

The two spoke little on the trip. For Major Shirley of the Welsh Guards and most recently of the SOE, this was his fourth mission into central Europe. He had been one of the first operatives recruited, trained, equipped, and sent into the continent to liaise with local resistance groups. The ideal candidate for such a mission, he was fluent in German, Spanish, French, and Italian. Having spent a considerable time growing up in Switzerland, the alias as an innocuous Swiss businessman and business manager to the baroness represented the ideal cover identity. It allowed the two to be seen in public without arousing suspicion. It also allowed him to operate independently of AGATHA under the cover of arranging her financial and other affairs. Additionally, since Switzerland was technically neutral, posing as a Swiss citizen allowed CHRISTIE to travel freely throughout central Europe—to Paris, Berlin, Prague, Budapest, and other key locations. Being a master of languages, he could change his dialect and accent in French or German to appear to be local when he needed to, a huge advantage for a secret agent operating behind enemy lines. While the mortality rate for other SOE agents was quite high, these advantages allowed CHRISTIE to survive in the highly dangerous espionage game. The German *Gestapo*, whose mission was to track down SOE agents and their local resistance counterparts, had no inkling of CHRISTIE, his missions, his identity, his location, and his successes over the previous two years.

CHRISTIE had other attributes that made him valuable for this mission. Like AGATHA, he was an athlete. In school he had played scrum half for the rugby club as he did at university. Skilled in all manner of sports, he was able to handle the rigorous, intensive training at Camp X with ease. He had also mastered other tradecraft skills. Agents operating inside the new German Empire had to communicate not only with their resistance contacts but also with home base. A great part of the training at Camp X was how to conceal oneself and yet still communicate effectively. CHRISTIE had become a master of coded messages, of surreptitious wireless transmissions, and passing intelligence information without detection. In short, he had mastered the art of operating in plain sight of the enemy.

Other assets included his looks. He was not considered overly handsome, rather he had a sort of plain appearance. In the intelligence and espionage world, this aspect was a huge asset. It allowed him to blend in easily with any sort of crowd and not attract unwanted attention. Because of his well-developed linguistic skills, he could adapt to any dialect, a skill that allowed him to blend into the countryside. Some might consider him unfriendly. In truth, he just simply was not a very sociable person. This personality trait represented a huge asset in that he could very easily disappear into a crowd unnoticed. He typically didn't socialize; there weren't many opportunities for the enemy, either a collaborator or German agent, to become suspicious or to detect any telltale signs that the man was not who he claimed to be.

In the spy game, agents who are too garrulous, outspoken, or social often give themselves away by making a small mistake that can become huge and deadly blunders if detected by an enemy agent or operative. In all his missions, that particular characteristic served to keep CHRISTIE safe from detection. For all these reasons, Gubbins, the Director of SOE Operations, chose this man to accompany the baroness on her mission to secure whatever information she could through her association (or hoped-for association) with Zimmermann.

The car came to a halt beside the white three-story guesthouse with brown clapboard shutters. They looked about a bit too anxiously for any sign of follower or observer. Both realized they had to be more discreet lest they give themselves away. Normal for the start of a new operation, nervous jitters could have onerous consequences down the road if not brought under control. Satisfied that they were safe and unobserved, they entered the inn through an old oak door with a wrought iron handle and into a main dining room.

The place had that earthy country inn feel and look. Wood paneling adorned the walls and ceiling with a dark patina of age. Layers of smoky soot from the warming fires in the stone fireplaces combined with that from many a pipe enjoyed with a drink after a hard day's labor in the fields and pastures covered the antique wood paneling. The heart pine flooring covered with careworn rugs dampened the noise of footfalls; nevertheless, the boards creaked as the couple walked softly through the foyer and into the main dining area. Wooden tables and chairs occupied most of the floor space and bright blue-or red-checked tablecloths gave the room the ambience of a traditional Italian restaurant.

Along the back wall sat booths with red-leather covered cushions. Clearly these tables were meant for the more private and intimate gatherings or even liaisons. Also along the back wall hung brightly painted coats of arms, including that of the Count of Fontenot, a local aristocrat and the current Swiss ambassador to Germany. He had recommended this rustic out-of-the-way inn for the meeting with PHANTOM. Other armorial bearings included the three green pine trees on a white shield representing the town's forest setting. Interspersed were the traditional arms of the Canton of Bern, the black bear on a yellow and red shield. Behind the bar hung row after row of beer steins, no doubt waiting to be filled as the local farmers and tradesmen drifted in. Through several open windows, a cooling spring breeze wafted in, causing the Belgian linen curtains to gently billow. Only the early morning sunlight lit the place, but with the many open windows, the inn was neither dark nor foreboding. Given the early morning, the place was still empty. The usual crowd would start arriving by noon, but for the moment the place was quiet.

"Willkommen die Herrschaften! Willkommen to the Löwen Gasthaus!"

CHRISTIE nodded a polite acknowledgment as his companion smiled and greeted the man who had just appeared from the door behind the bar obviously leading from the kitchen.

"*Guten Morgen, Herr* Innkeeper. Lovely day. Not many patrons this early, I see," said a smiling AGATHA.

"*Ja, die Dame.* You are unfortunately correct. With the war and all, we have many less travelers, you see. And it is still a bit early for the local farmers and herders. Aah, but you will receive my strictest attention." With that, the man broke into a broad toothy smile.

"*Danke,*" responded CHRISTIE, who had been surreptitiously scanning the place for any sign of their contact. "We are to meet someone here this morning." They had set the rendezvous time early by design so as to minimize the chances of being followed or shadowed. Anyone doing so would be immediately spotted amongst the empty tables and booths.

"*Ja, Ja.* I believe the gentleman is already here. Please do follow me," he said as he bolted from behind the bar while tossing a tea towel over his shoulder. From the looks of the three, he expected quite a fare this morning. He would not be disappointed.

As they rounded a corner, they spied a lone man sitting with his back to the wall, facing forward in a way that allowed for observation of the entire room. Additionally, an exit door was only a few feet away from the booth, the last one in the row. The lady smiled. This man knows his tradecraft—back to the wall to prevent a flank or rear attack, clear observation lines of sight across the room, and an emergency exit should things go badly. Yes indeed, good tradecraft.

As they approached, the man stood and extended a hand. Tall, elegantly thin, and oh-so aristocratic in a gray Harris Tweed suit with crisply starched white shirt and red foulard tie, he appeared every bit the model of a highborn aristocrat. He smiled broadly, causing the tip of his pencil mustache to turn upwards.

"*Willkommen* to Zimmerwald, Baroness and *Herr* Todt. Please, do join me." CHRISTIE shook his hand vigorously while the baroness curtsied ever so slightly as befit her aristocratic rank.

Clearly impressed by the importance of his customers, the innkeeper stiffened to attention, a broad grin on his round face. They all sat, the baroness first, followed by the two men. The greeter took his observation seat again with the two new customers across the table.

"What is your pleasure, *meine Dame und die Herren*?" We have tea and coffee and a wonderful assortment of delicious pastries just arrived from *Herr* Rhein, our magnificent baker."

The smell of freshly baked pastries and brewed coffee filled the room. CHRISTIE and AGATHA looked at the host, who leaned back and looked over at the innkeeper, still maintaining his stiff attention.

"How about coffee and tea for all and perhaps an assortment of the delicious pastries?" the innkeeper asked. Niven glanced back at AGATHA and CHRISTIE, who both nodded their concurrence.

"*Jawohl, Herr.* At once!" The innkeeper bowed and swiftly made for the kitchen behind the bar and, most importantly, out of earshot.

"Major Niven, David Niven. So glad to see the both of you. I trust the flights went well and without complication."

CHRISTIE spoke first. "Yes, sir. Well, indeed. No sign of enemy observation at least." Niven nodded.

"Yes, a somewhat important factor, I suspect." All grinned. Small talk followed as would be expected.

The innkeeper returned with a steaming pot of freshly brewed coffee, hot tea, milk, cream, sugar, and a tray of magnificent pastries. Once he disappeared again into the kitchen, the serious work began. Niven reached into his locked briefcase and pulled out a plain brown envelope. Out came a set of very official travel papers. All were genuine, courtesy of Count Peter Ruffener, the current Swiss ambassador to Berlin.

"Although the lads at Camp X produce very good false identity papers, I believe it is always better to have the real thing, don't you agree?" Niven smirked as the ends of his pencil mustache turned up with the broad smile that followed.

Niven proceeded to explain the plan. The next day, AGATHA and CHRISTIE would depart Bern by plane for Berlin in the ambassador's company. Traveling as his guests, there would be no interference from any overly eager customs or passport official. CHRISTIE was to travel as *Herr* Todt, the baroness's personal secretary and business manager. Traveling as herself, she had no need for an alias. INTREPID's masters of deceit had carefully planted the word among official Germany that although the widow of a Swiss citizen serving in the Czech forces who died as an RAF fighter pilot, the lady, though technically a Swiss neutral, was actually very pro-Nazi. The ruse and false intelligence worked so well that Admiral Wilhelm Canaris, head of the German military intelligence agency, the *Abwehr*, personally vouched for the lady. Even Hermann Göring and Heinrich Himmler asked to meet the Swiss baroness. Little did official Germany know that the lioness they were about to admit into their inner circle was in truth a highly placed British agent codenamed AGATHA. Perfidious Albion!

The plan called for AGATHA to attend a black tie and tails ball at the Swiss Embassy in Berlin, conveniently set up by the ambassador. Prominent on the guest list was the recent hero of the *Reich*, *Generalmajor* of the *Luftwaffe*, Peter von Zimmermann, Baron Zimmermann. The plot was a classic honey trap and AGATHA was the bait. She was to get as close—physically, if necessary—to the *Luftwaffe* man who had dropped the atomic bomb on Dartmoor and who represented, hopefully, the key to the German atomic weapons program. Whatever intelligence she could garner would be transmitted back to Niven in Zürich by CHRISTIE via the Swiss diplomatic pouch or by an intermediary in Berlin, who would transmit from a rural location that the German security services never suspected as a transmitter site. Messages would then go by cable back to INTREPID in New York. No direct communications with London from AGATHA, CHRISTIE or Niven could occur lest the Germans discover that supposedly neutral Britain was still in the game. The stakes for Britain and the world were simply too high.

Having finished the brief and a second round of the delicious pastries and coffee, the three departed the *Löwen* by separate vehicles—Niven back to Zürich, AGATHA and CHRISTIE back to Bern to prepare for the next day's flight to Berlin. As they were about to depart, AGATHA turned to Niven.

"Major Niven, did I not see you in a film before the war? What was it? I believe it was *Raffles*, just before the war?"

Niven smiled broadly. "Indeed, it was, Baroness. Not an Academy Award winner, I fear, but it certainly paid the rent that year!" All laughed as Major David Niven, late of the Highland Light Infantry, the Rifle Brigade, the General Headquarters Liaison Regiment with the current assignment to SOE, and an up-and-coming film star, reached out and swung open the door of the gray Mercedes.

PART II.
Breaking of Nations

CHAPTER 6

Danube Waltz

Berlin, 20 May 1943

Swissair Flight 210 departed Bern on time. Noted for its reliability and punctuality, the airline had grown in just a few short years to one of the major carriers in Europe. With Swiss neutrality, the air carrier could travel in and out of belligerent capitals with impunity. As such, it represented a potential vehicle for inserting clandestine operatives into Germany or Britain.

Despite the best efforts of the British and German security services, agents passed through without difficulty. The normal insertion for SOE agents linking up with the local resistance units was by parachute from the Whitley or Halifax bombers of No. 161 squadron—the "Moon" squadron—based at RAF Tempsford. For agents such as AGATHA and CHRISTIE, who would operate in plain view, the Swissair connection represented a vital resource in the spy game.

Few travelers deplaned from the Douglas DC-3 at *Tempelhof* Airport. The ambassador and his entourage, including AGATHA and CHRISTIE, were the primary travelers. There was a scattering of Swiss businessmen who still did trade with the Reich as well as the occasional German traveler returning home.

As they moved through passport control and customs inspection, the two British agents were surprised that a German military escort awaited the Swiss ambassador's party. Seeing the surprised and worried expression from AGATHA as they walked out of the passport agent's earshot, Ambassador Ruffener leaned over and whispered to AGATHA, "Not to worry, my dear. This is normal protocol. The Germans send an escort party to greet all incoming ambassadors."

Assured that all was well, AGATHA smiled sweetly at the SS officer in charge, who said nothing in response. Despite the ambassador's reassurances, she felt ill at ease until they were well clear of the airport. The SS security escort made certain that the ambassador and his party reached their limousines safely. Only when they were safely away from the airport did AGATHA feel more relaxed and at ease.

* * * * * * * *

As the 1939 Rolls-Royce Wraith limousine pulled to a halt outside the Swiss Embassy on *Otto-von-Bismarck-Allee*, the ambassador gave AGATHA her final brief. Both stayed in the backseat of the car as the driver stepped onto the pavement in front of the embassy and closed his door. The cool brown leather seats felt good after the somewhat bumpy flight from Bern to Berlin.

The chauffer stood guard on the sidewalk next to the car. This was a security measure to ensure that no one overheard the conversation. AGATHA was amused at the notion of the top-of-the-line British limousine driving around Berlin. The Swiss ambassador considered it something of an offhand insult to his German hosts. What they thought of the slight, he did not know, nor did he care. There is often great value in being in the middle during times of massive conflict.

"The driver will pick you up at eight p.m. sharp at your hotel. You will find everything you'll need already in your suite. I have confirmed that *Generalmajor* Zimmermann will definitely attend. I must add that it took some persuading and, frankly, a bit of intervention with *Generaloberste* Kline and Krause to convince the man that he ought to attend our little soirée. Good diplomatic relations and all that!"

"You are a charmer, Ambassador Ruffener," she responded with a smirk and a wink.

"*Danke*, my dear. *Danke*. We do what we can. By the way, Countess Ruffener eagerly looks forward to seeing you again. She will arrive in Berlin in a few days."

With the small number of Swiss nobility, they all knew each other quite well. AGATHA had not seen the countess in some years, but she remembered the lady as a charming and gracious matronly type. All in all, despite the tension of meeting the target for the first time, she vowed to enjoy the lavish diplomatic ball that next evening. After all, what a change from the spartan life at Camp X.

The plan called for CHRISTIE to remain as shadowy as possible. He would remain outside the embassy, hidden from observation, to detect any undue attention paid to the elegant, stunning, and charming baroness. They suspected that some agency of the *Reich* security services would be interested; CHRISTIE had to be not only the watcher but also a bodyguard.

As the ambassador stepped out of the Rolls-Royce, he turned back to AGATHA. "I shall see you then tomorrow evening, my dear. Good luck and good hunting." AGATHA smiled broadly. "*Danke, Herr Botschafter*. Until then."

With that, the limousine sped away, followed by the security detail and CHRISTIE in a separate car. Within minutes, they arrived at the palatial *Kaiserhof* Hotel on the *Wilhelmplatz*, which would serve as her quarters and operational base for the duration of OPERATION THOR.

* * * * * * * *

Swiss Embassy, Berlin, 21 May 1943

The Rolls-Royce limousine arrived right on time at the massive gray Regency-style building that had housed the Swiss embassy since the early nineteenth century. Greek-style columns adorned the exterior sides. Although not freestanding as later popular with the Greek-revival style of mid-century architecture, the columns still gave the impression of a Greek temple.

Located at *Otto-von-Bismarck Allee,* the embassy had been the hub of much of Berlin social activity since the war's start. Despite his dislike, if not outright hatred, for fascism, Ambassador Ruffener hosted many balls and less formal social events at the embassy since his appointment in 1939. In truth, his outreach to Nazi officialdom had a practical motivation. Surrounded on all sides by the new Third *Reich*, which included Austria and Czechoslovakia both absorbed into the Greater *Reich*, Occupied France, and Italy, Switzerland could not afford to antagonize Germany. Although every Swiss adult male was technically part of the armed forces as citizen militia and came well-armed, there was no real ability to resist an outright German invasion as had occurred in Czechoslovakia, Yugoslavia, and Greece. So the ambassador fêted the Nazi bigwigs and feigned support while all the while aiding British espionage activities and resistance groups. For Count Ruffener, it meant playing a dangerous yet vital role, and he did so especially well.

As the limousine pulled into the drive at the main entrance, an embassy clerk rushed to the ambassador's office with word of AGATHA's arrival. Ruffener proceeded down to the entrance to greet the baroness personally. For the honey trap to succeed, he had to take personal charge and facilitate the liaison with Zimmermann.

The aide opened the car door; Ruffener leaned in and whispered, "Are you ready, my dear?"

She nodded and took a deep breath. "As much as I will ever be, *Mein Herr.*"

He smiled. "Then let us go, you and I, and save the civilized world, shall we?" With that, she stepped out of the limousine, and with Ruffener cradling her arm, she was escorted through the massive entranceway and into an unknown destiny.

Meanwhile, CHRISTIE watched from the building across the street through powerful binoculars. Dressed as an average Berliner, he blended in with the background, allowing him the freedom to maintain his overwatch. He scanned the street and surrounding area with the binoculars searching for anything or anyone out of place that might indicate a threat. Seeing none, he dropped the binoculars to his chest and took a bite of the *knackwurst* and cheese sandwich that he had made up for dinner. He chuckled. *Well, my lady, here I sit with sausage and cheese while you dine this night on pheasant and caviar.* He made a decision. If they got away with this risky gambit, he would take the baroness to an excellent meal of good British beef at the Savoy Grill on the Strand in London once the war was over. With that, he bit down hard on the wurst sandwich.

"His Excellency, the Count of Fontenot, and the Baroness Ramsour-Fritsch," announced the embassy footman.

At most such functions, Lady Salome Ruffener would be introduced with her husband, but on this night she was at home in Bern nursing a bad bout of influenza. Normally, attendees ignored the formal announcement of new arrivals, but when the ambassador or other high officials came through the archway to descend the marble steps down to the ballroom, all paid attention.

The introduction was by design. To make AGATHA more prominent so as to enhance the official introduction, her arrival with the ambassador and host of the *Luftwaffe* ball was critical to the honey trap. It made AGATHA more than just another foreign socialite; it set her up as a highly important dignitary. It also made introduction by the ambassador possible. He would first introduce her to several of the *Luftwaffe* higher-ranking officers but would eventually reach Zimmermann. From there, AGATHA was on her own.

The affair glittered. Several dozen attended—generals down to some junior officers—all in their best formal dress uniforms. Silver and gold lace and various decorations for service or valor glinted in the warm glow created by dozens of cut crystal chandeliers and wall sconces.

AGATHA noted that most attendees appeared older. She knew why. The younger officers all served at the Eastern Front or North Africa these days. With the *Luftwaffe* stretched to the maximum attempting to hold back the Soviet Red Army, resurgent after the Stalingrad disaster, and to supply the *Wehrmacht* troops on the ground, most of the officers left in Berlin these days included various senior commanders, their immediate staff, and those assigned to operational units that flew out of the Berlin area, including *Luftflotte* 1.

This dynamic represented a subtle aspect of the plan. With a scarcity of men of her age, and with most senior officers married with families, that left few men available as targets for the affection of the stunning and imminently available baroness. That eligible group included one *Generalmajor* Peter von Zimmermann, now attached directly to the Air Ministry in his new and special role. INTREPID planned this operation well.

Following the arrival of guests and a cocktail social, all moved into the dining area. Several tables had been set with six or eight guests at each. A magnificent buffet included delicacies hard to find in wartime Berlin. But, as a neutral country with trade ties all over the world, the Swiss diplomatic corps always had the finest food at parties and social events. The buffet centered on a wonderful Swiss chocolate waterfall, much to the crowd's delight.

Ruffener intentionally did not introduce AGATHA to Zimmermann during the cocktail hour. They did not want to overplay their hand. Even though Zimmermann stood by himself slowly drinking a French champagne and seemingly bored, Ruffener and AGATHA avoided springing the plan too early. The introduction had to be more casual and look "unstaged." Rather, with control over the seating, the embassy staff intentionally placed AGATHA next to Zimmermann along with other married guests who attended as couples. Avoiding any hint of subterfuge, they paired up all singles, which made sense for a social gathering—married couples together with single gentleman next to single ladies. At her table sat three other much older couples, all *Luftwaffe* senior officers and their wives.

Zimmermann had already arrived at the table; he sat the champagne flute down next to his nameplate. He really didn't enjoy these affairs and preferred the company of a military club or officers' mess or just solitude with a pipe and a great work of literature. Nonetheless, as a senior officer, he felt obligated to attend and "grip and grin" as much as minimally required.

In truth, he initially planned to decline the invitation until *Generaloberst* Kline insisted he attend. Credit there went to Ruffener, who knew Kline quite well socially and made a point of insisting that such a great hero of the *Reich* absolutely must attend the *Luftwaffe* ball. Zimmermann hesitated until he received a call from Krause practically ordering him to attend. Thus, a key element in the plot unfolded, leading to the newest "Hero of the *Reich*" standing beside his chair as the ambassador and baroness approached.

"*Herr Generalmajor* Zimmermann, may I introduce the Baroness Amelia Ramsour-Fritsch."

The introduction caught him slightly off balance. In actuality, he had been thinking about how long this event would last and when it was prudent to depart. "*Ja* . . . I . . . *Ja*, Baroness Ramsour-Fritsch, how do you do?"

She curtsied in the most aristocratic manner and smiled coquettishly. "*Herr Generalmajor* von Zimmermann, it is so nice to meet you. I have heard so many wonderful tales of your flying exploits. You really must tell me all about them."

An odd look came over his face. AGATHA could not tell if it was surprise, dislike, or even contempt. But still, she knew she had sparked some reaction. The two just stared at each other for several seconds without speaking. Finally, Ruffener broke the silence. "Well, Baroness, *Herr Generalmajor*, I must see to the other guests. Please do sit and enjoy the evening."

"*Herr Botschafter*," responded AGATHA sweetly as Zimmermann pulled back her chair.

Other guests arrived at the table and the chitchat began. AGATHA had to pay attention to Zimmermann without making him suspect that he was actually a target. Despite his distaste for such social affairs, Zimmermann proved quite adept at the small-talk game. The other officers at the table clearly wanted him to discuss the Dartmoor mission; he refused. Instead, he focused on his previous experiences in France and on the Eastern Front. The three officers' wives all appeared bored with the war stories, but AGATHA paid rapt attention. One of the lessons at Camp X stressed finding the target's weak spots or interests that could be exploited to get closer to them. If the target feels closer to you as one of similar interests, a stronger trust bond is possible, leading to extracting more valuable intelligence. AGATHA then paid close, even keen, attention to the *Generalmajor* and his talk of life on the front lines.

The dinner was excellent. Once the tables had been cleared and the orchestra arrived for the dancing part of the evening's entertainment, Zimmermann had planned to bow out, claiming he had an early morning training flight or some such excuse. With that, he would have done his social duty, kept Kline and Krause from complaining, and thus been able to return to his regular routine. But something made him stay.

Perhaps it was the excellent food and drink. Perhaps it was the wonderful music from the orchestra. He could not remember having heard such excellent music since even before the war, what with the operational deployments and the long hours as the chief of staff. Or perhaps it was something about the lady with whom he enjoyed the finest dinner still available in Berlin. He found her to be most interesting, not only because she seemed genuinely interested in his military exploits but also because of something less obvious. She had a charm and wit that especially attracted him. Clearly the baroness projected an air of self-confidence and vitality that went beyond her physical attractiveness.

Truth be told, he was also struck by her ocean-blue eyes. She was quite attractive, one had to concede. Zimmermann had not missed the numerous sets of male eyeballs casting surreptitious glances at the lady in the ivory-colored silk gown replete with a magnificent strand of pearls and her honey-blonde hair topped by a jewel-encrusted tiara. Zimmermann chuckled to himself at the men's attempts to steal a glance at the baroness while not letting their wives see them. He noted that in more than a few instances, alert wives did see what was going on based on their glares at their indiscreet husbands.

The music began—a Strauss waltz. Couples joined up on the dance floor one by one until the ballroom became a swirl of elegant gowns and gold-and silver-adorned dress uniforms.

Initially, AGATHA and Zimmermann stood aside just enjoying another champagne. None of the other officers asked her to dance. The older men with wives dared not and the younger officers were clearly intimidated by the magnificent lady. Instead, they stood in clusters like schoolboys at their first mixed social, likely telling their own war stories.

Finally, after the third waltz began, Zimmermann set down his glass, turned to AGATHA, and asked, "Baroness, would you care to dance?"

She pursed her lips in a coquettish fashion as if considering the proposition. *Of course, I'll dance. That's the reason I'm here. Tally Ho the Fox!*

"Why, *Ja, Herr Generalmajor*, I would be most honored." With that, she extended a satin-gloved hand, and the couple proceeded on to the dance floor.

Zimmermann was not surprised at her ease on the dance floor. Smooth and graceful, her athleticism gave her great coordination and physical movement. Certainly, years spent at some of the finest girl's finishing schools in France, England, and Switzerland added polish to her dancing. Zimmermann, an excellent dancer as well, was impressed at how fluidly and effortlessly she moved.

Before the war, he and Ingrid had gone dancing on oh-so-many occasions, not just at their favorite cabaret but also at formal balls or just informal social gatherings. They enjoyed the new swing music coming out of America, which, since it did not conform to National Socialist cultural purity, had been discouraged. Nevertheless, he enjoyed dancing, and now, for the first time since Ingrid's death, he again enjoyed it with a partner of clearly great skill and grace. They danced for hours, and as midnight approached, finally sat, exhausted.

The crowd had thinned considerably by that time. Other officers did in fact have duties or even training flights early the next morning. The ambassador greeted every attendee as they departed and gracefully accepted their congratulations on the wonderful food and drink, how fine the orchestra had been, and so forth and so on. Finally, Zimmermann and AGATHA approached him as he stood at the top of the stairs leading out to the grand foyer. Zimmermann excused himself to retrieve his service cap and her mink wrap. AGATHA stood next to the ambassador as if expressing her appreciation for the wonderful party. In reality, she reported, "Mission success, *Herr* Ruffener. We have a date for tea tomorrow afternoon."

Ruffener nodded. "Understood, my dear. Good luck and be careful. You are amongst the wolves in this place."

Zimmermann arrived and thanked the ambassador for the wonderful party and for introducing him to the baroness. He escorted her out to the drive, and after shutting the door to the limousine and watching it speed away, grinned like a schoolboy who had just had his first kiss. With that, he strode toward his own car parked around the corner with a lightness of step not seen in him in months . . . if not years.

That night a coded message left the Swiss Embassy destined for Major David Niven in Zürich. It simply stated: "Danube Waltz," the code words indicating OPERATION THOR's first step had been achieved.

* * * * * * * *

Berlin, 22 May 1943

Some rubble still blocked part of the pedestrian walkway from British Bomber Command raids a year earlier. But since the attacks ceased with the armistice, Berliners felt more at ease in strolling the city these days. Cleaning up the rubble had pressed ahead regardless of the previous nightly raids; in fact, it had accelerated in the past few days. Nevertheless, there still were many parts of Berlin not yet clear.

One area relatively unaffected by the bombing was the *Tiergarten* District and the myriad of shops and outdoor cafés just on the park's edges. With the coming of spring's warmth and flowers all about, the shops and small cafés did a wonderful trade. Zimmermann had suggested one in particular. It sat on a side street off the main thoroughfare, but it had a good view of the River Spree. More of a tearoom than a full-blown restaurant, it was operated by an elderly couple from Regensburg. It had been one of his and Ingrid's favorite spots for a late afternoon rendezvous when he had been in town before the war. She always ordered a chamomile tea. He went for just a Brazilian coffee, straight, without any cream or sugar.

Ingrid always ordered a *sacher torte*. Being a Vienna native, she had grown up on these delicious chocolate delights. He shied away from such heavy sweets, preferring a plain strudel. It had become a regular routine for the young couple, even in the rough times that followed the previous war and the Great Depression that had devastated Germany. He instinctively chose this place for the rendezvous with the baroness. Why, he could not say. *Did it besmirch Ingrid's sacred memory? No, not really. It was just a quiet afternoon tea with a new and interesting friend.* But as he sat silently in the same chair he had always taken, staring across the simple wrought iron table at the chair Ingrid always took, he couldn't help but wonder if there was a deeper, subconscious need for him to go back to the spot they had shared so intimately so many times.

His train of thought was broken by a sweet voice behind him that shook him out of his remembrances. AGATHA had approached from an unexpected direction—more tradecraft training from Camp

X. Always approach from an unexpected direction. In that way, you will likely detect an enemy before he finds you. That gives you the option to surprise, engage, or leave, depending on the circumstances.

"*Guten Tag, Herr Generalmajor*. It is so nice to see you again. I trust you are well after our, shall I say, vigorous dancing last evening."

Zimmermann laughed heartily in an attempt not to blush. *Was ist das? What is this?* He had not really laughed like this in months, certainly not since taking up his new assignment.

"I see you have the better of me, Baroness. Fortunately, I have been able to keep my fitness up. But, I daresay, many of my fellow officers suffered last night. Too much excellent food, wine, and lack of exercise for the ballroom floor." Both laughed as Zimmermann leaned over and pulled out her chair. She sat as delicately as possible. After all, she was a lady of the finest breeding and had to play the role. It might not do if her companion this fine, balmy spring afternoon knew that the delicate flower sitting across from him could likely destroy him in a physical fight. Or, as one of the Americans at Camp X had boasted, he could: "Kick your ass twice on Sunday and give you change!" She was not quite sure what the peculiar expression meant, but she got the meaning, nonetheless. He pushed the chair back in and retook his seat.

Small talk ensued. It began in the usual fashion, discussing the weather and everyone's health. After a couple of minutes, a matronly lady arrived at the table. With rosy, cherubic cheeks, she appeared the perfect tea shop hostess. "*Guten Tag, Herr Baron. Willkommen* back to the *Edelweiss*. We have not seen you in so many years not since—" She stopped short. She knew of the tragic death of Ingrid. "Not since the war began, I am sure." *Nice recovery,* thought Zimmermann.

"*Nein, Frau* Schultz. I believe you are correct. It has been at least since before the war. But, as you see, I am back, and it is a wonderful day. Please, let me introduce the Baroness Ramsour-Fritsch, just arrived from Bern and before that, New York. She is a guest of the Swiss ambassador and will be visiting Berlin for a time." *Frau* Schultz curtsied gracefully . . . well, as graceful as one of her age and girth could.

"*Guten Tag*, Baroness, *und willkommen* to Berlin and my humble tearoom." The mature lady beamed ear to ear.

"How is *Herr* Schultz? Is he here today?" *Frau* Schultz's mood suddenly turned melancholy; all the previous cheeriness left her face. She bowed her head.

"I'm afraid, *Herr Baron*, my dear husband passed away last year. You see, our grandson Klaus was killed in the fighting in some place in the Ukraine, though we never were sure. He was an *Unteroffizier* (corporal) in the *Wehrmacht*. Herr Schultz never really recovered from the shock and just withered away. A stroke, the doctor said. I say it was a case of melancholia." Her mood then brightened. "But, *Herr Baron*, my daughter Katherina has helped me keep the tearoom going."

"I am most sorry to hear *Frau* Schultz, but I'm glad you seem to be doing well, despite all." The elderly lady smiled gratefully.

"Well then, *Herr Baron* and Baroness, what may I serve you today? Despite the war, we have a wonderful plum strudel."

There was a slight pause as Zimmermann looked over at AGATHA. She dipped her head as if to say "*Please order for me, kind sir.*" He got the message.

"We will have your magnificent plum strudel, and I shall go with a cup of Brazilian black coffee." He hoped that they still had Brazilian coffee. With the previous British blockade, there had been none since the war started. But with the recent armistice, trade with South America had started up again and beef from Argentina, pineapples from Panama, cigars from Cuba and Honduras, and, most importantly for him, coffee from Brazil began arriving again in German shops and restaurants. He looked back at AGATHA with the "over to you" expression.

"And, I will have a cup of chamomile tea, if you please, *Frau* Schultz," she responded. She hated chamomile tea. But she had learned that lesson well at Camp X—find out the target's likes and dislikes. Ferret out as much intelligence as possible and turn that back against them. The analysts at MI6 had developed an excellent file on *Generalmajor* Peter, Baron von Zimmermann. They knew exactly his habits, even the fact that his late wife always ordered chamomile tea at this particular outdoor café.

They sat and chatted for over an hour and a half. Both loved literature. Both had competed in the Olympics—he in the 1924 games in Paris in fencing and decathlon, and she in 1932 in Los Angeles and again in 1936 in Berlin as a swimmer and diver. Despite this common experience, they had never met. They discussed Victorian British poetry and the novels of the American Ernest Hemingway. That dynamic, they both noted but never said, was an interesting angle. Hemingway, the man of action and adventure, clearly appealed to the two, both persons of action, adventure, and risk-taking.

The more they talked, the more they realized how much in common they actually shared. As the afternoon wore on, the conversation eventually waned. Not that they had run out of things to say; rather, they had practically worn themselves out.

As Zimmermann pulled out of his wallet the cash for the bill of the many cups of black coffee and tea consumed that afternoon along with a more than generous gratuity, he suddenly stopped talking, his hand holding several *Reichsmark* suspended in midair. He stared at the lady sitting across from him at a little tearoom near the *Tiergarten* alongside the River Spree. An odd feeling came over him, one he had not felt in years. He could not really describe it, but it was there nonetheless, palpable and real.

Surprised by his sudden halt in midsentence and the hand suspended above the table, AGATHA frowned. "*Herr Generalmajor*, are you all right?" Her question shook him out of his momentary pause, and he dropped the money down on the table.

"*Ja*, quite all right. I was just saying, please call me Peter. I believe we have become familiar enough for some level of informality, do you not agree?"

"Of course, by all means. Peter it is, and please, I am Amelia." With that, she extended a hand across the table. He took it in his and felt a warm glow emanate from her long elegant, flawless fingers. "*Ja,* Amelia."

With that, the two went their separate ways. AGATHA returned to the Hotel *Kaiserhof* where she made out a report of the day's contact with the target. CHRISTIE then handed off the message to a reliable intermediary in Berlin, who then traveled out to his farm in the countryside to transmit it to Niven in Zürich, who then retransmitted it back to BSC in New York. Transmitting from a remote village miles out in the countryside avoided the routine *Abwehr* military intelligence vans that traversed Berlin looking for transmitters. From New York, INTREPID sent word back to London via secure transatlantic undersea cable, which the Germans had not tapped. Therefore, the more cutouts and subterfuge, the better. London could never be in the direct communications chain. While this transmission methodology might have seemed clunky and laborious, it was for good reason: there could be no hint of British involvement.

Meanwhile, Zimmermann returned to his flat on a side street just off the *Kurfürstendamm*. He rented the flat on an annual basis and thus had it available whenever he was in town, which had been more frequent these days. The Zimmermanns had done well in business investments in the past decades, unlike too many European aristocrats who assumed their landed and inherited wealth would last forever. The family invested heavily in mining, transportation, and manufacturing as Germany transitioned from an agrarian to an industrial society, such that they had amassed a large fortune. Thus, Zimmermann could afford to maintain an elegant flat year- round in one of the city's most fashionable districts, even when forward deployed to the battle fronts. The doors leading to the balcony faced west and across an open park, so he could see the magnificent sunset of red, orange, pink, yellow, and blue as he sat gazing at the colorful light show with a good brandy in hand.

As he watched the sunset's glow turn to a deep purple twilight, he swirled the brandy about in the crystal snifter, contemplating the events of the past two days. He realized he had encountered feelings not experienced in years. In a way, it frightened him. In a way, it thrilled him.

On the one hand, he was the most important military officer in the *Reich* at that moment. The Fatherland's destiny might lie with him over the next few months. How could he allow anything to interfere with that mission? On the other hand, he was fascinated with the Swiss widow. He had to admit, she had charmed him. He desperately wanted to see her again. Somehow, he had to reconcile the two courses of action and not allow the one to undercut the other. He took a last sip of the exceptional brandy, reached out to the telephone on the side table, and dialed the number for the reception desk at the Hotel *Kaiserhof*.

* * * * * * * *

For the next four weeks, they spent part of practically every day together, many times just walking in the parks and woodlands of Berlin that had not yet been damaged by the bombing. They frequented the *Edelweiss*, the little café near the *Tiergarten* that had become something of their place to rendezvous. The gossipers about town observed and made mention of the unusually close relationship between the widowed Swiss baroness and the widower *Luftwaffe* general, but there were others that had observed the apparent liaison as well. Men in trench coats and fedora hats pulled down low over their eyes seemed to be everywhere, as if following the couple. AGATHA noticed them but pretended not to. CHRISTIE also noticed them and, from a discrete distance, kept a sharp watch. He always carried a Walther PPK pistol cleverly obscured under a pants cuff just in case one of these watchers became too curious or aggressive. Zimmermann never noticed the watchers. Perhaps he had seen too much of these *Gestapo* thugs to even notice. After all, he had other issues on his mind, and one of those issues was about to become the fulcrum of his new existence.

* * * * * * * *

Office of *Reichsführer* of the *Schutzstaffel (SS)* Heinrich Himmler, 22 June 1943

The nervous little man sat quietly in the outer office. He did not know if he had been summoned to appear before *Reichsführer* Himmler for some infraction of the Party ideology or whether it might be for some important new assignment. *Ja. That must be it. The Reichsführer needs me for some new mission. Perhaps it's rooting out more Jews or sympathizers. Ja, that's it! After all, I am a loyal Party man and I have done great service for the Reich, the Party, and the Führer.* He crossed and uncrossed his scrawny legs as his posture took on an air of self-importance. Then, like a changing wind, he became nervous and ill at ease again. *What might I have done to distress the Reichsführer? Have I committed some discretion?* His right eyelid twitched as it did in moments of doubt or concern, as this event definitely was.

Sturmbannführer Johann Maas had failed at practically everything he ever attempted. He had tried teaching, but his pupils never took him seriously and the headmaster replaced him after only two academic years. He had tried military service during the Great War, and though rising to the rank of *Unteroffizier*, his commanding officers, and more importantly, his senior non-commissioned officers, never trusted him with any assignment or task of any importance.

Perhaps his worst moment came in 1917 at the Battle of Passchendaele. He had been charged with marching several British prisoners to the rear area for processing. He had not gone but a few hundred yards with his charges when one by one, the "Tommys" broke away and escaped. Of the 20 men he had been tasked to escort, only three remained, and they were the walking wounded. That incident resulted in his demotion. Though he later regained his rank while serving as a supply clerk in the rear area, no one trusted him on the front lines. So his brilliant military career, or rather, what he had envisioned as his brilliant military career, came to a crashing halt.

He had tried his hand at history research and writing. Much as Adolf Hitler failed as an artist in pre-World War I Vienna, Maas failed as a writer. His one book that did finally get published—a study of the Saxon invasions of the British Isles—was universally panned and dismissed. He received no further book contracts following that debacle.

Maas tried business but seemed to not understand that making a profit had to be an essential objective of any business enterprise. In short, the insignificant little man who now sat in the outer office of the head of the SS had been a complete failure in life until one day in 1928, when he found his true calling. He joined the *Sturmabteilung*— the SA known as the "Brownshirts" led by Ernst Röhm.

Maas found his mission as a thug. He especially enjoyed the gang beatings of anyone opposed to the rising National Socialist ideology. As the 1930s and the Great Depression gripped Germany, causing more and more angst with the accompanying anti-Semitism, he especially relished attacking helpless Jews, their homes, and businesses. In short, the SA leadership saw him as a useful tool, a man desperate to please, desperate to be seen as important, and bitter over his failures as a soldier, historian, author, and teacher.

With the "Night of the Long Knives," the purge and destruction of the SA instigated by Hitler and the Nazi hierarchy in 1934, it appeared that Maas's career as a party thug ended. He had luckily been home on leave visiting his dying mother and thus escaped the assassinations of Röhm and many SA men. But he had been noticed by Himmler, head of the rising *Schutzstaffel*, the SS, a Nazi Party organization ostensibly founded as Hitler's personal bodyguard but had essentially morphed into the Party's main security and enforcement agency. Himmler noted Maas's rough efficiency, particularly the brutality and lack of any empathy for his victims or targets. Himmler had said to Hitler,

"Maas is useful to the Party." Hitler agreed, so Johann Maas was spared and offered a position in the now dominant SS as an enforcer and one always willing to take on the often unpleasant or delicate missions. He had a primal desire to please, a need to prove his worth. The Party had need of such brutal men. He rose in the ranks over the years from *Schütze* (private) to *Sturmbannführer*, the SS equivalent of a major in the *Wehrmacht* or *Luftwaffe*. Thus it was that on this rainy, dreary afternoon in Berlin, he sat in the *Reichsführer's* office wavering between angst and arrogance.

"The *Reichsführer* will see you now," came a stern voice from behind him. Maas jumped, momentarily startled by the harsh voice of the *Reichsführer's* secretary. He rose quickly and straightened his tie. *I look fairly good*, he thought.

True, as he reached his mid-40s, he had put on considerable weight and appeared pudgy, as many men do at that age. Still, he felt physically able to do his job as an enforcer despite the limitations of age and a lack of exercise complicated by a too rich diet.

"*Jawohl*, I am ready. *Danke*." He followed the secretary into the *Reichsführer's* inner sanctum. Himmler sat behind a huge desk reading a report from a particular concentration camp in Poland called Auschwitz. A gleeful expression across his face indicated his pleasure at the highly effective efforts of his SS team at the "work camp." Himmler looked up and, almost with a sneer, glared at Maas, who seeing the *Reichsführer's* reaction to his presence, almost collapsed in fright. But, he didn't, and despite wobbly knees and a twitching right hand, he managed to throw up a hearty and overly loud "*Heil* Hitler" salute.

Reichsführer Himmler dropped his pen and grinned. No doubt he had managed to terrify another subordinate, a skill so valuable in his position. "Be seated, *Herr Sturmbannführer*. You may relax now." He looked up at the secretary who had stood behind Maas attempting to stifle a smirk. He had seen the *Reichsführer* do this intimidation act many times, and the reaction amused him. "That will be all, Steiner. *Danke*."

"*Jawohl, Herr Reichsführer.*" With that, the secretary turned and departed, leaving Maas alone to face the most feared man in the *Reich*. He sat frozen in the chair, still unable to tell if he was in desperate trouble or not.

"Relax, Maas. I trust you have been well?"

Maas did not know how to respond. Was the question a lead-in to the announcement of his demise? He could not read the *Reichsführer's* intent. It was a trick Himmler used often to throw off a target and to maintain his dominance.

"*Jawohl, Herr Reichsführer.* I have been well, sir," he responded nervously.

Himmler leaned forward and clasped his pudgy fingers together on the desk blotter. "*Sehr gut.*" He paused for effect. "*Herr Sturmbannführer,* have you heard of *Generalmajor* Peter von Zimmermann of the *Luftwaffe*?"

An odd question, thought Maas. "Why, yes, *Herr Reichsführer.* I believe he is the pilot who flew the glorious atomic attack mission against the British that forced them out of the war."

"Correct, Maas. You are quite right. The *Generalmajor* is in great favor with the *Führer* these days. In fact, he is about to be promoted to *Generalleutnant* (US major general/UK air vice-marshal) and awarded a Knight's Cross with Oak Leaves and Swords. What do you think of that?"

Maas was confused. *Why was I summoned to the Reichsführer's office just to discuss the career achievements of a Luftwaffe general? There is another agenda here that I do not understand.* He shifted uncomfortably in his chair, which was intentionally designed for discomfort. That feature played nicely into Himmler's domination game. Summoning all the courage he could muster, he asked, "Why do you ask *Herr Reichsführer*?"

Himmler only grinned again—the malevolent grim so famous these days. "Are you aware of the Baroness Ramsour-Fritsch, who has apparently become somewhat close to the *Generalmajor*?"

The question completely confused him. He hesitated.

Picking his next words cautiously, he responded, "*Herr Reichsführer*, I do not believe I know the baroness, nor do I know anything of her."

Himmler leaned back in his chair. "Then, *Sturmbannführer* Maas, you will soon know her quite well."

For the next half an hour, Himmler described the relationship that had developed between AGATHA and Zimmermann. It had become obvious to everyone; it worried Himmler and the Party leadership. What if she was a plant, either by the British or even the Soviets? What if she had been sent in to secure as much intelligence as possible on Germany's atomic weapons program? Certainly, she had known sympathies for the Third *Reich*, but were they genuine? The question concerned the men in the New *Reich* Chancellery, and they needed answers. As Himmler explained Maas's mission in more depth, Maas relaxed. He realized that he was apparently held in high esteem at *SS* headquarters.

He was mistaken.

From top to bottom of the high command of the *SS*, he was loathed. On the other hand, they understood that he was dogged, determined, and thorough. The *SS* had used him on other similar observation assignments and for special operations that ended in violence and brutality.

Although not spoken, Himmler made certain that Maas understood this imperative: If he was certain, without a doubt, that the seemingly neutral Swiss baroness was actually an enemy agent, he was to report that finding immediately. His mission was to observe as discreetly as possible her movements, whom she contacted, and whom she spoke with. Most importantly, did she compromise Zimmermann?

Himmler and the *SS* relied on Maas' need to please his masters. That meant that he would be dedicated to the mission to the exclusion of all other concerns. Himmler advised Maas that he must provide a daily report for Himmler's eyes only of his observations and actions. Should Maas uncover compromising information on the baroness that required violent action, he must contact Himmler and obtain direct authorization. In that case, though not specifically stated, there was the hint of violence to follow; that was Maas' forte.

Buoyed by the confidence shown in him by the head of the SS himself and puffed up with his self-importance, Maas departed SS headquarters on *Prinz-Albrecht-Strasse*. Himmler chuckled to himself. "What an insignificant little troll," he thought out loud. But he knew that the troll would be reliable enough and ultimately disposable once the mission was completed. After all, it simply would not do to assassinate a prominent Swiss citizen. Better that some rogue agent carry out any necessary action that could not be linked back to the official German government.

* * * * * * * *

Berlin, Air Ministry, 9 July 1943

As Zimmermann sat at his desk contemplating a depressing report of *Luftwaffe* casualties in the Leningrad sector, the phone rang. It was the boss, *Generaloberst* Krause.

"*Guten Morgen, Herr Generaloberst.*"

"Zimmermann, I trust you are well. Do you feel up to some travel?"

"Of course, *Herr Generaloberst*. Where might that be?"

"Zimmermann, you and I are going to the Messerschmitt aircraft factory at Augsburg. Be at *Tempelhof* not later than 0700 tomorrow morning. Don't be late. You will find me in the operations room. I'll brief you then." With a click, the *Generaloberst* hung up, leaving Zimmermann to wonder all night about the strange call and the apparent secret visit to a Messerschmitt factory in Augsburg, near Munich.

After an uneventful flight from Berlin, the *Generaloberst*, Zimmermann, and two staff officers arrived at the factory where a production manager led them to a large hanger guarded by several black-uniformed *SS* men. Inside, the manager flicked a light switch and hundreds of bright spotlights came on revealing a giant aircraft painted all black. Zimmermann's pupils grew bigger and bigger. He gazed in wonder at the airplane, the largest he had ever seen. Frozen in amazement, he simply stared at the machine with his arms hanging limp by his side. At this point he saw in his peripheral vision *Major* Pieper, grinning like the cat that ate the canary. He turned toward his copilot.

"Well, Hans. What have we here? What do we have here?"

Pieper grinned broadly. "*Herr Generalmajor*, here we have the instrument of our victory. This is the new Me 264 heavy bomber. Isn't she magnificent!"

Krause broke in. "Have a look. Go, have a good look at your new chariot."

Both officers walked hurriedly over to the new airplane. For the next two hours, they meticulously examined every aspect of the giant aircraft. They inspected every nook and cranny. They kicked the tires and played with the flight controls. Like two children with a new toy on Christmas morning, they were overcome with joy and curiosity. How did it work? What was this? Who operates that? Questions flowed from the two men and poured out to the Messerschmitt engineers who followed them about until all were simply worn down and exhausted.

The Messerschmitt Me 264 had been in the works for months, but Zimmermann's after- action report detailing the inadequacies of the excellent but limited He 177 as the atomic delivery vehicle prompted the Air Ministry to accelerate the development program. As the two poured over every detail of the aircraft, two engineers answered every question shot at them, often in rapid-fire succession, with great accuracy and authority.

The airplane's design originated in the late 1930s, but this model, known as the V1, represented the first flyable prototype. This plane was the Messerschmitt Company's entry into the *Amerikabomber* program, initiated in spring 1942. Even though the United States had been frozen out of the war by the Japanese recall of the *Kido Butai* Mobile Strike Force before it could unleash an air assault on Hawai'i— and more recently by the strike against Britain with the resultant armistice—Hitler demanded a multi-engine heavy bomber that could attack New York from bases in France. The *Amerikabomber* program sought to develop a heavy four-engine bomber with the range to reach North America, drop a significant bomb load, and return to base safely. Both Heinkel, with the prototype He 274, and Messerschmitt, with the Me 264, competed for the contract. Messerschmitt offered the Me 264, an all-metal, high-wing, four-engine heavy bomber. Powered by the Junkers Jumo 211 inverted V12 engines, the plane could zip along at a maximum speed of 546 km/h or 339 mph. The cruising speed was set at 348 km/h or 217 mph. With an operational range of 15,000 kilometers, or 9,300 miles, she could reach, bomb, and return from any target in Europe or the North American east coast. Although there remained some design features to be worked on, the prototype in the hangar that Zimmermann and Pieper now inspected was essentially combat ready. It could fly higher, faster, and longer than anything either pilot had ever flown before.

Zimmermann was particularly interested in the service ceiling. The engineers proudly responded—26,250 feet. That figure somewhat disturbed Zimmermann. Since the scientists advertised that the minimum safe altitude lay at about 25,000 feet, the figure given did not represent much leeway. If tasked to drop another bomb, they must reach maximum altitude well before the release so that a rapid bank to port or starboard would carry them safely away from the blast while the bomb descended. The crew chief had even recommended attaching parachutes to the device so as to slow its descent and allow more getaway time. Since the newest Yak-9 Soviet fighter could climb to 36,000 feet and then dive on the bomber, this aspect represented a potentially grave problem. They would still need maximum fighter cover for mission success. Still, they would work with what they had and make the most of it. Crewed by eight men and with an armament of four 13mm MG 131 machine guns and two 20mm 151/20 cannons mounted in remotely operated turrets and along the fuselage sides, the plane could make for a bad day for any Soviet fighter pilot bold enough to approach too close. Most significantly, the plane could carry 6,000 kg or 13,200 pounds of ordnance in the internal bomb bay at 8,600 km or 5,343 miles, more than enough range to reach any desired Soviet target or even major British cities should the UK violate the armistice agreement. To accommodate the eight-man crew on long missions, the plane even had mounted bunk beds and a small galley with hot plates.

"How do you like your new airplane?" asked Krause like a proud father presenting an extravagant gift to a favored son.

"I believe she will do," responded Zimmermann. "Is she ready for trials, *Herr Generaloberst*?" Krause shook his head yes.

"The chief designer and engineer tell me she is ready to fly. Your crew has been ordered to arrive in the next few days, and you may take her up."

At that point, a staff officer ran up to Krause and whispered in his ear as he shook his head in acknowledgment. "Gentlemen, you will excuse me for now. There is an urgent call in the office I must attend to. Please, continue examining the airplane as you wish."

"*Danke, Herr Generaloberst. Danke*," responded Zimmermann.

As the two pilots strolled back over to check out the plane again, Pieper turned to Zimmermann and asked, "*Herr Generalmajor*, she must have a name. What do you think, sir?"

Zimmermann stood staring at the monstrous aircraft, folded his arms across his chest, and beamed. "Hans, she will be called *Der Lindenbaum*—The Linden Tree."

CHAPTER 7

Bodyguard of Lies

Augsburg, Germany, Messerschmitt Factory, 12 July 1943
The crew stood silently as the giant aircraft rolled slowly out of the hanger. Like a new parent, Messerschmitt engineers and ground crew fussed and fawned over their creation. They had checked, double-checked, and rechecked again all systems since before dawn; now the time had come for the crew to board The Linden Tree for her maiden flight with a fully military crew. The Messerschmitt flight test pilots had taken her aloft several times; all systems operated smoothly and normal. But, as with all new systems, the real test lay in the hands of the actual operators.

Zimmermann stood off at a distance. Some of the crew whispered among themselves as they watched the plane role into place. Bigger and more complex than their previous He 177, it required more crewmen. Two new men, both experienced bomber veterans, had been added. In addition to Zimmermann and Pieper, *Oberleutnant* Fischer returned as navigator as did the crew chief, *Stabsfeldwebel* Weber. Four gunners manned the remotely and locally operated machine guns and 20mm cannons. Instead of the bombing officer, Zwilling filled that role.

As he looked over the crew, Zimmermann noticed that Zwilling seemed thinner and paler than normal. Known to be a nervous type anyway, Zimmermann assumed that the excitement and tension of the moment caused the physicist some distress. Still, like a mother hen, he would keep an eye on the nervous physicist and made a mental note to order the man to see the flight surgeon for a complete physical. But, for today, all those thoughts could wait for another time. The crew prepared to board their new chariot.

"You lot, over here! Line up for the photograph. Step lively, Wisniewski. You laggard!" shouted the crew chief, playing the role of senior man ever so well. The crew laughed as they jostled each other into position for the photograph.

It is an axiom among military of all nations that when a new ship, plane, or installation is about to be put into service for the first time, the crew gathers together for photographs to memorialize the event. For nautical men, these first crewmen are known as "plank owners." The same applies to airmen—they are all proud "plank owners."

The men gathered around the aircraft's nose. Bright sunlight glinted off the glass panes of the forward area—the cockpit and flight deck. The photographer shouted out, "*Bitte, bitte.* Move to your left. I have glare in my lens. *Bitte.*" The men shifted into new position. "*Wunderbar!*" the photographer shouted as he hid again under the black cloth hood that shielded his camera.

Zimmermann looked up at the area just aft of the cockpit windows. Painted in silver was *Der Lindenbaum*—The Linden Tree—the aircraft's name he chose to honor his home. Under the letters was painted an armorial bearing, a dark blue shield with a growling bear rampant painted gold, appearing as if about to strike a foe. In silver, under the bear, appeared three trees of a nondescript type, which captured the forest aspect of the Zimmermann family, who had begun as foresters and huntsmen; they had never forgotten their attachment to the forest. He approved.

One of the new gunners with a particularly talented artistic bent painted the shield. Paintings under a plane's cockpit were known as "nose art" to American aviators and tended to be more risqué and sexual. For the *Luftwaffe*, they tended toward the more formal. As with the submariners who painted some heraldic device associated with their commanding officer on the boat's conning tower, the bombers did the same for their pilot.

"And smile, my brave aviators!" shouted the photographer as he took several more photographs. Once developed, the best one would hang in a place of honor in the crew mess. In some ways it represented a grim reminder of men and aircraft lost either in training accidents or combat. In mounting the crew pictures taken alongside their aircraft, they were never lost, never forgotten, always remembered, and cherished by their comrades. So it was with aviators of every nation.

The crew clambered aboard and strapped in for takeoff as Zimmermann and Pieper methodically conducted pre-flight checks. Flap and aileron controls. Check. Oil pressure. Check. Electrical. Check. Communications with flight control. Check. On and on until the list was completed. Remotely operated turrets. Check. Navigation instruments operating normal. Check. Finally, all checked out satisfactory. "Ready for takeoff," Zimmermann radioed to the tower.

"You are cleared for takeoff on runway 240 Left, *Herr Generalmajor*. Good luck and good hunting."

Zimmermann turned to Pieper. "Hans, I believe she is ready to fly."

"*Jawohl, Herr Generalmajor*. She is ready to soar!"

With that, Pieper flipped four switches on the control panel above their heads. One by one, the huge Jumo 211 engines coughed, sputtered, then caught, throwing off clouds of grayish-blue smoke. Within seconds, all four engines hummed with power as the rpms revved up. Both men placed hands on the throttle controls located in the center panel set between the two pilots' seats and, on Zimmermann's signal, slowly pushed them forward. As the engines spun up, Zimmermann gave the signal to the ground crew, who raced in and pulled out the wheel chocks. Now unlimbered, the plane slowly edged forward as the pilots pushed the throttle toward the mark for takeoff speed.

Picking up momentum, she moved away from the hanger and onto the runway edge. Zimmermann turned the yoke, and the big plane responded easily and gracefully. With just a nod to Pieper, both pilots pushed the throttle forward. The engines roared louder, propellers spinning faster and faster. Slowly, slowly, then picking up speed, the bomber roared down the runway, gaining forward momentum with each second.

"Velocity 1," called out Pieper as the airspeed reached 60 k/h. Seconds later, he called out again, "Velocity 2."

With that, Zimmermann responded, "Rotate," as he eased the yoke back toward his abdomen. The flaps cut into the wind, creating aerodynamic lift. The plane slowly rose up over the tarmac, then, as Zimmermann pulled back the yoke all the way, the nose rose up into a sharper and sharper angle. Airborne!

"Gear up," ordered Zimmermann. Pieper reached over to the landing gear control. A whirring sound filled the cockpit as the automatic hydraulic system pulled in the tricycle landing gear. The Linden Tree soared off into the bright, sunlit Bavarian sky, the first of many flights to come that summer and a complete success.

* * * * * * * *

Speyer, Germany, 4 September 1943

Zimmermann and AGATHA strolled along the main street of Speyer, a picturesque city along the Middle Rhine River. Although they had been together constantly for several weeks, neither had taken any steps toward a sexual or physical relationship. To this point, though tempted mightily, they avoided such a relationship for opposite reasons, each valid.

For Zimmermann, he was laser focused on training his crew and preparing them for what he expected for their next mission. The massive assault by joint German air and ground forces to crush the Soviet Red Army in the salient that developed around the city of Kursk resulted in the largest, most deadly armor battle of the war. German forces of *Generaloberst* Walter Model's 9th Army pressed down from the north while those of Army Group South, under *Generalfeldmarschall* Erich von Manstein, assaulted in the south. Neither offensive yielded more than a few miles of ground gained. Massive German casualties resulted. The *Wehrmacht* lost a huge percentage of their operational tanks, many to Soviet aircraft. The IL-2 *Sturmovik* proved especially effective as a ground attack fighter-bomber, especially against plodding, slow-moving *panzers*. Carnage ensued. The offensive failed, and within a few days OPERATION CITADEL was canceled. German forces withdrew to recover, rest, and refit while the Soviets prepared to go on the offensive. Marshal Giorgi Zhukov had done a masterful job of preparing the Kursk defenses. Local citizens turned out by the thousands to dig tank traps and build fortifications. Hundreds of thousands of Red Army reinforcements moved into position. What had been designed by the German General Staff to crush the Red Army and restore the German offensive initiative instead turned into German tactical, operational, and strategic disaster. The *Luftwaffe* lost hundreds of aircraft. *Wehrmacht* casualties topped 50,000 men and, critically, over 300 tanks and assault guns in the six-week long series of attacks and counterattacks that summer. Germany now faced a crisis. With a second bomb nearing completion and operational capability, Zimmermann knew that unleashing the weapon on the Soviets could not be far away for him and the crew of The Linden Tree. It was in this frame of mind that that he gave the crew a much-needed 14-day leave after weeks of intensive training and familiarization flying. Perhaps he needed the break most of all.

He had spent time with AGATHA as much as the operational schedule allowed. Not only did they frequent the *Edelweiss* regularly, but with the wonderfully warm and sunny Berlin summer devoid of air attacks for the first time in years, they spent as much time as possible walking through the *Tiergarten* or boating in the city's lakes.

Despite his frequent trips to the factory in Augsburg, they still made time for each other. They attended the occasional social event but mostly stayed to themselves. Zimmermann did not particularly enjoy such soirées and AGATHA had to be alert to public missteps that might unmask her identity or compromise the mission. Spending so much time in Berlin was hazardous, but she needed to maintain her cover as a Swiss socialite enjoying the city's delights, and since Zimmermann's main office was at *Luftwaffe* headquarters, she needed to be in town when he operated from his office.

Meantime, CHRISTIE maintained his overwatch, never getting too close and avoiding detection at all cost. When asked about what had happened to her business manager who had arrived with her from Bern, she simply replied that he was still in the city managing her business affairs and that was that. They occasionally met at an out-of-the-way restaurant to maintain the cover that he saw to her business and financial affairs and periodically consulted in person with his client. Meanwhile, they employed a dead-drop system to communicate sensitive information needing passing to London via Niven and INTREPID. To also maintain the cover, she spoke regularly with CHRISTIE from her hotel suite phone fully expecting that the *Reich* security services kept a close watch on her, including tapping the phone. She was not wrong. Maas kept a constant watch on her and the couple and most days listened in on her phone conversations, but the troll was careless. While he may have been the consummate thug and enforcer, he had few skills as a clandestine operative. AGATHA detected him the first day. Amateurish acts such as turning his head away too quickly or walking too close behind and then making a sharp turn to avoid a direct confrontation gave away his presence. Because of his clumsiness and lack of any sort of capability for his new watcher role, it was quite easy for AGATHA to arrange liaisons with Zimmermann or contact CHRISTIE, leaving Maas frustrated. In truth, it had become a sort of game with AGATHA and CHRISTIE, but it was a decidedly delicate and deadly game as Maas became more and more furious and enraged that he could not detect any hint of espionage on her part.

It was in this environment that AGATHA found herself falling into a trap. Zimmermann was the target. She had to play the part—if not yet a lover, at least a friend and close companion. And yet, as each balmy summer day passed, she found herself becoming ever more attracted to the tall, stately, stoic, virile warrior-aristocrat. She resisted all temptation to carry the relationship further. That mistake could compromise the mission and lead to grave danger, possibly death. She fought the urge to become closer every time they were together. CHRISTIE noticed her dilemma and cautioned her to be ever more careful. Still, she struggled to maintain enough distance to avoid mission compromise yet still extract information. Although he had not revealed any secrets as to the atomic issue, he was quite talkative about the new airplane—too open in fact—a surprising dynamic considering that Zimmermann knew the importance of maintaining military secrecy, Every time he let out some new fact, even if just a routine "how was your day" type of detail, that information soon made its way to London. Even though Zimmermann never discussed the actual operational capabilities such as speed, ceiling, and so on, the intelligence analysts at MI6 soon had a good picture of the new heavy bomber, its capabilities, and its limitations. They collated the details provided by AGATHA with those from agents that worked in the Messerschmitt Company itself to derive a fairly accurate picture. But the golden fleece of intelligence—details of the German atomic program—still eluded AGATHA. She realized that she must ratchet up the pressure.

For Zimmermann, a different dynamic caused his reticence to give his heart completely to this incredible woman. Yes, there was still the devotion to Ingrid always playing in his thoughts, *but hadn't enough time passed? And had not sufficient mourning been carried out? Did he not deserve some new happiness to counter the horrors of war and loneliness of the past four years?* However much he tried to reconcile the dilemma, one overarching imperative remained. He was perhaps the most critical man in the Fatherland's military at that moment. He had delivered the killing weapon on the British. In all likelihood, he would soon deliver the killing weapon to the hated Soviets as well. Despite his growing feelings, perhaps even love for AGATHA, he had to keep in mind always that overriding imperative—*the mission, the mission, the mission; the mission must be paramount!*

Sometimes the folly of the heart overshadows the sensibility of the head. That is exactly what overcame both Zimmermann and AGATHA as summer's end approached. And that is what brought them to this lovely medieval city on the Middle Rhine—Speyer. *Generaloberst* Kline, in addition to his flying, which he rarely did anymore, was a keen sailor and yachtsman. In the early 1930s, he acquired a yacht, a beautifully crafted boat built 30 years earlier for a Scottish industrialist that had been through several owners over the years. Kline purchased it for perhaps more than it was worth in 1934 from a close friend, a Jewish businessman, who foresaw the future trend and emigrated to Canada. His friend was happy to find a good owner and Kline was more than thrilled with the new toy as well as helping a close friend.

Kline maintained the yacht in top order. Woodwork highly varnished, brass bright, kept shiny and polished on a daily basis, and the teak deck scrubbed down daily all meant a stunningly beautiful craft. The engines had been recently overhauled, and new instruments, especially communications and navigation, had been installed. The crew, expert to a man, all served in the *Kaiser's* Imperial Navy. The master had commanded a destroyer in the Great War and was decorated for his actions at the Battle of Jutland in 1916. Kline graciously offered Zimmermann the yacht for a Rhine cruise holiday. The older man saw the exhaustion and strain on the younger Zimmermann, and a river cruise in a luxurious yacht with a beautiful companion seemed the perfect tonic.

Zimmermann waffled at first, arguing, "*Herr Generaloberst,* I must not let our mission falter. I must—" He really couldn't turn down the offer. As dedicated a professional as he was, he finally realized that his leadership and military effectiveness would soon be compromised if he did not take some definitive action. After two days of pondering the dilemma, he relented and agreed to a two-week leave highlighted by a Rhine River cruise. For AGATHA, although she sensed danger in agreeing to the trip, her heart won out. In truth, she could see some possibility of attaining valuable intelligence in the more relaxed environment of a romantic Rhine getaway. She acquiesced.

The couple strolled down *Maximillian Strasse,* the broad avenue that formed the central street leading from the cathedral to the medieval portal. The city dated from 10 BC when the Romans first established the site as a military camp. Many Rhine west bank towns and cities started in this way. Most of the buildings dated from the early eighteenth century.

Much of Speyer had been devastated in the wars with Louis XIV's France in the late seventeenth century as he attempted to add the German Rhineland/Palatinate to his domain as did the later Emperor of France, Napoleon I. Alliances anchored by Great Britain under William III and Queen Mary, the Dutch, and a coalition of German states eventually pushed back the French invaders. The city again came under French domination until the final defeat of *l'empereur Napoléon.* The French invasion caused considerable damage in 1689 as it also did to Heidelberg and other cities along the Rhine. In place of the damaged homes and businesses, the industrious burghers and citizens rebuilt and created a magnificent array of architectural beauties. Zimmermann always loved Speyer and the Rhineland, so this city as a starting point for their cruise had great appeal.

At the eastern side of the city stood the magnificent Romanesque-style Cathedral of Speyer. Germany had many such beautiful churches and cathedrals, but the Speyer one always appealed to him. As he and AGATHA strolled through the various parts of the building, he realized that as wondrous as the building was, he was spending far more time staring at AGATHA. She detected his attention, but tried to if not ignore it, at least not react. It was damned near impossible. She wanted in the worst way to reach out and take his hand. The only thing that stopped her was that this man, gentle and kind though he may be, was the enemy . . . and an enemy to be defeated. At that moment, a dangerous thought crept into her subconscious although she would not yet acknowledge it. *What about after the war? What about when Germany is defeated and peace restored? What then?*

They exited the cathedral and then slowly ambled down the street lined with shops and family-run cafés. Stopping at one particularly attractive café, they ordered the usual. He had a coffee black and she had tea. Not the dreaded chamomile, though. She had many weeks back given up on that aberration. No, she had regular Ceylon black tea. With the British blockade lifted, such a treat was now readily available throughout much of Germany and certainly along the Rhine. Ships of neutral states brought in the cargoes to Dutch ports; it then came down the Rhine on cargo barges.

As she sipped her tea, looking over the delicate cup's rim as the steam rose from the delightful liquid, a thought struck her. Peace does have its positive points. But then the image of hundreds of thousands of men, women, and children disintegrating in an angry cloud of flame and dust flashed through her thoughts. She too had seen the photographs from Dartmoor, pictures of nothing but dust and rubble. Those images drove her on with the mission and her charge to extract from this man across the table as much intelligence as possible, intelligence that might bring him and his country down. *Still. . . .*

The cafe was striking. The exterior walls painted a dark rose color, the *Altpörtel Café* sat next to the medieval tower, the Old Gate, or *Altpörtel*, standing several stories high. A huge clock face in the tower situated high above the open plaza below struck the time. Part of the old city walls, the *Altpörtel* survived the French and anchored a lovely plaza where children played and couples dreamed of a real peace. Both were struck by the café's architecture. Built on four floors with three giant windows on the first floor to three windows then to two on the next floor and finally a single window on the top floor, the building reminded AGATHA of a wedding cake built layer upon layer with dark pink icing all around and an ivory-beige icing adornment. She wondered if that had been the architect's concept. *No matter. It's a pretty and striking building all the same.*

As the waitress arrived with their order, AGATHA gazed at the paintings adorning the walls. Mostly landscapes and pastoral scenes, they captured a more peaceful time before the world went insane. Would that they could just drift back into a painting of a more serene era. Given how relaxed she was at that moment, she made what might have been a fatal mistake.

"This café reminds me ever so much of the Crown and Anchor," she blurted out. *Alarm! Alarm! Alarm! Had she just revealed herself?*

"The Crown and Anchor?" responded Zimmermann quizzically.

She blanched. *Did Zimmermann see it? What have I done?* She squirmed in her seat nervously.

"That sounds like a British pub? Something from your past, I presume."

She tensed. *Strike now before the situation deteriorates!* "*Ja,* it is. It is no secret that my late husband chose to oppose National Socialism and died fighting in the RAF." She paused. She knew full well that he already knew that fact but reasoned that she needed to reinforce it. "I disagreed, vehemently as you know, but he was . . . well . . . truthfully, he was too stubborn and it cost him his life." She paused to gauge his reaction. Surprisingly, she saw no real reaction. *Perhaps just his notable stone-faced stoicism, but then . . .?* She continued, "That aside, when we lived in and around London, we often traveled into the city even during the air battle three years ago. Many shops and establishments closed up as one might expect, but there was one pub near Leicester Square that we particularly liked. That was the Crown and Anchor. Please understand, Peter, that that is in my past and has no impact on us now." She paused again—no real reaction.

"The Crown and Anchor in London, then? And this place reminds you of it?"

"*Ja,* Peter, it does. The Crown and Anchor had a nice pastoral feel just as does this lovely café."

Zimmermann looked directly into her eyes. "Amelia, Baroness Ramsour-Fritsch. I completely understand your past and do not really care for the details. I am more interested in now . . . and the future." There was a wistful, almost longing tone to the last statement. "Perhaps now that the war with Britain is over and once we win the struggle with the communists, we can both travel to London and you can show me this delightful pub called the Crown and Anchor just off Leicester Square." He took a sip of coffee. His look told her that she had not revealed herself as a British agent. But she must be ever vigilant.

As they sat silently sipping coffee and tea, enjoying some wonderful Bavarian pastry and reveling in the happy moment, she remembered a caution. Churchill had stated that "In wartime, truth is so precious that she should always be attended by a bodyguard of lies."[5] Vigilance and caution must be ever present. She had apparently survived this gross misstep. She could make no more such mistakes. The mission must succeed.

Their drinks and pastries finished, they strolled back to the yacht anchored at the docks just beyond the cathedral. That afternoon, they got underway, heading down river. Along the way they passed magnificent castles on either side. Built high on the cliffs overlooking the river, these bastions of the feudal lords that ruled the region lent an almost fairy-tale quality to the journey. Although many castles stood vacant and in some state of ruin, many were not.

The next day, late in the afternoon, Zimmermann and AGATHA both lounged on deck soaking in the delicious sunshine. Not quite awake nor quite asleep, AGATHA dreamily watched the beautiful

---

5 Plan Jael was the operational deception concept to make German authorities think the Allied invasion would be delayed for a year and that strategic bombing and Balkans operations would be the major Allied focus in 1944. The objective was to deceive Germany as to the invasion plans for France that eventually resulted in OPERATION NEPTUNE, the Normandy invasion (6 June 1944). At the Tehran Conference in late November 1943, Churchill made the statement on the necessity of operational deception. Plan Jael's name was then changed to OPERATION BODYGUARD. The phrase is so illustrative and so perfectly captures AGATHA and CHRISTIE's mission that it had to be used here! For details, I recommend the somewhat flawed but still excellent book *Bodyguard of Lies* by Anthony Cave Brown (London and New York: Harper & Row, 1975).

villages go by. The yacht began a gradual turn to port. Zimmermann sprang up in his chair and beckoned to AGATHA in that "come here quick" sort of motion. They were passing the Lorelei, the giant rock that jutted out into the river forcing the water to bend around in a wide curve.

"The Lorelei. What is the legend? Aah, yes, the maiden of the rock called out to the boatmen. Her song was so sweet that the sailors forgot all prudence, lost their wits, and crashed right into the cliffs. A sad tale, don't you think?" he said, smiling. The irony struck her. *Was she not the maiden of the rock luring the sailor to his doom?* The image both intrigued and, for just a moment, frightened her.

Just beyond the Lorelei, they passed two castles of great interest. *Maus* Castle (Mouse Castle) and nearby *Katz* Castle (Cats Castle). AGATHA laughed at the joke. Looking up at *Katz* Castle through a powerful set of binoculars, she noted a lot of activity that appeared to be military. Several vehicles—staff cars, some *Kübelwagen*, and other military transports and armored personnel carriers—were parked about the building. On the ramparts, she noted several armed sentries.

"That's quite interesting," she said as she handed the binoculars to Zimmermann. As he gazed through the powerful glasses, he turned pale and stiffened. *Most curious,* she thought to herself. "Are you not well, Peter? You've suddenly turned very pale and ashen."

He dropped the glasses to his chest and turned toward her with a look of anger she had never seen in him before. After a brief moment, he closed his eyes and color returned to his face. He turned back and gazed up at *Katz* Castle. Gripping the railing, he stood frozen for several moments without speaking. She just stood beside him, pretending to not notice his strange reaction and deeply troubled state of mind.

As the yacht proceeded on and *Katz* Castle receded in the distance, the steward finally broke the awkward silence. He appeared out of the salon, a proud smile on his cherubic face. "*Meine Herrschaften,* dinner is served." He bowed and stepped back into the salon.

Zimmermann turned to AGATHA and placed his hands on her shoulders. He stared into her ocean-blue eyes. She had never seen him so serious. "Amelia, we shall never again speak of *Katz* Castle." With that, they both turned and proceeded into the salon.

The salon was her favorite room of all. The highly polished light oak paneling reflected the candlelight from the brass wall sconces and crystal chandelier above the mahogany table. Deep red damask curtains covered the windows, giving the room a warm, cheery glow. A Persian carpet covering the entire floor gave it an earthy and friendly feel. The cook had done a masterful job. Noted for his skill with minimal ingredients, a dynamic typical in wartime, he had nonetheless created an amazing goulash with roasted potatoes and topped it off with a variety of pastries that rivaled the best of Paris. It was a simple meal and Zimmermann's favorite—goulash, *spaetzle*, and roasted potatoes—a magnificent feast. Afterward, they went out on deck. A cool breeze blew over them. Zimmermann took off his jacket and draped it over her shoulders. It was a wonderful night.

* * * * * * **

Der Gevatter Tod, East Prussia, 5 September 1943

Kwiatkowski and Mowak passed through the screening with ease. Despite the tremendous security arrangements at the atomic test and research site, the two Poles obtained access thanks to a superb forger in London, who, in exchange for a commutation of his sentence for blackmail, counterfeiting, and other crimes against His Majesty's kingdom, agreed to work for SOE supplying fake identity credentials. Both men now carried papers identifying them as Heinz Maurer and Johann Schilling, both medically discharged from the *Wehrmacht*, having served in Poland, France, and the Soviet Union. Both men spoke excellent and dialectically correct German and were thus able to pass themselves off as army veterans. More importantly, London provided them with special identity papers that cleared them for work at installations such as *Der Gevatter Tod* as first-class electricians. The papers allowed them access to the support facilities such as the barracks, mess halls, infirmary, and so on, but not to the research labs or the test site itself. Still, it was hoped that they could glean some vital information on the site. London had decided to risk the two Poles after they photographed the atomic test and managed to smuggle the photos to MI6. Thus, there were actually two intelligence operations working simultaneously—AGATHA and CHRISTIE in Berlin with Zimmermann and Kwiatkowski and Mowak at the research site.

Their assignment that day meant installing a new lighting system in Mess Hall A, where the SS guards took their meals and congregated in their off hours. The fact that the SS and regular army represented two distinct entities meant that the danger of one of the SS men asking "do you know" and thus suspecting the two Poles as not genuine was minimized. The unit the two men supposedly belonged to had been part of the German 6th Army, which had been wiped out or captured at Stalingrad. The cover story was that the two were wounded and medically evacuated earlier, before the Soviets closed the ring. This ruse reduced the likelihood that some veteran would discern that the Poles were phonies—or so it was hoped. The two men understood the danger, but agreed to go into the devil's lair nonetheless.

With all checkpoints successfully passed, they proceeded to the outside worker marshaling point. Once again, guards checked their credentials and, satisfied, ordered the dozen or so workers onto a waiting truck, which took them to the barracks compound. Along the way, they noted the vault-like entrance to the laboratory area. Both men were well trained in explosives, and when they sighted the heavy reinforced steel doors set into a solid concrete base leading down to underground rooms, their spirits sank. Kwiatkowski, as slyly as possible, looked over at Mowak and very slowly and unobtrusively shook his head as if to say "No go, mate. There is no way we could blast through that." Mowak got the message and acknowledged with two eye blinks, the pre-arranged a signal for "Yes, I understand."

Despite the realization that an assault on the laboratory and test facilities was not on, they decided to gather as much intelligence as possible on the support facility. They arrived at the barracks compound and went straight to work on the mess-hall lights. The plan called for chatting up the SS men in hopes they could obtain some actionable intelligence. They did. As it happened, one particularly friendly and talkative SS man became far too loose. It seems he had been cajoled into enlisting in the *Waffen SS* by his cousin, who had joined earlier. He would have much preferred to enlist in a regular army unit, but so be it, there he was. Once Kwiatkowski and Mowak realized they had their mark, they played the game. One would think they were all long lost friends after a few hours of conversation.

Two important things resulted from their time in the mess hall that morning. First, they had a fairly accurate idea of where the key scientists, technicians, and most important personnel lived when not actually in the highly protected laboratory compound. Second, the SS barracks Mess Hall A now had a superior new lighting system. That evening, both men discussed the next step in the operation over a fine meal of sausages, noodles, black bread, and pilsner at their local guesthouse. They were more than welcome as veterans of the Eastern Front. The locals had no clue that they welcomed into their company two top Polish SOE agents posing as *Wehrmacht* veterans.

Over the next few weeks, they visited *Der Gevatter Tod* several times, doing electrical work at various parts of the installation. In so doing, they identified vulnerabilities in the security system that could be exploited. They particularly noted a weakness in the security fence roughly a half mile from the barracks compound that housed the key scientists and technicians. They discovered that they could likely break through the fence unchallenged and surreptitiously make their way to the compound through the dense forest with little fear of discovery. This then would be the vulnerability to exploit and their axis of attack.

By the fourth week, they discovered other key weaknesses. Another overly talkative SS guard, who was having a liaison with a female technician working inside the laboratory compound, revealed that a single generating plant located nearby supplied the entire electrical power system, but it was not in the highly protected laboratory compound. Because it operated as a coal-fired generator, it had to be above ground. That singular vulnerability might be the way to, if not shut down the place, at least slow the weapons development and manufacture, thus allowing more time for the British to nullify the German program or for the Americans to develop a working weapon.

It was a dicey proposition at best but a necessary risk. If Germany developed an inventory of working bombs, they could threaten so much of the world that there could be no resistance. Therefore, delay, delay, delay became the watchword. If a direct attack on the production facilities, especially the equipment that refined U238 uranium into weapons grade U235 could not be mounted, then an attack on the support facilities might be the answer. A key had to be plausible deniability. Certainly, the RAF could carpet bomb the facility, but to what end? That action would simply restart the war with the likelihood of atomic attack on London and other British cities. Any ground attack had to have a misdirect component. What if it could be blamed on the Soviets? No one wanted to enmesh the former ally in a false conspiracy operation knowing full well the likely reaction. On the other hand, MI6 learned courtesy of CHARLEMAGNE that there were no bombs ready for deployment, but once the first one reached combat readiness, the target was either Leningrad or Moscow.

Always wary of sending too much vital intelligence to the enemy, CHARLEMAGNE avoided letting out anything that might cause Germany's defeat. Rather, he provided just enough to the British to check German plans or operations, but never enough to completely defeat them. Thus, the vital location and number of devices had to be determined by other means, which meant AGATHA through her budding liaison with *Generalmajor* Peter von Zimmermann.

With all the factors in mind, a decision was made—take out the electrical grid that supported the laboratories and manufacturing facilities at *Der Gevatter Tod* and blame the Soviets. The second part of the plan was equally perilous but vital. To seriously delay or disrupt the German atomic program, a concurrent step meant capturing or killing or somehow removing the key scientists and technicians. With the war in the east turning against Germany, the British operational planners led by INTREPID in New York and at Camp X hoped that the Soviets could cripple Germany before they could restart the program or complete any bombs already in production. It truly was a "wing and a prayer." But everyone in London understood that though there existed an armistice at the moment, once Hitler crushed the Soviet Union under atomic attack, there would be no stopping his aggression; the British Empire lay squarely in his sights. Therefore, a delaying attack on *Der Gevatter Tod* had to be risked, and the two men on the ground, Kwiatkowski and Mowak, represented the best hope.

A second aspect of the plan—removing the key players—involved AGATHA and CHRISTIE. The linchpin to the entire operation was Zimmermann. He was the one man above all that might supply the vital intelligence needed to neutralize the personnel aspect. Other key players such as *Generaloberst* Krause might have better knowledge of where vital laboratories and personnel were located, but there was no way to get at them. No, Zimmermann was the critical vulnerability and it was up to AGATHA to somehow wheedle the information out of him.

* * * * * * * *

Berlin, 17 September 1943

The cruise on the Rhine had been extraordinary—thrilling and wonderful. AGATHA saw a complete change in Zimmermann's demeanor. He relaxed completely . . . as if the war caused no cares or worries at all. Other than the tension as they passed *Katz* Castle, he had been calm and gracious for the entire trip. The food was outstanding. The fairy-tale scenery of the Middle Rhine was stunning and the yacht, magnificent. They stopped at town after town along the river, traveling in very slow stages.

At Koblenz, they turned on to the Mosel River and traveled through wine country. On the hillsides rising up from the river below grew row after row of grape vines—mostly the *Riesling* variety, which produced the white Rhine wine. AGATHA was amazed at how the vineyards operated at such steep angles with no terracing as often seen in mountainous agriculture. She wondered if the vineyard workers, mostly Eastern Europeans brought in especially for the harvest season, suffered from one leg shorter than the other. *Hazard of the job*, she suspected.

They reached Trier, the ancient city founded by the Romans centuries earlier, then sailed back down the Mosel to Koblenz, where the two rivers joined. From there they returned to Berlin.

The following day, Zimmermann reported back to Augsburg for another round of training flights with The Linden Tree crew. That night, a solitary lady strolled by a particular bench in a specific park. She sat after ensuring that no one was close enough to observe her actions, especially her regular watcher, the bumbling and indiscreet Johann Maas. Still, she needed to create a deception. Pigeons clustered about her feet in hopes of a handout. *Excellent! Thank you, birds, for your marvelous camouflage.* She had brought seed and scattered that about as more and more pigeons raced in to grab their share. Fluttering about, pecking at the ground and the thousands of seeds, the birds created a swirl of motion that masked her next action. Pretending to lean forward so as to toss some more seed to a group of pigeons gathering around her feet, she swiftly reached under the bench and placed a small wooden container on the underside of a bench slat. The motion occurred so quickly that the watcher hidden behind some bushes across the roadway never detected the deft movements. He didn't understand why this woman was so fascinated with the pigeons. They were only good for eating, and that, just barely. Yet every few evenings, here she went and sat on the same bench in the same park feeding the same pigeons. *Damn this woman!* He ought to be home feeding himself just now, not watching some damned aristocrat feeding the damned birds. Maas never, in all the times he trailed AGATHA to the park, figured out what she was about.

Hours later, a man in a black fedora wearing a dark nondescript raincoat with a drooping mustache sat on the same park bench. Looking about to ensure no one observed him, he reached under the bench and pulled out a small wooden box. Within hours, the cable went out from Zürich to New York with just a few words in a code unknown to the German cryptographers. It read: "Tisza is the key." In a moment of relaxation after far too much of the delicious *Liebfraumilch* wine on a warm evening as the two relaxed on the yacht's foredeck watching mile after mile of hillside vineyards pass by, Zimmermann made a mistake she had been waiting for. As he drifted off into a wine-induced stupor, he mumbled those four words and repeated them twice before finally nodding off: "Tisza is the key. Tisza is the key. Tisza is the key."

* * * * * * * *

Berlin, 19 September 1943

The phone rang. Reaching over to lift the handset from the cradle, she almost knocked over a water glass. *Mustn't be so clumsy.*

"*Ja?*"

"Amelia. There is a car waiting for you at the hotel entrance. Please be there in twenty minutes." Click. A moment of anxiety washed over her. *A car? Had he found her out? Was the game up?* She pondered what to do. He had always come for her personally or they met at some location such as a park, lake, restaurant, or the *Edelweiss* tearoom. And yet, there was no tension in his voice, despite the abruptness. *Twenty minutes.* She reached over to the side table, careful to avoid the water glass again. Opening her purse, she pulled out the Walther PPK, a small weapon, but with good stopping power. The perfect weapon for a ladies' handbag, it was light and easily concealed. She carried it always and, so as to not arouse suspicion, had shown it to Zimmermann. It just wouldn't do for a single lady to be out about town without some protection. He understood.

In truth, she carried the pistol more for protection against the *Gestapo* than any criminal assailant. Those people she could easily dispatch thanks to the excellent martial arts training at Camp X, particularly Fairbairn's *Defendu*. She put on slacks and low-heeled, flat shoes. Perhaps not as elegant as one would expect from such an aristocrat, it had a more practical purpose. Should trouble arise, she would be far more mobile in flats than in heels and in slacks as opposed to a dress. And, with the slacks, she could hide the Walther in a discreet ankle holster. Grabbing her handbag, she glanced in the mirror. *Good, all there. Onward to the fair!*

She recognized the driver—*Feldwebel* Holtzmann—Zimmermann's regular *Luftwaffe* driver. A nice young man, her worries of capture or confrontation instantly vanished.

"*Guten Morgen, Frau Baronin,*" said a chipper Holtzmann.

"*Guten Morgen*, Holtzmann. Lovely day is it not. And where might we be headed this fine morning?"

The airman grinned. "It is a surprise, Madame. A pleasant surprise. We are headed for Berlin-Staaken airfield. *Herr Generalmajor* will meet you there."

For the 40-minute drive to the airfield several kilometers northwest of the city, she engaged in a pleasant conversation with Holtzmann. She sensed no threat or tension at all. Still, the Walther PPK strapped to her ankle gave her some sense of security. They reached the airfield and, passing easily through the security checkpoint, drove out onto the tarmac and stopped finally by a Fieseler Fi 97 4-passenger monoplane where Zimmermann stood smiling. He reached out and opened the car door.

"Baroness, you look lovely today." They still practiced formality while in public so as to maintain the "close friend only" perception. They did not need the gossipers and wags chitchatting away about what they may or may not be about. "Let's fly, Baroness," he shouted above the noise of aircraft taking off and landing. The airfield was a hub of the *Luftwaffe* supply system and constantly active. Zimmermann chose to keep his private plane hangered and serviced there. "Come. Climb in," he said, extending a hand to ease her up and into the second seat next to the pilot's. He clicked on the ignition. With a wheeze, then a cough, then a roar, the engine revved up, pulling the plane forward. With a few words from the tower flight control, he was cleared as the plane picked up speed. It lifted off easily and gracefully; soon they zipped in and out of the puffy clouds hovering over the lush late-summer Brandenburg countryside.

Zimmermann, now completely in his comfort zone, traced a great arc in the sky, banking right and then left as he eased the yoke over. The plane began a graceful descent then leveled off.

"Would you like to try her?" he shouted over the engine noise and whistle of air passing over the sturdy wings.

"*Ja*, I would." It was one of the things she had never tried but clearly longed to experience. As with about everything else she attempted, she was adept. As he guided her through the steps, she grinned like a schoolgirl. Why she had never flown before she could not say, but here in the sky alone with Zimmermann and only the engine's hum, she felt completely at ease and relaxed.

* * * * * * * *

On landing, Zimmermann eased the plane toward the hanger. As the propeller spun then slowed to a stop, they stepped back out of the cabin. Zimmermann waved to Holtzmann, who had been patiently waiting with the Mercedes by the hanger. He turned to AGATHA and asked, "Tonight, we dine at Linden Hall. Are you ready to meet the family?"

A sudden chill made her shiver, though he did not notice. *The mission! The mission! Do not compromise the mission!* Asking one to meet the family represented a major new degree in a relationship. She knew why he had never asked her to Linden prior to this moment. What such a step meant she could not say, but as close as she believed herself to be loosening his secrets, this trip to the estate in the Brandenburg woods might result in finally solving some mysteries. She had already put bits and pieces together from a careless slip here or there. She tracked his movements, which allowed MI6 to gain tremendous insight into the German program. Although she had not seen it, his nonchalant small talk had given away many of the details of the new Me 264. Then there was the mysterious Tisza. "Tisza is the key." *What did it mean? Was he the key to understanding the German secrets?* But with all this, she still had not learned the most important intelligence of all—how many bombs did Germany have, where were they, and how could they be destroyed. Perhaps a trip to Linden Tree would be the answer. She would go. The mission now required it. She vowed that as often as possible, she would go flying with Zimmermann whenever he was back in Berlin from the training operations at Augsburg. She would learn how to fly herself. Not only did she enjoy flying, but that capability might play a vital role in her future.

* * * * * * * *

Linden Hall, Linden Tree Estate, Brandenburg, 19 September 1943

The Hall glowed warmth. The chilly early autumn wind could not dampen the place's spirit that night. They arrived about seven and the family greeted the couple in the Great Hall. His sisters Eva and Helga fairly fawned over her. Eva fired question after question at AGATHA, many to do with the world outside her cloistered existence in wartime Germany. *What was New York like? Did you see a show on Broadway? Was the Statue of Liberty really that tall? What about Zürich? What are the latest fashions in Switzerland these days? We see so little new fashion here!* On and on and on she fired question after question until finally the dowager baroness spoke up. "Eva.

Please allow the baroness to breathe, dear! My goodness." To all this, Zimmermann just grinned and said nothing.

After cocktails in the Great Hall, dinner was served in the family dining room. True to the eclectic nature of the place, which ranged from medieval castle to hunting lodge to seventeenth- and eighteenth-century ornate, the family dining room was totally different from the baroque Great Hall or the more elaborate rococo-style formal dining room where so many banquets had occurred in former times. In design, decor, and feel, the room retained the hunting lodge look of an earlier age. Rather than paintings of grand nobles in extravagant uniforms or ladies in ball gowns, the pictures represented pastoral life. Paintings of hunting dogs and sleeping cats, of farm animals and livestock, of game birds, of simple peasants harvesting the crops, and of woodlands and fields all adorned the walls. The furniture was simple—heavy oak, with the chair seats covered in a smooth, buttery-soft dark red leather. It had the feel of a true country house, one of the reasons Zimmermann loved the room so and why he refused to allow any changes to the décor.

The meal was excellent. Despite the war, there was still fine food to be had for the right price, and the Zimmermann family had the right amount. They feasted on a *Vesperplatte*, a simple platter of meats, cheeses, and rye bread followed by a delicious *sauerbraten* and finished off with a black forest torte. Practically everything except the wine came from the Linden Tree gardens and pastures. *It is the best meal I have ever had*, she thought as she took another bite of the wonderful torte. She had had fancier, more elaborate meals, but none as enjoyable. Afterward, Zimmermann took her for a tour of the house. She was actually surprised that they had been able to keep up the place despite the war and the shortages of men and material.

After the tour, more family conversation in the ladies' parlor ensued until well into the evening. Finally, the dowager baroness stood and exclaimed, "Peter, it's late and we all need a rest. Come girls, let's leave our two guests. I expect we will see you at breakfast, will we not? We serve at nine sharp. Don't be late. Heinz will be terribly disappointed if you are late." All laughed.

"Not to worry, mother. We will be there," he responded. With bows and curtsies, the three women left the parlor, leaving only Zimmermann, AGATHA, and a crackling fire in the marble fireplace.

Zimmermann said nothing. He stood over the fireplace with poker in hand staring into the glowing coals, deep in thought. AGATHA remained quiet, not wanting to disturb the man's thoughts. After several minutes, he placed the poker back in its rack, turned, and faced her as she stood behind him. He strode over to her, his eyes and face inches from hers. With no other words, he swung his arms around her petite waist and pulled her in toward him. She closed her eyes as he moved his lips toward hers.

The kiss lasted for many seconds. With no other sounds in the room but the crackling fire, he reached down, clasped his hand around hers and gently pulled her toward the open parlor doors and up the grand staircase toward the master bedroom.

* * * * * * * *

East Prussia, 10 October 1943

The Halifax bomber flew low and slow over the Baltic before making landfall a few miles from Danzig, the port city over which so much of German anger at the Versailles Treaty centered. In creating the Danzig Corridor to assure a resurrected Poland access to the Baltic, the corridor cut off an important part of East Prussia from Germany proper. Flying at under 1,000 feet to avoid radar detection, the Halifax zipped through the night undetected.

"Right lads. Drop in twenty seconds. Good luck and Godspeed!" shouted the crew chief, straining to be heard over the engine noise. The green drop light flashed. A cold breeze whipped through the bomber. The first man crossed himself and leapt out of the open door.

One by one in succession, each man jumped until all eight floated down toward Germany below. The crew chief stuck his head in beside the pilot seat after securing the open side door. "All a go, sir."

"Very good," responded the pilot as he banked right to get back over the Baltic as rapidly as they could but without attracting undue attention. From there, on to RAF Tempsford, home of No. 161 squadron, where a hot meal, a good ale, and a nervous INTREPID waited for their return and report.

INTREPID had brought the team over from Camp X. All had traveled by civilian airliner rather than British military aircraft. Despite the armistice, many German agents still operated in Britain seeking out any armistice violation. MI5, the counter-intelligence agency, knew most of them and kept a watchful eye, but there was always the chance of missing one. Actually, it would be easy enough to simply round them up, but they had some utility. MI6 regularly fed these German agents false intelligence that they dutifully transmitted back to Berlin. It was one of those sleeper agents that would play a large role in the drama to come.

In the control tower, INTREPID waited impatiently, a bit on edge. As the Halifax touched down, he patted the flight controller on the shoulder and nodded approval. In the operations room, the pilot reported that the entire team had successfully parachuted in and were presumed safe. With no apparent enemy activity, the mission went undetected.

Later that evening, an SOE listening station received a simple one-word message—"Agincourt"—the code word meaning all the team landed safely with no German reaction or detection. To reinforce the ruse that the action to come was a Soviet operation, each man had indiscrete items on him—a letter from the wife in Moscow, a good luck Russian coin, a photo of himself in Red Army uniform beside an obviously proud, beaming father. Additionally, the team carried a pouch containing a wallet and other personal items clearly identifying the owner as a careless Soviet operative. The plan was to accidentally "drop" the pouch near the attack site at *Der Gevatter Tod*, allowing the Germans to find it. Every man carried some incriminating evidence of Soviet origin as neatly prepared by MI6's resident forger. Should any man become a casualty, the apparent indiscretion would cast blame on the Soviets, not on Britain. Each man also carried two cyanide capsules. They understood completely that they could never be captured alive. Everyone volunteered for the mission. Everyone understood the risks.

INTREPID hated the thought of casting blame on the former Soviet allies, but it couldn't really be helped. Britain had to avoid any hint of an armistice violation. And, if CHARLEMAGNE was accurate, the next target as soon as the second operational bomb was combat ready was Moscow or perhaps Leningrad. If an attack on the electrical station and the scientists and technicians at *Der Gevatter Tod* delayed the program long enough to allow the Red Army to defeat Germany or, even better, allow the combined Anglo-American atomic program to come to fruition, then the ruse had been worthwhile.

The SOE crew comprised of Poles, Czechs, and even a former Greek naval officer made their way toward Rastenburg where a safe house had been prepared by Kwiatkowski and Mowak. Four of the men were explosives experts. They carried with them sufficient plastic explosive to knock out the entire electrical grid servicing *Der Gevatter Tod*. The plan called for these men to set the charges and timers while Kwiatkowski, Mowak, and the other four agents killed as many key personnel as possible. It was a deadly and brutal operation. INTREPID despised the fact that noncombatant scientists and technicians had to pay the penalty for Hitler's megalomaniacal dreams. But deep in his soul, he understood what Winston Churchill said about such hard choices: "It is no use saying, 'We are doing our best.' You have got to succeed in doing what is necessary."[6]

---

6 Robert Rhodes James, *Churchill Speaks: Winston S. Churchill in Peace and War: Collected Speeches, 1897-1963* (New York: Athenaeum, 1980).

CHAPTER 8

Michelangelo

Der Gevatter Tod, **East Prussia, 12 October 1943**

Construction at *Der Gevatter Tod* had almost finished up by the time Zimmermann and the crew received their orders to deploy to the new air station. A 10,000-foot runway along with a secure hanger, flight control tower, crew quarters, command center, mess hall, and all the other necessary accoutrements of an operational air station went up smartly throughout the early autumn. To anyone observing the activity, it became clear that the construction meant one thing—whatever was happening at the mysterious secret compound, it meant a shift in the war effort to the Eastern Front exclusively with all the *Reich's* resources. Rumors of secret war-ending weapons, especially among those that had witnessed the test detonation, ran rampant.

Along with the Kursk disaster following on closely behind the Stalingrad catastrophe, Germany needed a desperate play to, if not conquer the Soviets, at least hold them at bay. All who knew of the weapon's destructive capability, especially after the Dartmoor bombing, fully expected the next attacks to hit Soviet cities.

Interestingly, though the *Reich* demanded a British armistice and American neutrality, no demands had been placed on Moscow. That factor indicated that Hitler and the Party still intended to conquer European Russia, the Ukraine, and the Caucasus Mountain region for the Greater *Reich* and the sought after *"Lebensraum."* Despite the implied threat of atomic attack, the Soviets fought on. Stalin and the Red Army and Air Force high command fully believed they could defeat a wavering Germany. And, as suspected by the British and American intelligence services, the Soviets had well-placed spies in Germany, even at *Der Gevatter Tod,* who assured Stalin and the Politburo that Germany had the wherewithal to produce additional bombs, but it would be weeks or months before any could be operational. Accordingly, Stalin rolled the dice so to speak in hopes of a quick decisive victory on the ground. Kursk indicated he might be right.

Although Kwiatkowski and Nowak worked on the electrical wiring for the new airfield buildings, they still believed the personnel compound and the electrical generator power station represented the key targets. Without these components, no work could continue in the laboratories and test facilities for some time as Germany rebuilt its facilities and personnel cadre. However, the near completion of the airfield and support infrastructure indicated that at least one weapon was close to combat readiness. With the assault team in place and still undetected, the go signal had to be sent soon. Messages went out to Kwiatkowski and Nowak to be prepared for an assault within days. In the safe house, the assault team cleaned and recleaned their weapons, exercised to maintain top physical condition, and prepped the satchels of plastic explosive and detonators. All that remained was the go signal that consisted of a single line from a poem by T. S. Eliot: "In the room the women come and go talking of Michelangelo" from "The Love Song of J. Alfred Prufrock" to be broadcast by the BBC World Service. [7]

* * * * * * * *

---

7 T.S. (Thomas Steans) Eliot, *Prufrock and Other Observations* (London: The Egoist, Ltd., 1917).

While the rest of the crew made final preparations at Augsburg to transfer to *Der Gevatter Tod,* Zimmermann, Pieper, and Zwilling flew into the new airfield to inspect the facilities. Krause gave Zimmermann the final word as to when to make the transfer. He had to be satisfied that the new facilities could accommodate the heavy bomber and support the mission.

"As you can see, *Herr Generalmajor,* the facilities are quite nice. We are certain that you and your crew will be comfortable here," said the construction manager, beaming. Zimmermann looked left, then right, and shook his head in concurrence. He had to say, the crew accommodations were indeed quite well-built and comfortable looking. He had the same impression of the officers' quarters and the dining hall. All looked much nicer than he had seen in other forward operating areas. "*Ja,* you are quite correct. Your crews have done an excellent job with the facilities."

In truth, while the living quarters, command center, and control stations all were a cut above the norm and quite well-built, they were not his real concern. In the morning brief within the restricted compound where he had first met Pieper and Tisza months earlier for the initial detonation test, he heard something that troubled him. Only himself, Pieper, and Zwilling of the crew had actually been inside the laboratory and test compound; without any collusion or conversation among themselves, all three worried about the security aspect once the weapons became operational. The Dartmoor bomb had been brought to France by a special armored train that traveled only by night so as to be less of a target for British aircraft or detection by authorized eyes. Once the bomb arrived at Avord, it had been quickly loaded aboard the He 177 the night before the mission. Now, a new dynamic appeared. *As each device reached combat readiness, where would they be stored? How would they be secured and guarded?* The answers from the briefing officer did not make him comfortable.

"*Herr Generalmajor,* the devices will be stored in a special bomb-proof underground bunker at the airfield next to the main hangar. You will be taking a tour of that bunker this afternoon following a luncheon with the facility commander." The briefer smiled broadly, assuming he had assuaged Zimmermann's concerns. He had not. Instead, it only made Zimmermann more wary. He peered directly at the briefer, a *Luftwaffe* logistics *Oberst.*

"*Herr Oberst,* why will the devices not be stored here in this very well-protected and reinforced compound?" The question caused every head in the briefing room to swivel around from Zimmermann back to the briefer, eyes boring in on the poor man, now caught in the crosshairs, so to speak. He stuttered.

"I, well, *Jawohl, Herr Generalmajor* . . . that is . . . that is—" He paused, took a deep breath, calmed himself, and continued, "This decision was made personally by *Generaloberst* Krause. He is concerned that the transportation from this compound to the aircraft could be compromised. The *Generaoberst* desires that the weapons be stored very close to the aircraft." Regaining his confidence, he continued, "And, sir, in truth, we have no room. When this facility was constructed last year, we had no idea as to how much space would be needed for manufacture and storage. We found it to be quite adequate for the first weapon, but now that we are manufacturing more devices, we simply have no space." He obviously had regained his footing.

"And now?" shot in Pieper.

"*Ja, Herr Major.* We have learned much in these few months. By storing the devices remotely at the airfield bunker, we free up space in this compound for the future manufacturing process." He smiled again, sensing he had deflated the concern. In truth, he had raised the same issue with Krause only to be told to do his job and not question the decision.

Zimmermann breathed in slowly. *So be it. We will work with what we are given.* "Very well, *Herr Oberst.* We will see what your secure bunker looks like, shall we?" The briefer, now nervous again with the coldness of Zimmermann's response, could only reply meekly, "*Herr Generalmajor.* I am certain that you will find the arrangements to your satisfaction."

That afternoon, the airfield commander and the construction manager proudly displayed their new facilities. Following the accommodations, command and control facility, and dining hall tours, the group arrived at the aircraft hangar. Much larger than either pilot had ever seen save for the dirigible hangers, the pair was impressed. The Linden Tree would fit easily inside. There appeared to be plenty of workspace for maintenance and repair. But the next step worried Zimmermann. Next to the hanger sat the bomb storage and assembly building. Only the top appeared above ground. The bulk lay beneath the ground. Overhead, thick steel-reinforced concrete covered the building's top, similar to the U-boat pens at L'Orient, Brest, and other captured French ports on the Bay of Biscay. These submarine pens withstood British bombs, suffering little to no damage. The same idea prevailed here. The assumption that no British or Soviet bomb could penetrate the concrete barrier dominated. Add to that dynamic the time factor. With the situation in the Ukraine rapidly deteriorating, Germany needed to crush the Soviet war effort quickly; there had been little time to design and build a more robust, more bomb-proof structure. As the elevator took the party down from the entrance area to the bomb storage room, Zimmermann noted that was it was only a few meters deep. "*Herr Oberst*, how deep are we now?"

The officer, clearly chastised by Zimmermann's reaction in the morning brief, blanched. "*Herr Generalmajor*. We are now six meters below the surface. We would have preferred a few more meters deeper for the device storage space, but time, you understand, was an overarching imperative. This, I believe, is why *Generaloberst* Krause ordered the construction of the storage facility."

He was only partially correct. It was suspected that some of the staff at the laboratory or test site had sympathies not in line with proper National Socialist thought. While the *Gestapo* and *SS* intelligence unit had not identified any specific threats that in themselves validated the concern over sabotage, they simply did not know if a potential saboteur already operated in their midst. With the device stored in the same compound as all the research laboratories and production facilities, a single saboteur could do great harm. Removing the weapons to the new facility—isolated and well-guarded by reliable *SS* men—minimized concern over potential sabotage.

As he strolled through the storage space, Zimmermann looked up at the high ceiling. It seemed to him that if a powerful enough bomb or a series of well-placed bombs struck the concrete overhead just right, the entire structure might come crashing down and bury the devices under tons of concrete and steel rubble. He said no more on the subject, but his worry about the security of the structure bothered him intensely.

Finally, the tour ended, and with Krause's arrival at the hangar, a ceremony ensued. *Generalmajor* Peter von Zimmermann, Baron Zimmermann, stood at a stiff attention as the *Generaloberst* ceremoniously removed the gold coiled shoulder epaulets of a *Luftwaffe Generalmajor*. In their place, he attached the gold coiled with a single pip (star) epaulets of a *Generalleutnant* (equivalent to major general or air vice-marshal) of the *Reich's Luftwaffe*. He saluted the *Generaloberst* smartly as the older man beamed with pride. "Congratulations, *Herr Generalleutnant*. You must know that the *Führer* will personally award you the Knight's Cross with Oak Leaves and Swords at a ceremony in due course."

"*Herr Generaloberst*, I am most pleased and grateful to the *Führer* for his confidence in me."

With that, Krause promoted Pieper to *Oberstleutnant* (lieutenant colonel). Zwilling received the War Merit Cross, 2nd Class—the *Kriegsverdienstkreuz*—for exceptional war services to the *Reich*. The ceremony ended, and the trio prepared to board the Ju 52 for the flight back to Berlin.

As Zimmermann stepped through the passenger door, he turned to Pieper. "Hans, I'm concerned about this storage arrangement. I fear we will pay dearly for this mistake." Pieper merely nodded. He concurred. The storage facility was not adequate enough.

Two days later, The Linden Tree crew arrived and settled into their new quarters at *Der Gevatter Tod*. The flight from Augsburg had been uneventful. With dozens of training and familiarization flights over the past several weeks, the crew knew their roles and mastered the new aircraft. The gunners were particularly impressed by the remotely operated guns while Fischer reveled in the new state-of-the-art navigation and communications gear. One change had occurred. The engines had been changed out from the Jumo 211 to the more powerful and reliable BMW 801G engines in early September. Zimmermann insisted on the change. With the new engines, the service ceiling increased to 28,000 feet, still too low to avoid high-flying attacking Soviet fighters, but the extra 2,000 feet of altitude made the entire crew happier about the pullout. All remembered the bouncing about and terror of the Dartmoor mission and the fear that the onrushing shockwave would stall the aircraft. Plus, the extra 2,000 feet of drop time meant that The Linden Tree would be even further out of the blast field.

* * * * * * * * *

Berlin, 16 October 1943

AGATHA despaired. She had not learned anything of significance from Zimmermann in weeks other than that The Linden Tree and crew had transferred to *Der Gevatter Tod*. That intelligence had been transmitted successfully to INTREPID through the usual channel. While she felt disappointed in the intelligence, INTREPID took a different interpretation. The fact meant that a mission against Moscow or Leningrad was likely imminent. The team at Rastenburg reported ready for action, and INTREPID realized that the crucial moment had arrived. But what if in addition to the electrical grid and personnel, the team could destroy or cripple the bomber as well as shut down the new airfield and its support facilities? That might even further hamper or delay the German plans. Accordingly, directions went out to Kwiatkowski and Nowak—the assault plan changed. It was now time to strike.

Meanwhile, in Berlin, AGATHA grew more anxious. She felt in control of events while Zimmermann was in Berlin or with her at Linden Hall. At those times, she knew she could monitor events and pry for information. But when he traveled to Augsburg for training or now to *Der Gevatter Tod* for operational deployment, she lost what the military types call situational awareness—an understanding of the big picture. This dynamic frustrated her no end. She continued visiting the park and sending the coded messages to CHRISTIE through the bench dead drop. And she noted the regular appearance of Maas hiding in the bushes across the roadway. Surely, he must be getting bored with the operation and perhaps his inability to ferret out what she was actually doing. She decided to take action to break the doldrums.

Among her other qualities of intelligence, physical grace, and athletic ability, she had a streak of what the Yanks might call a "smart-ass sense of humor." All too serious most of the time, every now and then her oddball sense of humor broke through her usual serious demeanor. For example, one lovely summer day in New York, she suddenly felt the urge for a practical joke. Purchasing a large salami from the famous Katz Deli on Houston Street, she raced out into the line of traffic on Broadway. Running up to a man just sitting in his car, sweating, clearly irritated with the traffic and the heat, she shoved the salami through the driver side window and shouted, "Quick, take this to Grand Central Station!"

Without a pause or even a quizzical look, the driver slammed the car into gear and raced off toward the station. Not able to contain herself, she doubled over in hysterical laughter. As she raised back up, she glanced over at the sidewalk and saw about half the pedestrians laughing and half with a "What the hell just happened?" look. This made her laugh ever harder, almost to the point of tears. Such was her oddball sense of the ridiculous that occasionally struck.

Now, with Zimmermann at *Der Gevatter Tod* and not due back for several days, the urge for some offbeat practical joke struck her once again. The target? Well, it could only be the frustrated and really incompetent watcher in the bushes. She had a plan.

Going to the park bench, she fed the pigeons as usual, but instead of returning to the suite at the *Kaiserhof*, she took a different route. Though there was a chilly October wind with a hint of drizzle in the air, she just pulled the raincoat collar tighter around her neck and strode on out of the park. Confused by her action, Maas did not know how to react. He decided to follow anyway, which, of course, was AGATHA's plan.

She strolled down a major thoroughfare and then onto a side street into an area better known for cheap bars and houses of ill repute. Turning another corner, she came upon a drab, rundown gray concrete and brick building. She looked around, as if anxious that no one detected her movements. She really meant to see if the watcher had stayed up with her. He had. She snickered to herself and mumbled, "Let the games begin." She knocked twice.

Madame LaRue's House of Exotic Pleasures had been a staple of Berlin's lower social scene for two decades. Unlike other bordellos that catered to the higher orders of Berlin society, Madame LaRue's clientele included workingmen as well as university students. It was especially popular with servicemen stationed in the Berlin area or home on leave. She learned of the famed bordello one evening when she and Zimmermann sat in the veranda of his flat observing a wonderful late summer sunset. He recalled a phone call. It seemed that a former crewmember from his days early in the war as a *Gruppe* (group) commander decided to take in the city's sites and pleasures, most especially Madame LaRue's. For the unfortunate airman, he had difficulty with strong drink or, more succinctly put, he got drunk easily. It seemed the poor man became disorderly and out of control. The local constabulary was called in, and one can guess the outcome. His squadron commander, who desperately needed the man back for deployment rather than enjoying the delights of a Berlin jail, did the only thing he could think of at the moment—he called his old *Gruppe* commander, now a prominent *Luftwaffe* general. The upshot of the story was that not only did Zimmermann entice and convince the chief of the Berlin *Ordnungspolizei* that national security required the airman to report back to a squadron forthwith, but AGATHA learned a great deal about the delightful place—Madame LaRue's House of Exotic Pleasures.

Shaking off her watcher the previous day, she had slipped into the establishment. Madame LaRue, being a woman of keen business sense, was more than happy to accept the bundle of crisp *Reichsmark* "donation." All was arranged and now the trap sprung.

Maas could not understand why a baroness of such repute would sully herself by going inside such a place. Curious, he walked up to the door and tried to peer through the small portal, which slid open, revealing a set of overly mascaraed eyes. Before he could even speak, two huge bouncers emerged from the adjacent alley and grabbed Maas by the arms. They hustled him through the now open door. Meanwhile, AGATHA, her work done, slipped out the back door. Laughing as hard as she ever had, she gradually contained herself, pulled up the raincoat collar against a freshening wind, and strode back toward the more acceptable part of town and the fashionable suite at the Hotel *Kaiserhof* on the *Wilhelmplatz*.

Meanwhile, the hapless *SS Sturmbannführer* found himself bound, gagged, blindfolded, and eventually handcuffed to a bed post where he stayed for a full 24 hours, abused and "serviced" by the "employees" . . . and perhaps an animal or two. Though AGATHA never found out for sure, she was fairly positive that photographs of the events made their way to a certain *SS* commanding officer, much to the embarrassment and chagrin of *SS Sturmbannführer* Johann Maas. For AGATHA and her sometimes offbeat sense of humor and practical joking, it had been a delightful evening.

* * * * * * * *

Cabaret Paris, Berlin, 18 October 1943

Zimmermann had never taken AGATHA to the Cabaret Paris until now. One by one, the cords that so tightly bound him to Ingrid frayed as he fell deeper and deeper into what must be love. With each passing week, he resisted just a bit less until finally, on this autumn evening, he decided to take her to the place that had been so special. He had already broken the covenant with his dead wife very early on in introducing AGATHA to the *Edelweiss*. That represented a tentative first probing step. But the Cabaret Paris, where he and Ingrid spent so many happy and, yes, lusty moments, meant that now he was ready to go all in.

AGATHA understood the emotion. She knew of the cabaret and what it meant to Zimmermann. She never expected to cross that boundary with him, but now it happened. One by one, the barriers to their relationship fell.

In truth, she experienced both guilt and joy at the same time. She felt the weight of her mission. She understood how critical it was for her to gain key intelligence information from him, not only for revenge for her late husband but also for the world's sake. The Nazis simply could not prevail. But when she considered that the mission must drive all, more guilt crept in. She felt she betrayed him, that she only used him. And in return, he gave only genuine affection. Then, at times, she felt tremendous joy whether just strolling in parks, learning to fly in his private airplane, or simply sitting by a warm, cheering fire with a hot drink at Linden Hall, which they now visited often when he could break away from training and operational commitments. And, yes, now even a trip to the Cabaret Paris, perhaps the final turn in their growing relationship.

"*Guten Abend, Herr Generalleutnant; willkommen die Dame.* We have not seen you in so long. Please, please, this way. We have reserved a special table just for you," bubbled the *maître d'*. They followed him to the table which had always been his and Ingrid's spot. They ordered gin and tonics—not really an autumn drink, but since they both enjoyed it, why not? There was no lime—that commodity trade had not yet started up again. But the drinks tasted wonderful all the same.

He noticed that the place's style changed from his last visit earlier in the year. Gone were the trappings of Party and power. The place had become more subdued and, in a way, more elegant. Gone was the overly enthusiastic master of ceremonies, whom he had not really cared for anyway. Gone were the young dancers and their silver and black garish pseudo-Nazi costumes. Rather, there was a house orchestra, all properly attired in formal wear.

He did not know why the change but didn't really object. Perhaps it reflected a more somber mood in the country—a darker mood. Was it the losses on the Eastern Front? The euphoria that followed the Dartmoor attack and British acceptance of the armistice and the peace at least in North Africa, the North Atlantic, and Western Europe had dissipated as more and more families grieved for their fallen soldiers and airmen on the Eastern Front. Never in the previous two years since Hitler had unleashed OPERATION BARBAROSSA in June 1941 had Berlin been this somber. After all, the British and Commonwealth forces had been stalemated in the desert. The *Kriegsmarine* and *Grossadmiral* (grand admiral) Karl Dönitz' U-boats seemed to be winning the sea battle in the North Atlantic. Even though the British managed to hold out during the Blitz, Germany had been winning the war. That perception changed with first Stalingrad and now Kursk. The German public knew that the *Reich* possessed a super weapon. They did not understand what it was, but the public did question if Germany indeed had such a war-winning weapon, then why did the war drag on and on and on, and why had the Soviets not been defeated? He thought as he gazed at the house orchestra about to begin a beautiful waltz of all these things; he wondered if that darker mood meant the place's naughtiness and frivolity had turned to a more somber and formal tone. But, as he often did, he reconciled the horror of the atomic weapon and his role in its use and future with the understanding that not only would it bring eventual or, even better, swift victory to the Fatherland and keep it safe, but it would soon end this bloodletting. Those thoughts allowed him to carry on as he vowed to succeed in his mission.

As the orchestra began one of his favorite waltzes, he gazed into AGATHA's eyes. Any questions he had had about bringing her to this place dissipated as he stared into the face of a most enchanting lady. The dreamy chords of the *Schneewalzer*—"The Snow Waltz" —began. Not one of the grand Viennese waltzes of Strauss, the simple Austrian tune evoked the image of a gorgeous Alpine winter scene with towns-folk twirling and gliding under the lights to a simple, lovely melody.

Without saying a word, he extended a hand. She took it, and for the next two hours, they hardly left the dance floor except to swizzle a quick gulp of the excellent drinks. As if electrified, it seemed like sparks flew across the room from each to each. It was at this point that each had a revelation. They did not speak of it, but both had the same notion nonetheless. For Zimmermann, it manifested as a dream of the war's end and the possibility that he might be the instru-ment of peace rather than the destroyer of worlds. Then he could embrace this magnificent woman and build a life together, free from death and destruction. For her part, AGATHA visualized the same future for the couple except in her concept, peace came only when the world rose up, defeated the Nazis, and crushed the *Reich's* war machine. She too would play a part in that rising, only instead of the instrument of German victory, she would be the agent of the Nazis' destruction. With true peace restored rather than atomic extortion, she would spend the rest of her days not as a widow grieving for her lost warrior husband. Rather, she would embrace passionately this kind, gentle, honorable warrior-aristocrat. By different paths, they might reach the same destination.

As the couple danced the night away that autumn evening, a radio announcer stepped up to a microphone in a London studio. The BBC World Service announcer cleared his throat as the director gave him the sign –: "In three, two, one, on air." In a deep and sono-rous tone, the man announced that for tonight's poetry reading, the BBC World Service presented the American poet T. S. Eliot's "The

Love Song of J. Alfred Prufrock." Verse after verse came forth until finally the announcer said, "In the room the women come and go talking of Michelangelo."

* * * * * * * * *

Der Gevatter Tod, East Prussia, 20 October 1943

0430. With a snip of the wire cutters, the chain-link fence broke open. The team was surprised that it had not been electrified to keep out intruders or any of the many animal inhabitants of the forest surrounding *Der Gevatter Tod*. A dirt road ran completely around the facility. Their observations over the past several days revealed a pattern to be exploited. Every 20 minutes, a *Kübelwagen* with two SS men passed the spot Kwiatkowski and Nowak identified for their insertion. *Thank God for German preciseness!* They calculated that the patrol passed the spot never less than two minutes early or more than a minute late. The pattern never varied, regardless of which SS guards were on duty. The patrol occurred all day, every day. Once the team understood the pattern, they developed the insertion plan. They would assault at just before dawn. Historically, that time proved best for a surprise attack. At that time, humans are least alert. The team understood that dynamic, if not the human physiology behind it.

The *Kübelwagen*'s headlights bounced in the distance. It had been raining steadily for the past couple of days, turning the road from a dusty lane to a muddy quagmire. Fortunately, the rain had finally stopped, and though rough going the patrol was able to make the rounds with little loss of time. That factor was especially critical to the ten men in all-black clothing with burnt cork-smudged faces who crouched in the bushes and trees across the road from the chain-link fence. As the sentries passed, the crouching team heard one man complain to the other something about a cold, miserable night and only two more hours on duty. The two men in the *Kübelwagen* had no idea just how miserable their lives were about to become.

In pairs, six men raced across the road at intervals of 30 seconds between each dash. Two men immediately started snipping the links, while the other four took covering fire positions. The other four team members took up positions across the road. Should the patrol for some reason turn back or another come along, the enemy would be caught in a deadly crossfire.

After a few minutes, the cutters opened up a tear in the fence large enough for a man and the gear to pass through but still discreet enough to stay undetected except by very close examination. With a low whistle from the cutters, the remaining four men charged across the road. Within another minute, all were through the fence. Once the cutters pulled the fence links back together and bound them with lead wire seals so as to minimize the opening but allow for a rapid escape path, the team headed through the woods toward the three objectives.

Der Gevatter Tod was an odd installation, shaped like a barbell with heavy weights on either end joined by a narrow handle between. In the north, where the team broke in, stood the facilities compound and the entrance to the underground laboratories. At the far southern end lay the test site, 16 kilometers distant. The blast area had been calculated to be at least nine and a half kilometers.

Along the narrow "handle" between compounds and test site, a two-lane paved road and a narrow-gauge railway joined the two ends of the barbell. Underground, the corridor through which Zimmermann had first passed months earlier provided access and safety from aerial attack.

The new airfield with its outbuildings extended horizontally across the middle of the northern end. The personnel compound stood a half mile from the insertion point. If one looked down on the more or less oval-shaped northern end of the base, then the power station lay to the left with the personnel compound to the right. The airfield ran across the width of the northern end from right to left.

Based on the new target package, the teams split into three groups as they approached the personnel compound. Team A, headed

S.D.M. Carpenter

by Nowak, split off to attack the airfield. Team B, led by the Greek former naval officer, Stavridis, broke off toward the power station. Team C, led by Kwiatkowski, headed for the personnel compound. The combined teams covered the distance from insertion to break off point in just under 30 minutes despite the heavy wet foliage and deep woods. Before breaking off, they paused in the woods just north of the personnel compound to take bearings and ensure they had not been detected. All clear. After a five-minute pause with not a word spoken, Kwiatkowski raised his right hand and waved it in a circle. Each man knew the signal. Rising up out of the wet leaves and grass, each team quickly headed toward its objective.

Teams A and B carried most of the explosives. For Team B, the transformers, electrical towers, and generators represented primary targets. With electrolyte detonators attached to a timing device, the charges, when placed in position, would be set to detonate at exactly 0525. The same applied to the airfield. Team A's key targets included the flight control tower and command center, the Me 264 bomber in its hangar, the fuel storage tanks, and if the opportunity occurred, the crew of the bomber itself. For team C, their major objective was to kill or wound as many of the personnel as possible. Civilian scientists and technicians, though technically noncombatants, had to be the primary targets. No one liked the idea of killing civilians, but every man understood the critical imperative—delay and disrupt the enemy's atomic program. Since the laboratories were too well-protected, the physicists and their assistants became the target—dirty work, but it had to be done.

0505. Team A arrived at the end of the runway. In the ready room, illuminated by a glowing lamp inside, sat three SS men. No other guards appeared close. Nowak approached the ready room slowly, his Russian PPSh-41 submachine gun at the ready. As quickly as possible, he popped up for a quick look and then ducked down again under the windowsill. The three men had steaming coffee mugs on the simple wooden table in the middle of the room. They were playing a card game. Nowak thought to himself, *This is a surprising lack of vigilance from an otherwise efficient organization.* What he did not know was that these men from the *Waffen SS*, the combat military arm of the *SS* security service, had just returned from the Eastern Front and were relieved to be stationed at what seemed a very quiet zone. Accordingly, they relaxed their guard. They should not have.

Signaling to the team, Nowak set the operation in motion. One man raced toward the aviation fuel tanks while another carrying a satchel filled with explosives made for the flight control tower adjacent to the command center. Just as he arrived at the tower's base, he heard a crack behind them. Pressing into the side of the building, he heard footfalls from around the corner. A fourth *SS* man rounded the building corner. All four should have been on foot patrol, but the *Waffen SS* veterans decided on their own to patrol for a half hour each one at a time while the other three relaxed in the ready room. After all, they had suffered mightily at the front and, well, didn't they deserve a break at this cushy duty station?

Fatal mistake. The stiletto dagger blade of the Fairbairn-Sykes knife flashed out and caught the sentry squarely in the throat. Blood filled his throat such that he could not even cry out in pain or in warning. He fell limp to the ground, a gurgling noise welling up from his ravaged throat. Wiping the blade on the man's uniform tunic, the Czech replaced the knife in its sheath and waved to Nowak, who had seen the man approach but dared not signal to his team member.

Unobserved by the sentries engrossed in their card game, the other men set their charges and timers. A satchel was set on one leg of the control tower; the blast would easily topple it. More satchel charges were placed outside the control center underneath where the communications equipment was located. Antenna cables leading from the roof down the side of the building and into a specific window indicated where the airfield communications station was located. There had not been time to get the antennas and cables fully mounted and installed properly. The construction manager had been told the first priority was the hanger, the bomb storage bunker, the control tower, and the airstrip. Just make the communications work for now had been his direction. Charges were set on each of the three huge aviation fuel tanks that stood near the hanger. Another charge was placed on the fuel pump house that serviced the tanks. Nowak planted a charge under the ready room window. If nothing else, flying glass from the explosion would wound or cripple the three card-playing *SS* men, one of whom had just won a hand and a pile of *Reichsmark*. He held aces and eights—a winner! He had no clue that he held the "Dead Man's Hand." It would be his last one. Although the team might have wanted to blast open the reinforced bomb storage and assembly bunker, as with the laboratory complex, the heavily concreted facility with the underground rooms required far more explosive power than they could muster.

With the ready room charge set, Nowak sprinted out across the open space toward the hanger. With no roving sentry, he arrived undetected. According to the security plan, one of the four sentries should have been on duty at the hangar's entrance. Nowak breathed deeply after his sprint, grateful for the guards' slackness. He glanced at his watch—0520. He had five minutes to set the charge and clear the area.

Pulling out his last explosive charge, he taped it to the lock on the hangar main door. The plan called for the charge to blow open the hangar door enough for him to run through and toss multiple hand grenades at the plane, aimed primarily at the engines and cockpit area. They would've preferred to use regular charges for a more thorough destruction, but with the change of plans and the addition of the airfield to the target list, they divided up the precious explosives. Do as much damage with grenades as possible, admonished Kwiatkowski. We do the best we can. It will have to do. 0523. Two minutes to take cover and wait for the blasts.

0512. Team B reached the power station. They saw no sentries, although there must be some. They approached stealthily, spread out just enough to signal each other with hand gestures, but with enough distance to dive for cover should a machine gun open up and try to spray them.

As they reached just outside the main generator building, Stavridis shot his closed hand up. All ducked low. Inside the entrance-way to the main generator building, a lone SS sentry leaned against a doorway. With a sandwich in one hand and a coffee mug in the other, he clearly was not ready for action. Stavridis saw the man's lips move as he tapped his feet to a beat. That meant he was listening to music, which turned out to be the latest patriotic number from Berlin. Between the music and the attention to his breakfast, the man paid no heed and failed to see the whirlwind about to strike. A minute later, another razor-sharp Fairbairn-Sykes dagger thrust into another unwary, inattentive SS sentry. The body fell to the floor limp, still grasping the sausage and cheese sandwich. Stavridis stepped over the body and strode across the room, exclaiming as he entered the power station's main generator room, "Nice music, mate!"

Meanwhile, the other members of Team B raced about the electrical towers. Between them, they carried 12 plastic explosive devices. Since there were 20 individual electrical towers with transformers and with wires leading off in various directions to service the entire installation, they had to make a call as to which towers to actually destroy. The original plan called for placing an explosive on every tower, but due to the limited amount of explosives, they targeted the dozen most critical. On several previous reconnaissance trips while doing electrical installation, Kwiatkowski and Nowak identi-fied the most significant towers leading to the laboratories, the man-ufacturing area—especially the area where the uranium processing occurred—and the installation's command, control, and communi-cations centers.

With the charges set, the three men rendezvoused back at the rallying point. Once the charges went off, the plan called for them to sprint the quarter mile to the personnel compound and assist Team C with the unpleasant task of killing as many as possible. It was now 0524.

0504. Kwiatkowski and Team C arrived at the personnel com-pound. He had spent a great deal of time working in this area over the past few weeks and had become familiar with several of the *SS* men while in his guise as a *Wehrmacht* veteran. It depressed him that he now faced the same new acquaintances over the sights of his Russian assault weapon. It could not be helped. This was war. As the great Prussian theorist General Carl von Clausewitz stated decades earlier, war is the realm of chance and probability, marked by fog and friction, and ultimately, chaos.[8] These men conquered and raped his nation. He could have no empathy. Still, it bothered him immensely. But it would not deter him.

Kwiatkowski headed for Building 121, which housed the key physicists. He had only seen these men and women from a discrete distance. Their handlers made certain there was no contact between the civilian staff and the outside contract workers. He had only seen them at a distance as he transitioned from their quarters to the trucks taking them to and from the laboratories, the dining hall, and other compound buildings. He had not been assigned duties within Building 121, thus he was "flying blind," so to speak. Nonetheless, he would charge into the quarters and do as much destruction as possible.

Building 122 housed more scientists, though not the chief personnel. These men and women were the assistants and tended to be younger and less senior. Still, they were a critical part of the scientific staff. They did more of the labor tasks in the laboratories, leaving the senior scientists such as Tisza to think theoretically and technically and then actually design the equipment and devices.

Quarters 123 housed the technicians. These men did the hard labor jobs. They operated the manufacturing equipment, maintained the physical plant, and carried out various tasks in support of the scientists.

---

8 Carl von Clausewitz, *On War,* ed. and trans. Peter Paret and Michael Howard (Princeton: Princeton University Press, 1976).

Finally, Quarters 124 was the military barracks where a majority of the *SS* soldiers lived and quartered. The senior officers had much nicer quarters closer to the laboratory complex, while junior officers billeted in quarters just on the other side of the airfield. Officer quarters were not part of the target package. While killing off a few *SS* officers might certainly have appealed to the black-suited assassins now infiltrating what should've been the most closely guarded compound in the *Reich*, their value was minimal.

Lights were out everywhere through the compound except the main dining hall. The breakfast cook crew reported at 0300 and had been brewing coffee, slicing *Schwarzwälder Schinken* (Black Forest smoked ham), Gouda and Emmentaler cheese, salami fresh from Italy, and cracking eggs since well before dawn. Bakers prepared the black bread dough, a favorite for breakfast, along with sweet jams, butter, honey, and marmalade. With many of these treats so rare in wartime Germany, the cooks marveled at their good luck in getting such cushy duty. Their Wehrmacht comrades at the front rarely even saw hot meals these days, and here they were in the proverbial lap of luxury. They marveled at their good fortune.

Kwiatkowski ignored these men, all "rear echelon" types. If they resisted at all, it would be minimal and likely ineffective. The real danger lay in the *SS* personnel—hard, brutal men who would fight like banshees. Unlike the slack guards at the airfield soon to be all dead or debilitated, the rough men now asleep in the personnel compound presented a difficult problem. A few early risers stirred in Quarters 124, but more formal reveille occurred at 0600. There were no lights on in the building.

As Kwiatkowski and Nowak discovered in their many reconnaissance missions, the most intense security was provided for the laboratory complex, both in terms of physical construction and in security manpower. For this reason, they decided that the attack on the underground complex had no chance for success. Instead, the more cavalier security at the other three sites made better tactical sense. In truth, this lack of attention was the fatal flaw in the *Der*

Gevatter Tod arrangement. The decision makers from *Generaloberst* Krause on down assessed that any enemy attack or attempt on the facility entailed an assault on the laboratory complex. They completely overlooked the fact that a successful attack on the power grid and key personnel quarters would just as surely shut down the program. Kwiatkowski and Nowak, however, did not miss that fatal flaw.

0525. Within seconds of each other, explosions sounded all over *Der Gevatter Tod's* northern area, blowing out windows, collapsing walls, and creating its own form of hellish mayhem. At the airfield, the blast caved in the wooden wall of the ready room. Glass shards flew across the room striking the man who had just won the pot with his aces and eights. Blood spurted from his carotid artery, sliced by a chunk of flying glass. The other two men tumbled onto the floor, stunned and unable to move. A piece of weatherboard struck one in the temple, knocking him unconscious, while the third man's right arm hung limp, almost severed off by the blast. He struggled to raise up from the floor but collapsed into a bloody heap.

A plastic explosive satchel took out a leg of the control tower, causing it to lean then collapse, as if in slow motion. It fell atop the command center. The explosive set next to the command center blasted, shattering the wireless radio and telephone equipment inside. A second blast shot up the building's side, severing the cables running up to the roof-mounted antennas, which collapsed with an electrical crackling noise.

At the power station, one by one, the electrical towers fell, throwing up clouds of sparks and setting aflame a truck carelessly parked too close to the tower area. With that, the team of technicians and scientists working the night shift at the laboratory and production complex hunkered down in total darkness until emergency battery lanterns switched on, throwing a dim red glow over the compound. A voice of authority came over the general announcing system ordering them to shelter in place. No one thought they should do otherwise. They would ride out the attack, trust in the military men to protect them, and hope for the best.

0526. At the airfield, the explosive on the main hangar door failed to detonate. Not sure why, Nowak cursed aloud as he realized that without another way in, the Me 264 bomber would likely survive the assault. *Very well then. That being the case, the next best thing is take out the crew.*

On their last contract work at the airfield, they saw the huge bomber gracefully land on the new runway and taxi over to the hangar. The ground crew wasted no time in putting the plane inside its "cave." They had been mightily impressed with the aircraft, the largest they had seen, with its powerful four engines, gun turrets with no obvious space for a gunner inside, and painted all black. It truly captured the power and terror of the *Reich*. But with no crew, the plane might as well be a museum piece.

Cradling the grenade satchel under his left arm so as to not lose one to the jostling, he raced toward the barracks that housed the bomber's crew. He had earlier observed them coming in and out of the two-story white clapboard building and knew that is where they would be housed. Unlike the card-playing sentries, these men were likely all asleep this early morning. As he reached a position some 20 yards from the main entrance, he placed the grenade satchel by his feet and his assault rifle over the top of a pile of wooden pallets. If the crewmen charged out of the building, he would spray them with fire. If they stayed in the building, he would toss hand grenades through the windows. Either way, he was determined to decimate The Linden Tree's crew. As he set up his firing position, he noticed two things. One of his teammates, a fellow Pole, had set up a similar firing position a few yards to his right after his explosives had taken out the flight control tower and command center. But he noticed more movement. Emerging from one of the side buildings—a freestanding house that looked like senior officer quarters—a tall man in uniform trousers, boots, and a hunter's jacket raced out the front door, down the steps, and took cover behind the staff car parked next to the entrance. He carried what looked like a weapon. It was actually a *Maschinenpistole* MP 40 machine pistol with a hefty 32-round magazine.

Zimmermann awakened early that morning. Due to fly back to Berlin to brief Krause, he eagerly looked forward to spending some time with AGATHA for dinner that evening. Dressing in his uniform trousers, boots, and an undershirt, he felt a bit of the autumn chill.

Coming out of the toilet after shaving, he threw on the tweed hunting jacket kept by the door. Just then he heard the boom of explosions and instantly grabbed the first weapon possible—the MP 40 that hung beside the door—and bolted out the front to take up a tactical position. Zimmermann took aim at the closest man and fired off a three-round burst. Although splinters flew when they hit the wooden pallets, he missed Nowak crouching behind them. A spray of fire came at him from a different direction. One bullet grazed his left upper arm. Though painful, he soon realized he had not been badly hurt. But he realized that he was in a crossfire between the assailants. In his peripheral vision, he saw an additional black-faced man approaching from his right. He had to move. Letting off another three-round burst toward the man to his left, he rolled over, finding cover behind a large oak tree. When he found out that this house would be the quarters for himself, Pieper, Fischer, and Zwilling, he stopped the two workmen about to cut down the oak and insisted they leave it. Who was going to argue with a general? Now this ancient tree provided him some cover.

As he rolled behind the tree, a spray of fire hit the oak, knocking off big bark shards. Luckily, nothing hit him. He checked the clip. He had several rounds left, but no additional magazines. *It will have to do.*

By this time, he heard Pieper shouting from inside the house. The copilot had grabbed the phone handset and desperately dialed up the SS security desk to report that they were under attack—a useless move. Not only had the electrical tower serving the airfield been knocked down but also the one serving the personnel compound where the security watch stander normally posted. No one could answer.

At the security compound, the *Waffen SS* soldier manning the security communications desk heard the explosions coming from the airfield and power station. Grabbing his *Karabiner* Kar98k rifle, he raced out the front door only to be cut down in a volley from the Polish commando just outside the building. As other *SS* men, roused from their sleep and confused in the chaos, attempted to race outside Quarters 124 barracks, they met the same fate from the men in black waiting in ambush. From other areas in the civilian compound, screams of pain, terror, and rage erupted as the attackers charged into the quarters tossing grenades and spraying the rooms with bullets. No one—civilian or military—escaped the carnage.

One assailant, a Czech, wept and screamed apologies as he raced through the Quarters 123 building. He knew that, like himself, a simple automobile mechanic before the war, most of these technicians were working and tradesmen like himself. He knew they had been conscripted or forced to leave their homes, families, and businesses by the regime to work at *Der Gevatter Tod* due to their particular crafts and skills in engineering and high-end precision manufacturing. He also knew that most of these men were older. Many had already done their military service and had been mustered out or discharged due to wounds or injury. Many were just too old for military duty. He understood that many had children and perhaps grandchildren at home. As he raced through the barracks weeping and cursing, he screeched out, "*Gott verdammt* Hitler! *Gott verdammt* the Nazis! Burn in Hell!" With that he charged out of the building to join the Pole who had just entered the junior scientist barracks, Quarters 123.

At the airfield, unable to raise anyone on the phone, Pieper grabbed his service pistol and charged out the front door. He saw Zimmermann behind the oak letting off yet another burst of fire. Jumping over a newly planted shrub, he dove for the tree's cover just as a round zinged past his left ear. "Too close, *Herr Generalleutnant*! Too close!" He shouted.

At that point, both officers saw men rushing from the crew quarters. They ducked and covered; no one was hit, which amazed

Zimmermann. These were not infantry troops taught to advance and cover in their routine training. These were *Luftwaffe* men with a wholly different training regime. Later he found out that in those times when they were not flying The Linden Tree, the crew chief, one of the original 100,000 *Reichswehr* soldiers allowed by the Versailles Treaty, taught the crew the techniques he had learned in the Great War as an infantryman and in the 1920s before he transferred to the new *Luftwaffe*. He argued that should they have to ditch or parachute to safety; they must act like infantryman. The crew chief and one of the gunners wielded MP 40s and opened fire on the three assailants, who now had them boxed in. A fourth attacker attempted to outflank them, but fire from the gunner held him in check. Still, they received galling fire from three directions that blasted the side of their barracks to shreds and kicked up spurts of dirt and grass.

Zimmermann heard gunfire from around the side of the senior officer's quarters. Fischer ran out the rear door unseen, and in the melee retrieved his service pistol and extra clips. He lay down fire. A shout was heard from the left. Fischer hit one of the attackers, who now lay bleeding out on the ground. Meanwhile, two more of the crew had retrieved rifles and pistols from the armory and started laying down heavy covering fire. Realizing they were outnumbered and outgunned, Nowak raised his silver whistle to his lips and blew three short blasts—the signal to retreat to the rendezvous area. They had inflicted a great deal of damage to the airfield facilities and the installation's command, control, and communications centers. Time to retire.

An unhurt commando raced over to his comrade, now barely alive. The sucking chest wound meant he had no chance; both men knew it. Looking up at his teammate, the wounded man shook his head and whispered, "It is okay. It is okay. Time for you to go now." With that, he bit down hard on the capsule shattering the glass. Within seconds, ugly foam tinged pink with his blood poured from his mouth, a sign of cyanide poisoning. Before he left the man, though, the commando checked the dead man's breast pocket. The fake letter from his "wife in Moscow," now bloodstained, would stay with him. The operation had to deceive the Germans. With that, Nowak and the surviving men raced for the woods and disappeared.

Although they still heard gunfire from other directions, The Linden Tree crew emerged from their cover one by one. Looking pale in the half-light of sunrise, they huddled around the crew chief as Zimmermann, Pieper, and Fischer raced over. Zwilling had stayed in the house hidden behind a sofa. This action was for the military men, not a civilian scientist. He was the only physicist who kept the final coded numbers for the bomb he knew neared completion in the manufacturing complex. He dared not risk death or capture by the assailants.

The men all stared at Zimmermann, grim-faced, hollow-eyed, and many still in shock. After several seconds, he finally spoke in a low, almost inaudible voice. "Did we lose anyone?"

"*Nein, Herr Generalleutnant.* All are safe," responded the crew chief, who at that moment, noted blood dripping from Zimmermann's left coat sleeve. "*Herr Generalleutnant.* We must get you to the field hospital right away." He shouted orders to the men: "Find a vehicle! Make sure the assailant is dead! Help *Herr Generalleutnant* to the field hospital! Secure the airfield! *Schnell! Schnell!*" The command presence snapped the crew out of their stupor; they sprang about as the crew chief commanded. Order out of chaos.

Zimmermann turned to Pieper. "Hans, this will cause some heads to roll in Berlin; you may count on it."

Pieper replied solemnly, "*Jawohl, Herr Generalleutnant. Jawohl.*"

As action on the airfield raged, Kwiatkowski reached the end of the passageway of Quarters 121, certain that the death toll was high. What he could not know was the extent of the damage he had just done to the senior scientist cadre.

Of the four most critical physicists, only István Tisza survived. Asleep in his room when the gunfire erupted, he immediately bolted his door and crouched down behind an overstuffed chair, one of the few items from home the Germans allowed him. The three other senior physicists all clustered in one room, failing to consider that they now presented an easy target of opportunity. It should have been clear to them that key personnel were a target of this raid.

Kwiatkowski never realized when he tossed a grenade into the room that he managed to kill all three physicists—three quarters of the key scientists with intimate knowledge of how to refine the uranium and ultimately convert it into a workable atomic device. In his room alone, Professor István Tisza of Budapest, perhaps the most valuable member of the German atomic development program, trembled as he heard the heavy stamp of military boots just outside his door.

Kwiatkowski kicked in the door and pointed his weapon right at Tisza's head. But he didn't pull the trigger. Why, he could not say. To his dying day, he could not say. The trembling, terrorized man could only croak, "Please, please. I have a family in Budapest. The Nazis are holding them, forcing me to work for them. I can help, I can help you. Please, rescue my family and I swear I can help you make your own weapon. Please, I beg you." Tisza then broke down, sobbing.

Kwiatkowski lowered his weapon. A thought flashed through his mind. He had been overcome with rage and brutality as he made his way through the compound killing at will. Now, with a break in the rampage, his rational thinking returned. *Should we take this man with us? Can he really assist us?* He pondered for a moment until the growing din of shouts and cursing told him it was time to retire. Then he considered the man's plan. *If they took him, what of his family? They had made too many families grieve this morning. No. Leave him. But alert London. Perhaps they could rescue his family and then pull this valuable asset out of Nazi hands.*

"What is your name?" he shouted.

"Tisza. István Tisza, professor of physics at the Budapest University of Technology and Economics."

With that, Kwiatkowski raced outside and blew three short whistle blasts. But before he did, he carefully placed the pouch containing the incriminating evidence on the sidewalk where even the most inept person could find it.

As the team gathered at the rendezvous point, they counted heads. Other than the Pole who died by cyanide left on the airfield with the incriminating photograph, all made it to the rally point. Two men had slight wounds but could walk without aid. As swiftly as they arrived, they reached the fence line, and moving quickly and silently through, they raced back across the road and into the woods beyond. A further two-mile forced march brought them to their two vehicles on another road that ran parallel to the installation. Having camouflaged the vehicles under pine branches earlier that morning, they found them undisturbed.

INTREPID later learned their fate. Kwiatkowski and Nowak returned to Poland to operate as officers in the Polish resistance as did the other Poles. The Czechs did likewise, operating in the rural, backcountry training other resistance fighters. Stavridis, the Greek naval officer, made his way to Danzig. Expert in languages as well as special operations, he posed successfully as a stranded Spanish sailor and signed on to a Finnish freighter bound for Helsinki. From there, he made his way to Scotland and obtained a commission in His Majesty's Royal Navy.

Before the team broke up back at the safe house in Rastenburg, Kwiatkowski transmitted a simple one-word signal also from the Eliot poem—"Peach"—the message meaning "mission is accomplished." An hour later, a longer message followed in a code unknown to the Germans informing INTREPID of the exchange with István Tisza, professor of physics at the Budapest University of Technology and Economics. With their work done, he smashed the wireless transmitter, buried the parts, and made for Poland.

* * * * * * * *

London, 21 October 1943

A solitary man strolled under Marble Arch. It had been raining heavily that morning as it typically did in late October as autumn transformed into winter. He sat on a bench still holding up his umbrella to catch the drizzle. After several minutes, an elderly lady—the archetypal, matronly, British "mum" —ambled up and wordlessly sat on the same bench but at the other end.

"My, my, my. Such nasty weather. I do so miss the summer. But it is winter coming and spring will soon come again. Good day, sir. Must get on with the shopping, don't you know. Harry will be wanting his supper before long," she prattled on. Finally, she departed, leaving the lone man still sitting quietly. What no one but he noticed was the brown manila envelope left by the lady on the bench. He waited for several minutes ensuring there were no obvious watchers, snatched up the envelope, hid it inside his macintosh, and strode away. The German agent never realized that the chatty, matronly British lady was actually Mary Elizabeth Nesbitt, one of MI5's top counter-intelligence agents. The man fully believed that she was another German agent still operating in Britain. The message in the envelope made its way to Berlin, eventually to the *Führer* himself. The package provided the irrefutable evidence that the destructive raid on *Der Gevatter Tod* had been conducted by Soviet special operations forces.

CHAPTER 9

Carinhall

Berlin, Chancellery, 21 October 1943

Generaloberst Krause emerged from the room pale and shaking. Conferences with the *Führer* were never easy and often ended in the man screaming and threatening retribution upon those who did not share his interpretation of or perception of events. This conference, which started as a brief on the status of *Der Gevatter Tod* following the commando raid of the day prior, ended in the usual *Führer* screaming tirades about traitors, conspirators, etc. As usual, those accustomed to the behavior—including Göring; Himmler; Martin Bormann, the *Führer's* private secretary; Joseph Goebbels, *Reich* Minister of Propaganda; and *Generaloberst* Kurt Zeitzler, *Wehrmacht* Chief of the General Staff—sat silently with firm jaws but otherwise expressionless countenances. The upshot of the meeting, in a way, relieved Krause as he exited the *Führer's* inner sanctum. At least he had not been relieved of command as he had expected, nor had he been threatened with a court-martial. Rather, once the *Führer* calmed down, thanks largely to Bormann's more calculated, cautionary, and soothing words, the *Führer* tasked Krause to travel to *Der Gevatter Tod* to assess the damage.

He arrived at the site in midafternoon. Zimmermann, Pieper, and Zwilling met him at the airstrip, which had not been damaged in the raid. But the fuel storage tanks, command center, and the remains of the control tower still smoldered, giving off an oily, black haze. The Trimotor rolled to a halt as the ground crew raced to place wheel chocks. The three men stood silent several yards from the plane. Zimmermann still wore the same boots and uniform trousers as the morning before, but he had exchanged the torn hunting jacket for a uniform tunic. His wounded left arm hung in a sling. The installation medics did a good job patching him up. It would be painful for a few days but, fortunately, no great damage had been done. Krause bolted down the three-step ladder as soon as the ground crew opened the plane's rear door and placed the steps. Zimmermann and Pieper saluted. "Bad day for the *Reich*. Bad day for us all," he mumbled as he greeted the trio. Silently, the head of Project Armageddon gazed out across the destruction. He was appalled.

"*Herr Generalleutnant,* how could this happen?"

Zimmermann took in a deep breath. "*Herr Generaloberst,* I fear that with all the attention to the security of the laboratories and production facilities, we overlooked the support facilities." What he did not say—that statistic was soon to come—was that over a hundred key scientists, technicians, support workers, and SS security personnel had been lost, with another hundred in some state of injury.

Krause glared at Zimmermann. "What of the aircraft and your crew? Are they damaged?"

"*Nein, Herr Generaloberst.* We all survived, as did the aircraft."

"*Ja. Sehr gut.*" He pointed his walking stick, which he had hoped would be replaced with the baton of the *Generalfeldmarschall* someday, toward the storage and assembly building, its concrete walls and roof now blackened in places by smoke from burning avgas. "How did the building fare?"

"It was untouched, *Herr Generaloberst.* Apparently, the assault team targeted only personnel and easy to damage facilities such as the flight control tower and the command center."

"How long before the airfield is operational?"

"*Herr Generaloberst,* that is not yet known, but clearly the airstrip itself is undamaged. Engineers are on the way to repair and replace the damaged control tower and command center. That is not the primary concern here. We must replace the lost aviation gasoline and repair the tanks. That may take several days, but at the end, all will be operational again."

"Noted. *Sehr gut.*" Krause stared directly at Zimmermann. "But *Herr Generalleutnant,* you seem concerned. Why?"

Zimmermann shook his head. "*Herr Generaloberst,* we can get the airfield operational in quick order. My crew and the aircraft are intact, but the assault team destroyed the power generator and distribution center. The entire installation is without electrical power except for some emergency generators, but they will soon exhaust their fuel." He paused.

"And, *Herr Generalleutnant,* there is more?"

"Jawohl, *Herr Generaloberst.* There is more. All but one of the principal scientists were killed and most of the support staff and production engineers as well."

Krause blanched as white as the crisply starched shirt he put on before departing Berlin. The *Führer* conference had been so stressful that he completely soaked the clean shirt he had put on just that morning. After a few seconds, he responded as the installation commander and senior facility engineer arrived. "Then, gentlemen, we had best go and inspect the damage."

With that, the men all piled into the staff car, which whisked them out of the airfield and toward the personnel compound. The tour lasted several hours. The devastation was immense. Following that, the installation commander, a man who knew his career had ended and now only sought to preserve his life, presented a sobering brief in the headquarters conference room. The statistics were grim. In addition to the complete loss of the power station and the airfield damage, he reported a loss of 22 senior scientists and physicists, including the three killed by Kwiatkowski's grenade. A hundred and four technicians, junior scientists, and production staff perished as did 82 *SS* security personnel. As he exited the headquarters building, Krause turned to Zimmermann. "Very well, *Herr Generalleutnant*. As terrible as this episode has been, it appears that the devices are all secure as are the production facilities. The program must proceed. How soon will you be operational?"

Zimmermann looked at Pieper, then at Zwilling, who had been largely silent throughout the entire tour and briefing. Head bent down, staring at the grassy path below, he responded meekly. "*Herr Generaloberst, Herr Generalleutnant*. The devices are intact and unharmed. The intruders either were unable to break into the complex, or that was not their intention. The next device to be operational is about prepared. There are two that are almost ready. There are three more in some stage of production. I expect the first device to be operational within ten days."

With that, the pale young man again lowered his head. Zimmermann detected something, but he was not quite sure what it was. Zwilling seemed almost disappointed that the attackers had not destroyed or at least damaged the three devices now sitting in the production complex awaiting final assembly and movement to the airfield storage facility.

With the tour and briefings completed, Krause boarded the Trimotor for the short trip back to Berlin. He came away from the devastated *Der Gevatter Tod* with four essential impressions. He would brief the *Führer* and other high-ranking officials in due course. First, the devices were all safe, undamaged, and very close to combat readiness. Second, the bomber and crew were unhurt, and once the airfield was put back into action, a mission could be flown within a few days. Third, and of critical importance for the future, the enemy killed significant key members of the development and production team. Only Professor Tisza remained of the cadre, capable and knowledgeable in how to refine the material to weapons grade and then how to finally construct a workable device. There were numerous uninjured personnel remaining who knew certain aspects of the process, but for security reasons, only the four key physicists knew the big picture of how the entire system operated. Now, only István Tisza remained; he must be safeguarded at all costs. It would take weeks or perhaps months to rebuild the key personnel cadre around him. Finally, identification had been carelessly left on a dead assailant's body—a letter from the man's wife in Moscow. A pouch had been found with two documents of Russian origin inside, clearly indicating a Soviet operation. With this information in hand, Krause believed he was safe from retribution or charges, unlike the unfortunate installation commander, security manager, and SS detachment senior officers, who would be blamed for the security breach.

* * * * * * * *

Berlin, 25 October 1943

Zimmermann arrived back in Berlin three days after the attack. He managed to ring up AGATHA late in the afternoon before the briefing with Krause to alert her of the events and that he would be delayed but was unhurt. He lied. He failed to mention the wound. That knowledge would come soon enough; worrying her at this point had no point.

When he finally revealed the wound, she chastised him. Was she not strong enough to deal with something like that? After all, this is war. He laughed it off, exclaiming, "Not to worry, my dear. It's just another combat wound badge." She found the joke unamusing.

The following day, Zimmermann stayed at his flat to recuperate. He preferred working at *Luftwaffe* headquarters, but Krause ordered him to take several days of rest to fully recover. AGATHA came over to his flat to, as she stated, "Nurse him back to good health."

The phone rang. She answered. Krause paused for a moment, somewhat surprised that someone other than Zimmermann answered, but he had heard of the budding relationship between the attractive widowed baroness and the equally attractive *Luftwaffe* general. It bothered him a bit for potential security concerns, but he overall judged it a good thing. After all, he needed to keep his pilot happy and fit for duty, especially after the *Der Gevatter Tod* catastrophe.

"Herr *Generaloberst*. *Guten Tag*, sir." Zimmermann waved to AGATHA in an "I have it, *danke*" sort of motion. She understood the gesture, mouthed a silent "of course," and departed the room, closing the double doors behind her. What Zimmermann did not know was that once out of the room, she sprinted over to an extension phone in Zimmermann's bedroom and gently lifted the handset while holding her hand over the mouthpiece.

Peter, we have a problem. As you might imagine, the *Führer* is apoplectic. Heads are rolling, but fortunately, not ours."

"*Jawohl, Herr Generaloberst.*"

"We know that the Bolsheviks were behind the raid on the facility. Unfortunately, we don't know how much they know of the work conducted there. Nevertheless, it remains vulnerable. Do you understand, Peter? Highly vulnerable. Make certain that your crew is well protected. We have tripled the security force."

"*Jawohl, Herr Generaloberst.* I understand."

"Also, the *Führer* has ordered me to transfer Professor Tisza to the *Katz* Castle laboratory facility. That's where we will rebuild the team."

AGATHA took a deep breath. *Katz Castle! Tisza is the key!* She almost dropped the handset but managed to regain control before she made a crucial mistake. "Tisza will continue his work there. The devices are apparently well developed such that the technicians at *Der Gevatter Tod* can complete their assembly and make them ready for action. Be prepared for your next mission within the next two weeks."

"*Jawohl, Herr Generaloberst.*"

"Peter, I was assured that the *Katz* Castle facility is fully capable once Tisza and the replacement technicians and scientists arrive and he oversees the operation. That makes a second attack by the Bolsheviks practically impossible, you understand. Better to have the entire staff in hand at *Katz* than to lose them in East Prussia. That would set us back months, if not years. I'm arranging the transfer now along with some key equipment but, essentially, there will be no production capability at *Katz* for some time. The devices and all other equipment will remain in place for now at *Der Gevatter Tod*."

"*Jawohl, Herr Generaloberst,* I understand."

"Finally, Peter, the *Führer* wants to personally present you with your Knight's Cross with Oak Leaves and Swords. Be prepared to go to Berchtesgaden and meet the *Führer* there on November second. Do you have that? November second. More details will follow."

"*Jawohl, Herr Generaloberst.* Berchtesgaden on two November. I will fly in the evening prior in my own plane. Meanwhile, I must return to *Der Gevatter Tod* and see to my crew."

"Precisely, Peter. That is all for now. *Guten Tag, Herr Generalleutnant.*"

At that point, Zimmermann heard several clicks on the line. He held the handset out as if inspecting it. *That's very odd.* He looked at the handset cradled in his good arm, then at the double French doors leading out to the veranda, then turned his head to the office double doors. For a brief moment, he hesitated, curious, and actually a little alarmed by the clicking noise. He squeezed his eyeballs into a wince, and putting the handset up to his ear, finished the conversation. Where was Amelia? A moment of doubt crept back in. *No, no concern. Just the usual technical troubles caused by the previous bombing.*

"*Guten Tag, Herr Generaloberst.* I appreciate the information and all the caution. We will protect the program and the Fatherland. *Danke, Herr Generaloberst.*"

As the dial tone indicated that Krause had hung up, Zimmermann placed the handset back in the cradle, but he remained curious about the odd clicking on the line. In the bedroom, once she heard the dial tone, AGATHA quickly replaced the handset and raced back out of the bedroom into the main sitting room. She grabbed a book off at side table and hurriedly plopped down into a chair trying to appear as if she had been there all along quietly reading. She breathed in deeply to mask the effect of having raced in from the bedroom. The ploy worked, but her heart beat rapidly with nervous tension. *Katz Castle. Tisza is the key.*

* * * * * * * *

Carinhall, Near Berlin, 27 October 1943

The two men walked slowly through the hallway lined with antique tapestries, statues, and paintings by Old Masters. In the expansive Great Hall, A-shaped with great carved wooden beams overhead, Himmler, Goebbels, Bormann, Zeitzler, and Krause gathered around a highly polished mahogany conference table. Göring chaired the meeting. Zimmermann wondered why he and Zwilling had been invited; after all, this was a meeting of the Party "dinosaurs." More probably, it was because they represented the crew that would carry out the upcoming counterattack. Zimmermann feared what might happen here. Official Berlin had been aflame with passionate speech about eliminating the Bolshevik menace once and for all. He wondered if they understood the gravity of what they shouted for. As he sat at the far end of the huge table, he thought of the device safe in the complex that neared completion. Göring gaveled the meeting to order. Krause's presence, along with Zwilling and himself, told him that the next bomb, about to be moved to the airfield storage facility was soon to come into play.

"Gentlemen, welcome all. I think everyone has been briefed fully on the incidents at *Der Gevatter Tod*. All shook their heads or nodded affirmative. "Then we must react. But as both I and the *Führer* have advised, a reaction must be out of cooled passion and military necessity. It cannot be rash."

At this point, Zimmermann felt tension easing from both himself and also visibly from Zwilling sitting next to him, looking even paler and weaker than ever. *Perhaps they mean only a demonstration. Ja! That's it! Drop a bomb in a remote area or lightly populated region as a demonstration of Germany's power and resolve to use the new super weapon. Then offer an armistice to the Soviets such as the British had been forced to agree to. Ja, that's it. Perhaps they could agree to an annexation of territory already occupied by German forces. What an elegant solution. It ended the war, stopped the bloodshed, preserved the Fatherland, and rebuilt, nay, expanded the old Imperial Empire of the Second Reich before the disastrous Great War. And, oh, by the way, accomplished Hitler's goal of Lebensraum. Perhaps some Caucasus oil concessions might be thrown into the deal. Finally, some practical sense here!*

His hopes were soon crushed. In an instant, any hope of an "elegant solution" collapsed with the *Reichsmarschall's* next words.

"Accordingly, not only will we eliminate the Soviet cities of Moscow and Leningrad, but with the third device, we will obliterate London. While the British may protest innocence, it is the *Führer's* opinion, which I fully endorse, that the British are behind the raid on *Der Gevatter Tod*. No one believes the Soviets could carry that out on their own. Probably the Americans helped as well." Heads bobbed in agreement. Zimmermann stiffened. *The fools! The arrogant fools! What are you doing?* Zwilling's head sank further into his chest.

Göring continued, "Not only that, but the next three devices, which *Generaloberst* Krause assures me are well along in production at *Der Gevatter Tod*, will be ready for deployment soon. The targets will be Birmingham, Toronto, and New York."

With that, all perked up. Some resistance began to pop up, perhaps not so much from the morality, but more from the practicality. Goebbels spoke first, standing up and placing his hands palm down on the table and leaning in. "*Herr Reichsmarschall.* You say North America. How do you propose that feat?"

Göring beamed. "That is why we have here the chief pilot of Project Armageddon with us tonight." With a wave of his chubby hand, Göring indicated Zimmermann. "Please, *Herr Generalleutnant* von Zimmermann. Brief us as to why this feat would be quite possible."

Zimmermann slowly stood. "*Jawohl, Herr Reichsmarschall.*"

For the next 15 minutes, he outlined the technical features of the Me 264. The Linden Tree, he pointed out, could operate to a 28,000-foot ceiling, well above the blast area. More importantly, it had the range to launch from French airfields, fly to the North American east coast, deliver the ordnance, and return to base . . . all in one sortie. The Me 264 Messerschmitt entry in the *Amerikabomber* initiative had the legs to accomplish the mission. Additionally, he noted that the next two prototypes, V2 and V3, were almost ready for trials and could be available by the time future devices were combat ready.

The group was impressed.

"Danke, Herr Generalleutnant. Very well done."

As Zimmermann sat, he felt as if he had just signed the world's execution order. Göring blustered, as he did so well, "So, gentlemen, you can see our plan has merit. Accordingly, we shall now refer to each device by its target name—Moscow, Leningrad, London, Birmingham, Toronto, and New York."

At this point, *Generaloberst* Zeitzler posed a question. Although one of the chief architects of the disastrous Kursk operation, he had previously strongly advised Hitler not to issue the never withdraw order to Paulus and 6th Army at Stalingrad. As Chief of the General Staff, he had credibility and, as before, now voiced doubt about the viability of the plan for Soviet, British, and perhaps even American destruction. *"Herr Reichsmarschall.* Is it wise to target the United States? After all, we are not at war with the Americans."

Göring looked annoyed at first, then broke into a most malevolent grin. *"Herr Generaloberst* Zeitzler, the *Führer* has considered that very question and calculates that once we finish with London, there will be no need to attack the Americas. Remember that America is a weak, decadent society only interested in profit and luxury. They will fold when threatened, be assured of it. They are run by the capitalist and mongrel Jew moneychangers. They will not resist. If they have the temerity to resist, the *Reich* will crush them!"

As his voice rose higher and higher and louder and louder in his ridiculous tirade, Zimmermann could only think to himself, *Is this what we have come to? What monstrous hubris! Is this the Fatherland that I fight for and cherish?*

Finished with his histrionics, Göring calmed himself and stated quietly but menacingly, "Are there any other questions?" There were none. With that, he proclaimed the meeting adjourned and invited the attendees into the dining room for the most sumptuous banquet imaginable. Zimmermann gave his apologies to Göring, claiming that with so much work to accomplish before "Moscow" could be delivered on the enemy capital, he and Zwilling needed to return to Berlin. As they passed back through the corridor toward the main entrance—the corridor lined with exquisite artwork stolen from so many innocent Jewish families or looted from the museums of Occupied Europe—he considered the *Reichsmarschall's* words. "Decadent and luxury-loving Americans indeed," he mumbled to himself and no one in particular.

Zimmermann and Zwilling stood in the steady rain waiting for the staff car to arrive. The younger man shivered. It was not especially cold that evening, but the rain and fog made it seem more so. *Still the man has little tolerance for cold, almost as if he is ill*, thought Zimmermann. He worried about Zwilling. The man's health clearly deteriorated week by week. Perhaps it was the stress of the attack on *Der Gevatter Tod* or just the tension of the onerous position he played in the war and the world's fate. Though not really certain why, he knew that Zwilling suffered terribly.

Zwilling detected the unease in the *Luftwaffe* general as the meeting had become more and more bizarre. Threats of exterminating every Russian, then vaporizing the entire British nation followed by their evil allies, the Americans, had truly unnerved both men. The depravity of the threats emanating from the very top of the Nazi regime frightened the young physicist. He had had such qualms ever since that day over Dartmoor where he witnessed his and his fellow scientists' handiwork. With each event piling one on the other, his concern grew. Had they created a monster that would soon eat them? Had they foisted on the world the instrument of mankind's ultimate destruction? Since that day at Dartmoor, he had transformed from a scientist beaming with pride and enthusiasm for his creation, like Baron Frankenstein of fiction and film, to a man shocked and stunned by what he had created. With the Carinhall brief, he had finally broken. He had to say something. He sensed in Zimmermann a similar concern. Perhaps it was fear—the same fear as his own. Perhaps it was the general's essential morality and humanity. He did not know, but he knew he had to finally speak of his concerns. He shook violently with the chill made worse by the tension. Zimmermann grabbed him by the shoulders.

"Franz, Franz. Are you well? Are you all right?" Zimmermann looked directly into his eyes. Zwilling's lips trembled.

"*Herr Generalleutnant,* I must say this. We have . . . Germany . . . we have gone mad . . . insane. We developed this weapon . . . naïvely, I suppose . . . to end this war and ensure that Germany survives. Now it has totally become the instrument for setting off Armageddon."
The irony of the project name had not escaped Zimmermann. He stood statue-still, just looking at the trees beyond the drive swaying in the misty, cold drizzle.

Zwilling continued, "I do not know if I can continue in this . . . thing . . . we have created. Understand, sir, that atomic energy can light up the world if used well. But in the hands of a man like Adolf Hitler and the masters that we have, it can only be a terrible curse. I understand that now," he exclaimed, tears rolling down his ashen cheeks. Zimmermann still said nothing. He just kept staring at the swaying trees in the distance.

The car arrived. Holtzmann leapt out to the side and swung open the door. "*Guten Abend, Herr Generalleutnant, Herr Doktor Zwilling.* Terrible night, sir."

Zimmermann only grumbled. It had indeed been a terrible night. He had learned that he was to be the instrument of destruction of perhaps millions of souls. To the Prussian warrior-aristocrat, honed in the ideals of country, honor, duty, and integrity, what he had heard that evening in the extravagant palace that Göring built for himself shocked him beyond anything he'd ever experienced. As the Mercedes sped away from Carinhall, windscreen wipers slapping away the now heavy raindrops, he came to a decision—the most important decision of his life. He leaned over to Zwilling, who sat sad and hunched in the seat beside him looking even more dejected and distraught. "Franz, I have a plan. We shall talk in the morning."

"I understand, *Herr Generalleutnant*. In the morning."

* * * * * * * *

Garmisch-Partenkirchen, Bavaria, 29 October 1943

A lone figure slowly ambled down the cobblestoned street. He appeared to the casual observer as just another elderly gentleman with no particular place to go. The early snow concealed the streets and walkways of the Bavarian alpine town nestled neatly near the Austrian border. All the shops had already closed for the evening as tradesman and merchants headed home for a warm dinner and a refreshing beer. Business had been good lately. With the lifting of the blockade, goods started to flow again, but the mood remained dark. The government had built a military hospital nearby, and that provided substantial trade for the local economy. Additionally, the *Luftwaffe* opened an airfield to service the hospital and supporting military activities.

Despite all this, many wondered why the war went on. Many became increasingly anxious about the future. As each month and year went by, the public in this idyllic little Bavarian town that hosted winter Olympic games in the 1930s worried more and more about the edicts from Berlin coming one atop the other restricting who could do what, when, and how. They worried that maybe they had granted the National Socialist party entirely too much power over their lives. And what about their neighbors, friends, and families who seemed to disappear on a regular and unexplained basis. These thoughts worried the people of Garmisch-Partenkirchen. Given that worry, no one would question the lone elderly man walking in the snowy twilight and headed into St. Martin's Catholic Church. Perhaps he had lost close friends or relatives in this never-ending war and probably went into the church to pray or seek solace for his loss.

He entered and headed directly for the confessional that sat off to the side of the pews, intentionally obscured so as to reduce the chances of confessions being overheard from any nearby pew. The man shambled up to the confessional and opened the heavy wooden door. He stepped in and sat down while unwrapping the heavy wool muffler that gave him the impression of age. He sat for about a minute, silently, breathing slowly in and out as if truly in religious contemplation until finally, the man on the other side of the barrier spoke.

"*Guten Abend.*"

The man responded, "*Guten Abend,* Herr CHARLEMAGNE. You have something for me?" He heard a deep sigh from the other side of the confessional barrier.

"It is a heavy, onerous thing to betray one's country, is it not? Still, when we deal with an evil so great as our beloved *Führer* and his minions, one must take a stand."

The man did not respond. *What does one say? How would he react if in the same situation?*

The German continued, "Evil must be confronted and crushed, you understand, and there must be of those of us willing to do whatever is necessary, however harsh or distasteful. Do you not agree, *Mein Herr?*"

The Briton shifted in his seat. He wanted to get a glimpse of the man known to British intelligence only as CHARLEMAGNE, but the German refused to allow it. "That is quite so, *Herr* CHARLEMAGNE. Quite so. What can you tell me tonight, sir?"

The German coughed, no doubt catching a cold in this early taste of winter after such a warm, sunny summer. "You will be interested to know that *Herr* Professor *Doktor* Tisza, who has been working on our Project Armageddon—" He paused. "Project Armageddon. How appropriate, don't you agree? In any case," he continued, "*Herr Doktor* has been moved to the research facility at *Katz* Castle on the Rhine. It seems that the Soviet raid on our little project in East Prussia killed all our chief atomic scientists but him. Is that not interesting?" The German coughed again.

"Why might that be of interest to my superiors?" fired in the man, already fully aware of the answer. The German coughed again and chuckled. "Why, why you ask? Perhaps it may be because of how *Herr* Professor *Doktor* Tisza came to be our chief physicist in the first place. The *Gestapo* is holding his family hostage at their home in Budapest. *Herr* Himmler made it quite clear that any, shall I say, lack of cooperation on his part will result in dire consequences. I don't believe I need to elaborate, do I?"

"No, quite clear. So Tisza works under duress. Nonetheless, his work was demonstrated by your little affair on Dartmoor."

CHARLEMAGNE paused. "*Ja*, you are right. Our little affair that may be the death knell for the world if the Nazis are not stopped. Here are the two things you may well be interested in, sir. I do not say these things lightly. I wish no harm for my country, but I fear for the Fatherland if this maniac in Berlin continues to destroy. He must be stopped, so hear me well. It is not well-known among our Nazi masters, but Tisza has indicated that if you, British or Soviet, it matters not . . . if you rescue his family and somehow can spirit him to safety, he will gladly work for you or perhaps the Americans to develop a weapon that counters Germany's. With such a technology, Hitler would not dare use the weapon he has developed. It is rather like a stalemate at chess, you see, a sort of mutual destruction. No one dares use their bombs, and we then have a true peace."

The man on the other side tensed. This intelligence certainly had been worth the risky trip across the border from Switzerland through Austria and finally into Bavaria but, in truth, he was the only one that CHARLEMAGNE trusted with this incredible intelligence. "*Herr* CHARLEMAGNE, you said there was another piece on this chessboard?"

"*Jawohl.* There is. At the Masurian Woods site, there are three bombs now almost operational. Hitler, to the delight of some of his followers, has named them Moscow, Leningrad, and London. You can perhaps figure out why. But there are three more in production code-named Birmingham, Toronto . . . and New York. You see the problem. But here is a solution, *Mein Herr.* Tisza is now the only one capable of finishing the construction of the devices. So tight was our security that only four scientists, Tisza and three Germans, had the full knowledge of how to produce the explosive material and thus make such a weapon. Thanks to you . . . or perhaps, the Soviet raid . . . Tisza is now the lone survivor. You have a very slight window of opportunity to free him or neutralize the man."

The man shook his head. He understood that Tisza was the key. Captured or killed, he represented the linchpin. "Understood."

"Tisza is now at *Katz* Castle on the Rhine, but the security there is not very robust yet. That will change in the next few days. An additional *SS* security detail is being sent to ensure no more raids. You understand . . . only a few days. After that, well, after that, who knows? Remember that all six devices are either close to ready for use at Masurian Woods or in some state of completion and that only Tisza can direct their completion. Haste, haste, post haste, sir."

"Understood." The man leaned back into the confessional, close to being simply overwhelmed by the gravity of what he had just been told. A creaking noise came from the other side as CHARLEMAGNE shifted in the seat, indicating perhaps the conversation had ended.

"You must go now, sir. There is a poem by an American . . . the name escapes me now: 'The woods are lovely dark and deep...and miles to go before I sleep.'[9] Go now and Godspeed!"

---

9 Robert Frost, "Stopping by Woods on a Snowy Evening," in *The Poetry of Robert Frost,* ed. Edward Connery Lathem (New York: Henry Holt and Company, Inc., 1969).

The British agent replied, "And you, Herr CHARLEMAGNE. Would you grant me absolution were you actually a priest?" A cough and a chuckle came from the other side.

"Say ten Hail Marys and put some *Reichsmark* in the poor box."

With that, the Briton wrapped the muffler around his head and shoulders, opened the confessional door, and shambled out, appearing again as simply an elderly gent seeking solace in church and confession. As he neared the station to catch a late train, he picked up the pace. After all, Major David Niven, late of the Highland Light Infantry, the Rifle Brigade, the commandos, and currently seconded to SOE had a train to catch to Innsbruck and, thereafter, the late train to Zürich. Later that following morning, a message went out to INTREPID with the newfound intelligence followed by a message immediately back to CHRISTIE in Berlin.

* * * * * * * *

Budapest, Hungary, 31 October 1943

The hulking man kicked in the door to the elegant flat in the upscale section of Budapest, his weapon raised high in a ready firing position. The two *Gestapo* men sitting at the kitchen table had no chance. One wheeled about, desperately attempting to draw his *Luger* from the shoulder holster. A round struck him in the left temple, thrusting him against the kitchen stove behind them. The second *Gestapo* man dove for the floor, desperate to get out of the line of fire. Too late.

Two more men dressed in all black charged through the door and opened fire. One bullet struck the second *Gestapo* agent in the shoulder. He cried out in pain but only for a brief moment as another round caught him directly under the right eye that blew out the back of his head, scattering brains and blood against the kitchen wall.

In a back bedroom of the luxury flat, a woman clung to her two children, having heard the door crashing, the shouting, and gunfire that followed. She immediately covered the two young children with her arms and upper body, expecting the worst. After a few seconds, the shouting and gunfire went silent. Only the sobbing of the two small children could be heard in the room. A moment later, a tall, somewhat thin man with a sporty pencil mustache appeared at the bedroom door.

"Madame Tisza. I am Major David Niven. Please, gather your most important things—valuables, jewelry, money, documents, and some traveling clothes. We must be off as soon as possible. Please hurry, Madame." He turned and strode back into the kitchen to help the two rough men clean up the grotesque scene.

With the *Gestapo* agents properly disposed of, the blood and brain matter scrubbed from the kitchen floor and walls, and with Madame Tisza and her two children protected at the SOE safe house in Zürich, a short message went out to Berlin direct to *SS* headquarters. The routine report sent every two days by teletype from Budapest used a special code developed for just this operation. Niven had located the codebook among the dead *Gestapo* agents' belongings. *Damn bloody careless sods,* he thought to himself. The simple message, when translated from the special code, merely stated: "Package secure. No problems" along with the date and time. The portable teletype machine, designed to patch into a standard landline telephone, and the codebook for the next 30 days accompanied the Tisza family and Niven back to the safety and comfort of Zürich.

Hours later, CHRISTIE received a message from INTREPID, which he scrambled to pass to AGATHA. The pair held periodic meetings to maintain their cover where she appeared as the wealthy Swiss baroness with significant financial interests in Germany, with CHRISTIE as her business manager. The message from New York simply read: "Tisza family freed and safe. In Zürich. PHANTOM sending to Lisbon under guard, then to NYC."

* * * * * * * *

Berlin, 1 November 1943

The phone rang. AGATHA lifted the handset gingerly, hoping it was Zimmermann on the line. It was not. CHRISTIE, her "business manager" asked if she was alone. She was. Zimmermann had flown to Berchtesgaden that morning in his private plane for the medal ceremony at Hitler's Bavarian Alps retreat and where the *Führer* spent every free moment he could spare with his paramour, Eva Braun.

"We need to meet, Baroness. I have come across an especially interesting and potentially lucrative business investment you will most assuredly want to hear of." Those were the code words for something "hot" and critical just arrived from INTREPID.

"*Ja, Herr* Todt. Shall we say ten o'clock at the usual place?"

"Most agreeable, Baroness. Ten it is. I look forward to meeting as always." He rang off. She held the phone handset to her ear and then slowly dropped it back into its cradle. She wondered. That code phrase was reserved for only the most delicate or important issue. Looking at the Louis XVI-period clock on the mantle, she realized she had best hurry along. Already, it was just past 8:00 a.m.

Zimmermann departed early that morning for the Berlin-Staaken airfield. Although the ceremony was scheduled for the following day, with the early November weather, one might get a balmy, sunny day or a blizzard. He always traveled a day ahead to account for any such delays. Besides, there was a wonderful little *Gasthaus* and restaurant in Berchtesgaden that he and Ingrid had stayed at years earlier. He checked when Krause announced the ceremony place and date, and, yes, the same owners ran the inn and restaurant. He would stay two nights before returning to Berlin and then back to *Der Gevatter Tod* to check on progress. The *Luftwaffe* ground crew had already rolled out the Fieseler Fi 97. They fueled and warmed it up as Holtzmann drove up onto the tarmac just outside the hanger.

"It looks to be a nice day for flying, *Herr Generalleutnant*."

"Indeed, Holtzmann. Take the car back to the flat. If Baroness Ramsour-Fritsch requires any transportation, please provide it and then relax until I return on the third. Then we have much to do."

"*Jawohl, Herr Generalleutnant.* Have a safe and successful journey."

With that, Zimmermann strode across the tarmac, turning up his greatcoat collar against a chilly breeze. The warmth in the cockpit felt good. With clear weather and light winds, it would be an easy and comfortable flight to Berchtesgaden.

* * * * * * * *

She picked up the handset again and called for a taxi, which arrived in only a few minutes. By just before 10:00 a.m. she arrived at the restaurant used for their "business meetings." CHRISTIE sat in the usual table in back that provided some measure of privacy. She made a show of greeting him. "*Herr* Todt, good to see you as always. I understand you have some potential business investments for my consideration?"

"*Jawohl,* Baroness. I do." He bowed his head appropriately, stood, and slid her chair back in. He then sat down and opened a briefcase making a show of extracting a sheaf of papers. No one but an accountant or attorney might have noticed that these were the same documents they had used several times over the past months. To the smiling, affable restaurant owner behind the bar washing up beer steins from last night's dinner guests, papers were papers. He didn't intrude on the baroness and her financial manager when business called.

In a low voice, he whispered, "Signal from INTREPID. Tisza has been moved. He is at the *Katz* Castle laboratory now. More importantly, he is willing to come over to us with what he knows if—" he paused.

"If?"

"If and only if we ensure his family's safety. They were being held hostage for his cooperation and good behavior at their Budapest flat. PHANTOM sent in a team yesterday and pulled them out. They are safe in Zürich now and will be sent to Lisbon and then New York. But in order to rescue them, the team killed two *Gestapo* agents.

PHANTOM may be able to fool the Jerries for a bit, but how long is the operative question. We have to move fast and extract Tisza from *Katz* Castle straight away before the *SS* or *Gestapo* figure it out."

"Is INTREPID sending a team from Camp X? How can we assist?"

"Aye, there's the rub. We know from Niven's highly placed *Abwehr* contact that the *SS* is moving a huge security detachment to the castle. But that is still a few days away. Tisza is there now, setting up his new laboratory. The Jerries are worried about having him at the Masurian Woods site lest . . . ahem." He cleared his throat. "Lest the 'Russians' pull off another raid."

He chuckled. He had trained with most of the Polish, Czech, and Greek team members at Camp X. He continued. "That likely means our window of opportunity is less than forty-eight hours. Amelia, my love, it looks like we are at bat for this one." A serious expression on his face made the point; it was imperative to snatch Tisza from *Katz* Castle right away, and they were the team to accomplish the extraction. What they had to accomplish their mission was essentially their physical ability, courage, and brains—and little else.

"INTREPID informed us that there is a man in Sankt Goarshausen, the town close to the castle, who is a member of the German resistance. He is conveniently a victual contractor—a meat and produce distributor. He is well-placed and already has a contract to provide fresh produce and meat to the castle, so there is a way in. He also was tasked by MI6 last year to keep a watch on the place once we found out something scientific and technical had started up. We now know, of course, it was an alternate atomic lab and research facility. Presumably, they also intend to produce the bomb material there as well. But Tisza is the key."

She jerked back ever so slightly. *Tisza is the key. Tisza is the key.* Those were the words she heard Zimmermann mumble in his alcoholic stupor weeks earlier as they drifted down the Rhine. But she also remembered his anxiety and rudeness when they passed *Katz* Castle. Since then she had learned why. *Very well, then. How do we mount this operation? Driving a car across Germany in the best of con-*

ditions would take far too long. Then, a thought occurred—why not fly? She had gained sufficient experience and knowledge to handle a simple aircraft in calm weather. That would not last. She knew a cold front bringing a late autumn snowfall was expected in a few days. *Decision time.* She perked up. "We fly!"

CHRISTIE had a quizzical look on his face. "We fly?"

"Yes, we fly." She pulled a piece of paper and pen from her purse and scribbled a name, address, and phone number. Handing it to CHRISTIE, she explained, "This is the information for *Herr* Dellinger at *Tempelhof* Airport. He runs a flying school for civilians and also rents out aircraft to his students. When Zimmermann is away, I have been going to Dellinger's for flying lessons. He is a most pleasant chap and very accommodating for an attractive and very persuasive aristocratic lady." Both grinned broadly.

"He has good taste," remarked CHRISTIE.

She smiled. "Cheeky bastard! Now ring him up and hire an airplane, a Messerschmitt Bf 108 *Taifun*. It has four seats and will do. That's what I have been flying. Use my name and make sure he knows you are my business manager. Hire it for four days. We must be out of the country by then. Leave him a hefty deposit for the plane. Tell him we are going for a brief holiday, in say, Vienna. That's all he needs to know. File a civilian flight plan. Then we will rendezvous at *Tempelhof* at 1300 this afternoon and, God willing, will make this plan work."

With that, they made a show of shuffling papers, signing some, and so forth, mainly for the restaurant owner's benefit. He brought over their usual pastry and coffee. By 11:00 a.m., they departed, AGATHA back to the *Kaiserhof* and CHRISTIE to Tempelhof to arrange the aircraft.

* * * * * * * *

Sankt Goarshausen on the Rhine, 1 November 1943

The flight to Sankt Goarshausen was uneventful. CHRISTIE was impressed at how well AGATHA handled the airplane, but he expected no less. They landed at a small private airstrip just north of town and only a couple of miles from the castle.

Karl Reinhardt had been a good German, a good Party man early on. Wounded on the Western Front in the first war fighting as an artilleryman, he seethed at Germany's humiliation. Without employment or a future, he briefly joined the *Freikorps* in the early 1920s, those groups of soldiers released from active duty, but without any prospects. They readily joined in bashing those they blamed for the defeat, especially anyone identified as sympathetic to the Russian Bolsheviks. He even joined the early National Socialist Party with its rising star, the army veteran Adolf Hitler. But as the 1920s rolled into the early 1930s, he became more and more disenchanted with the Party's excesses. He had no qualms or quarrel with his Jewish friends and neighbors. By the mid-1930s, he had established a thriving grocery and victualing business in the Middle Rhine area. Many of his customers, employees, and business acquaintances were Jewish. The final break came when his only son, Otto, an airman in the *Luftwaffe*, had been lost over the Channel in the early days of the Battle of Britain. He harbored no ill will or hatred toward the British; they defended their homeland, just as he had done in 1914. Rather, he directed his grief for a son's loss and the resultant rage and hatred at the Nazi regime. He vowed to do all in his power to destroy that regime and became a key member of the secret German resistance movement in the Middle Rhine region. Due to his past as a decorated veteran and a Party member (at least still on paper), he obtained the clearances to enter into contract to supply food to the new secret research laboratory in *Katz* Castle in 1942. Now that access became a crucial advantage as AGATHA and CHRISTIE prepared to assault the castle to free the most important man in the world at that moment. For Reinhardt, here was his chance to strike back at Hitler, the Nazis, and the entire National Socialist regime.

Reinhardt warned that castle security was very tight; he couldn't allow them to go in with him and his assistant. Only those employees already vetted could get inside. There was no time to do that.

The assault required a direct insertion and exfiltration. He had a plan though. While inside, he pretty much had the run of the place. He would conceal a rope knotted in several places for climbing in the bottom of a vegetable box. Once inside, he would attach the rope to a railing in an unused area of the castle on the southwest side facing the river. There were two large paneled doors leading out to a balcony from what had been the master bedroom apartment. It was a steep climb up from the cliff, but doable for anyone in as fine a physical condition as AGATHA and CHRISTIE. That would be the insertion point. Once inside, they would then dispose of the rope by hiding it in a location where they could retrieve it later if needed. They did not want to endanger Reinhardt by leaving a rope hanging from the balcony. How else did it get there but by the food contractor was a great question no one would want asked.

Reinhardt, in his many trips in and out bringing food, had put together a fairly accurate picture of the castle's layout. He observed Tisza two nights in a row, having his dinner in his quarters at about 8:00 p.m. Presumably, that is where he would be at that time. Once AGATHA and CHRISTIE snatched the scientist, they would make their way to the kitchen where Reinhardt and his assistant, Deppen, would meet them. Vegetables came in large wooden boxes more like crates. These would be emptied and carried back out the kitchen entrance on the castle's rear. The kitchen stood well away from the quarters and laboratories as was customary in pre-modern buildings. It stood close to the woods and under the 40-meter-tall medieval watchtower called the *Bergfried*, the surviving part of the original fourteenth-century castle. That area was relatively unobserved from anywhere else in the compound and had the paved road leading up to the castle just outside the kitchen doors. There, the team with Tisza could be spirited away quickly in the delivery van. Tisza would be stuffed in one of the empty vegetable crates. AGATHA and CHRISTIE would put on smocks as if they were Reinhardt's assistants. The fact that two people entered the castle with the crates and four went out should not be a problem unless, by some quirk, the security guards that checked them in and dutifully inspected the goods happened to be lurking about the kitchen area. A risk, yes, but one that had to be taken.

From the castle, Reinhardt would spirit them to the airport where the Me 108 was parked By flying very low they should avoid any patrol planes. Once on the ground, they would meet up with Niven, who would spirit AGATHA, CHRISTIE, and Tisza out of the country via Zürich to Lisbon and then to New York. Mission complete. As to Tisza, they would leave evidence that he bolted on his own so as to protect Reinhardt and his crew from suspicion of complicity. It was a risk, but the man was willing to take it.

But as with all plans, danger, risk, and that inconvenient probabilistic nature of war might just intervene. It was well to recall the admonition of *Generalfeldmarschall* Helmuth von Moltke the Elder, chief of the Imperial German General Staff during the Wars of German Unification in the 1860s and 70s: "No plan of operations extends with any certainty beyond the first contact with the main hostile force."[10]

Earlier in the day, as AGATHA revved up the engine of the hired plane awaiting tower clearance for takeoff, a man in a black leather coat and a dark gray fedora hat placed a call from the terminal to *SS* headquarters in Berlin, attention *Sturmbannführer* Johann Maas. The short message simply stated: "The baroness has hired a private airplane and is departing Berlin with a declared destination of Vienna."

---

10 "On Strategy" (1871)/"Über Strategie" (1871), *Moltke on the Art of War: Selected Writings,* trans. and ed. Daniel J. Hughes and Harry Bell (New York: Presidio, 1993), 92.

CHAPTER 10

Knight's Cross

Berchtesgaden, Bavaria, 2 November 1943

"*Heil* Hitler!" Zimmermann's right arm shot up in perhaps the crispest Party salute he had ever delivered. He hated it, but when in Rome, etc., etc. Besides, it would not do at this stage to antagonize the *Führer* and his closest advisers. He had finally determined his course of action. It had been a long time evolving, but the Carinhall meeting confirmed for him what must now be done to preserve the Fatherland.

The man with the funny mustache looked much smaller in person then Zimmermann had imagined. Perhaps it was the effect of the staging wherever the *Führer* spoke. Leni Riefenstahl had captured the image of the greater than life, messianic crusader for the Aryan race and the Greater *Reich* in the films she made of the Party rallies at Zeppelin Field in Nuremberg in the 1930s. Wherever the *Führer* appeared, it was always on a raised stage or platform; if others stood beside him, the organizers made certain to lower them on the platform.

The much taller Zimmermann looked down on the much shorter leader of the *Reich*. Standing at attention with jaw firmly set and staring straight ahead at his most military and strict attention, he could only see the top of Hitler's peaked service cap. That's just as well, he concluded. *Do not even look the bastard in the eyes, which might give away my disdain for this "Bohemian corporal."*

"*Herr Generalleutnant* von Zimmermann, your country, your Party, is proud of you and your singular accomplishments not only on your latest mission but also in your entire history."

"I am most honored to serve, *Mein Führer.*"

Hitler shook his head briskly. "I understand that you served in the infantry on the Western Front in the first war."

Zimmermann lowered his head to look into the face of evil, but never revealed his emotions of the moment. "*Jawohl, mein Führer.* That is so. I commanded a company of the 1st Prussian Guards in France. Like you, *mein Führer*, I was wounded in action and decorated for valor."

Hitler beamed. It thrilled him no end when these Prussian aristocratic types had to acknowledge his own military accomplishments. To Zimmermann, Kline, and others who played the game, it was all understood to be nothing but a game. It did one well to just stroke the ego of the world's most powerful and dangerous man. Curse him in private, but praise him in public had been Kline's advice when he heard of Zimmermann's promotion and new decoration in recognition of the Dartmoor mission.

"Just so, *Herr Generalleutnant.* Just so." With that, Hitler turned to the aide trailing behind who opened a gold and black ornate wooden box. He extended the Knight's Cross with Oak Leaves and Swords—a bit of silver and black enameled metal suspended from a red, white, and black ribbon. As Hitler held the medal up, Zimmermann dipped his head. Hitler placed the ribbon over Zimmermann's neck. As he raised back up, Hitler straightened the medal hanging at Zimmermann's throat. The *Führer* thrust his hand out. Zimmermann clasped it, and with two firm shakes, the deal was done.

"Congratulations, *Herr Generalleutnant.* We expect great things from you in the future."

"*Danke, mein Führer.* I am always at the service of the Fatherland. It is an honor and a privilege." Perhaps he should have said *Reich* or the Party, but he couldn't. He fought for Germany, the German people—the Fatherland—not the strutting gang of Nazis. He simply could not dignify that. Hitler or the entourage neither noticed nor cared as they all clapped in unison.

After several congratulatory handshakes and even a few pats on the back, they all retired to a lounge area where pastries and coffee were served. Hitler, Göring, Himmler, and the others did not stay long. They retreated to an office with the door shut. *No matter,* thought Zimmermann. *That's just as well. I'd rather not make small talk anyway.* Instead, he engaged Eva Braun and some lesser functionaries in mindless chatter, calculating that he needed to stay at least an hour or so and be sociable for protocol's sake. And the pastry was excellent. He had not eaten at all, even that early morning before the flight, and thus partook of more than one of the delicious strudels and tortes.

The event complete, he walked out to the waiting staff car for his trip back into Berchtesgaden. As he exited the doors leading out to the drive and turned up his greatcoat collar against the chill, he looked up at the clouds racing by. *Cold front moving in. Likely snow tonight. It's good that I'm staying over the night. Foolish to try to fly in this weather.*

* * * * * * * *

Sankt Goarshausen, 2 November 1943

1900. The team prepared for the assault. Dressed in all black so as to be less detectable at night, AGATHA and CHRISTIE hid in the back of Reinhardt's delivery van under several crates of fresh vegetables. Reinhardt drove while the assistant, also a member of the local resistance and a World War I veteran, sat up front. They had made the vegetable and meat delivery at the same time every other day. Normally, he would have made daytime deliveries, but the head chef at the castle, a pompous but extremely talented cook, insisted that he and his staff not be disturbed during daylight hours. After all, they had to prepare meals for over 50 civilian scientists, technicians, and SS personnel three times a day. They could not be bothered by tradesmen trudging in and out of the kitchen and storerooms disrupting the cooks. "Therefore, *Herr* Reinhardt," he directed, "you will deliver your goods at precisely 1930 every other evening." Reinhardt did not like the arrangement, but now, with the necessity of striking at night—the overriding imperative—the delivery timing looked prescient.

The delivery van jostled over the rough road leading from Sankt Goarshausen to the castle. *Riding under a ton of vegetable crates might be the most uncomfortable half hour of her life,* thought AGATHA, *but all for the mission.* A few hundred feet from the drive that led up to the castle kitchen, the van stopped momentarily. The assistant leapt out of the front passenger seat and quickly unlocked the rear cargo door. Within seconds, AGATHA and CHRISTIE bounded out and disappeared into the woods.

Surrounded on the north and east side by heavy woods and facing the river on the south and west sides, *Katz* Castle sat atop a huge promontory over a steep cliff down to the Rhine. Originally constructed in the fourteenth century by Count Wilhelm II of Katzenelnbogen as an outer defensive fortification for *Rhinefels* Castle and a station for collecting the Rhine toll, the bastion also provided protection from *Maus* Castle down the river in the electorate of Trier, an often unfriendly neighbor. Napoleon and the French blew up the fortification in 1806, but in the 1890s, a private owner restored the castle's grandeur as a personal residence. At that time, the watchtower, the *Bergfried*, and part of the Great Hall were all that remained of the original structure. The buildings overlooked the town of Sankt Goarshausen, where Reinhardt worked and lived. In the distance further up the Rhine stood the Lorelei Rock, dominating all river traffic. The regime converted the castle to a research facility in 1942 when the Party seized the building for use as a test facility and alternate production site for a scientific program known as Project Armageddon.

AGATHA and CHRISTIE ducked low through the heavily forested area surrounding the castle until they reached the southwest face. Meanwhile, Reinhardt and Deppen, the assistant, easily passed through the security checkpoint as they had so many times previously. The friendly security guards knew and liked the men and truly respected them for their military service in the First World War. Step one complete. The two men proceeded around to the van parked by the kitchen entrance accompanied by a guard, who peremptorily inspected the produce crates. "All good. Same as usual, *Herr* Reinhardt. Have a good day and check with us before you depart," the friendly sentry assured them.

With a smile and a handshake, the security man departed while Reinhardt and Deppen unloaded four heavy crates of vegetables. While Deppen unloaded a crate of carrots, Reinhardt removed the coiled rope from underneath a cabbage crate and, wrapping it about his substantial waist, he concealed it with an oversized jacket. Reinhardt then headed quietly up the stairs toward the empty master bedroom apartment with the double doors leading onto the balcony. The master bedroom had been recently renovated with the intention of establishing the command center there and, thus, no one was about in the vicinity. The *SS* guards not on duty all gathered either in their mess for dinner or in the makeshift lounge, playing cards, backgammon, or reading. A radio blared out the latest screed from Goebbels' propaganda ministry, a voice no one really listened to. However, the noise provided Reinhardt some cover as he crept up the stairs to the master bedroom. Meanwhile, AGATHA and CHRISTIE waited tensely at the foot of the high wall below the balcony. A rope came over. The end bounced on the rocky ground at their feet. Looking up, they saw Reinhardt wave as if to say "All clear." CHRISTIE pointed to the rope and grinned. "Ladies first."

AGATHA gave him what might be called "the evil eye" and then smirked. "Always the gentleman. That means I will be the first to be shot!" With that, she grasped the knotted rope and with a great push, scaled the wall, hand over hand, feet firmly planted against the rocky face and blithely walking up the wall. Standing below, CHRISTIE was mightily impressed. He then did the same, grateful he had maintained his physical fitness while undercover in Berlin. Step two completed.

On cats' paws, they padded through the upper chambers area after hiding the rope in a box of carpenter's tools in the master bedroom. They hoped they would not need it for their escape. Passing the Great Hall, they heard singing and laughter. The *SS* men watched a new musical comedy extolling the *Reich* and ridiculing the Russians, which they enjoyed immensely. The evening's entertainment included catcalls and off-key singing. *Good*, thought AGATHA. *The caterwauling masks our movements.* Most of the scientific and technical staff had retreated to their quarters after dinner and closed their doors. For those whose doors remained open, a quick peek inside first ensured that no one saw them as they scampered across. No one did. As Reinhardt returned to the kitchen, AGATHA and CHRISTIE arrived at Tisza's room. The door was slightly ajar. CHRISTIE reached out and grasped the wrought iron handle slowly and pushed the door open.

Hearing something odd, Tisza whirled around. He had been staring out the window at a barge making its way around the Lorelei and dreaming of home. Mouth agape, he stood facing the two black-clothed intruders both with Walther PPK's pointed directly at his head. He gulped hard. *An assassination. I should have expected it.* Then, in a surprise move, the woman raised her forefinger to her lips in the universal sign for silence. He opened his mouth to challenge the pair, but now he stood frozen in place, mouth open, not daring to say a word.

"*Doktor* Tisza. Please be silent. We are here to get you out. Quickly, grab any valuables and leave with us, now, sir," whispered CHRISTIE.

"You are British, then?"

"It is of no matter. Come, quickly . . . your things, sir," admonished AGATHA.

The man folded his arms across his chest defiantly. "*Nein*, I cannot go. My family in Budapest is not safe. I must remain here, or the Nazis will harm them!"

AGATHA shook her head no. Earlier in the day in preparing the extraction at Reinhardt's, they received a call from Niven in Zürich. Madame Tisza and the two children were safely on their way to Lisbon where the team would escort them to New York and safety. But, he cautioned, they might fool the *Gestapo* for a couple of days, but not likely for much longer. A later phone call from Niven came in as they prepared to depart for the castle. Once they had Tisza in hand, they were to return to their plane and fly to Garmisch-Partenkirchen in the Bavarian Alps along the Austrian border. Avoid the military airfield. There was a private airstrip owned by a Swiss businessman who agreed to leave a car at the unmanned and unpatrolled airstrip. The Nazis had not yet figured out that this airstrip was often used to insert or extract operatives. They were then to proceed to St. Martin's Catholic Church in the village where he would meet them and then escort them out of the country on the early morning train to Innsbruck, then on to Zürich. He held all their diplomatic papers in hand, including one for Tisza identifying him as Anton Haus, a Hungarian businessman with whom the Germans had considerable business dealings. Should they be challenged at the castle or in Garmisch-Partenkirchen and thus become known fugitives, then Niven would bring alternate identity papers as a backup. It was risky, but INTREPID considered all the angles before sending the fake credentials in the Swiss diplomatic pouch from New York to Bern. Niven also provided the code word to give to Tisza to assure him that his family had escaped and was safe.

Every plan requires a backup—a plan B. In case the team could not make it to the church or if they were on the run and threatened with arrest if seen in Garmisch-Partenkirchen, they were to meet at a remote cabin high in the mountains above the town in a high alpine meadow where shepherds took sheep and cattle for summer grazing, Niven arranged for food, water, and other items to be hidden there.

That would sustain them until he arrived with reinforcements. It was a delicate plan.

"Doctor Tisza. Your family is safe. They were rescued by our people in Budapest two days ago and are now safely on their way to Lisbon from Zürich. There you will meet with them, and all four of you will fly to safety in New York. Now, sir. We must be along. Be a good chap," admonished CHRISTIE.

Tisza stood motionless, still aghast at what transpired. He had dreamed of freedom and safety for so long and now it seemed at hand. Now the British agent gave the correct code word that only he and she knew—"Lissa" —for the famous Austrian naval victory over the Italian Fleet in 1866, which meant that she and the children were safe.

"Please, *Doktor* Tisza. We must hurry!" added AGATHA. Finally out of his momentary shock and stupor, he responded, "*Ja*, quite right. Must go, *Danke*." With that, he marched over to the chest of drawers by his bed and, grabbing a valise, stuffed everything of value inside. He turned to AGATHA.

"There are important papers in my laboratory—critically important papers that your scientists will need to . . . to . . . negate the German weapon. I offer them to you."

AGATHA and CHRISTIE looked at each other. *Was it worth the risk? The entire operation could be compromised. Did they need to exfiltrate right away?* AGATHA turned back to Tisza. "*Doktor*, where is the laboratory, and can we get there without being discovered?"

He beamed. "Most assuredly, Madame. You see, the lab area is still off-limits to all but myself and my key assistants, and they both have not yet arrived. It is a clear path from here to there, and there should be little chance of being seen."

AGATHA shook her head. "Then, let us go, quickly. First, though, please sit and write out this letter." She dictated as Tisza scribbled on a piece of stationary with his name and title displayed prominently as a header. The letter was brief, but to the point. As a moral man and despite the danger to himself and his family, he could no longer participate in the ruinous destruction caused by his work on the atomic weapon. Therefore, he would flee the castle while he could and would die before returning to work on Project Armageddon. Hopefully, the letter would be sufficient to shield Reinhardt and Deppen from suspicion. After all, were they not both loyal Party members?

The three proceeded out into the hallway and along a corridor, down three flights of steps, and finally to the locked laboratory. Tisza fumbled with his keys while AGATHA and CHRISTIE took up firing positions should they be discovered. Finally, a click indicated Tisza had found the right key, and in he went. Two minutes later, a beaming Tisza strode back out of the lab holding a bulky briefcase high in the air. He whispered, "Behold, the mighty *Führer's* super weapons program. May he rot in Hell!"

"Right then, off we go. Quickly and quietly back to the kitchen," said CHRISTIE. The three arrived at the kitchen just as Reinhardt and Deppen finished stowing the produce. AGATHA and CHRISTIE shucked off their black clothing and donned the simple work clothes and white apron of a tradesman's assistant. Then they loaded Tisza into one of the vegetable crates, while his briefcase containing the atomic secret papers and valise went into another. Likely, no one in the Anglo-American scientific community could object to the papers reeking of raw onion, thought AGATHA in a flippant moment as she shut the crate and heaved it up into the back of the van. As they loaded the rest of crates into the van, Reinhardt checked out with the security guard, the same genial SS man as when they checked in originally. No problems. Making good the escape, they stopped briefly at Reinhardt's home to change back into the clothes appropriate for a baroness and an upper-middle class Swiss businessman, then on to the airstrip. Step three completed.

* * * * * * * * *

Over Bavaria, 3 November 1943

0300. The small plane pitched, rolled, and yawed violently. AGATHA could hardly keep control as the wind buffeted the aircraft. The wintry weather arrived earlier than expected. Even at 6,000 feet, which should have been above the clouds, she could scarcely see ahead. The wipers flapped furiously but could not keep the windscreen clear. They flew blind into the worst of the storm front. CHRISTIE gritted his teeth while Tisza turned a light shade of lime green. Fortunately, he did not lose his dinner. In the small cockpit, that would have been most unpleasant. The weather was rough, but AGATHA worried more about navigation. She had flown a straight course for Garmisch-Partenkirchen, which would be fine in clear, calm air. But with the wind and buffeting, she had no clear idea how close they were or if they even remained on course for the town in the mountains. Then, of course, what about the mountains? Flying across the Bavarian flatlands presented no danger, but as they approached the Bavarian Alps, her worry increased. Crashing into a mountain-side wasn't really the proper way to end this mission. If they did get to the Garmisch-Partenkirchen area, what about the *Zugspitze*, Germany's tallest mountain at over 9,000 feet. They might well slam into it without any warning. She dared not increase the altitude. Flying out of Sankt Goarshausen's tiny airstrip, she climbed quickly to 5,000 feet, but with wind screeching by at upward of hurricane force, she had to ascend to 6,000 feet to find somewhat calmer air. Still, as they approached southern Bavaria, she knew she had to climb to altitude soon.

0400. Tisza had nodded off. He had become better acclimated to the altitude and the rocking and rolling. CHRISTIE checked his watch. They had been airborne for over three hours and though they had topped off the fuel tanks on arrival at Sankt Goarshausen, the fuel-state level steadily headed toward pegging out at empty. That concerned them both.

"Perhaps we should have landed at Stuttgart and refueled," said CHRISTIE, now visibly worried.

"Perhaps, but with our flight plan for Vienna, how would we have explained being that far off track? Pray God we have enough fuel. If we miss Garmisch-Partenkirchen, we may have enough fuel to make Innsbruck, but no further," she added.

"A risk either way." He went quiet and silently prayed, something he had not really done in months.

0430. The weather cleared. They passed through the storm front's leading edge. Below, they saw the white, pristine landscape covered in new fallen snow. A light shone every now and then telling them that they were over the southern Bavarian plain. But, clearly, the elevation changed. She descended to 3,000 feet to try to find a visual navigation aid or something recognizable. At that altitude, they seemed to be barely above the ground. AGATHA began a slow, gentle climb, trying to avoid using too much fuel.

The mountains appeared ahead, stark and foreboding. Decisions had to be made. Should they find a road or a pasture to set the plane down or should they continue on into the Alps and an unknown future? They looked at each other apprehensively. Lights from the small villages below twinkled in the moonlight—a full moon.

"Let's press on ahead," she finally said. A nod from CHRISTIE told her he agreed. "After all, what's an adventure without a bit of danger?" Gallows humor to be sure. To save fuel, she slowed to the bare minimum speed to avoid a stall. It made for an agonizing rest of the trip.

0615. *Lights ahead. Many lights. Off to the left, a runway brightly lit.* She calculated that they must be close to Garmisch-Partenkirchen at this point. *Perhaps? Perhaps?* At that point, a Junkers Ju 52 flew under them a few hundred feet below. *A military plane! A logistics aircraft.* They peered out the windows and followed the aircraft as it descended rapidly toward the well-lit runway below. *Garmisch-Partenkirchen! They made it.* She knew from the directions that at this point, make a port turn of 20 degrees, and then find the private airstrip roughly 15 kilometers from Garmisch-Partenkirchen on a bearing of 110. If they were fortunate, there would be some runway lighting. They would have preferred to wait until dawn, but checking the fuel state, they had to go in now.

0645. As they approached where the airstrip ought to be, CHRISTIE shouted, "Look! There. Off the starboard side. Lights in a row!"

AGATHA grinned, never as relieved as she was just now. She turned the yoke and the small plane banked right. Their contact had turned on some lights before he departed, having delivered a sedan to the airfield. There were not many—just a few on either side, but it was enough to at least outline the runway, which was really just a straight, flat field.

What they did not and could not know was that when they failed to arrive at Vienna in accordance with the filed flight plan, Maas suspected the worst. Fearful of losing his quarry, he put out the word to all *Gestapo* and *SS* stations in the *Reich* a notice to be on the alert for the couple, especially at small, private airfields. Having received the alert, the local *Gestapo* agents in Garmisch-Partenkirchen decided to check out the privately-owned airstrip just outside of town. As they approached the airfield, they became suspicious. *Why would the runway lights be on this night? Who was flying in, especially with threatening weather promising heavy snow on the way?* As they reached the small wooden building that served as a sort of terminal and storage shed, they grabbed their MP 40s and gingerly checked out the building. They heard the roar of an engine—a small plane lining up to land. *Perhaps it's just the airstrip owner returning from a business trip. Perhaps not.* They walked out toward the end of the runway.

"Tisza. Quick! Down! Get down and stay out of sight!" shouted CHRISTIE above the engine noise. He spotted the two agents and realized they carried weapons, never a good sign. He looked at AGATHA. She sat stone-faced and grim. "We have to land now or we crash. Fuel state is fumes. No choice."

With that, CHRISTIE checked the clip in his Walther, slid it in his trouser waistband, and buttoned the outer coat concealing the weapon. Once back at Reinhardt's, but before driving to the airstrip in Sankt Goarshausen, they had changed back to the clothes they departed Berlin in two days earlier. Just on the off chance that the two men standing next to the wooden shed posed no threat, he did not want to let on that they were armed, however minimally.

The plane came down hard on the grassy runway. Landing was a skill AGATHA had not yet quite mastered. Nevertheless, they made it successfully. Thankfully, the snowstorm had not reached the area yet and they were able to visually line up the lights and see the landing strip. In the east, a clear dawn broke. To the west, ugly, puffy snow clouds appeared that would arrive overhead soon. But, as pilots always say, any landing that you walk away from is a good landing.

As the plane taxied to a halt a few yards from the building, AGATHA cut the engine. They sat there for several seconds.

"Well, here we are. And there they are." AGATHA reached behind her to make sure the Walther was securely tucked into her skirt waistband covered by a nicely tailored jacket.

"Right you are. They have *Schmeissers* and we have . . . well . . . we have these," he responded, touching the Walther's grip cradled in his waistband. "I suggest we bluff our way out if we can. After all, you are the Baroness Ramsour-Fritsch. Who knows?"

She smiled. "Quite right, *Herr* Business Manager Todt. Let's do."

With that, after ensuring Tisza stayed hidden under a blanket in the passenger seat, they opened the cockpit doors and stepped out. CHRISTIE raised a hand in a friendly greeting, hoping the two armed men were just checking out who was landing in Garmisch-Partenkirchen this early morning. He was wrong. One of the men shouted, "It's them! It's them!"

Despite their strict orders to simply observe and report, the other man panicked. He raised his MP 40 and let off a burst. Several rounds tore through the fuselage and shattered the right side window. One struck CHRISTIE square in the abdomen. Panicked, the other man opened fire as well, but his rounds went high and right. Clearly, though they were *Gestapo*, they were not the sharpest of agents, which is likely why they had been posted to such an isolated, out-of-the-way duty station.

As CHRISTIE staggered backwards, he managed to pull the Walther from his belt and open fire. He hit a man in the thigh. He quickly doubled over, screeching in agony. The other man sprayed the plane again, blowing out windows, but still not hitting Tisza, who crouched down as low as possible. By this time, AGATHA had rounded the front of the plane, which shielded her from the first two volleys. She ducked down beside a wheel for cover, took careful aim at the unwounded agent, and let off a two-round volley. He immediately doubled over in pain and screamed to his wounded partner to get to the car quickly. Even though they had superior firepower, their courage faltered and within a few seconds, the car sped back down the road as fast as it could move.

AGATHA, seeing CHRISTIE now sprawled out a few feet from the plane, raced over to him. Still conscious, he grimaced. "Hurts like bloody hell!" he exclaimed. She tore open his shirt. The bullet had entered his right abdomen just above the waistline. She started compression to staunch the bleeding, but it did little good. Although she had taken rudimentary first aid and battlefield emergency medical training at Camp X, she was not quite sure how to respond. At that point, Tisza, now out of the plane and unhurt, hovered over them. He bent down and looked at the wound, examining it from various angles.

"My dear. Before I became enthralled with the physics of the universe, I studied medicine in Vienna. I can help him."

With that, he crouched down as AGATHA stepped aside. "We need bandages."

"Shirts," she shouted, "we packed dress shirts when we left Berlin just to maintain cover."

With that, she bolted toward the shot-up airplane. Tearing at CHRISTIE's travel bag, throwing useless clothes here and there, she pulled out two crisp white dress shirts. Finding her purse still in the shattered cockpit, she rummaged about and pulled out a pair of scissors and began furiously cutting patches. She raced back over to Tisza and CHRISTIE, who was still conscious, though just barely. She thrust the patches into Tisza's outstretched hand and he immediately applied the makeshift patch over the wound.

"Fortunately, it looks like the bullet passed in and straight through. That is good. And I don't believe it hit any vital organs. Still, if we don't stop the bleeding, he will not make it."

AGATHA looked down at CHRISTIE. "Sorry about your shirts. Your tailor will be so out of sorts."

CHRISTIE managed to chuckle. "Well," he gasped, "almost made it. Damned bad luck!"

Then AGATHA had a thought. "*Herr Doktor.* I always carry a sewing repair kit in my travel bag. It's only a few needles and thread, but might that help?"

The physicist looked up at her. He now looked surprisingly upbeat considering their situation. "My dear Baroness, you might have just saved his life. Quick, get the sewing kit." CHRISTIE groaned.

With that, the medical student turned physicist turned hostage and now back to healer stitched up both the entry and exit wounds and stopped the bleeding. CHRISTIE passed out halfway through the procedure, which was likely best.

AGATHA spotted the car on the other side of the building. No stray bullets had hit it and the fuel gauge showed a full tank. There was no way they could go into town to rendezvous with Niven at the church. Plan B kicked in. They would follow the directions and find the alpine meadow cabin to await reinforcements and rescue. Bundling CHRISTIE into the sedan's backseat as best they could, they drove toward the turn off of the main road leading up into the high Alps.

What they did not know was that the two wounded *Gestapo* men had made it back to a local hospital. From there, a call went back to Berlin to *Sturmbannführer* Johann Maas. Now that he had his prey sighted and probably cornered, he called down to the team he had assembled. The five men raced to *Tempelhof* airport where a Ju 52 was already turning over its engines on the tarmac bound for the Bavarian alpine village of Garmisch-Partenkirchen.

* * * * * * * *

Garmisch-Partenkirchen, 3 November 1943

0830. The car crunched to a halt in the newly fallen snow that accumulated up to about six inches but was building rapidly. They had found the turnoff that led up to the pasture above the town. What they did not know until now was at this point, the road ended and turned into a trail that wound up the mountainside with tall pine trees on either side—much too narrow for even a small vehicle. Cattle, sheep, man, or dog had to pass in single file up the trail for a couple of miles before reaching the high meadow.

The path was by design. Deep woods on either side inhibited animals from wandering off the trail, thus creating a natural fence. At the far end as it emptied onto the meadow, a six-foot wide wire gate sealed off the meadow quite nicely.

"Damn, we walk it from here," exclaimed AGATHA, frustrated as she slapped the steering wheel. She glanced over at CHRISTIE, who was conscious and somewhat alert but clearly in no shape to hike it by himself. She stared ahead at the narrow trail and the tall pine trees on either side. For a brief moment, she considered turning back and taking a chance on finding shelter somewhere in the village and perhaps finding more medical attention. Then again, by now the word had to be out. With the town containing so many military personnel due to the hospital and the airfield, the chances for hiding were minimal. So she made a decision—get to the cabin and await Niven and his rescue team. *Had the plane not been shot up in the airfield melee, they might have managed to fuel it up, take off, and fly to Innsbruck or even Zürich, only about 250 kilometers away. No option there. They might just drive as far as possible into Austria, perhaps Innsbruck, and catch the Zürich train, but to what end? And how far would they get with a clearly wounded man? No, the best course of action lay in sticking with the original plan B. Niven would realize that they had not reached the church. He likely would have heard the word about town of a strange plane landing at the private airfield followed by a shootout with the Gestapo and assumed they headed for the rendezvous at the cabin on the meadow. Yes, she finally concluded—best course of action.*

"*Herr Doktor*, are you ready for a hike?"

They trudged up the mountainside with CHRISTIE supported on their shoulders. She was surprised at how well the 50-ish scientist held up. Clearly, he managed to stay in somewhat decent physical condition while working at *Der Gevatter Tod*. They paused every couple of hundred yards. The thin air at this altitude clearly made the trek more difficult. They covered at least two miles, and by 2:00 p.m., reached the gate.

Stretching out for hundreds of yards in an oval shape, the high alpine meadow seemed as serene and picturesque as a Swiss postcard. The snow had piled up to at least a foot, and though the hike up the trail had been difficult, at least the trees somewhat held down snow accumulation on the trail itself. They also worried about frostbite as the temperature dropped hour by hour. The storm brought both cold air and snow, and other than their outer coats, they had little in the way of warm clothing. Reinhardt had outfitted Tisza with a heavy coat knowing where they were headed and having heard of the storm coming. He helped AGATHA and CHRISTIE with some heavier clothes as well, but in the frigid high alpine air, they now suffered. Adding to their misery, they had to carry Tisza's valise and briefcase containing valuable scientific notes that had to be preserved. Thus, they trudged up the mountain yard by yard and finally sighted their objective. In the distance, they spotted a small log cabin at the far end of the meadow.

"Right, then boys and girls. We made it to Shangri-La," muttered an almost delirious CHRISTIE as AGATHA lifted his arm over her shoulders, and Tisza did the same with his other arm. She said nothing—too much energy wasted to respond.

It took over an hour to reach the cabin. It started to dim as the late afternoon turned to early twilight. It would have been rough enough going through the foot-deep snow regardless, but with supporting CHRISTIE, the trek was exhausting. They found the cabin door unlocked, and once inside, AGATHA and Tisza simply collapsed. There was a single camp bed by the fireplace and, as gingerly as possible, they eased CHRISTIE down onto the cot. He passed out again. Tisza commented that sleep was good for his recovery as he changed the blood-soaked bandages. Meanwhile, AGATHA rummaged for wood and matches and built a fire in the stone fireplace. It felt wonderful. She finally warmed up for the first time in hours. True to the plan, Niven had arranged with the local contact to leave food and drink as well as plenty of firewood in the cabin. The man had also refilled the kerosene lanterns and left several boxes of matches. A pile of quilts, beautifully stitched by the contact's wife, were piled in a corner. At least they would stay warm and dry through the long alpine night.

As CHRISTIE slept, AGATHA and Tisza ate a meal of *Würstchen* sausages, cold potato salad, Muenster cheese, and black bread with a bottle of surprisingly good local wine. They talked of his family and his career. She told him of her first husband and about his death. But she decided better of talking about her relationship with Zimmermann. Exhausted from the hike and the day's tension, they both passed out. But, despite all, they were still alive, warm, and safe . . . for the moment, at least.

* * * * * * * *

High Alpine Meadow above Garmisch-Partenkirchen, 4 November 1943

0700. Dawn in the Alps brought a chilly, crisp morning. The storm had passed on, leaving over 18 inches of fresh, powdery snow covering the high alpine meadow and the cabin. AGATHA was the first awake and she brewed coffee. With luck, Niven would arrive that day. By noon, he had not, and AGATHA worried. So she devised a plan should he fail to find them.

Assuming that the car was still parked at the trailhead and not disturbed, they would remain at the cabin for two more days or so to allow CHRISTIE to somewhat recover. By that time, the furor in town over the wrecked plane and the wounded *Gestapo* men hopefully would have died down on the assumption that the fugitives were long gone. They could attempt to enter the village, if nothing else to obtain food and medical supplies. Then they could execute plan C—drive to Innsbruck, which was only about 50 kilometers from Garmisch-Partenkirchen, and finally catch a train to Zürich and safety. That was the thinking, at least, until they heard a voice, a shrill, angry voice, shouting from outside the cabin.

"Baroness. Baroness Ramsour-Fritsch. We know you are in there. You will come out, hands up. Leave your weapons inside in plain sight. Otherwise, Madame, we will come in and execute all of you. Do you understand me?" Johann Maas's intention could not be clearer.

He had arrived with his team from Berlin the afternoon before. A search of the village failed to locate the three refugees, but an offhand comment from a resident that night at a local inn gave Maas a clue. The man, a shepherd, maintained a high alpine meadow for grazing his sheep in the summer. He said if he were on the run, that's where he would seek shelter and a hiding place. Charged with that clue, Maas and two of his team located the car at the foot of the trail and headed up the mountain early the next morning. Seeing smoke from the cabin's chimney, he knew he had found his target.

"Baroness, please. All come out now and you will not be harmed," he shouted.

AGATHA parted the heavy cloth serving as drapery for a window just enough to peek out and see the three black-uniformed SS men. Between the two Walther PPKs and an extra clip, they had a few rounds, but the SS men all carried MP 40s. *If she opened fire, she might hit one or maybe two, but what then?*

While she contemplated a plan of action, a fusillade plowed through the window above her head, shattering the glass. Shards fell down on her. Another burst followed, striking the stone chimney, sending bits of rock and bullet clattering about the cabin. Tisza took cover under the table and had not been hit. Neither had CHRISTIE. With no response, Maas ordered his men to spray the cabin as all three MP 40s fired round after round into the building. The log walls stopped most of the bullets, but several came through the windows and door and whizzed by her head.

At that moment, she contemplated surrender. *Clearly the pudgy little man outside and his two cohorts do not intend for us to survive. Not a good plan!* "Now or never," she screamed, and thrusting the Walther barrel out the broken window, fired three shots in quick succession. An amazing thing occurred. A bullet struck one of the SS men directly in his chest. He keeled backwards, but his finger still wrapped around the MP 40 trigger. It kept firing. As he fell backwards, the machine pistol sprayed bullets out in a wide arc. Two struck the other SS man, one in the chest and one in the head. Maas dove for cover behind a woodpile and fired off another volley at the cabin that shattered the plates and cups neatly stacked the night before on a shelf above the table.

For the next several minutes, gunfire echoed about the meadow, breaking the stillness of a peaceful winter morning. Emptying the clip and the backup one, AGATHA skittered across the floor as low as possible and retrieved CHRISTIE's pistol. It still had several rounds left, but she did not know if he had a spare clip. She had earlier put the one spare in her purse, and that was now expended. Moving to another window to get a different angle, she took careful aim at Maas's head that appeared just above the top of the wood pile. She pulled the trigger, but the rounds struck only the top of his silver and black peaked service hat, the one with the death's head emblem of the SS. He howled in pain as the bullet grazed his balding head, and he ducked down low. For another couple of minutes, they exchanged fire, but she could never get a kill shot. Then, she heard a dreaded sound—click—the clip was empty. No more ammunition. In the clear, crisp, chilled air, such sounds travel far. Maas heard it too and giggled. A minute later, with no more rounds fired from the cabin, he stood up, a malevolent grin across his face.

"Baroness, Baroness. You seem to be out of ammunition, are you not? Time to come out . . . or I shall come in to get you? What do you choose, Madame?"

The sound of Maas slapping in a fresh ammunition magazine told AGATHA that he meant execution, not capture. She looked about the shattered room. CHRISTIE was still barely conscious on the cot while Tisza, a sad expression on his face, crouched underneath the table, his knees up in the air and arms hanging limp by his side with an expression of utter dejection.

"I'm coming to get you now, Baroness Ramsour—"

He never finished the statement. A single shot from a *Pistole Parabellum Luger* of Great War vintage, an infantry officer's side-arm, rang out. The noise reverberated off the cabin walls. She heard a shout, a moan, and then silence. She held her breath for several seconds, her back against the wall just to the window's left. Slowly, she pivoted around and peered out the window.

On the ground in a heap with a rivulet of blood flowing out of his bald head lay a man in the black and silver uniform of an *SS Sturmbannführer*. Behind him stood a tall stern-faced man in the bluish-gray uniform of a *Luftwaffe Generalleutnant*. Smoke still rose from the muzzle of the pistol in his right hand, the same one he had carried throughout the first war two decades earlier. She stared at Peter von Zimmermann, Baron Zimmermann, for several seconds and then saw in the distance, trudging as fast as they could through the deep snow drifts, three men, one of whom appeared to be Niven. She dropped the Walther and raced out the door shouting, "Peter! Peter!" They embraced as they had never before. Neither said a word. Only the flapping of a bird flying overhead broke the stillness.

* * * * * * * *

Earlier that morning, as Zimmermann prepared to depart the guesthouse in Berchtesgaden, the proprietor told him of an incident that had just happened the day earlier in Garmisch-Partenkirchen. It seemed that a woman and two men landed a small plane hired in Berlin at the airstrip there, and after a shootout with the *Gestapo*, had fled, presumably into the mountains.

As he sat staring at his breakfast and just swirling the spoon in the coffee cup, a feeling of dread came over him. He whispered, "Amelia. Amelia!" Why, he could not say, but he knew this was her. Perhaps the other man was her business manager, and who knew who else? Despite no evidence or hard information, he instinctively knew. This was Amelia, and she was in deep trouble. He bolted up, startling the proprietor just returning to refill his coffee cup.

"I must leave immediately." He paid his bill, leaving a generous gratuity, and raced out of the inn. A taxi to the airfield followed. He had called the control tower as the innkeeper prepared the bill and ordered that his plane be pulled out of the hanger, fueled, and warmed up. As the taxi reached the control tower, he threw a handful of *Reichsmark* into the front seat, thanked the driver, and raced for the plane.

He arrived at the *Luftwaffe* airfield by late morning, and being of general officer rank, he demanded a vehicle. The base commander was more than pleased to provide his personal car.

Zimmermann sped out of the base with tires screeching. When he arrived at the *Ordnungspolizei* station in Garmisch-Partenkirchen, the officer on duty indicated he believed that an *SS* officer with two men had headed up to the meadow in search of the refugees from the airport incident. *Amelia. It must be,* he thought to himself.

Obtaining the directions from the policeman, he drove up the mountain road and found the two vehicles at the foot of the trail. Walking hurriedly and at times jogging, he raced up the trail after hearing gunfire from up ahead. At the gate, he saw three black-clothed men firing burst after burst at a cabin. Charged by rage now, he raced across the open meadow as fast as he could run. Only a few yards ahead, he saw the man behind the wood pile stand up and slam in another magazine.

"I'm coming to get you now Baroness Ramsour—"

Zimmermann raised the pistol, and taking careful aim at the back of the bald man's head, squeezed the trigger.

* * * * * * *

Zimmermann and AGATHA continued embracing as Niven and the two Austrian resistance men came up behind them. Niven halted and raised a hand. The three stood back several yards from the embracing couple. Finally, Zimmermann and AGATHA turned to Niven.

"I fear you have me, sir," he said to Niven in a soft voice.

"Holster your weapon, General," Niven responded.

As Zimmermann replaced the *Luger* in the holster, Niven and the two men lowered their weapons. Niven raced into the cabin. CHRISTIE, now fairly alert, sat up in the cot. Still pale, he looked better than he had the night before.

While Niven and the Austrians packed up Tisza and CHRISTIE, AGATHA and Zimmermann talked softly outside. When Niven reappeared holding the briefcase, Zimmermann smiled. He spotted Tisza standing behind the British major. Tisza's face appeared as immobile as a Greek statue. Zimmermann could not tell if it looked like hatred or just relief. He would not blame the physicist for either emotion.

"*Herr Doktor* Tisza. I know you well. But, you, sir?" He looked directly at Niven.

"Niven, Major David Niven, sir."

Zimmermann pursed his lips and paused for several seconds. "Well then, Major Niven, would you do me the courtesy of delivering a letter?"

Niven looked surprised and puzzled, raising one eyebrow as if curious at what he had just heard. "To whom, General?"

"To your prime minister, Major Niven."

With that, the two men proceeded into the bullet-ravaged cabin. With a back sweep of his arm, Zimmermann cleared the broken glass, shattered dishes, and wood chips off the table. He sat and pulled a pen and stationery from his greatcoat pocket. He wrote slowly, considering his words. Looking about, he noticed a candle on the shelf above that had survived the fusillade. Lifting it, he lit the wick, allowed it to melt for a moment, and then dripped hot wax on to the folded paper, sealing it. Then he pressed his signet ring into the warm, gooey wax making the impression of a roaring rampant bear surmounting three trees, the Zimmermann family arms. He handed the sealed letter to Niven. "For your prime minister only, sir. If you would be so kind." Niven nodded affirmative.

With the site completely sanitized, the SS bodies stripped of their uniforms and insignia and buried under mounds of snow where they would not be discovered until the spring thaw, they prepared to depart. AGATHA, CHRISTIE, Tisza, and Niven would head back to Zürich by way of Innsbruck in the sedan left by the contact. Meanwhile, the two Austrians would dispose of the SS car before catching the Innsbruck train to Salzburg, posing as workmen returning home. Zimmermann would return to the *Luftwaffe* airfield to fly back to Berlin. He had a mission to fly in two days.

As they embraced one last time, Zimmermann whispered to AGATHA, "When this is done, I will meet you at your Crown and Anchor pub in London. Leicester Square, did you say? Save us a table."

She smiled. With that, they trudged back down the mountain as the afternoon sun disappeared in the west, throwing a shimmering radiance across the majestic mountains in the distance.

Messerschmitt Me 264
"Amerikabomber"

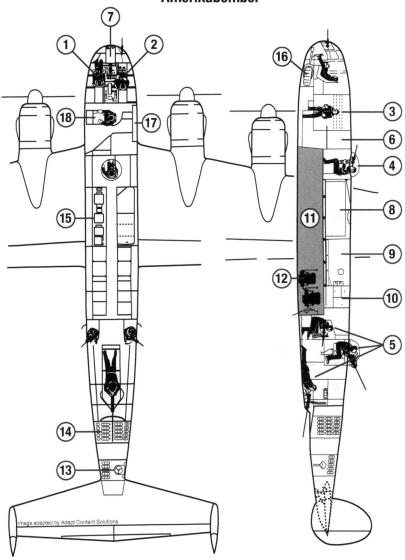

Image adapted by Adept Content Solutions

1 - Pilot
2 - Copilot
3 - Wireless Operator
4 - Flight Engineer/Crew Chief
5 - Gunners
6 - Navigator Station

7 - Cockpit/Flight Deck
8 - Lubricants Container
9 - Crew Bunks
10 - Galley
11 - Bomb Bay
12 - Cameras

13 - Master Compass
14 - Oxygen Cylinders
15 - Radio Gear
16 - Nosewheel
17 - Main Switchboard
18 - Wireless/Radio

CHAPTER 11

The Face of God

Oh, I have slipped the surly bonds of earth,
And danced the skies on laughter-silvered wings;
Sunward I've climbed and joined the tumbling mirth of sun-
split clouds—
and done a hundred things You have not dreamed of—
wheeled and soared and swung high in the sunlit silence.
Hovering there I've chased the shouting wind along
and flung my eager craft through footless halls of air.

Up, up the long delirious burning blue
I've topped the wind-swept heights with easy grace,
where never lark, or even eagle, flew;
and, while with silent, lifting mind I've trod
the high untrespassed sanctity of space,
put out my hand and touched the face of God.

> "High Flight"
> Pilot Officer John Gillespie Magee Jr., RCAF
> 1941

***Der Gevatter Tod*, East Prussia, 7 November 1943**

0430. The massive gray steel hanger doors clanked and rattled above the low-pitched hum of electric motors. The glow of a hundred light bulbs spilled out of the widening chasm into the damp early morning air. Zimmermann stood before the widening hanger gates, hands folded behind his back.

A solitary figure, grim in countenance, he stood alone in the glowing light from the mammoth building. Before him towered the awesome engine of destruction. As he stared up at the airplane, it reminded him of a medieval knight cloaked in full jousting armor astride a huge black charger, ready for combat to the death if required. The bomber's still propeller blades, bright silver, sparkled with the light, casting shadows on the concrete deck below. The Linden Tree. It occurred to him that here was the steed of the German warrior— the knight standing silent before the open doors. A freshening breeze lifted the collar of his leather flying suit, flapping it gently.

Inside the hanger, the ground crew ran about vigorously, pulling wheel chocks away from tires and opening crew and maintenance hatches for last-minute checks. There could be no mechanical mishaps on this flight.

"A great bird, is it not, *Herr Generalleutnant?*"

Momentarily startled out of his daydream, he had not heard the approach of the copilot now standing beside him.

"*Ja*, Hans . . . a great bird . . . whose belly will disgorge a most unusual egg."

Both men stepped aside as the plane began moving, pulled by a towing tractor, her wing tips swaying to and fro. With a momentary groaning noise, the plane gave way and crept forward out of the cavernous hanger. Above the roar of the tractor's diesel engine could be heard the shouts of the crew chief giving last-minute orders to the ground crew, engine mechanics, and fueling crew.

Before anyone was even really aware, there appeared a new presence. From around either side of the giant hanger came armed men, black-uniformed, with the double lightning bolts of the SS on their collar tabs, grim-faced men, worried men, anxious men who would be happy to see the great bomber lifting off, absolving them of their onerous responsibility for safeguarding the bird and her deadly cargo. As The Linden Tree rumbled onto the tarmac, the *SS* troops spread out and took their positions around the plane, one man every two meters, escorting her to the takeoff position. Discretely, a few meters away, the crew gathered behind the two pilots. They stood silently, faces numbed by the chill in the air, each in his own private meditation. Without a word, Zimmermann walked toward the idling tow tractor, the collar of his flight suit still flapping in the early dawn breeze.

"Pre-flight checks complete, *Herr Generalleutnant*. She is ready to fly."

"*Danke*," he responded to the ground crew chief.

Raising his hand, he motioned to the crew. One by one, each man hoisted himself into the aircraft by the front hatch and took his place for takeoff. Three gunners took their position in the rear while Zimmermann and Pieper strapped up in the cockpit. Fischer, the navigator, and the wireless operator took their seats just behind the cockpit while the crew chief and the other turret gunner vaulted up into their seats in the fore and aft machine gun turrets. Zimmermann entered the bomb bay and began unbolting the bomb casing and removing the arming device box.

Two staff cars emerged from behind the airfield command center, still showing the signs of bomb blasts from the raid days earlier. The *Luftwaffe* erected a temporary flight control and command center in the undamaged part of the building. Out of the first car stepped *Generaloberst* Krause. From the second car, two civilians—the two most senior scientists to survive the raid on the compound only because they had been on duty in the laboratory complex—stepped out and fell in behind the *Generaloberst*. Reaching the plane, they each climbed the ladder just aft of the cockpit up into the fuselage and entered the bomb bay where Zwilling had placed the box on the fold-down table. Only one man could enter at a time through the narrow hatch that opened up into the navigation and wireless compartment. The *Generaloberst* went first and keyed in his two numbers to the arming device—the pod —as Zwilling observed. Stepping back out of the bomb bay, without a word, he tapped the first scientist on the shoulder, who entered and keyed in his code. The second scientist did likewise. Zwilling placed the arming mechanism back into its cradle in the front section of the bomb casing but did not key in his part of the arming code. That last step only occurred just before the weapon was released. Without those final two digits, the bomb was nothing more than a huge piece of steel, wires, and minerals. With the two numbers, it became the most destructive force on earth. Zwilling's hands shook as he replaced the pod in preparation for takeoff. He bolted the cover back in place and collapsed into the canvas jump seat that had been installed in the bomb bay.

As the two scientists clambered back down the ladder, Krause thrust his head up between the pilot's seats. Taking off his right glove, he shoved the hand toward Zimmermann, who had sat silent through the entire arming process. Zimmermann looked down, saw the hand and removed his fur-lined flight glove. He grasped the *Generaloberst's* extended hand and shook twice.

"*Herr Generalleutnant* von Zimmermann, you are already a hero of the *Reich*. Today, you become the savior of the *Reich*," exclaimed a beaming Krause.

Zimmermann forced a smile. "*Jawohl, Herr Generaloberst.* For the Fatherland."

With that, Krause headed back for the hatch and patted a grinning Fischer and the wireless operator each on the shoulder and climbed back down the ladder. The ground crew chief removed the ladder and slammed the hatch shut. The Linden Tree was now ready for flight.

Zimmermann keyed the private intercom that went only to the bomb bay. "Franz, is our passenger ready to fly?"

"*Jawohl, Herr Generalleutnant.* All pre-flight safety checks are complete and the bomb is prepared."

Zwilling stared at the ugly blunt nose of the bomb as he strapped himself into the canvas jump seat directly in front of the bomb. Bonded with the special cargo, he would sit, monitoring all functions and movements. The *Luftwaffe* did not fully trust the scientists who said nothing could go wrong with the beast until it was fully armed. Nonetheless, they installed the jump seat and rigged an intercom to the pilot just to keep a watchful eye on the device until it was ready to be dropped.

As his seat harness clicked into place, he heard the rumbling, then sputter and wheeze, then the roar of engine No. 1 as it caught, silver blades biting into the cool, damp air. He cringed for a second or so at the thought of what was to happen today. He looked up at the overhead, with its tangle of electric cable runs, hydraulic lines, and assorted aircraft paraphernalia. He sat right under the crew chief manning the fore gun turret and heard gears whirring. The crew chief was testing the turret mechanisms. *Good German aeronautical engineering,* he thought as his eyes skimmed over the overhead, then down as he stared at the device, built for a single purpose—massive destruction. He shut his eyes hard and tried to think of less challenging things—a good pilsner or a deliciously spiced sausage, the soft skin of a beautiful girl. The moment passed as an engine on the other wing came alive, giving balance to the symphony of vibration and humming. A gentle tremor moved through the innards of the great beast as she strained forward to join the fray, ridden into battle by the warrior-aristocrat at the controls.

* * * * * * *

0500. The sun came up over the East Prussian landscape as The Linden Tree taxied into takeoff position with all four BMW engines humming smoothly. Clearance came from the flight controllers in the makeshift control room. Zimmermann turned and looked over at Pieper, whose left hand hovered above the four engine throttles. Unlike their first mission, the man's hand did not quake or twitch.

"Ready, Hans? Here we go."

With that, Pieper pushed the throttles forward. As the rpms revved up, the plane began its run down the strip into the rising sun.

"Velocity 1," called out the copilot. Seconds later, he called off again, "Velocity 2."

Zimmermann pulled back on the yoke; the plane slowly rose. "Gear up."

Pieper reached out and toggled the landing gear switch. With a whirr and then a slight bang as they reached their in-flight position, the tricycle-style landing gear retracted. Another set of hydraulics pulled shut the landing gear doors, which settled with a slight bump. Airborne. At 5,000 feet, she turned to a northeasterly heading directly for a spot over the Polish countryside for a rendezvous with her men-at-arms.

* * * * * * * *

The internal intercom hummed. It was the wireless operator. "*Herr Generalleutnant.* I have the escort commander on Channel 2A."

"Very good. Patch it up to me."

"*Jawohl, Herr Generalleutnant.* At once."

A second later, there was a resonance in Zimmermann's earphones, followed by electromagnetic induced static. He keyed the handset.

"Pony, this is Stallion, over."

Silence.

Pony, this is Stallion, over."

"This is Pony. *Guten Morgen,* Stallion. A fine day for a ride, *Ja?*"

Zimmermann smiled. It was *Oberst* Klaus Boorstein, another great *Luftwaffe* luminary, a fighter pilot of incomparable skill, daring, and ruthlessness, who had over 60 confirmed air combat victories. They had fought many air battles together since 1939. His *Geschwader* (fighter wing) would escort the black bomber on the first leg of its flight to Moscow until handed over to a new wing west of Smolensk. A total of six wings would rendezvous along the route to provide cover, especially against high-altitude Soviet fighters. While less numbers of escort wings could actually make the journey, in this way each wing had sufficient fuel to engage the enemy in a classic dogfight should that be necessary. The He 111 chase and photo plane joined up just after takeoff. All proceeded according to plan, on time, on target.

"*Ja*, Pony. Hopefully a profitable ride as well."

None of the fighter pilots now taking station on the bomber knew officially what the Me 264's mission really was. All could surmise. This airplane and its weapon represented Germany's solution to the stalled Eastern Front campaign and the instrument of victory over the despised and stubborn Russians. The Soviets had to be bludgeoned into submission.

A Me 109, with a bright scarlet nose cone and a Bavarian blue and white checkered tail fin, zoomed by The Linden Tree, its wings waggling. In the cockpit, a flight-helmeted face grinned and his gloved hand waved as it peeled off and took station ahead and above the bomber at 12 o'clock high. Boorstein. The fighters of II/JG26 and III/JG26 (*Jagdgeschwader* 26) formed a movable box around The Linden Tree, not only to protect against any foolhardy Soviet pilots but also to absorb any ground anti-aircraft fire. Over Poland, though, there was no chance of either. Within minutes, the box was complete.

"Too bad we couldn't have had this protection over England in '40, eh, Hans?"

"*Ja*, indeed, *Herr Generalleutnant,* but the fighter boys would have peeled off just as soon as the Spitfires arrived. Glory hounds! They would rather tangle with the Spitfires and Hurricanes than protect us plodding bombers." Both men chucked softly.

"Still, it is comforting to be so very well-liked."

It was dark humor considering the monstrosity lying only a few feet aft of them.

"*Herr Generalleutnant,* please come to new heading 085 in precisely thirty seconds," said the navigator over the intercom.

"Stallion to Pony. I'm coming to new heading 085 in twenty seconds, over."

"*Ja*, understand 085, out," responded Boorstein.

The fighters conformed to the bomber's movements, executing the course adjustment flawlessly and effortlessly. The rising sun blazed over the bank of clouds below as the formation headed due east toward the Soviet capital.

"At time 0545, I make us twenty seconds ahead of track, *Herr Generalleutnant*," came the navigator's report.

"*Ja, danke.*"

0600. Zimmermann leaned over to the copilot, who stared out the window at the Polish countryside below, and tapped him on the shoulder. The man's head whipped around, startled out of his aerial daydream.

"Hans, why don't you go back for a cup of tea and a stretch? I'll take it for a few minutes."

"With pleasure, *danke.*"

The copilot unstrapped from his seat, ducked down to clear the overhead combing, and disappeared below into the radio space. The galley sat above the bomb bay. Pieper nodded to the crew chief as he passed the man, who was looking at the fuel state numbers and doing calculations. He passed by the lubrication oil tanks and crew bunks to get to the galley, which was just ahead of the gunner's compartment.

Just as he reached for the kettle, he remembered that he had brought aboard his favorite tea but had left it in the cockpit. He whispered softly to himself, "Why didn't I stow it in the galley yesterday when we loaded stores. Aah, well, *sehr gut*. Not to worry."

With that, he turned about and headed back toward the cockpit.

Zimmermann stared straight ahead into the rising, anvil-shaped cloud formation ahead, transfixed on a spot in space. His breathing became shallow and quick. His jaw tightened. He closed his eyes, pressing his eyelids tight together. After a few seconds, he slowly, carefully released the pressure of the jaw muscle and began to relax. He opened his eyes to barely a slit, just enough to sense the sunlight spilling into the cockpit despite the heavily tinted Plexiglas. It was dazzling, as the glass acted as a prism, diffusing and refracting the early morning sunlight. Then, puffs of wispy smoke-like clouds raced past, crowding out the sunlight. And then it was dark, solemn and dark.

They passed through a cloud, a high, dense, ghostly gray rain cloud. The bomber barely noticed the turbulence and reacted with only a slight waggle of its ponderous wings. The plane tore through the other side of the cloud and into the clean, pure, fresh blue air. The hot white sunlight flashed through his eye slits. The shock of it shook him from his trance. He turned his head away from the windscreen, now glowing in the radiance. He pulled the tinted goggles down over his eyes to shield them from the high-altitude sun. It was time. He keyed the special circuit rigged to the bomb bay, which only he and Zwilling could communicate on.

"It is time, Franz."

"Jawohl, Herr Generalleutnant. It is time."

Zimmermann reached into the zippered thigh pocket of his black leather flight suit. His fingers fumbled around amongst the objects there—a survival package, notepad and pencil, a good luck charm, and an ever discreetly small Beretta .25 pistol. He found the object of his search and pulled out a set of needle-nose pliers, the kind used to twist and bend electrical wiring. He cupped the delicate tool in his gloved hand and looked back down into the navigator's space below the flight deck. No one was coming, no one was looking. The crew chief was still hunched over a small, fold-down desktop, intensely calculating fuel consumption figures. He would not interrupt.

Zimmermann bent down and forward, his other hand feeling along the row of wires and cables running along the deck just below his feet. He felt them, tightly banded together, until he found his objective. Just before the bundle of colored wires entered the cockpit display panel, they began to untangle and head off in various directions, feeding information to the panel gauges and displays. He found the object of his search—four tiny green wires. They were banded with red wires that encircled each green wire every few centimeters. He fingered wires numbered one and three and gently eased his forefinger between the two wires, pulling them away from their bundles.

He eased the tips of the pliers under the two tiny wires stretched taut over the tips of his glove and snipped.

On the cockpit display panels, the phosphorous-covered orange needles of four gauges whipped about, pegged to 0. The oil pressure gauges, two on each panel, pilot and copilot, showed no oil pressure for engines No. 1 and No. 4, one on each wing. The oil pressure fail-safe designed into the airplane ensured that there would not be a cat-astrophic loss of oil pressure to all four engines at once and that two separate pumps supplied oil to one engine on each wing.

Replacing the pliers in his thigh pocket quickly, he tucked the two dangling red and green wires back into the bundle, disguising them as best he could. He cursed to himself for forgetting to bring any electrical tape to properly secure them. The tuck would have to do. What he could not see and thus didn't know was that Pieper, returning from the galley, observed the last part of the sabotage. Zimmermann had not expected the copilot back for several minutes. But, at least for the moment, Pieper was not sure what to make of his commander's action. *No matter. It's nothing.* He bounced into the seat and strapped in.

In the navigation compartment, the crew chief, who also served as the flight engineer, noticed something wrong on his oil pressure gauges. *"Scheisse!"* He flung down the clipboard and raced up the two steps onto the flight deck. He stuck his head into the cockpit between the two pilots.

"Herr Generalleutnant! We've lost oil pressure to No. 1 and No. 4 engines. Look at your gauges!"

Pieper peered at his gauges showing no oil pressure. "He is cor-rect, *Herr Generalleutnant.* We have lost oil pressure. Pieper leaned forward and put his face up to the cockpit glass looking for any flames shooting from the starboard-side outboard engine. Nothing. The engine seemed to be running normally. Zimmermann already knew the gauges would read zero oil pressure to the two outboard engines, but to maintain the ruse, he looked out at the port side out-board engine No. 4. No flames yet. Immediately, he reached over and toggled off the fuel pumps that serviced both engines, standard procedure to avoid a flameout. Had it been an actual oil pressure casualty, he would have taken this action immediately, but for the ruse to work he had to get validation from the copilot and flight engineer before taking such drastic action. In short, he needed witnesses to the problem for his actions to be credible. The huge propellers slowed as he feathered the blades to reduce wind drag.

"Pony, this is Stallion. I have an oil pressure catastrophic casualty. Execute Hands Off immediately. I say again, execute Hands Off immediately, over."

"Stallion, this is Pony. Understand Hands Off and will execute, out."

Already, the Me 109s to the bomber's rear detected the sudden loss of air speed and pulled away to avoid a mid-air collision. In rapid succession, the fighters pulled off and away to take up new screening positions at a safe distance from the bomber.

Down below in the bomb bay, Zwilling dropped a pair of needle nose pliers back into the breast pocket of his flight suit. While Zimmermann cut the wires for the cockpit gauges, Zwilling snipped those for the flight engineer's display. They too now read zero oil pressure in engines No. 1 and 4. Alarms clanged.

Having returned to his fold-down table in the compartment below the flight deck, Weber called back up to the cockpit over the intercom. "Sir, we have lost all oil pressure to engines 1 and 4. The pump alarm is screaming down here," shouted the flight engineer.

Zimmermann bit his lower lip. *It is done, then.* Once Zwilling severed the wires that passed through the bomb bay overhead and into the flight engineer's display in the navigation compartment, the blaring casualty alarm blasted out the warning—catastrophic loss of oil pressure.

"Chief, can you redirect the oil flow to the affected engines?" Zimmermann already knew the answer.

"*Nein, Herr Generalleutnant.* There is no cross connect. It would reduce the total oil pressure too low for one pump to service all four engines."

"Can we stay aloft, then?"

"*Jawohl,* sir, but at reduced altitude and speed. We must descend to 2,000 meters." Already, the air speed had dropped to barely 180 knots and the plane descended from 6,000 to 5,000 meters.

"Pony, this is Stallion. I am descending to 2,000 meters. I think I can hold her there, and at 150 knots, over."

"*Jawohl,* Stallion. Understand 2,000 meters, 150 knots. Pony out."

Ever so gently, he pushed the yoke forward. The Linden Tree lurched and vibrated, then nosed down in a slow, gentle descent. At 2,000 meters, Zimmermann leveled her off.

"We can hold her here, Hans, but we must abort the mission."

Pieper could only concur.

The plane was designed to fly on only two engines with no bomb-load or full crew and on three engines when fully loaded. But even if they could restore oil pressure to one engine, it would not allow the plane to reach the required altitude. Better to return to *Der Gevatter Tod* and try another day.

Despite all efforts, the plane could not maintain altitude and slowly descended. They would never make base. Zimmermann made a decision that, in truth, was already part of the plan. He ordered the escorts and chase plane to break away and return to their bases. The crippled bomber represented a hazard in the air, and being over German-held eastern Poland, there was no danger yet from Soviet fighters. Once the escorts cleared well to the north and south, he ordered the crew to bail out.

He keyed the internal intercom. "This is the pilot. I am aborting the mission. I repeat. I am aborting the mission. We cannot maintain sufficient altitude to safely drop the weapon." There was a pause. Not a man spoke, not even to acknowledge the general's instruction.

"Navigator, mark this area. We will notify the local authorities of your location. Bail out on my mark. I shall stay as well as *Doktor* Zwilling. All acknowledge except copilot."

One by one, the crew acknowledged, their voices not even bothering to disguise their disappointment.

"We shall try to return to *Der Gevatter Tod* safely. If we should not make it, you must know that you are the finest air crew in the *Luftwaffe* . . . in the world. Good luck. God bless the Fatherland." Again, silence.

One by one, through the now open bomb bay, the gunners jumped, followed by the crew chief. Then Fischer too leapt out after plotting a direct course back to *Der Gevatter Tod* and advising Zimmermann of their precise position, All the while, Zwilling sat strapped into his canvas jump seat claiming it was his duty to stay with the device no matter what circumstances arose. No one challenged that claim.

"You as well, Hans. That is an order."

Pieper looked straight at the pilot, his jaw firmly set. "*Nein, Herr Generalleutnant*. My duty is here. You cannot pilot this crippled airplane by yourself. It is a two-pilot task. We must save the aircraft and the device, and you need me to help land safely. I shall stay."

Zimmermann gripped the yoke so tight that his knuckles turned white, though no one could see them through the thick, fur-lined flying gloves. *This is not part of the plan. For his own safety and reputation, he must bail out. He cannot remain.*

"Very well, Hans. Stay with us for a few kilometers while I stabilize her without the crew weight. Then you too must bail out. Understood?"

With an expression of frustration that indicated he did not like the order but would obey, he responded, "*Jawohl, Herr Generalleutnant.* I understand."

For the next few minutes, the plane continued on but at reduced speed and altitude. Now, minus the crew weight, she would make it home.

Then, with no warning, it hit. The plane struck a huge air pocket causing a sudden drop in lift. Zimmermann pulled back on the yoke as the altimeter spun around. The wings bounced like a balloon in a summer wind as the plane literally fell from the sky. In seconds, the bomber fell to 700 meters before she steadied out, having landed on a plateau of cooler, heavier air.

Zimmermann's hands trembled. He sucked in and slowly let out his breath to calm himself and regain control. His heart raced. Beside him, just below his knee, two severed green wires had flopped out and aimlessly flapped against the fuselage. Zimmermann did not see the telltale wires. Pieper unstrapped his belt and leaned over for a closer inspection.

"What is it, Hans?"

Pieper pointed to the two dangling wires. The cleanly cut, exposed shiny copper wires could only mean one thing. *Sabotage! The Linden Tree had been sabotaged! But the general . . . his general . . . von Zimmermann . . . had been there the entire time. No one could have done this without his knowledge.* Pieper's head exploded in pain . . . confusion . . . disbelief. His general had betrayed the *Reich. How, why . . . terrible!* Pieper's jaw dropped as if he were a drugged, stupefied man. Zimmermann looked down at the tell-tale wires, then at the gasping copilot.

"You do not understand, Hans. You cannot interfere!"

"I understand treason, *Herr Generalleutnant.* I understand that!" he shouted, his composure returning. Pieper reached for his service pistol in the holster strapped across his chest. His hand barely reached it when two bluish-gray puffs of smoke shot out into the cockpit as the Beretta sent two rounds into Pieper's chest. There were two small perfectly round holes in the waist pocket of Zimmermann's flight suit out of which the smoke drifted. Pieper slumped to his right, his head banging against the copilot's window. A tiny rivulet of blood emerged from the corner of his mouth and trickled down onto his collar. From deep inside his throat came the sickening, gurgling sound of his death rattle. He stared wide-eyed and glassy-eyed, an expression of shock and bewilderment on his face. Then, just as he keeled over onto his control panel, perhaps in a last gasp effort, he withdrew the *Luger* and fired a single round before the pistol fell to the flight deck. It rattled around as it struck the copilot's foot pedal controls. Pieper's bullet struck Zimmermann in the side, penetrating the liver and a kidney. He did not yet realize it, but he would likely bleed out within the hour. There was no hope.

"I'm so sorry, Hans," he gasped. "This was not how it was meant to be. I'm so sorry."

The makings of a tear welled up in his eyes and then rolled down his cheek. A tear for a fallen comrade—a tear for another good man sacrificed to the Nazi lunacy. He had not disliked Pieper even though he knew him to be a devoted Party man and suspected since the first time they met at *Der Gevatter Tod* that he had been sent to spy on him and to ensure loyalty and obedience to orders.

He unstrapped and engaged the autopilot. The Linden Tree now flew straight and level, finally out of the turbulence. Zimmermann pulled the dead copilot back into an upright position and arranged him with his hands in his lap and his neck square against the head rest. With his silk scarf, he wiped clean the congealing blood on Pieper's jaw, throat, and collar, then stuffed the soiled scarf into the man's breast pocket. He pulled the man's goggles down over his face. The dark tinted glasses, designed to protect their eyes from the flash of the bomb's detonation, now concealed the dead man's lifeless eyes. To cover the two holes in the leather flight suit, Zimmermann's shifted Pieper's right arm around until it appeared to be in a normal position for piloting yet disguised the bullet holes. Inside the flight suit, blood spilled from the wounds. Nothing to be done for it—it would not be a problem.

He sat down in his seat heavily. The exertion and tension drained him. Breathing now came in short, shallow bursts. He squeezed his eye lids shut. *Concentrate. Concentrate, Verdammt! Get control.*

Slowly, like a man coming out of anesthesia, his mind cleared. His pulse and breathing slowed. The crisis of Pieper's discovery passed.

The crisis of the mortal wound in his abdomen now dominated his thoughts. He reached down and touched the wounded area. Pulling his gloved hand back up, he saw fresh blood covering the palm and fingers. The recognition struck him that their plan to fly the bomber with the device to Britain was no longer possible. He now knew he had little time left.

Zimmermann conceived the plan outline that night following the Carinhall brief but agonized over it as he pressed ahead with the medal ceremony and preparations for this mission. He decided to not brief Zwilling as he promised until he determined his actual course of action. When questioned the following morning after Carinhall, he demurred and claimed that he would brief Zwilling at a more appropriate time. That time came at the cabin on the high alpine meadow above Garmisch-Partenkirchen two days earlier as he stood over the lifeless body of the SS troll, Maas. He could no longer support the National Socialist regime. The maniacs at the Chancellery in Berlin must not have the atomic monopoly. If Britain and the United States had the weapon as well, they could checkmate Hitler. But there were more bombs becoming operational within weeks. *No, the only solution was literally treason.* He knew he would fly the Moscow mission. What if instead of dropping the weapon, he faked a casualty to the plane and ordered the crew to bail out to safety? He could fly the plane to British airspace and land with an intact weapon. British scientists, and probably the Americans as well, might reverse engineer the bomb and speed up their own development programs. More immediately, they would have an operational weapon ready to use, a weapon that Germany no longer possessed. Having blackmailed Britain and the United States into neutrality, they could return the favor—not an "elegant solution" perhaps, but a workable one, nonetheless. How to rationalize his treason? That was the conclusion he arrived at as he stared at the evil little man bleeding out in the snow. His treason might be against the Nazi regime, but his patriotism was for the Fatherland and the German people.

Now another decision loomed. He realized he would bleed out soon. The night before, he and Zwilling had finally had their conversation. From the physicist's actions and words, Zimmermann surmised that the man would be a willing accomplice. Zimmermann had seen the proud scientist deteriorate into despondency and melancholia from the moment they dropped the first weapon on Dartmoor. That evening, Zimmermann learned two things. First, Franz Zwilling, though a good German patriot who loved his country, could no longer support the Nazis possessing such a weapon. He had been instrumental in developing that weapon; now he was determined to somehow balance the books. He just did not yet know how until the evening before the mission. Second, Zwilling revealed the reason for his seeming declining health. Zimmermann credited it to tension and stress, and while contributory, it was not the sole reason. Zwilling had been diagnosed with terminal pancreatic cancer a week before the Dartmoor mission. He had said nothing to anyone, fearful of being pulled off the project and losing whatever leverage he might have. He told Zimmermann that, at most, he had two to three months left. With those two dynamics in play, the young, talented, patriotic, idealistic physicist wholeheartedly agreed to be Zimmermann's accomplice. Over a bottle of fine Hennessey Napoleon brandy, they made their plan to sabotage the plane once airborne, have the crew bail out, and then fly to eastern England with a landing somewhere in Kent, Suffolk, or Essex. That part of the plan had been noted in the letter to the British prime minister that he hoped Niven would deliver. Finally, the afternoon of the fifth, he received a phone call from the Swiss ambassador in Berlin. Count Ruffener, the man who first introduced him to the Baroness Ramsour-Fritsch at an embassy ball at what seemed eons ago, just wanted to inform the honorable *Generalleutnant*, that the baroness sends her regrets at her sudden departure from Berlin but that she had urgent financial business back in Zürich and would then fly to New York on the Pan Am Clipper from Lisbon.

His jaw muscled tightened again, then relaxed a few moments later. Pieper's devotion to duty and the mission had not been accounted for and it cost the man his life as well as Zimmermann's and the plan itself. He turned off the autopilot, gripped the yoke, and made the decision.

Zwilling, who sat strapped in the bomb bay jump seat, heard the gunfire and suspected what had happened. Unstrapping, he bolted through the hatch, raced through the navigation compartment, and up to the flight deck. An expression of anguish across his face, he stared at the pool of blood forming just below the pilot's seat and the wet trickle dripping from Zimmermann's side. Then, he turned to the silent copilot, who never moved. His head slumped to his chest, knowing that the plan was now undone.

"It's just us, Franz."

"Jawohl, Herr Generalleutnant."

"It's time to go home."

"I understand, *Herr Generalleutnant.*"

Zimmermann gently turned the yoke to the left and moved his boots on the pedals below, changing the angle of ailerons and rudder. Slowly, gracefully, the bomber heeled over to the left and made a slow turn to its new heading back to *Der Gevatter Tod* while climbing to 2,500 meters.

Returning to the bomb bay, Zwilling removed the arming mechanism box out of the bomb casing and placed it on the makeshift fold-down table. Reengaging the autopilot on the new course, speed, and altitude after restarting the two engines, Zimmermann clambered down into the cramped bomb bay. He moved too quickly, and weak from blood loss and the intense pain welling up from his side, he almost hit his head on an overhead strut. He paused and breathed in deeply despite the thin air. At this altitude, they did not need oxygen masks but, still, sudden physical exertion needed to be avoided or lightheadedness occurred. His heart raced. *Must get control, must be calm. Cannot make a mistake. Must be calm.* Once in the bay, he nodded to Zwilling, who returned the greeting. It was time.

Zwilling's hands trembled as he opened the small box lid. Inside lay a numeric keyboard and eight rotors—the detonation arming device. Unless all eight numbers were set in the prescribed sequence, the detonator could not be armed, nor could the altitude for detonation be confirmed. The plane swayed in a downdraft, then steadied out. Neither man spoke. They had practiced this drill over and over. Zwilling's hand quivered then steadied. He touched the rotors running the tips of his ungloved fingers over their smooth surface. The rotors were surprisingly warm in spite of the chill of the altitude. Or maybe . . . maybe it was just the pounding of his heart, pumping, pumping, pumping feverish blood through his hand. He moved the far-left rotor for the first number—8—and depressed the enter key. From inside the metal box, they sensed but could not hear, the movement of tiny, precise gears. *Good German engineering,* he thought, *good and precise.* He then rotated to the second numeral—5—and punched the enter key. The arming mechanism was now functional.

"Three hundred meters?" asked Zimmermann.

"*Jawohl,* three hundred meters."

On the weapon's front was a depression with several female type connections, somewhat like a very large electrical outlet. Zwilling positioned the pins on the back of the arming mechanism in the depression and pushed it flush up against the bomb casing.

With the interlocks inside the detonator removed, the bomb was now armed. At precisely 300 meters of altitude, the wrath of man would detonate, gouging a moon-like crater into the earth with horrendous heat vaporizing all about it. The creation of Hell. Zimmermann leaned back against the forward bulkhead, his breath now shallow.

"It is done. It is done, *Herr Generalleutnant,*" he whispered. Both men sat immobile for a full minute.

"It's time for you to bail out, Franz. I'll mark and report your position. At least you will have a few weeks more," gasped Zimmermann as he slowly and agonizingly rose to return to the flight deck.

"*Nein, Herr Generalleutnant. Nein.*"

Zimmermann stared into his eyes, now seemingly blazing in fury. "I'm going in with you."

"That is foolish, Franz. Suicide is an Oriental virtue, most unbecoming to the new Aryan man."

"Perhaps so. Maybe they will think that a terrible accident occurred. Maybe not. What kind of life would I have for the next three months, if that? What happens when they interrogate me, as I know they will? What horror comes to any one of my friends, family, or associates if they break me?"

"The British or the Americans, you can—"

"Can what? Defect? Then what? Will the British do any less, once they know who I am? God knows what would happen if the Russians got their hands on me. I fear that I am just not that strong. *Nein, Herr Generalleutnant von Zimmermann,* this is the only way. I am now at peace with myself. I have made my peace with God. You are a soldier, a warrior. To die in conflict is glory for you. I am a scientist. I must live or die with my creation. Do you understand?"

There seemed a look of tranquility on the scientist's face. Zimmermann would not force the issue. Zwilling would stay aboard the bomber. The point of impact had to be precise. There was no margin for error. He would fly the weapon on target with all the skill he had gained over years of flying. *So be it.* The two men would go in together.

Zimmermann sprang up with surprising vigor despite the wound. A pool of blood puddled on the deck below. While they armed the device, Zwilling noticed but said nothing. Zimmermann stretched out his hand toward the scientist, who clutched it. They shook in silence. Zimmermann turned, crawled out the hatch, and climbed up the ladder back to the flight deck. There was work to be done yet.

He spun the dial on the tactical radio for the *Der Gevatter Tod* flight control frequency and keyed the transmitter.

"Corral, this is Stallion, over." Silence. "Corral, this is Stallion, over."

The air to ground distance was still significant, and the voice was weak and scratchy, but readable.

"Stallion, this is Corral. Go ahead, over."

"Corral, I have lost oil pressure to two engines. I have aborted the mission, over."

Silence on the net. After several seconds, the air controller, his voice hesitant and nervous, responded. "Stallion, this is Corral. Understand you have lost two engines and are aborting the mission, over."

"That is correct, over."

"Stallion, what are your intentions, sir, over."

"I am returning to Corral. Request you evacuate all personnel from Corral immediately in case of unintended accident, over." Zimmermann did not elaborate further.

The *Feldwebel* manning the air traffic control circuit did not know the exact nature of the huge airplane or the very odd scientists who clustered about it, but he had a pretty good idea. The notion of this thing coming back with the beast still in its belly made him most uncomfortable.

"Stallion, this is Corral. Wait, out." The man's hand jabbed for the black telephone behind him. His watch supervisor must be informed at once.

Zimmermann visualized the scurrying and scrambling about now going on in the makeshift control center. He even managed a smile and a chuckle. He grasped the yoke with both hands. The Linden Tree responded nimbly and gracefully. A click indicated the autopilot had disengaged. He took positive control once again. He would pilot the bird himself on her last mission . . . and his.

Through all of the years flying anything he could get his hands on, Peter von Zimmermann, Baron Zimmermann, had never lost his passion for flying. It was his first, only, and last mistress, at least until he met Amelia Anne Marie Ramsour-Fritsch. He thrilled to the touch of the yoke and throttle every bit as much on this November day as he had first on a hot July day in 1923, 20 years before. *Amelia. Amelia.* His head drooped.

They passed through a cloud bank, thick and smoky white. The bomber jostled and shook in the unsettled, moist air. It also shook him out of his thoughts of Amelia. But the blood loss now told. He knew delirium would soon overcome him. He pushed the throttle forward for more airspeed. *Mustn't pass out yet.* Surprisingly, he now felt little pain, but was sure that would change soon with a bullet lodged in his liver. He keyed the intercom.

"How is our passenger, Franz?"

"No difficulty," came a surprisingly laconic response from the scientist.

Sunlight sparkled again through the tinted cockpit glass, throwing a magnificent light show across the flight deck. He began to drift off. He thought about the last time he had seen Amelia on the high alpine meadow—beautiful, blonde-haired Amelia with the delicate porcelain skin and ocean-blue eyes. He could see her clearly from that morning days earlier at his flat in Berlin. One long lovely leg not covered by the satin sheet, mounds of luxurious blonde hair spilling over the pillow as she slowly breathed in and out, blissfully asleep in his bed. She had the most beautiful legs of any woman he had ever known.

His head jerked back up. He unzipped the leather flight suit down to the waist. Perhaps it was just his imagination, but it was getting very warm in the cockpit.

An outside observer would have been surprised to have seen his uniform. It was not the bluish-gray jacket of Hitler's *Luftwaffe* with the distinctive yellow flashes on the lapel. Instead, Zimmermann wore his gray field uniform from the First World War—a captain of the Prussian Foot Guards—an Imperial German Army uniform, with high collar and epaulettes. Around his neck hung three swatches of ribbon, dangling from each a symbol of his heroism and dedication to the Fatherland. There was the Iron Cross 1st Class. The Crown Prince himself had presented it. Just beneath this was a more recent decoration—the Knight's Cross of the Iron Cross with Oak Leaves. He earned it over the skies of France, Poland, and the Soviet Union. Then, just beneath, lay another, more sinister medal, a Knight's Cross of the Iron Cross with Oak Leaves and Swords suspended from a red, black, and white ribbon. Hitler had placed it around his neck days earlier in recognition of his piloting the Dartmoor mission. At this moment, though, it was not a badge of honor to Zimmermann. Rather, it was a token of barbarism.

Next to him in the copilot's seat, Pieper's hand fell off his lap, jolted by the swaying caused by a sudden air pocket. The hand dangled at his side with fingers spread, swaying to and fro with the plane's movement. Zimmermann reached behind his neck, grasped the Knight's Cross ribbon and eased it over his head. He placed the medal over the dead man's head.

"For you, Hans. May God have mercy on your soul."

He looked away, fighting back the tears welling up again in the corners of his eyes, swallowing hard against the choking feeling in his throat.

"Stallion, this is Corral." He heard the clear, powerful voice of *Generaloberst* Krause. "What is your status, over."

Summoning up all his strength so as to not sound weak, he responded, "*Guten Morgen* Corral. I have lost two engines. Catastrophic oil pressure loss. My crew has bailed out except for the special crewman. I am aborting the mission and returning to you, over."

"I understand Stallion. Is your cargo safe, over."

"*Jawohl*. Safe. Safe. No problem, but I cannot maintain altitude, over."

Krause paused, then keyed the microphone again. "Are you declaring an air emergency, Stallion, over."

"That is correct. Request fire and rescue appliances standing by and that all traffic be cleared from the area. Please evacuate all unnecessary personnel, over."

"That will be done. What is your time to arrival, over."

Zimmermann mentally calculated his time and distance based on current air speed. "I do not have my navigator, but by dead reckoning, I estimate . . . estimate TOA in three two minutes, over."

"Understand, Stallion. All will be cleared by then. Do you require anything further, over."

"*Ja*, a good bottle of schnapps when this is all done, over."

"Consider it done, Stallion. Check in on this circuit every few minutes, over."

"This is Stallion. I will comply, over."

Krause signed off while Zimmermann passed the bail-out position coordinates provided earlier by Fischer. He made the point forcefully that the local authorities in Poland must be notified immediately of the crew's whereabouts. Ten minutes later, the flight controller reported back that the area military and police authorities had been notified; they would search for the crew straightaway.

The fish took the bait. For the next 20 minutes, the bomber hummed along, steady on course, speed, and altitude. *By now, the phone lines between Der Gevatter Tod and Berlin must be hot with frantic activity,* he thought. On The Linden Tree, though, all seemed calm and serene, punctuated only by the occasional radio chatter as he called in his position. *No change in status, holding steady.* The radio homing beacon made an occasional blip but, otherwise, all remained silent.

"Franz, it has been a pleasure working with you."

"*Jawohl, Herr Generalleutnant,* with you as well."

There was no more talk. Each man needed to be alone with his private thoughts. As the bomber came out of another low cloud bank, the Masurian Lakes appeared off to port, blue sapphires surrounded by emerald-green forests. He thought again of Amelia and her ocean-blue eyes.

Zimmermann banked left and pushed down on the yoke for the final descent. The air- traffic circuit chattered away with last-minute instructions until Zimmermann requested silence on the net so as to concentrate on his glide path approach. The tower complied. He ordered them to evacuate as far away and as fast as possible just for caution and safety. He thought of the fire and rescue crew patiently awaiting his landing as well as those who did not get the evacuation word or who tarried too much. He felt more angst for the soldiers and airman and less for the strutting *SS* men and even less for the scientists and technicians who had designed and built this device. It could not be helped. In war there are casualties. Clausewitz was right. War is the realm of chaos and probability.

As the plane descended gradually, he began to sing. *"Deutschland, Deutschland über alles, über alles in der Welt, Wenn es stets zu Schutz und Trutze brüderlich zusammen hält, Von der Maas bis an die Memel, von der Etsch bis an den Belt, Deutschland, Deutschland über alles, über alles in der Welt!"*

He keyed the intercom to the bomb bay. "Sing with me, Franz."

"Herr Generalleutnant?"

"Sing with me . . . please . . . *Deutschland, Deutschland über alles. . . ."*

As The Linden Tree descended steadily down toward *Der Gevatter Tod,* it resounded with the voices of the two men, both singing as loud as they could, almost as if they wished for the Fatherland they both adored to hear their song of adulation . . . and triumph.

In the command center, the flight controller, who had stayed at his post along with Krause and the airfield commanding officer in spite of the evacuation order, realized that something was amiss. The bomber had veered away from the runway approach and headed toward the laboratory and production facility complex. Suddenly panicked, he grabbed the airbase commander's coat sleeve, who spun about in anger that dissolved to abject fear as he saw where the gaping-mouthed controller pointed. The Linden Tree passed clear over the airfield and descended toward the laboratory complex. He grasped the microphone and keyed it in desperation.

"Stallion . . . Stallion . . . *was ist—*"

In the cockpit, Zimmerman whispered the airman poet's lines: "I have slipped the surly bonds of earth . . . put out my hand and touched the face of God."

The altimeter clicked to 300 meters.

PART III.

The time has come," the
Walrus said,
"To talk of many things:
Of shoes – and ships – and
sealing-wax –
Of cabbages – and kings –"

Lewis Carroll, "The Walrus and the Carpenter," from
Through the Looking-Glass, and What Alice Found There
(London: Macmillan & Co., 1871).

CHAPTER 12

Cabbages and Kings

Crown and Anchor Pub, Leicester Square, London, 10 November 1943

AGATHA sat silently at a corner table underneath a reproduction of a William Turner landscape labeled "The Forest of Bere, c. 1808." The pastoral setting with grazing cattle and a solitary horse peacefully drinking from a brook with a beautiful forest in the background reminded her of the pastoral paintings in the café in Speyer and, more directly, of the family dining room at Linden Hall. She took a sip of the tea she earlier ordered.

Two men entered the pub lit only by the midmorning sun. November can be raw in London, but on this day, dawn broke sunny, warmer than normal, and with just a few fleecy clouds. The room was empty except for AGATHA and the pub owner washing glasses behind the bar. The early lunch crowd had not started arriving. *Just as well*, thought AGATHA, alone in her thoughts and memories of the past few months. The two men, one on crutches dressed in civilian clothes with a noticeable bandage encircling his abdomen, and the other, a dapper gent in an officer's uniform with the SOE code name,

PHANTOM. The two men spotted AGATHA, came over and took a seat, leaving one empty chair across from her.

"It's confirmed, Amelia. Total destruction," said CHRISTIE, shaking his head at the gravity of that statement.

Niven shook his head as if confirming the statement.

"Zimmermann?" she asked, hoping, but already knowing the answer.

"The Jerries are calling it an accident. MI6 is certain he flew the bugger right in. We intercepted wireless transmissions from the plane to flight control only seconds before the blast and—"

She raised her hand and cut him off in mid-sentence. "Yes, quite. I understand. Thank you."

"Well, old sod. We had best be getting along. There's a brief with 'CD' (SOE Director) shortly," Niven said, looking at CHRISTIE. He turned to AGATHA and smiled, the ends of his mustache turning up at the corners. "My dear, will we see you there?"

"Of course. I'll be along in a bit. You had best help this cripple along," she said, a broad smile breaking across her face and pointing to a grinning Major Kevin Shirley, aka CHRISTIE.

With that, Niven and CHRISTIE departed, leaving AGATHA alone at the corner table. The barman hobbled over. "Another tea, Miss?"

She thought for a moment. "Do you have a *Riesling*, a Rhine wine by any chance?"

The publican smiled. Not many of his patrons ever requested wine, let alone that variety.

"Why, yes we do, Miss. A very good Rhine wine, in fact, from the Mosel region from just before the war—a very fine vintage. I'll bring you a bottle, straightaway."

She nodded as he turned and headed toward the back storeroom leaving her alone with her thoughts. He returned a minute later and poured out a glass of the clean, crisp light tan liquid, placed the bottle on the table, and returned to the bar to finish washing up glassware.

Amelia Anne Marie Ramsour-Fritsch, Baroness Ramsour-Fritsch, aka AGATHA, raised the glass, swirled it around for a moment, and then extended her arm toward the empty chair across the table as in a toast. A single tear rolled down her cheek.

"To you Peter Christian von Zimmermann, Baron Zimmermann, with love and admiration. For the Fatherland. For all of humanity."

The Oval Office, The White House, Washington, D.C., 11 November 1943

"Mr. President, General Donavan and Mr. Stephenson are here," said the crisp voice on the intercom. Brigadier General William J. "Wild Bill" Donovan, head of the Office of Strategic Services (OSS), more-or-less the American equivalent of Britain's Special Operations Executive, had continually monitored OPERATION THOR through his close confidant and ally, William Stephenson, aka INTREPID, head of British Security Coordination.

"Good. Send them right in."

Franklin Roosevelt leaned back in his chair as the two men entered the Oval Office. Cordell Hull, the Secretary of State, stood as did the Secretaries of War, Henry L. Stimson, and the Navy, William F. Knox. The group in the room included all the Joint Chiefs of Staff—General George C. Marshall, Army Chief of Staff; Admiral William D. Leahy, Chief of Staff to the Commander-in-Chief; the President's primary military adviser, Admiral Ernest J. King, Chief of Naval Operations and Commander-in-Chief, United States Fleet; and General Henry Arnold, commander of US Army Air Forces. Brigadier General Leslie Groves, head of the Manhattan Project, sat in the back under a bust of George Washington. Behind the president stood the Speaker of the House of Representatives, Samuel F. Rayburn, as well as the Senate Majority Leader, Alben W. Barkley.

"Well, General Donavan, Mr. Stephenson?"

"It's confirmed, Mr. President. The entire installation is gone. These photos were taken twelve hours ago by an RAF recon flight."

Donovan placed the photos on the desk and spread them out in order as INTREPID handed a package each to Hull and Stimson, who proceeded to pass them about the room. There was nothing, simply nothing except a huge crater in the earth. Other photos showed remnants of some concrete ruins and the torn and jagged remains of an airfield runway. But there was nothing left but the lifeless crater where the *Der Gevatter Tod* laboratory and production facility once stood.

"Did it get everything, General?" asked the Secretary of State, gazing incredulously at a photo.

"Yes, Mr. Secretary . . . everything. It got not only their two other close to operable weapons but also their entire stock of processed, enriched uranium; their reactors; research and assembly labs; and, most importantly, all of the project scientists."

"All of them, General?" asked the president, his teeth clenched around the cigarette holder, now pointed straight toward the ceiling.

"Yes, sir, every one of the bastards was there. That is, all except Doctor István Tisza, who is probably the most important one of the lot. We now have him safely tucked away. He now works for our side."

Roosevelt pursed his lips and grunted. "Hmm, excellent. Excellent! How did it happen?"

Donovan deferred to INTREPID.

"Accident? Perhaps. We know that the bomber was over Poland when she lost two engines. We know the target was Moscow. The mission commander, a General Peter von Zimmermann, aborted the mission and returned to the installation they called *Der Gevatter Tod*, which, quite ironically roughly translates to Godfather Death or, you might say, the Grim Reaper."

"Sabotage, Mr. Stephenson?" The president's eyebrows lifted quizzically.

"Possibly, Mr. President. Possibly. By whom, I doubt we'll ever know. The Germans haven't a clue and are assuming an accident. We know this from our well-placed source inside the German military establishment, who also confirmed that the German atomic program is, in his words, completely 'kaput.' The only thing left is the facility at

Katz Castle on the Rhine. A heavy bomber raid will see to that easily now that we have confirmed its presence and function. Nor does it matter how it happened. The result is the same, sir."

Not everyone in the room was cleared for knowledge of CHARLEMAGNE, thus INTREPID tiptoed around it.

"General Groves, what of this fellow Tisza?" inquired Roosevelt.

"Mr. President. Professor Tisza and his family are now safely at Los Alamos. He has already begun working with the team, and Dr. Oppenheimer reports that with Tisza's cooperation and the diagrams and data he brought with him, they anticipate being ready to test a device at the Trinity site in about two months."

"Indeed, yes!" The president jabbed a finger in the air as he leaned forward in his chair, elbows on the desk blotter.

"Cordell, is the ultimatum ready?"

"Yes, it is, Mr. President. It only needs your signature."

Roosevelt swiveled around to face the Speaker of the House and the Senate Majority Leader. "Mr. Speaker, Senator, are the proposed declaration of war documents prepared and are we set for me to address the combined Houses of Congress should they all reject the ultimatum as expected?"

The House Speaker piped up first with the senator nodding concurrence. "Yes, Mr. President. We will schedule you at any time or date. At that time, you will request that Congress declare that a state of war exists between the United States, the Empire of Japan, the German *Reich*, and the Kingdom of Italy. There will be very few nay votes. The German provocations, the use of the bomb on southern England, and the Japanese invasion and seizing of the Philippines are the *casus belli*. The isolationist wing has largely repudiated neutrality and will fully endorse the war declarations."

The president nodded. "Then I recommend Cordell that you call in the German, Italian, and Japanese ambassadors straight away." He swiveled back to face Marshall.

"General Marshall, Admiral King?"

Marshall stood as did King. "Mr. President. We, the United States, British, and Canadian forces, are trained, equipped, and prepared to execute OPERATION TORCH within the month. That is an amphibious landing at multiple points along the Moroccan and Algerian Mediterranean and Atlantic coasts that puts us immediately into the rear of Field Marshall Rommel's German and Italian forces. Simultaneously, British, Australian, and Commonwealth forces under General Montgomery will assault from out of Egypt. The intent is to catch the enemy in a pincer movement and literally squeeze him out of North Africa in this combined operation. Planning is already underway for follow-on operations against France and the European continent itself. We will hold in the Western Pacific, build up our forces, and then counterattack against Japan."

Roosevelt leaned forward and looked straight at King. "Well, Admiral King, can the US by God Navy support these multiple operations?"

King smiled. "Indeed yes, sir. As a result of the appropriations that Congress passed and you signed in summer 1940, the first of the new *Essex*-class aircraft carriers and *Iowa*-class battleships are already, or will soon reach, operational capability. By early next year, Pacific Fleet will outnumber the Imperial Japanese Navy in all regards by a substantial margin, especially in capital ships and combat aircraft. We will then launch the rollback operations if they have not heeded the ultimatum and evacuated their forces from all their conquests in the Far East, the Western Pacific and China. We are ready, sir."

"Excellent, Admiral King. Excellent!" Roosevelt leaned back in his chair with a broad smile that was well-known by the public. "Gentlemen, we have much to do and little time to do it in. Thank you, and let us press ahead with this crusade. The world awaits us."

Across the room, a match struck, sending out phosphorous fumes and smoke. In the light of the flame as it touched the tip of his Havana cigar, the cherubic eyes of Winston Churchill twinkled in the match light. In his hand, he held a letter sealed with candle wax. The stationary was particularly fine. At the top left the paper bore the roaring bear rampant surmounting three trees, ancestral arms of the Prussian baronial House of Zimmermann. On the top right, it bore the insignia of a *Luftwaffe Generalleutnant*. The very last line read: "Sir, I quote your great statesman Edmund Burke: 'The only thing necessary for the triumph of evil is for good men to do nothing.'"[11]

The man in the blue pin-striped suit exhaled another smoke ring that drifted toward the ceiling and said softly, "Mr. Hitler will sleep uneasily tonight."

THE END

11 The quote is attributed to the Whig Member of Parliament, Edmund Burke in the 1790s in reference to the atrocities in France during the French Revolution that began in 1789. While often attributed to Burke, it is not known for certain if he actually penned these exact words, but regardless, they capture the spirit and tone of his reaction to the French Revolution's excesses.

Author's Notes

A question I am often asked is where and how do ideas for historical fiction originate. Sometimes, that is an easy answer.

For example, with the *ANTIMONY* series of historical fiction, the idea for the original *Resurrection of ANTIMONY* novel came from reading the chapter entitled "The Zany Saga of the Zamzam" in the "Battle of the Atlantic" volume of the Time-Life Books World War II set that came out in the 1980s. The story centered on the sinking of the SS *Zamzam*, an Egyptian-flagged merchant ship bound from New York for Alexandria with over a hundred American passengers in March 1941. My brother Larry supplied the idea of a British field agent from the First World War—code name ANTIMONY—coming back on active duty in World War II to watch over an American nuclear physicist embarked on the *Zamzam*.

For the second in the series, *Genesis of ANTIMONY*, which introduced the agent in his first mission in World War I set in German East Africa, the idea came while admiring the posters and decorations at Disneyland in line for the Jungle Cruise with two of our granddaughters. Yes, sometimes ideas come about in the oddest ways.

For *The Linden Tree*, it's not quite as clear. I can say that the concept first occurred to me of a patriotic German *Luftwaffe* pilot who gives up his life to save the world from the Nazis having the atomic bomb monopoly as I stood in a copier room at LSA, Inc. offices in Crystal City, Arlington, Virginia, in 1990. Between Navy active duty and returning to graduate school for my doctorate in British history in 1991, I worked for several years as a contractor on Navy satellite communications and command and control systems. Having said that, the first several chapters of *The Linden Tree* were written in the 1990–92 time frame and then, as with many writers, I allowed the project to go dormant. Life happened. My first child came in January 1992, and everyone knows how that changes even the best-laid plans.

But, through the years, the saga of *Generalleutnant* Peter von Zimmermann and Amelia Ramsour-Fritsch popped into my mind every now and then; I made mental notes on the plot structure for some future writing date.

With *Genesis of ANTIMONY* in 2018 and my latest study of strategy in the War of American Independence—*Southern Gambit: Cornwallis and the British March to Yorktown*—published in early 2019, I again took up the pen to complete the story. As the head of the Strategy and Policy Department in the College of Distance Education at the US Naval War College in Newport, Rhode Island, I have traveled extensively to the College's non-resident Strategy and War seminars across the country presenting case study lectures and conducting seminar assessments. Since these are graduate evening seminars, I found extensive time during the day to write while traveling for the College. Over the years, I found numerous and now favorite writing places ranging from Hospital Point at Naval Station Pearl Harbor, Hawai'i; to the Mormon Battalion Monument/Fort Stockton Park overlooking Old Town San Diego, California, to Deception Pass Park on Whidbey Island, Washington, to Corral Canyon Park above Malibu, California, to Crystal Reservoir on Pike's Peak, Colorado, to overlooking Surrender Field at the Yorktown National Battlefield Park in Virginia. All of these writing locations played a huge role in making the story of Zimmermann and the baroness come alive.

As a military historian, I am keen on historical accuracy. The great imperative with any historical fiction based on actual events and personages is this: The writer has a moral and ethical obligation to avoid having a character say or do anything that is completely out of character. Given that the dialogue and action must largely be imagined and then created by the author, it is incumbent that the writer stay true to the actual person and not create a caricature that is totally out of sync with the actual person.

Sadly, the film industry is all too often guilty of violating this ethical imperative. If you need a villain, invent one. Don't make a real person something they never were. On the other hand, with actual evil villains such as Adolf Hitler—well—there's lots of room to maneuver there.

With all this in mind, I have found it helpful to the reader to present in these author's notes a bit of the historical record on people, places, and events. I hope that you enjoy these historical tidbits and that they help flesh out the persons, places, and events around which this alternative history novel is constructed.

The German nuclear weapons program, officially the *Uranprojekt* (Uranium Project) and unofficially as the *Uranverein* (loosely translated to Uranium Society or Club) started well ahead of the British and American efforts but soon lagged due to official neglect. In January 1939, two German chemists—Otto Hahn and Fritz Strassmann—published an article in the German scientific journal *Naturwissenschaften* (*Natural Sciences*) claiming that they had bombarded uranium, a radioactive mineral, with neutrons and produced the element barium. Two physicists, Lise Meitner and Otto Frisch, conducted their own experiments and validated that the uranium atom could indeed be split by neutron bombardment. They called the process "nuclear fission." Frisch and Rudolf Peierls also calculated the critical mass of the uranium isotope U235, which created a benchmark as to how much material would be needed for an actual explosion.

Based on these positive results, other scientists began experimenting in April 1939, but the experiments essentially ended with the start of the war in September when Germany invaded Poland. However, the possibility of using atomic energy for military purposes intrigued German authorities, especially in the military. Accordingly, on 1 September 1939, the *Wehrmacht Heereswaffenamt*, the Army Ordnance Office responsible for military weapons logistical administration, took over project coordination. Under military control, the project then had official sanction as well as funding. Three separate efforts resulted.

One effort strived to develop a nuclear reactor or *Uranmaschine*, whereby in a controlled setting, nuclear fission occurred and plutonium 239, a fissile material that can be used in a weapon, is produced. The bombs used against the Japanese cities of Hiroshima and Nagasaki in August 1945 were of two kinds. The Hiroshima bomb was uranium-based, while the Nagasaki bomb used plutonium.

A second effort sought to procure the necessary uranium as well as manufacture heavy water, which contains a larger than normal amount of a hydrogen isotope, deuterium. Heavy water acts as an inhibiter in a nuclear reactor, slowing down the neutron movement, thus making them more likely to react with the fissile uranium U235 atoms. The attacks by British and Norwegian commandos on the Norsk Hydro heavy water manufacturing facility in Norway in 1943 and 1944 inhibited German access to this vital part of the nuclear reactor process.

Finally, the third thrust—uranium isotope separation—sought to enrich the material by stripping away isotopes from U238 leaving the highly fissile U235 isotope used to create the powerful nuclear fission and subsequent explosion. The U238 form of uranium cannot sustain a nuclear chain reaction, whereas the U235 isotope does. When a sufficient amount of the fissile U235 is thrust together rapidly, a chain reaction and massive nuclear explosion results. This is called achieving "critical mass."

By early 1942, the *Heereswaffenamt* decided that nuclear fission had no real military utility and though the effort remained somewhat funded, the army turned control over to the *Reichsforschungsrat*, the *Reich* Research Council. Once the central coordination flagged, the effort was divided among a number of research laboratories and universities and essentially never developed beyond the research and experimentation stage. A key in the change in focus came from the eminent Nobel-prize winning physicist Werner Heisenberg, who advised Hitler that it would take at least five years to produce a useable fission weapon. Thus, the regime turned its focus to other, more immediate weapons systems such as rockets and jet engines among other scientific initiatives.

Although Germany built an experimental nuclear reactor under Heisenberg's direction, they were never able to make it produce the fissile material. The Alsos Mission, an Allied consortium of military, intelligence, and scientific personnel that stood up in 1943 to track German scientific advances, especially in nuclear energy, discovered the experimental reactor in a raid on 23 April 1945. The team found the reactor, but there was no uranium or heavy water, indicating that Germany was far from developing an atomic weapon.

For the alternate history plot in *The Linden Tree*, the fiction starts with the building of a successful nuclear reactor at the Kaiser Wilhelm Institute for Physics in December 1939 under Heisenberg's leadership where they successfully split the atom in July 1941, as Zwilling briefs Zimmermann at Avord Air Base in chapter 4. That is where fiction takes over from fact.

The Heinkel He 177 *Greif* (Griffin) heavy bomber used in the initial attack on Dartmoor in this story was a German attempt to develop a strategic bombing capability. First designed in 1936 as a heavy bomber, the plane suffered from the German operational concept for force employment that emphasized ground close air support, unlike British and American air doctrine that emphasized strategic bombing of the opponent's infrastructure and industry. The main aircraft used for bombing in the battles of 1939–41 against Poland, France, and Britain was the Heinkel He 111 medium bomber, which had limited range and bombload capability. While Britain and the United States developed a heavy bomber force (e.g., the Avro Lancaster, the Boeing B-17 Flying Fortress, and the Consolidated B-24 Liberator), Germany focused on airpower in support of the land war. This combined arms approach empathizing rapid encircling movement, psychological paralysis, and the integration of infantry, armor, and mobility based on mechanized troop movement, artillery, command and control, and close air support, came to be called *"Blitzkrieg"* or "Lightning Warfare." Strategic bombing did not fit this mode of operational warfare and the *Luftwaffe* focused on developing air superiority fighters such as the Messerschmitt Me (or Bf) 109, the Focke-Wulf Fw 190, and ground attack fighters. Aerial bombing in support of the land battle was supplied by aircraft such as the Junkers Ju 87 Stuka, the He 111, and the Dornier Do 17 light bomber, all carrying relatively small bomb loads with limited range. Also, the change in the He 177 mode of high-level horizontal bombing to "glide bombing" ("dive bombing" but at a much flatter angle) created many technical problems with the He 177 and retarded its operational viability.

Once the need for a more robust strategic bomber was recognized, Heinkel fielded the He 177 in April 1942. It was a two-engine aircraft powered by the Daimler-Benz DB 610 24-cylinder liquid-cooled piston engine producing 2,900 PS (2,860 hp; 2,133 kW) and consisting of paired DB 605 V-12 engines. The initial engine design suffered from many casualties due to the engine nacelles being too constricting, which resulted in engine fires. Crews referred to the aircraft as *"Reichsfeuerzeug"* (*"Reich's* lighter") or *"Luftwaffefeuerzeug"* ("Air Force lighter"). With a crew of six, it had a maximum speed of 351 mph at 19,685 feet, which made it highly vulnerable to high-flying American, British, and Soviet air superiority fighters. It had a combat range of 830 nautical miles (960 statute miles). For Eastern Front service, where the plane was primarily used, it had to be operated from airfields already inside occupied Soviet Union to reach any viable Soviet industrial targets that had been moved further east. The *Luftwaffe* found that operating in the Soviet Union, especially in winter with temperatures so low that lubricants turned to the consistency of putty, made the new bomber less than ideal as a strategic bomber. As the *Wehrmacht* and *Luftwaffe* were driven further west after the Battle of Kursk, range became more problematic.

The He 177 was well-armed for self-defense and carried an assortment of machine guns (7.92mm MG 81 and 13mm MG 131) as well as a 20mm 151/20 cannon. The bomber had what was known as a "fishbowl nose," meaning that the entire nose area was glass, thus giving the pilot maximum visibility. The same concept was used on the American Boeing B-29 Superfortress. It had a ceiling of 26,000 feet and carried a bomb load of 15,000 pounds. With the engine replacements and modifications, the bomber became more reliable toward the end of the war, especially on the Eastern Front, but by that time, Germany had clearly lost the struggle and the He 177 never made a great impact.

The Messerschmitt Me 264 represented the Messerschmitt Company's attempt to field a four-engine heavy bomber with sufficient range and payload to reach North America. It was the company's entry in the *"Amerikabomber"* program established in 1942 with the purpose of attacking North American east coast targets. As such, the Me 264 represented the ideal vehicle for Zimmermann's aircraft, The Linden Tree. A few details on the Me 264 are interesting, a picture of which appears on the book's cover.

On 23 December 1942, the first prototype Me 264, the V1, rolled out of the hanger at the Messerschmitt factory in Augsburg, near Munich. Powered by four 12-cylinder, liquid-cooled Junkers Jumo 211 J-1 engines, the plane overcame the problems of power and lack of engine redundancy of earlier aircraft such as the He 177; it represented the first truly "transatlantic" German bomber. In late 1943, the V1 was retrofitted with BMW 801G 14-cylinder air-cooled radial piston engines, which delivered 1,290 kW (1,750 hp) of power. In the story, The Linden Tree is retrofitted with the BMW engines in September 1943, in time for the Moscow mission in November. The design speed was 339 mph at 20,000 feet with a cruising speed of about 217 mph. The service ceiling was 8,000 meters or roughly 26,000 feet. Depending on the type of external fuel tanks, the range was between 13,000 and 15,000 kilometers or roughly just over 9,000 miles, more than enough to reach North America and return. With a crew of eight, the plane had sleeping accommodations and a galley as indicated in the drawing in chapter 10, which is based on a Messerschmitt design office drawing. Armed with four 13mm MG 131 machine guns and two MG 151/20 20mm cannons, the plane had significant self-defense capability. The bomb load depended on the range and could vary from 6,000 to 13,000 pounds. As a "transatlantic" aircraft, the endurance was over 40 hours with extra fuel tanks attached to the wings.

Ultimately, there were only three prototypes labeled V1, V2, and V3. V1 was heavily damaged in an air raid on 18 July 1944 and never repaired. V2 was destroyed in an earlier 1943 raid, while V3 was never completed. Had Germany actually developed a working atomic bomb, the Me 264 was the right platform to deliver the weapon on target. Although the Me 264 as a long-range bomber was overcome by more advanced but never fully-developed designs, the *Kriegsmarine's* need for a long-range maritime patrol aircraft to replace the Focke-Wulf Fw 200 Condor kept the program alive until late 1943, when the Navy opted for competing designs.

Camp X, or more formally, Special Training School No. 103, was a training camp for Allied Special Forces, located in Ontario, Canada, on the northwestern shore of Lake Ontario between the towns of Whitby and Oshawa. Established by William Stephenson, Director of British Security Coordination (aka INTREPID), on 6 December 1941 as a training camp for covert and clandestine agents of the Special Operations Executive, the camp was also used by the American Federal Bureau of Investigation (FBI) and agents of William Donovan's Office of Strategic Services (OSS). The OSS was the forerunner of the post-war Central Intelligence Agency (CIA) and the American equivalent of the British SOE. Note that for this story, Camp X opened the very day that USS *Swordfish* detects and reports the Japanese *Kido Butai* strike force nearing Hawai'i. The camp taught several hundred agents before being closed in 1944. It was jointly administered by BSC and the Canadian government, especially the Royal Canadian Mounted Police (RCMP).

In 1942, Lieutenant R.M. Brooker, a British Army officer who appears in chapter 5, took over as camp commandant. Instructors William E. Fairbairn, called "Dangerous Dan," and Eric A. Sykes, inventors of the Fairbairn-Sykes combat dagger, taught close combat skills to the students. Additionally, Station M designed and manufactured covert devices for use by clandestine agents operating behind enemy lines.

Hydra, established in May 1942, a highly capable telecommunications relay station, operated at Camp X. Due to its geographic location, it was able to transmit and receive communications, both radio and telegraph, to and from Europe and the Americas easily. Since Hydra had direct lines to the Canadian government as well as Washington, D.C., and since it was in North America and safe from German surveillance, it represents the perfect vehicle for INTREPID, as the coordinator of OPERATION THOR, to maintain instant communications with both Niven in Zürich and AGATHA/CHRISTIE in Berlin through Swiss diplomatic cables or even commercial telegraphy.

As with all historical novels, certain persons are real. One of my favorite characters is INTREPID, who also appears in *Resurrection of ANTIMONY*. Sir William Stephenson (INTREPID), hailed from Manitoba, Canada, A Royal Air Force fighter pilot and ace in the First World War, Stephenson proved a remarkable and successful businessman and was one of the founders of the BBC in the 1920s.

Interestingly, one of his reputed 12 air combat victories before he was shot down and captured was over Lothar von Richthofen, (younger brother of the Red Baron), who scored 40 air combat victories. Prime Minister Winston Churchill personally recruited Stephenson to head up all British Western Hemisphere intelligence operations (interestingly, over the objection of General Sir Stewart Menzies, wartime head of all British intelligence operations). Traveling to New York in June 1940, Stephenson established British Security Coordination, headquartered at Rockefeller Center in New York. Posing as a passport control officer, he coordinated all hemispheric intelligence operations and became a personal representative of Churchill to President Franklin Roosevelt. Stephenson worked closely with William Donovan even before the United States officially entered the war in December 1941.

Another historical character, and my all-time favorite actor, is David Niven. One of the Hollywood stars who volunteered for military service in World War II, he headed back to England the day after Britain declared war on Germany in September 1939 and rejoined the British Army. As a 1930 graduate of the Royal Military College, Sandhurst, and a former officer in the Highland Light Infantry, he was recommissioned as a lieutenant in February 1940 in The Rifle Brigade (Prince Consort's Own). He soon transferred to the Commandos, the special forces created for raiding and intelligence collection, and was initially assigned to Inverailort House in the Scottish Highlands, a commando training base. He later commanded "A" Squadron, General Headquarters (GHQ) Liaison Regiment, better known as "Phantom." Interestingly, one of his best-known film roles was as Sir Charles Lytton, "The Notorious Phantom," in the Peter Sellers film *The Pink Panther.*

Niven arrived in Normandy several days after the D-Day landing and Phantom operated in France gathering intelligence on German positions and movements throughout the battles in France and Germany in 1944 and 1945. He also did film work for the Army Film and Photographic Unit and appeared in two movies designed to build public support for the war effort: *The First of the Few* (1942) and *The Way Ahead* (1944).

Niven ended the war as a lieutenant-colonel, showing that he had tremendous leadership and command as well as acting skills. In *The Linden Tree,* he has been "seconded" (the term for being detached from a home unit for a temporary assignment) from the Commandos for duty with the SOE as the point man in Zürich. In 1943, he would have not yet been promoted to lieutenant-colonel, so he appears as a major in the story.

As always, I wish to thank my lovely wife Linda, who perseveres while I write and then takes time from her busy schedule to read the manuscript, check for grammatical errors and faulty logic, and make comments and suggestions, all of which is hugely valuable. Additionally, I would like to thank Susan Carpenter, a good friend (and not a relation), who also read the manuscript with the eye of a copy editor and provided invaluable suggestions for improvement. An old colleague from my days at LSA, Inc. and a former submariner or "Bubblehead" (as we Surface Warfare types affectionately refer to our shipmates in the undersea warfare world), Radioman Senior Chief Petty Officer (RMCS (SS)) Mike Klein, helped immensely with submarine procedures and terminology. I am ever grateful to my colleague, Professor Donal O'Sullivan at California State University (CSUN), Northridge, California, who is half-German, half-Irish, has two doctorates in German and Russian history from elite German universities, and teaches history at CSUN as well as the Naval War College Fleet seminar in Port Hueneme, California. Professor O'Sullivan reads all my World War I and II manuscripts and corrects my absurdly awful German grammar!

Suzanne Lawing does magnificent artwork and cover designs, and Lori Martinsek at Adept Content Solutions provided the excellent adapted diagram of the Me 264. Additionally, my thanks to the staff at Clovercroft Publishing, especially Gail Fallen, the copy editor, who do a wonderful job and could not treat authors any better.

Everyone has persons in their life that made a difference or influenced their personal and professional lives. Most of my career has revolved around the US Navy as a 30-year serving officer on both active duty and Navy Reserve as well as nearly 22 years as a Professor of Strategy at the United States Naval War College. To pay tribute to some of those remarkable folks from my Navy past, I have used their names (or versions of) for the key characters in the prologue on the USS *Swordfish*. Those shipmates include Commander Tim Garrold, USN (Ret.), who is now the Deputy Dean of the College of Distance Education at the US Naval War College; the late Captain Zeke

Newcomb, USN, my second commanding officer on USS *Josephus Daniels* (CG-27); Captain Charles McDaniel, USN (Ret.), to whom I had the good fortune to serve as his XO at NCSO WESTLANT 409; Captain Rich Nolan, USN (Ret.), who as OOD when I was a rookie JOOD, taught me the ropes; and the late Radioman Senior Chief (RMCS) Albert H. Smith, my first leading chief petty officer as a brand new communications officer, who taught that young ensign so many valuable lessons in leadership.

Finally, I thank you, the reader, for persevering and taking the time to read my scribblings. I trust that you enjoyed the tale of a patriotic German warrior-aristocrat and the Swiss baroness agent caught up in the chaos and maelstrom of a world at war.